Praise f

'An impressive debut, with vivid period atmosphere, colourful personalities and stirring action' *Sunday Telegraph*

'Pip Vaughan-Hughes has given us a monk, a corpse, a sinister Templar and a terrific adventure that romps across medieval Christendom. A great read!' Bernard Cornwell

'An audacious plot ... suffused with intelligent writing ... a satisfying read' *Book & Magazine Collector*

'A debut that will hopefully spawn many sequels ... a rattling yarn from an author who knows his history, *Relics* is high entertainment readers will relish'
Waterstone's Books Quarterly

'*Relics* is a great fix ... it packs power, fear, rage and revenge into a fine 13th-century thriller ... it's the answer to your prayers' *Ladsmag*

'An absorbing, exciting tale' *Good Book Guide*

'Gripping narrative and so steeped in atmosphere you can almost smell what they're up to. Pip's pulled out another corker in what will surely be a long line of epic books'
Sunday Sport

'A complex and geographically wide ranging novel that sweeps through early mediaeval Europe ... the finely woven plot, although complex, never confuses the reader'
Crime Squad

'Vaughan-Hughes portrays Petroc's adventures with lip-smacking relish, conjuring up a colourful cast of pirates, cut-throats, scoundrels ... all things considered he has a whale of a time. And by and large, so do we'
Yorkshire Evening Post

Pip Vaughan-Hughes grew up in South Devon. He studied medieval history at London University and later worked as a reader for a literary agency when he wasn't dabbling as a bike messenger, food critic, gardener and restaurant owner. He now lives in Vermont with his wife and daughter. Pip's first novel, *Relics*, is also available in Orion paperback.

THE VAULT OF BONES

PIP VAUGHAN-HUGHES

An Orion paperback

First published in Great Britain in 2007
by Orion
This paperback edition published in 2008
by Orion Books Ltd,
Orion House, 5 Upper Saint Martin's Lane,
London, WC2H 9EA

An Hachette Livre UK Company

A CIP catalogue record for this book
is available from the British Library.

Typeset by Deltatype Ltd, Birkenhead, Merseyside

Printed and bound in Great Britain by Clays Ltd, St Ives plc

The Orion Publishing Group's policy is to use papers that
are natural, renewable and recyclable products and made
from wood grown in sustainable forests. The logging and
manufacturing processes are expected to conform to the
environmental regulations of the country of origin.

www.orionbooks.co.uk

To my parents

Acknowledgements

My thanks go to: Tara, Jon Wood, Christopher Little,
Emma Schlesinger, Genevieve Pegg, Angela McMahon,
Tabby Bourdier and Paul Wyncoop.

Prologue

The moon was very bright, so bright that the feathery leaves and umbels of the water dropwort under which I lay painted my body with crisp, trembling shadows. Spiders were busy looping their silk between blades of iris, and each new strand blazed like the trail of a falling star. I raised my head and breathed in the clean, sweet scent of the plants. Something flopped wetly in the shallows of the river, and my head cleared. The river. It stretched away from me, straight as a blade of damasked steel, towards the dark hump of the city that squatted away to the north. I stood up lazily, only to be startled by a mighty confusion of noise: I had roused a heron, and, screeching, he blundered into the air, clapping his wings hollowly. The river broke into a ferment of colliding ripples.

I had fallen asleep, that was obvious. Had I been fishing? I could not recall, although I must have had something more than water to drink for my thoughts to be so muddled. I would have to dodge the Watch to get back into Balecester, and I had to be back before dawn: Magister Jens began his class promptly after Vespers, and to be late meant a tongue-lashing in his excruciating Swabian-tinged Latin. I looked around for a bag or a fishing-pole, but could see nothing in the flattened greenery. I had left a man-shaped dent in the tall grass. The dew was already settling, and I found I was soaking wet. My head was cold, and I was brushing the dewdrops from my tonsured pate when an awful peal of thunder shook the ground beneath me and the distant, shadowed city burst into a great roil of fire. A fountain of destruction it was, too bright to look at, brighter than burning pitch or the fire of the Greeks, that burns even on water. For a moment the buildings stood out in the heart of the pyre like children's toys: the cathedral, the castle, the bishop's palace, until the flames poured over them like a tide and they were consumed. Scorching air billowed around me, and my clothes, damp and clinging an instant ago, stuck to my flesh like molten lead. The water dropwort was burning and the fronds and flowers turned to white ash before my eyes. I opened my mouth and fiery air rushed in. Flames blossomed in my throat, my chest, my belly. My teeth turned to glowing coals. With my last strength I threw up my arms and screamed forth a gout of fire.

I was choking, and as I had that thought a voice above me said, 'You are choking him.' I opened my seared eyes and saw a man's face looking down at me. His forearm was across my neck and he was pinning me down to the burned earth, but as I twisted and turned to see what I thought would surround me, I saw not the ashes of the water meadows of Balecester but rumpled bed linen and, further away, the walls of a chamber, lit by rush lights and by the glow of a dying fire. The man was watching me intently. His face was familiar: black arched brows, brown almond-shaped eyes. I could not place him, though, and let my head sink back into what I found was a sweat-soaked bolster. I let my eyelids fall, and for just a few more seconds the river was running once more, and everything was green and still. Sweet fronds of water dropwort bowed and danced.

'Patch. Patch! Do you hear me?'

The green fronds became fingers waving inches from my

nose. I opened my mouth to protest, but only a strangled croak came forth.

'He wakes. Piero? Please fetch the Captain.'

It was not an English voice, nor an English face. I blinked, and it came into focus again. The mouth was smiling.

'Patch, can you speak?'

I shook my head. At once, a strong hand was lifting my head, and a cup touched my lips. I let icy water slip across the charred leather of my tongue and down my throat, then gulped until I gagged and spluttered.

'Who am I?' I gasped.

PART ONE

London

Chapter One

Late December 1236

We came to London on Childermass Day, blown up the Thames by a snow-filled squall out of the Low Countries. It was an ill-omened day, to be sure: Herod massacring the innocents, best forgotten; or perhaps worth remembering after the heedless roistering of Christmas. But despite the nasty weather I was all aquiver with the excitement of seeing London for the first time. It is the heart of England, and every Englishman feels its pull, even the meanest villain who has never ventured further than the edge of his master's land. So to finally behold the great city ... I admit that, like a child, I ran about the ship, getting in everyone's way, and at last volunteered to climb the mast and keep look-out. I had not seen England since that day, two years and more ago, when I had been taken aboard the *Cormaran*, a wretched, wounded fugitive. And so now, when the wet snowflakes stung me I did not care, and when the first houses came in sight around the great bend of Stepney Marsh, although they were but mean eel-fishers' hovels, I thrilled at the sight. And when the dark, spiked bulk of the Tower resolved itself out of the grey distance I all but fell off my perch to the deck below.

Anna, meanwhile, was snug in the cabin, wrapped in furs, reading. She cared not one whit about London, so she said,

and she had been teasing me gently about my boyish anticipation since we had set sail from Bruges. She did not come
on deck at my cry, although many of the crew rushed to the
prow, as London was reckoned a good landfall by all sailing
men, and these ones had been promised a long shore-leave.
And she did not emerge as we slipped through the open
gates of London Bridge. Only when we were safely tied up
at Queenhithe Wharf did she deign to step forth, sniff the air
and wrinkle her nose, and give me her hand.

'Oh dear,' was all she said, as she looked up at the sooty
buildings that rose around the basin of the wharf, itself fairly
muddy and stinking, for it was here that all the fish sold in
the city came ashore; and as I later discovered, it served as a
public privy, a great jakes for any Londoner to use. So Anna's
royal nose had reason to object, but despite the stink and the
snow I was all afire and bustled her up the water-steps. It was
a half-mile to our lodgings at the Blue Falcon in Cheapside
so a litter was found, and as the two footmen – under the
cold eye of Pavlos the Greek, once a bodyguard of Roman
despots, now devoted heart, soul and sinew to his *vassileia*,
his princess – jolted Anna through the teeming streets I
jogged alongside, chattering, while she swatted flakes of
wet snow from her face. I was an outlaw in this country,
but I gave it little thought, for my face had come into the
lines of manhood and my skin was burned dark from the
sun, and indeed I was as like the terrified, lost little monk
who had fled these shores as the butterfly is to the crawling
worm.

That first day was a flurry of organising, greeting, paying
calls, and it was not until the next morning that we could
take our ease, if only for a short hour, in the big, faded private
chambers that we were to share with Captain de Montalhac,
his lieutenant, Gilles de Peyrolles and Pavlos, who, as well

8

as her bodyguard, was also Anna's devoted, self-appointed manservant.

The others having left to call on some important merchant or other, Anna and I sat in the Blue Falcon's not-quite-comfortable chairs and broke our fast on fresh bread, smoked fish, gulls' eggs, sweet butter, warm goats' milk and cold, bitter ale. Being still full of a good night's sleep and so somewhat heavy and contented, I watched as my love ate and drank. Her night-black hair was loose and hung about her shoulders and back. Her face was brown, with a constellation of darker freckles scattered across her cheeks. When I had first laid eyes on her, high on a lonely island hilltop, she had been pallid from years in the ghastly climate of Greenland and several weeks in the pitch-black hold of the *Cormaran*, on to which she had been smuggled in a load of whalebone. But the sunlight had quickly given her back the complexion of her people, and the only reminder of those grim days was the space in her mouth where the scorbutus, the sickness which had blighted us all as we crossed the endless Sea of Darkness, had stolen one of her teeth. Her front teeth had a little gap between them as well, in which she liked to work the tip of her tongue when she was thinking hard about something. Her eyebrows were black ink-strokes above her brown, almond-shaped eyes, in which the mercurial tumult of her humours played like the reflection of the sky in still water.

I loved her for all this: for all that lay on the outside, the flesh that clothed her, the scent that was hers alone, the way her hair shimmered like the nape of a jackdaw's neck. But most of all I loved her for what lay within, for like a great city Anna held within her a powerful complexity – a tumult, as I said – that had its cause, in part, in the way her life story had skipped like a stone just above the dark waters of disaster.

But the other part was Anna's own self, for – to me, at least – she was a creation without peer. The blood of emperors, of old Romans, flowed hot and furious in her veins, and I believe she felt her ancestors' presence very keenly. Certainly they would appear to me in flashes of anger or joy, the face of some long-dead queen or warrior usurping her own features to glare out at a strange world before vanishing back into the past.

The days passed pleasantly enough. The weather improved, indeed it became quite warm, and the stench from the filthy kennels that ran down the middle of every street made itself known to us. What time I had that was not spent in affairs of business I spent with Anna, and we explored high and low, from the vast, ugly hulk of Saint Paul's Cathedral to the Tower perched upon its mound. We squinted at the heads displayed on London Bridge, marvelled at the goods on display at the markets, and lost ourselves in the roistering crowds at Smithfield. Anna grudgingly admitted that London was worthy of at least a little admiration. She was always grudging with praise for anything Frankish, as she called everything outside her homeland of Greece. Franks were barbarians, boors, bloody-handed primitives. She made an exception for me, thank God, and for most of the *Cormaran*'s crew, but on the whole she resented the fate that had decreed she must pass her time in Frankish lands, and dreamed – every night, so she said – of the day that she would return to her home in Nicea and even, perhaps, see the greatest city of them all, lodestone of her heart: Constantine's city, Byzantium.

We had passed a week in this manner when the captain asked that I make a journey down the Thames to Deptford to buy a new anchor for the *Cormaran*. I would be gone a day, no more, and I bade Anna farewell with a kiss and a fierce embrace, knowing full well I would be back in those arms by nightfall. I took a wherry downriver, enjoying the boatman's skill as he manoeuvred us through the water traffic and shot the foaming race under London Bridge. It was a sunny day, and I stepped on to the bank at Deptford at around the noon hour. I took a mug of ale and a hot pie at a tavern, sought out the ironworks and paid for a fine anchor. The ironmaster was a voluble Kentishman, and before any money had changed hands a big flagon of cider appeared and we passed it between us in the blazing heat of the forge. Kentish cider is no match for that of Devon, and I told him so in good humour. That set him talking all the more, and before long we were in his cider store, eating great lumps of hard cows' cheese from the downlands of Sussex and sampling the contents of various barrels and tuns. My head well and truly fuddled, I at last conceded that a thick, mouth-puckering scrumpy from the Weald would not be laughed out of the fine county of Devonshire, hugged the man like a brother, and staggered off to find a wherry bound for London.

But there was no wherry. I had spent far too much time at the ironworks. Now it was dark, it was snowing again, and the tide had turned. Cursing, I made my way to the inn, an ancient pile of wattle and daub that the breath of the river had all but dissolved, and enquired after a boat, but there were none to be had until the morrow. And so I reluctantly took a room – there were plenty free – and hoped that Anna would not take my absence amiss. The place was pleasant enough, in truth: there was a hearty fire that hissed and crackled with the jolly song of burning flotsam, good ale and hot wine to chase off the cider hangover I was already suffering. I took myself off early to bed, where I had to curl up tight against the creeping damp of the linen, feeling a little sorry for myself, but not overmuch: for I was playing truant, as it were, and that is a pleasure all to itself.

The pot-boy woke me some time before the fourth hour, while the mist was still thick on the face of the Thames. There were stars in the sky, and marsh birds shrieked and piped out in the foggy desolation. There was a wherry-man up and about, said the boy, and when I had jogged through the mist to the edge of the river, I found an ill-tempered man, a boat and a favourable tide. As the bells of the city were chiming the eighth hour, I was whistling up Garlick Hill on my way to the Blue Falcon.

I crossed the threshold of the inn expecting a ghastly tongue-lashing from Anna, but when I found her in the parlour, perched upon a settle by the window, she greeted me with a soft, distracted smile. I sat down warily opposite her and poured out the apology I had been constructing since my wherry had passed the Isle of Dogs.

'I am glad you had a nice time,' she said, stopping me with a hand to my lips. 'But now I have a puzzle for you. Can you make head or tail of this? It came just after you left.' And she handed me a letter, a neatly folded square of vellum sealed with an anonymous, blank blob of wax. The seal was broken, and I unfolded the vellum and scanned the neatly written words within.

To Her Majesty the Vassileia Anna Doukaina Komnena, respectful greetings.

I humbly ask that you will receive a petitioner who will make none but the briefest imposition upon your day. If you would care to hear words from a place that perhaps is still dear to your heart, please receive this humblest of supplicants, who shall call upon you at the hour before noon, tomorrow.

The letter trailed off into florid politenesses that tried but failed to disguise the fact that the writer had not signed his name.

'Who brought this?' I asked. Anna shook her head.

'A tall man,' she said. 'So the pot-boy says. When pressed, he claimed the fellow was not a poor man, to judge by his clothes. That is all.'

I read the letter again. It was in French, which gave no clue, although I thought perhaps it might be the French of Paris, and not London French.

'Not a Greek, then?' I puzzled. 'I mean, this would seem to be from a Greek, would it not? "A place dear to your heart?" Nicea, I suppose.'

'That is what ... oh, Mother of God, Patch, I can't go on being this calm! Who knows my name, outside our good shipmates? No one! And all this about my heart! Of course it is someone from ... someone sent by my uncle,' she finished, her voice sinking into an involuntary whisper.

'I doubt that,' I said, soothingly. 'Are there Greeks in London?'

'There are,' said Anna. 'Of course there are.'

'Well, then.'

'He was not a Greek,' said Anna. 'I asked. I said, "Did he look foreign?" Apparently he did not. This is Frankish writing, and a Frankish choice of words.' She plucked the letter from me and dropped it on to the settle between us.

'Did you tell the Captain?' I asked, searching her face. Her brows were furrowed and her mouth was drawn into a tight line. She shook her head.

'No. I do not wish to.'

'I think you should.' She shook her head again and gave me a look in which nasty weather was brewing.

'I do not wish to trouble him. He suffers my presence in his company very prettily, and in return I shall not pester him with annoying flea-bites such as this.' She pinned the letter down with her downturned thumb and gave me a look that said the matter was closed. I knew her well enough by now, though, to judge that it was not. But I let it lie, for my love was no mean judge of the world, and prowled around its snares and ambuscades as deftly as any cat.

'Well, what shall we do today, then?' I asked, happy to change the subject.

It was early yet, before nine bells, but Anna had heard of a spice merchant in a street nearby who promised the freshest and strangest oddities from Ind and Cathay, and then perhaps a visit to a silk-seller. They were not really shopping trips, these excursions, but rather Anna's way to justify long and rambling explorations, a passion I shared with her. Whenever the *Cormaran* brought us to an interesting landfall we would lose ourselves in streets and alleys, twisting and turning, chatting to townsfolk in cookshops and taverns, until we thought we had found the heart of the place. London was our greatest challenge so far, and so far we had only dipped our toes in its roiling, limitless waters. So we set out, and quickly found the spice merchant, whose wares were as withered and overpriced as we had expected. Finding ourselves near the Hospital of Saint Bartholomew, we strolled out beyond the walls to the great, stinking plain of Smooth Field, where the kingdom's farmers bring their animals for slaughter and butchering. There were no cows today, merely a churned-up expanse of muddy grass rank with dung and old blood, and a small town of rude huts and some grander houses of wattle and brick, peopled, so it seemed, by filthy children whose play was blows and vile oaths, and by men and women crippled either by drink or the drip. Driven back inside the walls by a reeking host of beggars, we wandered some more, past ancient churches and grand houses, hopelessly entwined in the tangled net of streets.

Or so I supposed, until, turning a corner, I found that we

had come back to Cheapside, and that our lodgings were only a little way away, across the teeming street.

'How did you manage that?' I asked Anna, amazed. She said nothing, but looked smug and tapped her head wisely with a finger. Then I realised.

'It is almost noon, is it not?' I said.

'I could not resist,' she said. 'You do not mind, do you? If I do not find out who this fellow is, it will drive me mad.'

'But ...' I began to protest.

'You will protect me,' she said, smiling. 'And we will spy, only that. Peer at the fellow from behind a door. Do not worry: if there is trouble, I will tell the Captain, I promise. And, you well know, if trouble is coming, it will find us anyway.'

I could not argue with that, so I huffed peevishly and set off after her. I knew her well enough to know that if her mind was made up, nothing I could say or do would change it, short of binding her hand and foot. Cheapside was crowded – it was always crowded, but at the middle of the day it seemed as if all the people in the world were hurrying along it, on foot, in carts or on horseback. Anna was hurrying along, heading for the place where a stepping stone had been laid in the kennel, for that foul and stinking runnel of shit and night-water was almost too wide to jump over. She stopped and waited for a haywain to pass, and when it had creaked by, she darted out, shouldering her way past a stout countrywoman shuffling along with a yoke and two baskets of dead geese, heads lolling, thick pink tongues jutting from their open beaks. Looking past her towards the Blue Falcon, my eye was caught by a man who had paused at the door, and who seemed to be looking in our direction.

He was quite tall, and crop-headed like a soldier, and even from this distance I could tell that his face had suffered in battle, for the thin winter sun caught the silver trail of an old scar as the man turned his head. But if he recognised Anna, he made no sign, and kept his place at the door. Still I hurried to catch up with her, for now we could not go into the inn through the front, if we went in at all. I had almost caught her when she stepped neatly around two fat burghers talking loudly about money and skipped up on to the stepping stone. Now I was blocked by a man with a barrow, who swore at me absently, the quick-tongued foul geniality of London. I was about to curse him back when the words seized in my throat, for a beast was screaming, high and sharp, and a woman's voice had joined it. I shoved the barrow-man aside with my shoulder in time to see Anna, in the street beyond the kennel, raise her arms high over her head as if to grasp the great hooves that flailed there, for a great piebald horse loomed above her, dwarfing her, and then all at once her slim shape was for an instant caged in the living bars of its legs before it reared up again and came down upon her with both hooves, dashing her to the mud. The rider seemed to be grappling with the reins and let out a despairing cry as the horse came up again, seemed to walk for an instant like a man upon its hind legs, before plunging forward and setting off down the street, rider clinging to its back like a ragdoll.

Anna was lying crooked in the mud, pressed into the paste of earth and dung, one arm beneath her, the other flung back behind her head. Her hair was across her face and trampled into the filth like a dead crow. I knelt, babbling, cooing wordlessly to her in my panic, and brushed the hair away. She turned and looked at me, and I gasped with relief, for our eyes met and her lips parted, to tell me it was all right, it hurt a little bit here, and here. The world stilled, I reached for her, told her not to move, for her leg was broken; slid a hand beneath her head, bent my own head to catch her words.

Then her good leg gave a kick and her neck shuddered beneath my fingers. Her eyes fixed on mine for a moment longer and then slid away, seeming to flutter across the hedge of muddy legs that surrounded us. No words came, only a throttled, rattling hiss. I pulled her from the mud and tried to cradle her head in my lap, and found that my hands were wet with blood. I could feel it, flooding hotly across my legs. Her leg kicked again, like a snared beast, and the world started its heedless dance once more, and the London sun trickled down upon us, pale as piss, while an apple bobbed past down the kennel.

She was alive when we carried her into the Blue Falcon, myself and a page, an egg-seller and the barrow-pusher, and laid her on the bed she and I had awoken in two mornings ago. Captain de Montalhac burst in with Gilles, just that moment returned from some business out in the city, and a doctor was sent for. I relate these things as if I were aware of them, and I was, though only as a reader is aware of the tiny painted figures crawling about the margins of a book. For Anna did not move, though a woman came and sponged the blood from her face and chafed her wrists, and I whispered in her ear and stroked her cold forehead. She was still, save for the rise and fall of her chest, and silent, but for her breath, which hissed and creaked and held not the slightest hint of her voice.

The doctor came, a grey old monk from that same Hospital of Saint Bartholomew we had passed just an hour or two ago. He came to the bedside and ran his hands gently over Anna's head. She did not stir, nor did her breathing change its timbre. He peered into her ears, put his ear to her chest, and lifted her eyelids with a careful thumb. Then he looked up and met my desperate gaze. He patted my hand where it lay upon Anna's collarbone, and sighed.

'A kick from a horse, was it?' he said. 'There is little to be done. Perhaps ...' and he paused, and raised his hands. I thought he was about to pray, and my heart shrank within me, but instead he interlaced his fingers. 'The bones of the skull are fitted together thus, like the vaulting of a stone roof. The lady ... her skull is shattered in one place, and the vault is collapsing in upon her brain, which is inflamed and has started to swell. There have been seizures?' I told him of her kicking leg. 'They will worsen, until ...'

'Is there truly nothing to be done?' I croaked, searching his grey eyes and finding nothing there save resignation.

'I could attempt to remove the pieces of bone, which might relieve the pressure upon her brain.'

'Then do it, for God's sake! Do not hesitate!'

'I do not have the instruments with me, my child,' he said gently. 'And I fear that if we try to bring her to the hospital, the motion ...' He looked at the faces gathered around the bed. 'I will fetch my tools, but I fear that this poor child will not live even until I return.'

I saw the Captain's face go grey. 'Go, sir,' he said. 'Maybe she is stronger than you think. Fetch your instruments, we ... the company begs you.'

The doctor nodded gravely. He patted my hand again and took his leave. After he had gone, the room was silent save for Anna's laboured breathing. I had laid my forehead on the cool linens to calm my battering thoughts, when Pavlos gasped. Anna's eyes had opened. At once I bent over her, and tried to meet her gaze, but to my dismay I saw that it wandered, now slowly, now flickering aimlessly across the ceiling beams. But here, surely, was a sign, for she had awoken! Where was the surgeon and his cursed instruments?

I whispered in her ear and held tightly to her hand, but still her eyes searched calmly amongst the cobwebs. Somewhere nearby, a bell rang the quarter-hour. A serving-girl looked in at the door and, seeing our stricken faces, hastily withdrew. As the latch snicked, Anna's left leg gave a twitch and then a kick. Her fingers began to flutter and pluck at the sheet, and then her spine arched and a terrible gasp burst from her. Her eyes were still and wide, and were looking straight into mine. Then both legs began to thrash madly, and I threw myself across them. Pavlos choked out a prayer and took her shoulders, pressing them into the mattress. Gilles knelt beside me and took Anna's right hand, and the Captain grasped her left. She gave another gasp and thrashed again. There was a terrible strength in her legs, but it was not willed, was not Anna's. I called out to her and fumbled my hand under the Captain's, reaching for her fingers. They twitched and shuddered, her nails scrabbling at my palm, and then they were still.

One of her eyes was open. It bulged through the bruised lids like a blood-streaked pearl, lustrous but not alive. Blood had burst from her ears and her nose, and a red froth clung to her mouth. But all the blood had left the skin of her face, and a livid red mark curved from her smashed right ear to the corner of her mouth, and under the skin the contours, all the lines and declivities that I had mapped out upon my own heart, were wrong. I beheld a ruined country, and there was no map for it.

I lay there for an infinity, one hand in Anna's, the other cupped around her chin, that grew cold even as I held it. I pressed my face into the muddy silk of her dress, her scent already fading, the clumsy vapours of death gathering. When at last I lifted my head, strong hands grasped me and helped me stand. The Captain stood there, and he drew me to him in an embrace that all but squeezed the air from my lungs.

Then he took my face in both his hands and kissed me hard on the forehead.

'She is dead,' he said, his hands still on my face. 'You must leave her, just for a little while, for she must be attended to.' I searched his eyes, but they were black and hard as coal. So I stepped away from him and turned to where the flat white glare of the London winter was lighting up the dingy room.

'An apoplexy,' I heard the doctor say wearily behind me. 'The brain swelled and burst its vault of bone. Thus the eye was forced ...'

Words I had not spoken in long years, words from a life that might have belonged to another man, welled up in me: *Deus, in adiutorium meum intende. Domine, ad adiuvandum me festina. Gloria Patri, et Filio, et Spiritui Sancto. Sicut erat in principio, et nunc et semper, et in saecula saeculorum. Amen. Alleluia.* The prayer at Vespers: 'O God, come to my assistance. O Lord, make haste to help me.' But I had abandoned such help. 'Glory be to the Father, and to the Son, and to the Holy Spirit. As it was in the beginning, is now and ever shall be, world without end.' The world had destroyed my love, turned her fiery beauty into a mask of ruin. That terrible, blind and staring eye would never close again, world without end. Without end. Amen.

Gilles and someone else helped me to an outer chamber and sat me down, brought me wine, took a wet towel and wiped Anna's blood from me. They talked to me as men talk to animals, soothing, empty words, and I did not listen, but stared at the plaster of the walls while my thoughts thrashed like a rabbit flayed alive. Horst came in, and Zianni, and many others of the *Cormoran*, some angry, some weeping, some merely dumb.

'It must have been a destrier,' said Horst to Gilles. 'A war-horse. Patch said it took her with its forelegs – no untrained beast would do such a thing! Well, have *you* ever heard of it? I know: I have ridden those creatures into battle. An ill-tempered riding horse will kick out with its hind legs, yes, but ... Christ. Some knight's battle-shy mount, I'd guess. Those creatures should never be taken out in the common street. I'd like to find the fool ...'

'There was a man,' I started to say, but I trailed off, for the fellow with the scar had not been looking at Anna, not been waiting for us at all, and in truth I had all but forgotten why we had even returned to the Blue Falcon, for now I felt night falling upon me. Except it was not dark, it was a silvery, cold oblivion, drowning me like quicksilver. When at last the Captain came for me I rose like a man in heavy iron mail and plodded after him, each footfall a labour.

Anna lay there on the bed we had warmed for each other just yesterday, dressed in white linen. Tall candles burned at each corner, the flames invisible in the sunlight. Her face was covered with a square of white muslin, and her brown hands were folded on her belly and held a golden cross. Pavlos the guardsman knelt at her feet, his face buried in the coverlet. He was weeping, and I saw he had torn his clothing. Like a man drugged with henbane I walked, infinitely slowly, through the empty light, until I could see the outline of the face beneath the cloth. With numb fingers I tugged it away.

One eye was still open. It jutted from its distended socket, an obscene thing, an abomination. The terrible bruise on her cheek and temple had turned a dark, turgid red. Tendrils of black hair pushed from beneath the white strip of cloth that bound her jaw and clamped her mouth into a disapproving line. Gently I placed my fingers upon her cold lips and tried to form something I recognised, some illusion of Anna, of her smile, but they sullenly reset themselves. I bent and kissed them anyway, eyes closed to block out the terrible white orb.

21

The Captain was pressing something into my hand. I looked down: it was a thick plait of black hair, tied with thread of gold, no bigger than my thumb. But it glistened with the oily sheen, the crow-shine, the dark light that always hung around Anna: her own stormy nimbus.

I tried to pull the cloth back over her face but one of my fingers brushed her eye, and at the touch of it I came undone. I tried to gather her rigid form into my arms but whether I did, and what I did after I cannot tell, for I do not remember. There is a memory of a terrible sound that perhaps tore itself from me, and a confusion, as comes with a dreadful, racking fever, and then nothing. I will relate what came to pass in the days that followed, but it will be a cold telling, for I was not really present. Everything had become a grey blur. Anna's strange letter was put away with her things and I forgot that it had ever existed. I walked and talked, but my soul had followed Anna down through whatever appalling drift had engulfed her and I had no more life in me than does a revenant.

We buried her in the Church of Saint Faith Under Saint Paul's. *Cormaran* gold bought the services of a reluctant, hand-wringing priest, for only the communion of money could induce the Church to treat the mortal remains of an unwed, schismatic woman with any sort of deference. The only mourners were the *Cormaran*'s crew, but even so the little church, which stands in the shadow of the great, ugly cathedral, was full. The Greeks could not teach our poor priest how to bury Anna in her own faith, but every man kissed her farewell, and Pavlos stood and chanted in his tongue some spoken hymn, words I do not recall that rose and fell like the waves of the sea, or starlings wheeling and flocking at sunset. Anna lay in state before the altar dedicated to the service of a faith she despised, and was laid to sleep in a stone tomb in the heart of a land she felt nothing for, surrounded by the bones of reviled Franks. But she has a fine slab carved with Greek letters in the custom of her people, and there she will rest for all time.

Whatever business we had in London was concluded, I presume, and days later, or perhaps weeks afterward, the *Cormaran* slipped down the Thames, past the brown marshes, the desert of hissing reeds, the frost-painted meadows grazed by sheep, the towns where folk were living and dying; and out into the bleak oblivion, the cold comfort of the sea.

PART TWO

Rome

Chapter Two

'Do you not mean "*Where* am I?" or perhaps "Who are *you*?"?' asked the man. I shook my head. Thoughts were whirling around my skull like flying ants around a summer lantern. I took another draught of water. One by one my thoughts began to take hold of one another. Faster and faster they spun until they were one thought, and at that instant my reason returned to me.

'You are Isaac,' I told him. 'I am ...' My mind throbbed. I thought of the city of Balecester, that was destroyed. No, not destroyed: that had been a dream. But I had been in those water meadows, once. I had washed up there, after a madman had killed my best friend – or so I had believed – and knocked me senseless into the river. Balecester was lost to me, sure enough, as certainly as if it had indeed been consumed by fire. I had stolen a holy relic and been accused of murdering a priest. Then I knew myself. I was Petroc of Auneford, monk of the Abbey of Buckfast in Devon, erstwhile scholar, fugitive, outcast. My home was a ship called the *Cormaran*, and for two years I had known no other.

'I know who I am,' I said. 'And we ... but this is not London, is it?' My last memories were of that great, stinking town, of rummaging through a market with the Lady Anna Doukaina at my side.

27

The man put down the cup and clapped his hands, then raised them, palms up, towards the ceiling. 'God be praised!' he laughed. 'Praised indeed! I did not know if it was the fever that had broken, or your spirit. No, we are not in London. We are in Rome.'

'But that is … oh.' I tried to sit up, and found my backbone as weak as a poppy-stalk. 'How long have I been …'

'Ten days. There was a storm off Oran, and you fell from the mast. You landed on your head – a hard head, to be sure, as it did not break. But you fell into a deathly sleep. My dear friend, I feared we would be burying you in the blue water.'

'Ten days? From a knock on the head?'

Isaac shrugged. 'You developed a brain fever.' I shuddered. A brain fever had carried off both my parents when I was very young. 'That I could treat, and the lump on your pate. But there was something else working in you, I think. You really remember nothing?'

'No,' I said impatiently. Then I did recall the ghost of a memory, 'Is Anna nearby?'

Even in my addled state I saw that Isaac's smile had frozen on his face. He grimaced, and feigned an itch alongside his nose. I jerked upright, and my head swum horribly. But I seized him by the sleeve and feebly shook his arm. Isaac said nothing, but looked grave, the way doctors do when they must tell you that your running nose will kill you within the day. He gently eased his arm from my grasp and, going over to a table in the corner of the chamber, poured a dark liquid into a goblet. To this he added something from a small vial. When he held it to my mouth I found it was wine, with something bitter and sharp mixed in. But the wine was strong and gave me some warmth, so I drank down half of it. To my surprise, Isaac drained the goblet himself and sank down on to the pallet next to me with a sigh.

28

The wine was closing in on my reason like thick ivy around an old ruin, and I felt my eyes grow heavy, although I desperately willed them to stay open. Perhaps I had not heard Isaac properly. I opened my mouth to speak, but he placed his palm on my forehead, and his fingers pressed gently into my temples.

'Sleep a little, and then things may be a little more clear,' he murmured.

I tried to protest, but a deep, soft darkness was engulfing me. It was the friendliest oblivion, and I gave up struggling against it. But just as the last spark of light went out in my skull I glimpsed an image. It was Anna, a dark cloak about her shoulders, tears painting streaks of kohl down her cheeks. She turned from me. Turned away, and stepped through a great stone doorway into shadow. Darkness swallowed her, and then it swallowed me.

When I woke next, it was morning. At least, I supposed it was morning, for the light was coming in through the window at a sharp angle and lighting up the walls of my room. Without thinking I swung myself out of bed, only to find that I had no strength in my legs. I slumped on to the bedcovers, and then managed to haul myself upright. Leaning against the wall, I shuffled over to the window. The sunlight was strong, and blinded me for a moment. I blinked, and saw, stretching away below me, a field of tumbled stones and ruined walls. My heart gave a lurch as I remembered how I had seen Balecester destroyed. Had it really happened? Then I blinked and saw goats clambering over the stones, and the silver-green of olive trees. I rested my elbows on the cold stone of the windowsill. Tears started to prick my dry eyes, and then I heard a noise behind me. I turned and found that I had not been alone. Captain de Montalhac was seated in a narrow chair, his long legs thrust out before him. He had been sleeping, I supposed, for now he yawned and rubbed his hands through his greying hair.

'Good morrow, young Patch,' he said thickly. 'I suppose it is the morrow? I believe you had a better slumber than me.'

'I did not see … How long have you been there, sir?'

'Since Isaac put you out with his finest sleeping draught. And that was a little after sunset yesterday.'

'Isaac took a little of his own medicine,' I said absently.

'And well he might,' said the Captain, standing up and stretching. 'He had not left your side for nearly two days and nights. We thought we were losing you, boy. Your life was smouldering like wet peat, and Isaac tended you without pause.'

'When I awoke then, I could remember nothing,' I whispered. 'But now … everything is pain.'

'You nearly died,' said the Captain.

'Would that I had!' I cried. 'I understand nothing, and yet she is dead, which I seem to know, and I … I am alive? Dear God, how has it come to this?'

'Pain is to be expected. But Isaac told me that your pain might be beyond the reach of his skills. Indeed we both wondered whether your body was sick at all, for it seemed that, even though you were hurt from your fall, you grew far more sick than your injury merited. Isaac wondered if you had lost your will to live.'

'I wish to die.'

'Indeed. But you still live…'

I sat down heavily on the bed. 'I can see Anna turning away from me, and a door closing. Then nothing until I woke last night. Yet I know she is dead.'

'Well, you seem to have lost a full three weeks of your life,' said the Captain. Then he attempted a grin. 'Good riddance,

30

I'd say. They were unalloyed misery for you, lad. You had been sunk in a deathly gloom since we left London.' Then the grin vanished as he dropped his head into his hands and rubbed his eyes cheerlessly.

I did not reply, but lay down and turned my face to the wall. I hardly cared that the Captain was still talking, indeed his voice faded away into a thin, distant hiss, for I had been engulfed by a swift, searing tide of pain. It was the returning memory of all that I had forgotten, and it travelled like cold fire along every nerve, every vein, every bone in my body. I shook as if with the ague, and tears dropped from my eyes and soaked into the sheets. Perhaps I might die now, I thought feebly. Please, let this be death.

But it was not death, at least not mine. As one feels a knife-thrust first as simply a dull blow, the pain coming along with the realisation that there is a blade in one's flesh, so I was first stunned by the remembering of my loss, then pinned and writhing, the blade of memory twisting in my heart. I closed my streaming eyes, and through the tears, as if in a scrying glass, I saw it all.

I came to my senses later. The room was empty, and the day was fading outside. Sparrows were chatting on the windowsill. I raised my face from the wet bolster, to find something there that shone warm in the dimming light. I reached for it.

It was Anna's locket, a square of filigreed gold that enclosed a tiny panel of ivory, upon which some careful hand in the time of Constantine had placed the image of Saint George spearing his dragon. It was cold to the touch, of course. I had never felt it so, for its rightful place had always been the freckled hollow where her breasts began to rise. I opened it. Inside, like a tiny window on to the blackness beyond the stars, lay the plait of Anna's hair. I lifted it to my face and

31

inhaled the scent that still clung, strong as life, to the dead strands: gillieflowers, Anna's own smell.

Time does not stand still, nor does it run backwards. But for an instant I felt her fingers again, warm on my cheek, and heard her slow, deep laugh, so full of delight and passion. Then the sparrows commenced some little war over a crumb, and I was alone again but for the ethereal breath of gillieflowers.

The next day I awoke half-fogged with pain and confusion, and could not even lift my head. Isaac attended me with his bitter draughts, but they did nothing, for it seemed I was filled up with bitter already, as if my blood had turned to wormwood. Muttering about the balance of my humours, he retired to consult his books, for I was not feverish, merely clubbed with malaise, and my mind, infected with the same bitter gall, wandered through the cold, stinking mists of London in search of Anna that I might close her staring eye.

So I lay, my room dark, while visitors came and went like wraiths, their voices nothing but faint hissing in my ears. I was racked by nervous pains and stabbings, but I could not move, for I was rendered immobile by an invisible pall, heavy as chain mail, that pinned me to the sheets. I do not know how long this state of affairs continued, but candles had been lit, so the day must have slipped away when I opened my eyes to find a grey face staring down at me. Grey skin, grey eyes. Thick, beetling eyebrows the colour of pewter. A black hood pulled tight under a grey stubbled chin.

'Are you with us, boy?' The voice was strong, gravelly. The man spoke in English, but he was not an Englishman.

'Who are you?' I said. 'Why can't you all leave me alone?'

'Feeling sorry for yourself, my lad. Good. Oh, very good, indeed. Self-pity is the strongest of all the emotions save love, and even then … Can you move your limbs at all?'

I tried. I could, feebly, like a beetle on its back.

'The paralysis is passing off. Close your eyes. What do you see?'

'Nothing.'

'Nothing at all?'

'No. Darkness.'

'Darkness is not nothing.'

I opened my eyes again. My visitor was peering at one of Isaac's physic bottles. He sniffed it, and grimaced, a clown's mask of distaste. I laughed. At once the man's eyes fixed themselves to mine and held me there.

'Who are you, Master?' I asked once again.

'Michael Scotus,' he told me. Of course: he was a Scot, although his tongue was much laced with the lilts of other, warmer places.

'Who summoned you?' I wanted to know. 'Isaac? Do you know Isaac?'

'I did not know your worthy Jew before today,' he replied. 'Although we have much in common, for we both studied our art in Toledo, and we have passed a fine afternoon in discourse while you lingered in your shadows. You have been in excellent hands. I was, I daresay, not needed at all.'

'Then ...'

'I am here at the bidding of His Holiness the Pope. His Eminence heard of your indisposition, and wondered if my humble talents might be of some service to you.'

'The pope? What cares ... I mean to say, I am exceedingly grateful. But ...' I struggled to sit up and succeeded in propping myself against the bolsters and the wall. Michael Scotus was regarding me.

'You occupy a small but important corner of a surprisingly small world, lad.' He laid a long, long-nailed finger alongside his nose. 'So: you are well. Isaac has cured you. You are young,

33

your body is strong. If you were going to die of your fall, you would have done so by now. So. What ails you then, lad?'

'I grieve,' I blurted out. I did not know this odd doctor, if doctor he was, but something about him made words leap from my mouth.

'Grief. You have lost someone.' I nodded, praying he would ask no more.

'Whom did you lose?'

'My love,' I muttered. 'My lady love.'

'How do you feel?' His eyes seemed to reach into my head and force the words out of me.

'If I could vomit up my soul, and have it drop into the palm of my hand like a golden coin, and then pitch it into the deepest, blackest well that has ever been, I would not feel so bereft,' I said.

'It dizzies you, then.' He seemed to be pondering, though what was so complicated about my state I failed to see.

'Listen to me, sir,' I began. 'My woman – her name was Anna – is dead. She was barely one and twenty. She was kicked in the head by a horse and died of an apoplexy.'

'And could you have saved her?'

I took a deep breath. 'It was fate. If I had been quicker, perhaps the horse would have kicked me instead. An instant more, an instant less, and the hooves would have missed her. I ... it is not that I could have saved her, sir; it is that I was not ...'

'She died alone?'

'No, no, sir. I was with her. Many of us ... It was beyond the art of man to heal her wound. Her skull ...' I broke off, wincing.

'And so you saw her die?'

'I did.'

'And it was dreadful.'

34

'She had not found, ah …' I choked back a sob. 'Repose. She was, my friend – whoever you are – ruined. As perfect a creature that ever blessed this world, mangled by a horse, by a fucking dray horse in a shit-splattered London alley. And I cannot see her as she was in life, but only as she lay, all cold and stiff, her face stove in, her eye – oh, Christ! You speak of being dizzied? Her eye will not close, sir! I cannot close her eye!'

The doctor leaned forward and laid his hands on my shoulder. His gaze was scalding. 'Look into that eye. What do you see?'

'No! I cannot!'

'Look!'

I shuddered and kicked as a white orb, slick and silken as a pearl, swelled and grew dull like some ghastly night-sown fungus, an earthball pregnant with spores of death; then it was the winter moon, then a great cloud, seething and mounting up over sea and land, roiling. I managed to shriek feebly, like a coney in a snare, then Michael Scot was holding a basin for me as I puked myself raw.

'There, there. It is over. You are done. Good lad, good lad.'

I gulped and gagged, then found my breath. The chain-mail quilt seemed to have left me.

'You are not sick, lad: you are haunted.'

'Haunted? Do you mean that Anna …' I tried to shake the thought from my head. In my land, folk believed that those who died badly could not let their loved ones be, but harried and hunted them to death. People, healthy, young people, sickened and faded and died for no reason. I had seen it happen. As a novice monk I had sung my first mass over a ghost-struck corpse. But I did not feel her near me. I felt nothing. 'She might possess me?'

35

'No! Dear God, no. Why, do you believe she does? That would be altogether too simple, I think. No, you are possessed by a great melancholy – ach, half a lifetime spent studying in the finest schools in Christendom, to bring you that diagnosis!'

I laughed despite myself, which set off another bout of retching, which in turn brought Isaac clattering into the room.

'Good Master Michael! What are you about?' he cried, seizing my wrist and feeling for my pulse.

'Good Doctor Isaac, I have made my diagnosis – lad, what did I say ails you?'

'Melancholy, apparently,' I replied, submitting to a barrage of prods and probings from Isaac's anxious fingers. Truth to tell, I was indeed feeling considerably better.

'Well, well, well,' Isaac answered, seriously. 'Who would have thought it?' Then he straightened up and turned to Michael. 'He is prone to it,' he told him. 'There was a bad episode – not as bad as this, mind – two or so years ago.'

'And you treated it how?' the Scotsman replied, deferentially. Then to my surprise the two men turned away and began to mutter excitedly in what I realised was Arabic. The only word I understood was *Aristotle*, who both mentioned again and again, although what that obscure old Greek had to do with my affliction I could not imagine. Feeling bold as only a man with a brimming basin of vomit sloshing in his lap can, I called out to them that this was no philosophy school.

'Ah, Patch. The good Michael here was discussing a theory of Aristotle concerning black bile, and I was countering with the teachings of the great ben Maimon, whom you know as Maimonides. Do you like the music of lutes, dear friend?'

'I do not know. I have never really thought about it. Why?'

'Ibn Sina – your Averroes – prescribes the music of stringed instruments for your particular sickness,' Michael Scot put in. 'Shall I send some musicians?'

'I pray you, do not!' I insisted.

'He is much recovered,' mused Isaac. 'What exactly did you do?'

'I merely applied that which is set out in the *Poetics* of Aristotle and developed by Averroes. To whit, I challenged the dark humour by holding up a mirror to it.'

'And only that? Extraordinary.'

'It is a beginning. I believe I may accomplish a complete cure, but I will require some time to prepare. Master Petroc, I will see you again.' And without another word he embraced Isaac, turned to regard me for another piercing instant, and stalked from the room. I had not noticed until that moment that he was tall, and though he must have been all of sixty years if not more, he did not stoop, and moved like a man half his age.

'Is that it? Who was that very odd fellow?' I demanded of Isaac as soon as the door had closed.

'Michael Scotus,' he spread his arms wide, palms open to heaven. 'A prodigy, and a gift from ... I know not where.'

'You know him, then?'

'His fame is, one might say, legendary,' said Isaac with a touch of professional hauteur.

'Nevertheless ...'

'No, no, you are right. Famous to those such as myself. He was still spoken of at Toledo, although he had been gone two decades or more when I was a student. Strange, though. I believed he had died.'

'Plainly not.'

'Quite so. But there were reports ... quite definite ones. The pope – this one, Gregory whatever he is – recommended him for Archbishop of Canterbury, but the English would not have him. 'Tis said he returned to his homeland and died of disappointment.'

'Why wouldn't they have him?' I enquired, feeling strong enough at last to move the reeking basin on to the night stand.

'Um. Well, the ignorant often ... our profession is ill-understood by the mass of humanity, my friend. Our services are needed but feared, for – so it seems to them – we hold sway over life and death. Would that it were so,' he added, pouring me another draught of some noxious, syrupy physic. 'But in the case of our worthy Scot, whose talents and interests stretched much, much further than the healing of the sick, the ignorant painted him with their most foul slur. Not so incredible, perhaps: he spent many years at the court of the Emperor Frederick, who is so repellent to the pious amongst your people. But this was a man, Petroc, who knew the greatest minds of his age, who understood Ibn Sina, Ibn'Rushd, Maimon, whose intellect reached back deep into the pagan ages to discourse with Aristotle ...'

'But what was the charge?' I rasped, my throat flayed by whatever I had just swallowed.

'Sorcery. What else?' he answered, picking up the basin and leaving me to my thoughts, which, suddenly unencumbered by the crushing weight of melancholia, were circling and cawing like gulls about a herring boat.

Whatever Michael Scot had done to me – and I could not recall him having done anything at all, save make me puke – I began to recover, for in truth there was barely anything the matter with my body, and my strange doctor had, I thought, somehow released my natural energies so that the vitality of youth, and the impatience, began to flow once more. So in

38

a day I had left my room, and before another three days had passed I was pacing about the rooms that the Captain had taken for us, and which seemed to occupy an entire floor of some ancient and labyrinthine building. Most of the crew had stayed with the ship, but Horst the Swabian, Zianni the Venetian and a couple of others had come to help with city business. My wanderings had begun to annoy my companions, I would guess, for I was pestering Zianni one afternoon when he snapped his fingers under my nose.

'Listen, my invalid, you are more irritating than a bot-fly. Why do you not go outside?'

'I ... I do not know this city,' I stammered, taken aback. Indeed, why had I not left the building? 'I was waiting for Isaac to give me a clean bill of health, I suppose.'

'Right, then, I shall see to it that he does, immediately.'

Isaac did indeed pronounce me free of his care that very afternoon, and did so with a smile in which I detected a hint of relief. He sent me to see the Captain, whom I found in his room, talking with Gilles, who had just returned from a couple of days with the *Cormaran*, which lay at Ostia.

'What cheer, lad?' he asked brightly. I hunched my shoulders.

'None at all, but I am up,' I said.

'Have you told Gilles of your strange physician?'

'I have not,' I said, and gave him the story. It left him exchanging looks of frank puzzlement with the Captain.

'*The* Michael Scotus?' said Gilles at last. 'He is dead.'

'So Isaac told me. Was he a revenant, Patch? Did he carry a whiff of the grave?'

'Not at all. He was as lively as a foal.'

'But terrifying, surely?' Gilles pressed. 'His reputation is – Good Christ, I have known of him since first I learned to read!'

39

'Not terrifying, but very *intent*, I would say. I felt as if he peered right inside me. In fact ...'

The Captain interrupted, fortunately, and saved me from reliving the horrible vision the grey man had stirred up in my mind's eye. 'Sent by Pope Gregory himself. Is that not curious? I did not think we merited such favour.'

'Nor did I. Curious that His Holiness even knows we are here – but he is a customer, so no doubt he has been expecting us.'

'Indeed, I did send word of our arrival to the Lateran Palace,' said the Captain, looking unconvinced. 'If indeed old Gregory is even there. And of course we do have some ... some items that will interest him. But to send his own physician ...'

'He loves us, it is plain,' said Gilles. 'But in point of fact, Scotus is not the pope's physician. That is a fellow by the name of ... oh, I forget. A Cypriot, very fat. And so far as I know, Scotus was the emperor's man, his tutor, I believe, and of course his necromancer, if you believe the chatter of the mob. Nonsense, of course, but ... No, I have it. He died five years ago, in Edinburgh.'

'Another Michael Scotus, maybe?' I ventured. 'But Isaac thought he was the real article. And how could he be a necromancer if the pope marked him as Archbishop of Canterbury?'

'Necromancer or not, he has mended our Patch,' said the Captain, and squeezed my shoulder.

Later, after we had dined on hotly spiced ox-tails, various strange but delightfully chewy entrails and an assortment of bitter greens washed down with a pale, somewhat thin wine, the Captain wiped the gravy from his beard.

'Now then, Gilles. It is high time we introduced our young friend to the city of Rome.'

My last clear recollections were of the grey, muddy streets of London, so stepping out into the warm afternoon light of Rome was perhaps the greatest shock I had yet received since waking from my long slumber, and from the numb revenant's existence I had led since Anna's death. For almost my whole life, Rome had been like a lodestone to my thoughts. The greatest city on earth, where Peter and Paul and countless other martyrs had met their glorious deaths. Seat of the Holy Father, and the place where Caesar had walked, and Nero, Cicero, Virgil ... And my journey here had been like a miracle. I had been borne here, unconscious and unknowing, and my awakening had been a sort of resurrection. These and a cloud of other portentous thoughts were whirling around my head as I waited for a servant in sober livery to unlatch the huge, studded street door. Then it swung open, and we strode out into the city.

Perhaps I had been expecting angels, or stern-faced ancients in togas, but as my foot landed in a pile of fresh donkey-shit and a swarm of filthy ragged children seized me around both legs and held their hands up to me in eager supplication, chattering like sparrows, and as the scent of cooking grabbed me by the nose and filled me up with the promise of garlic, herbs and roasting meats while a passing tradesman yelled at us in fury or brotherly greeting – it was impossible for me to tell which it might be – I had my first inkling that this city was indeed the centre of the world, but not in any spiritual sense. For Rome, although it is the home of God's representative on earth, is above all else the centre of the world of men, and here is concentrated all the glory, chaos, beauty and squalor that man has ever created.

'Dear God!' I squeaked.

'Somewhat absent here,' said the Captain, shaking an

urchin from him and waving to the tradesman, who had been greeting and not cursing. 'Despite the presence of His vicar. Throw some coin to get rid of these little ones, Patch, and let us make haste.'

And so began my life in Rome. From that day on I began to roam its streets, sometimes with a crewmate, more often alone, gorging myself upon its strangeness, its age, and the ferocious, frenzied humanity of its citizens. It would take a whole book just to tell what I saw, and since the *Mirabilia Urbis Romae* has already been written I shall not repeat what it says. Sufficient to relate, I lost myself in the clamour, the filth and the beauty, and in so doing I began to blunt the cruel edge of memory, and to accept that the sun could still warm my skin while another's would never be warm again.

I had no adventures, save with the local food, and soon learned my way around the maze of streets. I was strolling through the Borgo one morning after a visit to Saint Peter's, marvelling as ever at the myriad stalls that crammed the streets close to the great church, devoted to nothing else but fleecing pilgrims. Gawping bumpkins from Frisia and Ireland were handing over their last groats for worthless lead badges, and shrewd-eyed Catalans were striking what they believed were bargains for vials of holy water that had been Tiber fish-piss this very morning. Englishmen and Welshmen groused to one another about the local food, Danes gave directions to Basques, Hungarians argued with Swiss. It was like a county fair peopled by all of Christendom, a carnival for the gaily credulous, and I found it darkly fascinating, for was this not my company's business, writ large?

Wearying of the crowds I turned off the main street, for I remembered a small market in a square I had found a few days before that sold fine sausages from the countryside, and I thought I would bring some back for the dinner table. The market was busy, although here the crowds were local folk, women buying fruit and all the spiky and leafy vegetables the Romans love so well. I bought some sausages and had turned to leave when I heard a woman cry out behind me in anger. There was nothing unusual about that, except that the voice was English – I could have sworn it was English, and London at that, but when it came again the words were Italian, in some dialect I did not know. There she was: a slender figure with a cascade of yellow hair, over on the other side of the square. Curious despite myself, I began to wander towards her. She was standing, hands on hips, facing a thickset man in gaudy silk clothes. As I watched, the woman shook her head defiantly. Then, so quick I barely saw it, the man's hand darted out and caught the woman a hard blow on the side of her face. She fell as if hamstrung, and lay for a moment among the feet of the marketgoers, all shuffling now to get out of her way, or to get a closer look. She rolled over slowly and got on to all fours, head hanging; her hair falling about her face like a veil and trailing on the dusty cobblestones.

Her man looked down upon her. He had a crudely handsome face, somewhat florid – from too much wine, perhaps – and freshly shaved, for he had an oily gleam about the chops. His eyes were narrow and his eyebrows bristled above them like battlements. His nose had once been broken and his mouth had a proud downward curve at its corners; and his thick, curly brown hair was fashionably long. He was obviously a nobleman or a rich banker, judging by his clothes, which were the finest, no doubt, that could be bought in Venice – for by their cut I took him for a Venetian, and he was certainly as noticeable here as a pheasant amongst pigeons. And yet he had the look of a brawler, and it was not just his flattened nose that said this, but the loosely coiled way he held himself. He gave off an intelligent yet brutal menace, scanning the crowd as if daring someone to challenge him. Then he turned and stalked off.

The girl knelt, and pushed the hair away from her face. It was flushed and there was an angry red patch, already blue-ing, around one eye. Her nose was running and she wiped it, uncaring, with a sleeve. I shoved past two leering boys and was about to offer her my hand when she stood up and began to brush half-heartedly at her sullied clothes. I drew back, not wishing to embarrass her further, and the crowd began to drift away, pretending it had seen nothing, feigning no interest in the disputes of yet more mad foreigners. The girl – she was no older than me, I saw, swayed a little, then gathered herself and looked around. Her eyes were very blue, the colour of forget-me-nots, and one of them stood out, blazing from a purple halo of bruised flesh. She had a sharp nose, which she wiped again, and a wide mouth, twisting as if she were about to cry. But she did not, and with a defiant shake of her head she put her nose in the air and flounced off between the stalls and out of my sight. She plainly had not needed my help. She had been beautiful, though – no, not beautiful, but sensual. Reflecting that I had no doubt avoided making a fool of myself, I left the market, and by the time I had reached the Palazzo Frangipani I had forgotten all about the Venetian lord and his wench.

Chapter Three

A nd thus my life meandered for the next month or so
– nay, I am being too casual with time. For although
my days were lacking in both form and purpose I believe
I noted the passing of every minute, for grief ordered my
hours as strictly as any hour-glass and calendar, and I still
spent my idle time meditating upon the stark text of Anna's
death. Time passed in the world, and passed at another pace
entirely within my head. And in Anna's tomb in heartless
London, it did not pass at all. So it was not a month or so: it
was exactly three weeks and two days, while the numberless
bells of Rome were ringing out Sext, when Zianni caught me
on my way out of the Palazzo.

'Horst and myself have been invited by our dear Captain
to join him tonight at his favoured tavern. It is not far from
here. Fine food, abundant wine, brave friends. You will come
too.'

It was not an invitation, it was a command. And I had
to accept. I knew full well that my shipmates – for if things
were a little different now that we were on land, and matters
did not move in the rigid order that perforce they had to at
sea – had been putting up with me for far longer than I had
any right to expect. In ship's terms I was a useless mouth, a
non-paying passenger. I did no work – there was no work
for me to do, but that is never an excuse for idleness – and I
was not even amusing company. Plainly the time had come

to stop indulging myself, and besides, what could befall me but good food and drink, and fine company?

But now, with that perversity that so often comes when the humours are disturbed, I began to feel apprehensive. So I took to my room again and paced there until Zianni, taking pity on me, came in to help me make ready. He picked out my clothes, for Zianni was Venetian to his fingernails, and regarded the world beyond the Rialto as no more than a rabble of uncouth and unfashionable savages.

'We will show them,' he muttered, rummaging in my sea-chest and pulling out a handful of bright silk, at the sight of which my heart lurched.

It had been a gift from Anna. She had bought them for me in Bruges: a tunic of white damask, striped with black and gold, with sleeves that tapered to hug the forearm; a sleeveless tunic of the sort called cycladibus, cut from a rich bronze silk ringed from neck to hem with broad bands of deepest midnight blue. The hem itself was scalloped and, like the neck, edged with bronze ribbon, and it was very – indeed immodestly – short. Then there was a pair of hose the hue of very old clary wine, woven so that, although all of one shade, they appeared striped; and a coif of saffron-coloured linen, worked at the edges with silver thread.

That night I had worn my Venetian finery for the first and only time, feeling horribly aware that my calves, resplendent in their striped hose, were on display. The height of fashion it might be, but I was more comfortable in the kind of things a rich Devon farmer might wear to Totnes Market. Soon afterwards we had set out for London, and soon after that the time for fine clothes was past. And yet Zianni had unerringly pulled out every item that Anna had selected for me. Perhaps it was a sign. Trying hard to banish the pain of memory, I dressed myself, and buckled on Thorn, my jade-handled Moorish dagger. Zianni sat back and whistled appreciatively.

'*Que bella figura!* Almost a Venetian, my dearest shepherd. I will have to dig deep to best you, but I shall, never fear!'

I will admit that I had no fears on that account, for when I descended to find the others I saw that Zianni had rigged himself up in an even more preposterous bedizenment. His hose were flame-coloured and he was within two inches of exposing his knees to the gaze of all, and his own cycladibus blazed in shifting hues of red: blood, rubies, fire. I could barely look at him.

'Do you like the colour?' he asked me, as one dandy to another. 'It is called *sakarlat* – Persian, you know.'

'Very nice,' I replied, glancing at the Captain, who honoured me with the ghost of a wink. As ever, he was dressed in plain black. Horst, dowdy, German and impatient, snorted.

'Time to drink,' he said.

We made an *amen* and strutted down to the street door. 'I hope no one laughs at my legs,' I muttered to the Captain.

He led us under a low archway, so low that I could feel my head brushing against the moss that grew beneath it, and into a narrow street lined with stone colonnades. The sun had almost set, but in here it was already night. Like everything else here, the buildings seemed to be sinking into the soft earth, and when we came to the door of the inn I realised that this place had once been at the level of the street, but was now all but underground. Following my friends, I found myself in a long room made of stone, great, honey-coloured blocks of it, lit everywhere by oil lamps and tapers, and by a fire that burned, festooned with cook pots and loaded spits, in a huge fireplace. There were people everywhere, making a great and lusty noise. The owner, a villainous fellow with

47

close-cropped hair and a much-broken beak of a nose, gave a genuinely reverent bow when he saw us, and ploughed through his customers to seize the Captain in his arms and plant two fervent kisses upon his cheeks. Then, giving the rest of us a regal nod, he led us to an empty table over against the far wall, and sent over three surly pot-boys to ask our pleasure. I was feeling almost faint with hunger, and with the shock of being outside and in Rome, and so when a boy brought over a hot, greasy pie filled with what proved to be peppery, vinegary tripe I wolfed the thing down, felt slightly sick, and leaned back against the cool stone wall. Life began to ebb back into me, and after a few minutes spent watching the comings and goings around us, I was ready to join in.

The evening flowed happily on from there. It emerged that our host had once served in the Captain's company, although long before the time of any of us present – before, if such a time were imaginable, the *Cormaran* herself had first set sail. But the man, who delighted in the name of Marcho Antonio Marso, was plainly still a confidant of his old captain, for after we had been shown our table the two of them vanished into a back room together, and emerged a little while later with the intent look that comes after a deep conversation. Business, I imagined, and why not? Marcho Antonio kept a fine house. The wine was good, if somewhat sweet, and the food was abundant and tasty. I was beginning to gather that the Romans liked to eat every last bit of their beasts, from snout to ballocks, and indeed I had eaten both snout and ballock, I believe, by the time I was sated. I leaned on my elbows, picking at a dish of rice balls stuffed with cheese, watching the crowd ebb and flow and listening absently to my friends.

Zianni was explaining the finer points of Venetian etiquette to the Captain, and to Horst, who seemed to have fallen in love with a tart called Clementia he had met the day before. He had described her every charm to me at least six times already since we had left the palazzo. I thought of Anna, of course, but trying to banish such thoughts I pushed my chair back on its hind legs and stretched noisily. And in another instant I was scrabbling at the table as a jolt of shocked surprise sent me off balance.

For two men, soldiers by their weathered faces and cropped heads, had appeared behind Zianni and were looming over him, hands to the hilts of their swords. Between them appeared, as if by a mountebank's trick, another face. It was young, very young: a boy's face, smooth and slack, as if the puppet-strings that life weaves behind our visages had not yet taken hold there. I will call him a boy for that is how he always seemed, although when I first saw him he was in his twentieth year, married and already provided with a son and heir. He met my eyes, and smiled. His hands squeezed Zianni's shoulders and he looked down at the Venetian's coiffed head.

'Well met indeed, Jean de Sol,' he said. Zianni sat, a marble idol of himself.

'Have a care, my lord huntsman, before you blow your horn,' said the Captain evenly. 'Do not sound the kill, for you do not have your prey, nor even know him.' Then he turned to me. 'Do you know what manner of man stands before us?' he asked. It was not a question I could answer at that moment, for I swung, unbalanced, between the safety of the table and the unknown void behind me, my right hand – even while my left hand reached for the table's edge – grasping the cool stone of Thorn's hilt. The Captain took my flailing hand and pulled me upright. In answer to his question I shook my head, never taking my eyes from the stranger's face.

'Not a man at all, in fact,' said the Captain. With a touch

49

of his finger on my hand he pushed Thorn back into her sheath. The whole place had suddenly fallen silent, and with an almost painful surge of relief I heard her neat little click.

'No, not a man. And not *merely* a boy. This is an emperor.'

The emperor blinked. He had large blue eyes that looked neither innocent nor malign; rather, they were the guileful eyes of a spoiled child forever trying to get his own way. I was staring full into them. He blinked again. I did not.

'Emperor of where?' Horst asked the Captain, taking no pains to keep the rudeness from his voice.

Now the boy's hand was on his sword – he was wearing a short sword, I now noticed, and so were his two men, and their hands were ready too. Horst had pushed his chair against the wall. Zianni's knuckles were white as he gripped the table's edge. The Captain looked past me and raised a casual finger, as if calling for another jug of wine.

'To your left, my lord Emperor,' he said. We all looked. The proprietor was leaning calmly on the marble counter, aiming a small crossbow steadily at the boy in green. The three pot-boys had cleared the floor and faced our table, legs apart, one holding an iron mace, one weighing a cudgel and one slowly swinging a gigantic falchion. The Captain turned back to me. I felt him release my knife hand.

'You were saying, Horst?' he said.

'I merely asked, emperor of where?' he replied thinly.

I was staring at the boy again. He had released Zianni and I saw pride, anger and fear ripple over his face, which settled at last into a mask of resignation. It was not the look of a man who has been thwarted on the point of success, rather of one who, in his heart of hearts, never expected to succeed. Suddenly he looked very young indeed, and rather desperate. He turned to his companions.

'Wait for me outside, my good lads,' he muttered in

French. They backed away like two big, angry dogs before turning and shouldering their way out through the crowd, who were watching the scene as if waiting for a cock fight to begin. Then the boy turned back to me.

'I am not about to trade words with anyone,' he declared. He spoke a very noble French, tinged with something that sounded much warmer.

'There is no trade, and no purchase,' replied the Captain politely. 'My colleague would like to know who you are. Please understand that if you part with this information you will receive nothing in return, except perhaps your life. Tell me: apart from those two strapping fellows you brought with you, will you be missed? Think carefully.'

The boy took a deep breath and blinked again. I was beginning to feel almost sorry for him.

'Perhaps you are accustomed to a herald,' said the Captain. The boy looked up with something like a flash of anger.

'It seems I must needs be my own herald, then, now as always,' he said, and drew himself up to his full height, which was not considerable.

'Well then, know that I am Baldwin de Courtenay *Porphyrogenitus*, Emperor of Romania and Constantinople, Margrave of Namur,' the boy declaimed.

I sensed more than saw that Horst had slipped his knife from his boot and was holding it flat against the underside of the table. He glanced at the Captain.

'An emperor, this one?' he asked in his German-slanted Occitan. We had all been speaking French, and to hear the familiar tongue of the *Cormaran* was startling. 'He is telling us shite, yes?'

'Not at all,' answered the Captain. 'Has he answered your question, my Horst?' He nodded. 'Then I thank you, but you can put that away.'

Horst let go of his knife, still scowling. I felt surprising anger, although whether it was aimed at this strutting boy's presumption, the menace of his companions or the result of my own confusion I could not tell. Meanwhile the Captain nodded seriously. He turned back to the boy.

'Against my better judgement and the good advice of my colleagues, I will trade with you after all, Baldwin de Courtenay. A seat at our table in return for your name.' He waved again to the proprietor, and the pot-boy laid his falchion with a clank upon the counter and brought over a chair. As quickly as they had appeared, all weapons vanished, and the proprietor began yelling at his customers as if nothing at all had happened. In another moment I began to wonder if it had all been a dream as the inn settled down to business once again. Meanwhile the boy seemed to weigh his options and chose, with evident relief, to sit down at the end of the table. A cup appeared before him, and another jug of wine.

'Drink with us,' said the Captain. 'You are in no danger here. Not any more, that is. I must admit that I am delighted to meet you at last, but I am a little surprised to find you are in Rome. I thought you were in Venice, and the world believes you to be in France, yes?'

'You will forgive me, but I still do not know to whom I am speaking,' said Baldwin de Courtenay. He hesitated for a moment, then shrugged and took a long gulp of wine. His shoulders relaxed a little, and he risked a glance around the table. 'I believed myself to be in disguise, but even here I am recognised, and by the owner of a ... a tavern. This is your house, sir, is it not?'

'In a manner of speaking, yes,' said the Captain.

'But you said you were delighted to meet me *at last*, and I do not know what you can mean by that.'

'It is simple,' said the Captain, and he looked enquiringly

at the boy. 'It is most simple.' Baldwin shook his head in confusion. 'You seek a man, do you not?' asked the Captain, slowly.

'I do,' said Baldwin. 'I believed I had tracked him to this place. But ...'

'And whom do you seek?' the Captain ploughed on.

'He goes by many names, so far as I can tell. In France they call him Jean de Sol, and it is in France that I heard of him from ... from a dear friend.'

'And who is he, this Monsieur de Sol? What does he do?'

'He is a trader. No, hardly a trader, for that would be an insult to his stock-in-trade. Rather, he is a purveyor, a middleman. He expedites the sale of delicate ...' Baldwin was almost wringing his hands. I could tell that he was either trying to find a particular word, or frantic to avoid saying it. 'Delicate, wondrous *things*,' he managed.

'And you, as ruler of Constantinople, are well known for having a large – a very large – number of such *things* in your possession.'

'Good sir, you mock me!' said Baldwin stiffly. 'If I were not at your mercy here, I assure you—'

'Peace, peace. I do not doubt you. Far from it. I am simply amazed that you have sought me out.'

'Sought *you* out, sir? Your pardon, but I have simply made a mortifying error. I thought I had found this de Sol here, and seeing this gentleman' – he nodded politely at Zianni – 'who is the most magnificently attired person in the room, I assumed, most foolishly and carelessly, that he was the man I had been hunting for. Now I beg your pardon once again, and by your leave ...' He rose, but the Captain reached out and patted his hand.

'My dear sir, be at your ease. Your hunt was a success. You have found Jean de Sol.'

53

Baldwin jumped to his feet. 'He is here?' he cried, looking around wildly.

A hand came down on the table and made the cups dance. 'For fuck's sake, my lord Emperor, or whoever you are, just listen.' It was Horst, and his appalling French chopped through the air like a blunt hatchet. 'This is Jean de Sol, this one here. Sit down, drink your wine, and listen.'

Baldwin de Courtenay sat down with a bump. He had blushed crimson to the roots of his thick blond hair. Now, finally, I did feel sorry for him. And evidently the Captain did too, for he turned back to the boy, folded his hands in front of him, and treated us all to a great, sunny smile.

'Now then, gentlemen all, let us drink a toast of peace and friendship. Even ill meetings can have happy outcomes. So: to new understandings!'

We clinked our cups together, a little sullenly to be sure. Zianni alone seemed to find the whole thing amusing. He was also, I knew, of all of us the one most likely to have put a sudden end to the young emperor's reign. He carried a stiletto, a peculiarly Venetian dagger as long and thin as a blade of grass, and it was that knife, or one like it, that had got him banished from Venice six years ago. He was a merry soul, a happy rake; but he had the quickest hands I ever saw, and a temper like fire and quicksilver thrown together. The boy was luckier than he would ever understand.

'So it was the blaze of *sakarlat* that drew you to me?' he asked Baldwin. 'Like a moth to a candle, eh? That is a little worrisome. Come, though: you are no leper yourself, in that greenery. Where did you get it? I should like some.'

If nothing else, Baldwin de Courtenay was scrupulously polite, and to his credit he swallowed his imperial pride and allowed this banter. As I have said, I was beginning to feel sorry for the lad, so I joined in.

'Peace, Master Zianni: I saw it first. Indeed, I have been wondering how I might have a bolt for myself.' I threw him what I hoped was a conciliatory smile. To my relief, he chose to take the bait.

'It is from Constantinople, where we have the finest silk in this world,' he said. 'I would be glad to make you a gift of some. A gift to both of you, if that would not cause a falling-out between friends.' He cocked his head a little slyly. 'And now, Monsieur de Sol, I am at a horrifying disadvantage. I beg you to introduce me to your ... colleagues.'

'Gladly. The gentleman you mistook for me – and I am most flattered that you would suppose me to be so elegant – is Signor Giovanni Canal. This is der Junker Horst von Tantow. And this other young dandy here is Petrus Zennorius.'

'Well met indeed,' said Baldwin graciously. 'Allow me to beg your forgiveness for my earlier rudeness. My eagerness to make your acquaintance overcame my manners. And I am most eager, Monsieur de Sol, to be acquainted with you.'

'So I have gathered,' said the Captain. 'If you would care to speak a little of your reasons for this eagerness, I assure you that these men are my trusted confidants, and I could not keep my private matters from them even if I so wanted.'

Baldwin took a thoughtful sip of wine. Horst, as a peace offering, pushed a dish of rice balls in his direction and the boy took one, bit into it and made a face.

'Rather dry, are they not?' I asked sympathetically.

'Somewhat,' he agreed, finishing the thing and reaching for another. I saw that he was very hungry.

'Monsieur, you said that the world believes me to be in France, and indeed it has been my misfortune – my *life's* misfortune – to have the world taking an interest in my affairs. I was, until lately, indeed in France, a guest of my cousin Louis. I believe that most think I am still there. I pleaded

55

urgent business and left Paris for my fief of Namur, from whence I slipped away.'

'You had a hard ride, then,' said the Captain. 'How did you get through Lombardy? The Holy Roman Emperor holds everything from the mountains to the shores of the Venetian lagoon, and Emperor Frederick is no friend of Louis.'

'Frederick von Hohenstaufen is also a cousin of mine,' said Baldwin, a little pompously. 'But I felt it prudent to go in disguise, nonetheless. His captain in those parts is a monster, so one hears.'

'Ah, yes – Ezzolino da Romano. But it is his job to be monstrous: he is merely very good at what he does.'

'You jest with me again, monsieur. If you had ridden through the burning towns and seen the butchered corpses he leaves behind him ...'

'Yes, yes. You can see the smoke from the campanile on a fine day, so I hear,' said the Captain dismissively. 'Given all that, finding your way past the monster's army was no mean feat.'

'Well, I decided it was too dangerous to pass myself off as a simple Ghibelline, as allegiances change every furlong or so between the mountains and the sea. Besides, I am, as you know, rather well known as a Guelf, and my personal affairs are all over *fleurs de lys*. No, that is a dangerous game to play, so I posed as a knight journeying to the East to save Constantinople from the Turks. As that is the truth, I was not putting my immortal soul at risk.'

I poured myself some more wine. This evening had taken a strange turn indeed. A simple fight would have been quite a normal end to the night's proceedings; fights, although I did not enjoy them, had ceased to surprise me, and I knew how to look after myself. But this: this was something so far outside my ken that I might as well have been supping with the man in the moon. Here, seated at my right hand, was a real emperor, and a hungry one at that, gossiping about his royal cousins and about the great war that had burned up half of Italy as if it were nothing of greater moment than a day at the fair. What I knew about the Empire of Romania was slight: Anna had fizzed with rage at the very thought of Frankish Constantinople, but let me know that the thieves who had captured the greatest of all cities were no better than beggars, paupers who held her uncle – who was, of course, the true emperor of the Romans, although at present he ruled from Nicea – at bay only through luck and by prostituting themselves to any barbarian or infidel who rattled their purses.

It confused me that, while he was cousin to both Louis of France and Frederick von Hohenstaufen, he put himself in the Guelf camp, that is, a supporter of the pope's cause against the claims of the emperor, rather than an ally of Frederick, or Ghibelline, as they have begun to call themselves. *Fleur de lys* and eagle: this war between flowers and birds had already spilled blood enough to redden every whitewashed wall in Italy. Indeed I could not quite see why an emperor would have to take sides at all. It did not seem prudent to ask, however. Baldwin had finished the rice balls and was delving deep into a stack of ham, and although he was trying to seem courtly it was plain that hunger had mastered rank, at least for the moment. The Captain was letting him eat and watching carefully. He was wearing the look that had reminded my friend Will of a great owl watching mice scurry below him on the floor of his barn, and not for the first time that evening I felt a – very small – tug of pity for Baldwin de Courtenay.

'Good sir, I can perhaps guess what you are hoping to talk to me about,' said the Captain after Baldwin had polished off the ham and sat back, looking rather stunned and wiping greasy hands on the wondrous tunic. 'Your cousin Louis is a collector, of course.'

'Monsieur, by your leave! You speak of the King of France, the heir of Charlemagne, not some … some ploughboy!'

'Peace, dear friend,' said the Captain calmly. 'That most pious king and I have a long acquaintanceship: I daresay I know him better than you do yourself.' He held up a hand to silence more protest. 'Louis Capet is not a proud man, nor overbearing, nor is he a zealot for pomp and ceremony. I have conducted most of my dealings with him seated at his side beneath an oak tree, and he would not wish me to dissemble otherwise.'

Baldwin sighed. 'You are right. The King of France has ways and habits that are beyond the understanding of …' he glanced nervously around the table. 'Beyond my under-standing, certainly. But as to piety, there, sir, do we have the matter itself.' He sighed again, and placing his right hand on the table, seemed to fall into sad contemplation of it.

'Baldwin de Courtenay, I believe I can find the heart of this matter that plainly weighs heavily upon you.' The Captain was leaning forward, looking past me into Baldwin's eyes. It was like watching a baby rabbit mesmerised by a stoat. The boy swallowed painfully. His eyes were very wide.

'In your palace of Bucoleon in Constantinople, there is a chapel. That chapel's name is Pharos. I know every single thing, great and small, that resides within the Pharos Chapel.'

Baldwin looked for an instant as if he had been run through the heart with Zianni's stiletto. Then, as the shadow of a cloud moves across and leaves a summer hillside, his face crumpled into a grimace of the most intense relief. His shoulders slumped and he put his two hands together as if in prayer and kissed his fingertips.

58

'I knew it, gracious Lord,' he whispered, finally. 'I knew You would bring me to this man. Thank You for guiding me this night.' I was puzzled for a moment, then I realised that the boy really was praying. I had not seen a man pray in earnest in many, many days and it struck me that prayer, a habit I had learned at my mother's breast and had performed as naturally as breathing every day, every hour of my life until I had joined the *Cormaran*, was now as strange to me as the habits of some grotesque from the pages of Herodotus. I looked around at my fellows. Zianni was smiling indulgently and a little wolfishly at Baldwin; Horst was scowling. The Captain's face was unreadable. Baldwin de Courtenay finished his prayer and crossed himself extravagantly. I believe the Captain was the only one of us who did not flinch.

'I am most flattered to be taken for an answered prayer,' he said. 'However, I am usually thought by most to be a businessman. I would be delighted to talk business with you tomorrow – I will come to your lodgings, if you would care to name a time.'

Baldwin blinked in surprise. He was forever being taken by surprise, this one, I thought.

'As you wish, monsieur,' he said. 'But I ...'

'Please stay a while and order some more food – in fact I shall see to it. We must be elsewhere, unfortunately. And tomorrow?'

'Yes, yes. I am lodging at the *Locanda della ... di ...*' he snapped his fingers in frustration. '... in any event, the Sign of the White Hound, in the Borgo. I will await you ...'

'At terce, if that suits.'

'It does, it does.' Baldwin rose, and we followed his example. I thought he was about to push past me and embrace the Captain, but he stood fast. He was younger than I had thought, or perhaps relief had softened him, but I saw that, had I acted on my base, angry instinct I would have killed a child. As I left the table I bowed my head politely. He gave me a bland look in return that I could not read. With Zianni and Horst I pushed through the crowd and stepped out into the street. It was raining, a warm mizzle, and Baldwin's two men were standing across the way, sheltering in the mouth of a covered passageway. At the sight of us they squared their shoulders and stepped into the rain. Horst held up a hand.

'Be of good cheer, lads – your emperor is within, filling his belly. I should join him before he scoffs the lot.'

If he had intended to sweeten matters with the honey of peace, it was obvious that his words had achieved the opposite effect. Both men stopped short, threw back the cloaks they were wearing and clapped hands to hilts. In another instant they would have drawn, had not the Captain stepped in front of us.

'I am the man your master sought,' he said, and his voice rang against the stone walls around us. 'Well, he has found me, and we are to meet again tomorrow morning. He bid me summon you to his table, where you will find food and wine. You are my guests, good fellows: I ask you to eat no less than your fill. We will see you on the morrow, and there will be no more thoughts of war. Good night to you.'

And he opened his arms as if to sweep them into the taverna. Horst, Zianni and I stepped back to let them through. One, taller than his mate and with the close-cropped hair of a soldier, whispered to his partner and stalked to the doorway. He peered inside. Looking over his shoulder I could just see the boy-emperor mopping a plate with a hunk of bread. The soldier turned and gave us a look that was more puzzled than angry. Then he beckoned to the other man, who walked past us, biting his lip and with his narrowed eyes on the ground. They stepped through the doorway and did not turn back.

'Gentlemen, I am sorry our evening has been cut short, but the circumstances are …' the Captain paused and rubbed his nose. 'I need to think things over. Thank you, dear friends, for not skewering that half-grown kinglet. I dare say we may never have a more fortunate meeting again, though we live as long as Adam. If you would care to take a cup of wine at the palazzo, you are welcome.'

Zianni shook his head. He was grinning. 'Captain, you are a prodigy of this age. Merely by sitting quietly in the midst of the city you draw the greatest fish of all into your net. I'll bid you good night and hide my fair locks, I think. I don't want to feel any more hands upon my shoulders.' And with a wave, he set off up the street towards his lodgings.

'By your leave, friends, I will see if my little Clementia is still awake,' said Horst.

'It is late to be calling on a lady,' I scolded him in my monk's voice.

'She'll not mind if I wake her,' he said seriously, and hurried off after Zianni. 'Hold up, boy,' we heard him call. 'Come meet my little pigeon.'

We watched them turn the corner. I was about to make my excuses as well, but the Captain took my arm and we began to stroll. He was silent for a few long minutes, then as we were crossing a little square he paused. The square was small, a black pool in a ravine of towering stone walls. In its centre stood a piece of ancient marble carved like a fish, from the mouth of which flowed a thin stream of water. It had stopped raining. An archway led out of the place, and beyond it people streamed to and fro along a busy thoroughfare, but where we stood we were surrounded by looming slabs of shadow. Voices and laughter reached us with no more form or substance than the piping of bats. I listened to the water trickle behind us.

'The world passes by,' murmured the Captain. I looked at him. He was staring at the shadows. I could not think of a reply, and perhaps none was needed, so I kept silent.

'You are a country lad, Patch,' he said finally. 'You must have remarked, a thousand times, how of a summer's evening great clouds of midges hang in the air, and that when you walk through them it is like passing through a curtain: the creatures part for you, and form themselves again behind your back. And save for one or two, perhaps, who have become entangled in your hair, it is as if you had never disturbed them at all. I have always thought of the world in that way.'

I looked at him. 'Like gnats,' I said, cautiously.

'Look over there – and everywhere in this city and over the whole face of the earth – at how they swarm. I pass through them, and they part, and re-form as if I had never been.'

'I have had that very sensation,' I said quietly.

'Perhaps every man does. They seek to find a pattern in the swarm, to descry meaning. Perhaps they call it fate or destiny. Usually they choose to see God in the meaningless whirl. But there is no form. My faith teaches me that all life – all matter itself – is the creation of the Dark One, and to contemplate it is worthless and corrupting.' He shook his head. 'And I know that to be the truth. But then from out of the vast cloud, the whirling chaos, steps Baldwin de Courtenay, who holds the key to the Pharos Chapel. Patch, tonight I am like a disenchanted alchemist who, out of sheer habit, peers into his alembic and finds the Philosopher's Stone. The great event, the goal of goals, that one gives one's life to prepare for while never really believing it will come to pass … The Pharos Chapel is that to me, and its key is my magical Stone. The world is not behaving itself, Patch. This smacks of fate, and I do not believe in fate.'

'Surely there is no deep mystery here, Captain,' I said,

trying to sound light-hearted, although my mood was indeed guttering. 'Baldwin has been looking for you. He was fortunate, or skilful – though that seems doubtful – and found you. After all, you do not hide yourself, at least not here.'

He sighed. 'Good sense, Patch, as always. You are absolutely right. What is troubling me is that this night's events are like nothing so much as the answer to a prayer. And I do not pray.'

'Baldwin does,' I told him. 'So what will you do?'

'Do?' He laughed, and all at once he seemed to grow cheerful again. 'What will I do? What would the alchemist do, who finds the Philosopher's Stone?' He spread out his arms, and his cloak flew up around him like wings. For a moment the Captain was a magus of night, binding the city to his command. Then the cloak settled, and he was a man again.

Chapter Four

The bells of every church in the Rione Campus Martius, with all the other belfries in the city, began to chime the nine bells of terce.

Gilles had awoken me at dawn. Opening my eyes, I found him squinting at me down his nose, like a surgeon in a mummer's play.

'You are rested? Not still in a drunken stupor? The Captain has need of you.'

'I was not so drunk – I hardly drank anything last night,' I rasped indignantly, my leathery tongue giving the lie to my protest. And then, 'Has need of me? How so?' I asked, curious despite myself.

'He is taking you with him to see Baldwin.'

I all but choked.

'Why, O Gilles, is the Captain taking *me*? It is much too weighty a matter,' I protested when I had recovered my breath.

'Aha!' he said, chuckling. 'Your perfect manners.' He smiled. 'Listen, Patch: I will not say more now, but I can at least tell you this. The Captain has a great liking for you, lad, as do I. You are a brighter light than most; you are young, and you have proved that you have the liver for our sort of work. If the Captain chooses to take you along to an important audience, perhaps he means you to learn something. Eyes open, yes? Eyes and ears.'

'And mouth shut tight?'

Gilles merely laughed, and, seeing that my unsteady hand was shaking ruby droplets on to the bed linen, reached out to steady my cup.

'Look upon it, then, as your reward for having the hardest head on the *Cormaran*, and for returning to us despite all,' he said. 'By the bye, you will be Peter of Zennor, of course.' I nodded. It was the name I had assumed in London, where my own name was likely to lead me to the scaffold.

Gilles had ordered a set of fine clothes laid out for me. I dressed hurriedly, all fingers and thumbs, and although I heard a commotion beyond my door I was too nervous to join in with what was clearly a rowdy breakfast. When at last the Captain knocked, I was pacing in front of the window, watching the goats play-fight amongst the stones. After that I broke my fast on raw eggs, cheese and good bread with the Captain, who all but ignored me, instead leafing through a sheaf of old parchments. But at last he poured me a mug of small beer and one for himself, toasted me with a warm smile, and drank.

'That is better,' he said, wiping the foam from his beard. 'Well, my lad, are you ready for the off? An emperor is waiting for us.'

I followed him out into the already bustling street. Striding through the Campus Martius, we came at last to the bank of the Tiber, and nervous though I was, my heart leaped to see it, running fast over a bed of weedy, tumbled stones. Perhaps I had been expecting something as grand and majestic as the Thames, but here was a stream much like my own River Dart back in Devonshire. But that was merely the river itself. If it seemed friendly and familiar, what lay along its banks was not. We passed a dark, lowering building spiked with gibbets that overhung the bank of the Tiber, a brace of leathery cadavers swinging there seemingly unnoticed by those who walked beneath them, and crossed a great stone bridge that led over the river to a strange, circular castle that guarded the far bank.

'This, Patch, is the Pons San Petri,' said the Captain. 'The Romans built it – the old ones, mark you – and they built that thing as well,' he said, pointing to the castle. 'That is the Castel Sant' Angelo, the fortress of the pope. Grim, is it not?'

'Not as grim as the one behind us,' I said.

'Ah yes, the Tor di Nona. That is where the Holy Father has his enemies strangled in the dead of night. Up there,' he pointed up the hill across the river, where I could just make out the long roof of a great church, 'that is Saint Peter's, from where the Church extends its control over the souls of men. But here we stand between the symbols of its power over their bodies. The pope is also a prince, lad. Old Gregory is also Ugolino, Count of Segni.'

My strength was ebbing under the baleful watch of the bodies dangling from the Tor di Nona. I began to feel weak again. What was I, a bumpkin, a pipsqueak from the boggy moors, doing here? I followed the Captain like a whipped hound into the tangle of streets that made up that part of Rome called the Borgo, which lies beneath the walls of Saint Peter's Church. Saint Peter's! The dangling cadavers of the Tor di Nona had all but driven the thought of her from my head, yet there was the mighty arched tower of her bell tower, there the great flight of steps up which pilgrims were crawling, and rising in the distance, the basilica itself. I stopped in my tracks, slack-jawed with wonder yet again, until the Captain tapped me on the shoulder.

It was not hard to find the Sign of the White Hound. It was directly across a square that stood before the church of

Santo Spirito in Saxia, the biggest church hereabouts, whose bells were beating the air with their din; and the two French soldiers from last night were standing self-consciously in front of the door, pretending not to guard it. They recognised me straight away: there was no mistaking my finery, which the Captain had bid me wear. As always, he himself was dressed in simple black, almost priestly garb, with a cloak thrown about his shoulders and a black coif covering his greying hair. Only when you came very close would you see that what seemed to be homely cloth was in fact damasked with strange creatures and plants, with subtle workings of silver thread. This morning it was I whom the two bodyguards fixed their blue eyes upon, and seeing this, the Captain leaned and whispered in my ear.

'They look no happier than they did last evening,' he said. 'Go to, Patch: win them over.'

I licked my suddenly dry lips and stepped forward. The taller one was grasping the hilt of his sword in a businesslike manner, and it was true: neither of them seemed overjoyed to see us again. Not quite knowing what to do but remembering how I had seen courtly folk act (the few times I had been anywhere near such people), I strolled towards them, halted a few paces from where they stood, pointed my right toe in front of me and bowed slightly from the hip. Straightening up I spread my arms wide and smiled, in what I hoped was a friendly manner. Last night I had been angry and withdrawn and quite eager – as my late friend Will would have said – to get stuck in, and now I wanted them to know I was harmless, or at least in a better mood. Happily they seemed won over, for my true harmlessness was no doubt all too apparent, and both smiled faintly at my display. And now they take me for a prize poltroon, I thought. Nevertheless I cleared my throat ostentatiously.

'Good morning to you, sirs,' I said in French, which luckily I spoke tolerably well – luckily, that is, for apart from a smattering of Latin, French was the only tongue that Baldwin and his entourage had at their disposal. 'We are here at the hour appointed by your master. Pray tell: is he within?'

'His Majesty the Emperor of Romania is within, and he awaits you,' said the tall one in courtly French, and it was then I realised that he and his mate were not men-at-arms, but knights. They had made an effort to disguise themselves in rough attire, but I now saw, as I had not last night, that they wore golden rings on their fingers, and their belt buckles were golden also, and worked in the outlandish fashion of the East. The tall man had taken a sword pommel or shield-edge on the nose once upon a time, and an old scar trailed from his temple to his mouth.

'You are welcome,' added the shorter man, who had seemed so possessed with fury outside the inn. He had grey hair and age or a fight had robbed him of two front teeth. 'And we beg you to forgive our intemperate manners at our last meeting. It was poorly done.'

'No, no: if my manners were surly, the fault was mine alone,' I said graciously, trying not to sound as relieved as I felt. 'I was mistaken in my assumptions, and somewhat on my guard, as I am not yet familiar with this place.'

'Then we shall be friends, in that at least,' said the tall man. 'Though I took you for a native son of Italy last evening, you are an Englishman, I think.'

'Do I know you, sir? I mean, aside from last night?' I asked politely, for there was something familiar about him that I could not place.

'I do not think so, good sir,' he replied.

'Bruges, perhaps?' I was racking my brains.

'Alas! I was whelped not far from there, but I have not

68

been back these twenty years or more,' he exclaimed with a sad smile. Perhaps he simply looked Flemish, I thought, and let it be.

'Now let us make haste,' said the other man. 'The emperor is anxious to talk with you. Monsieur de Sol,' he called. 'I bid you welcome in the name of His Majesty Baldwin, Emperor of Romania and Constantinople. Please, come inside.'

The Captain shot me an approving look as we made our way inside the inn. The Sign of the White Hound had seen better times, but it was not quite so insalubrious as its surroundings promised. I caught sight of a couple of bright whitewashed rooms with long tables laid for the midday meal, and a pretty serving-maid in a clean apron was bustling around. We were led upstairs to a suite of modest rooms panelled in painted wood, with dark wooden ceilings. There were tapestries on the walls – I guessed they were Baldwin's, for they were creased and somewhat clumsily hung – glass in the windows, and fresh rushes underfoot that filled the air with their sweet scent. An ornate but travel-worn chest stood against the wall, and I glimpsed another in the adjoining room, where there was a bed and a somewhat grander hanging, upon which a cross in gold thread shone on a field of red cloth, surrounded by a pattern of smaller golden crosses. Baldwin was sitting in a high-backed chair with his back to the largest window. A shield – a war-shield in size, but bearing no marks of war – hung behind him, and on it a black Flemish lion pranced on a field of gold behind a diagonal red band. The sun was coming in and it was obvious he had chosen this spot so that anyone facing him would be dazzled. The tall man offered us two stools that had been placed in front of Baldwin's would-be throne, but the Captain winced as if in pain.

'I am not a young man, and my bones are as old as I am,' he said ruefully, making his way to another chair set off to the side. 'If you will permit me, I will be more pleasant company if my back is straight.' I pulled one of the stools next to him and sat down. We heard a hiss of exasperation as Baldwin heaved his chair around to face us. He was no longer a commanding shadow half hidden in light but merely a young lad in a rented room. He put a brave face on things, though, and called for wine and food. Then he raised a pale, lordly hand in greeting.

'Gentlemen,' he said, 'you are most welcome. Monsieur Jean, last night you spoke of my palace of Bucoleon. I wish with all my heart you were my guests there, rather than here, but expedience ... no matter. And already I am remiss. Let me introduce my two most faithful of men: this,' he said, indicating the tall knight, 'is Fulk de Grez, and here is Gautier de Bussac. These most excellent knights have been my faithful companions as I have made my way from one chilly northern land to another – we all miss the sun, eh, boys?'

Fulk de Gréz glanced at us with something almost like mortification in his eyes. These men, I saw, must be from Outremer. They had probably fought hard their whole lives, against the Infidel, pestilence, the sun itself, and this was their reward: handmaidens to this half-emperor. Yet they played their parts with exceedingly good grace. Gautier de Bussac brought a silver dish with water and clean linen towels, and we all washed our hands. The serving-maid came in with a silver flagon of wine, a tray of glass cups and a dish of little honey cakes. Only when everything was set to Baldwin's satisfaction did they retreat to an inner chamber.

'At last,' said the emperor, when we all had a glass in hand. 'I have been waiting for this moment.'

'I am honoured that one so illustrious should be so eager to make my acquaintance,' said the Captain gravely.

'Forgive me, but I am an impatient man,' Baldwin went on, then paused. He took a sip of wine, which was rather poor stuff, and sighed. 'That is not true at all,' he said. 'I have already learned that you are more perceptive than most men, Jean de Sol, and very well informed about my affairs. So you will know that I am nothing if not patient. I waited for years for my Regent to hand the throne over to me, or at least to die, but like Methuselah he clung to life like a strangling vine. Now he is dead at last, but I must wait patiently by the thrones of my rich cousins while they decide whether or not they will grace me with a little gift. I am patient because I need their gifts, not for myself, but for my empire. This you already know, I think, but the Empire of Romania is all but destitute. Venice took everything at the very start, and they hold all the choicest land. They squeeze the trade-routes like a wolf's jaws around the throat of a lamb. When the crusaders took Constantinople they set up their empire and left it supplied with nothing more than promises while they moved on to other deeds. My brother Robert, who was a besotted fool, died nine years ago, and if old John de Brienne had not been named Regent there would no longer be an empire. We are beset on all sides: by John Asen of Bulgaria, by John Vatatzes of Nicea, by Thessalonika.' He sank back in his chair as if the very act of telling these things had exhausted him. 'My barons are loyal when it suits them so to be. My Greek subjects, to a man, loathe me as they loathe all followers of the Church of Rome. So I need money, a great deal of it, and soldiers. I have not been home for two years, and yet I am still empty-handed – no, I have my hands full of promises.' And he held up both fists and shook them. His knuckles were white.

'But what do you wish to discuss with me?' asked the Captain. 'I am no Henry of England or Louis of France. I have no armies and no treasury. You have all my sympathy, but I believe you want a little more than that.'

'Straight to the mark, sir – thank God. You know what is in my mind, so let us be direct with each other. You know of the Chapel of Pharos.'

'I do.'

'Do you know what it contains?'

'The relics of the Passion of Our Lord Jesus Christ, so I understand.'

I all but choked on my wine at these words, so carelessly uttered. If I had not held a goblet I would surely have crossed myself with reflexive piety, but I did not, and in another moment the training of my new life had overpowered the habits of the old one. Meanwhile, Baldwin brought his hands together and kissed his fingertips. I had seen the same gesture last night.

'Those wonders have been guarded there since the Empress Helen brought them out of the Holy Land a thousand years ago. It is beyond ...' He shook his head.

'Forgive me, but I am as overcome as you are by even the mention of such relics,' said the Captain with great care. 'The greatest wonder is the Crown, is it not?'

'The Crown of Thorns itself,' Baldwin breathed. 'The thorns that pierced His flesh, that were doused in His blood. Yes, that is the treasure of all treasures. But there are more.'

The Captain was silent. He leaned back in his chair, as calm as if he were alone in the library of the Ca' Kanzir. He regarded Baldwin with no more than polite interest. Only the slight tilt of his head showed that he was paying attention.

'Yes, more,' Baldwin went on, becoming somewhat carried away. 'The Crown is chief of them, but the chapel holds the Spear that pierced His side, the Reed, the Cane, the Sponge, the Chain that bound Him; His Swaddling Bands, His Tunic,

His sandals, a part of the Shroud that wrapped His body …'
He was rattling away, counting relics off on his fingers. I
fought back a grin.

'… the Towel He used to dry the feet of the Holy Apostles,
the True Cross – pieces of it. The head of the Baptist, and
Saint Clement's, Saint Simeon's, Saint Blas' heads. The very
staff of Moses!'

'But the Passion relics themselves,' said the Captain. 'Your
pardon, but I am fascinated. As you know from your cousin
Louis, I have helped with the translation of a number of relics
over the years, and for many clients, including Louis himself.
But to hear of such things, and from a man who has seen
them with his own eyes …' The Captain passed an expressive
hand over his face. 'I understand the very Stone that blocked
the mouth of the Tomb is there?'

'Supposedly … that is, indeed it is. The *Sudarium* also …'

'Your pardon again, Sire, but is this *Sudarium* – the face-
cloth from the Gospel of Saint John, I believe? – is it not part
of the Shroud you mentioned?'

'No, I don't think so. The …'

'No matter, no matter. You are speaking of wonders and
I am acting the pedant. There is no doubt you possess a
formidable collection. I think you wish for my professional
opinion?'

'Indeed,' said Baldwin, his voice almost cracking with
relief.

'Well then. The Pharos Chapel holds the most formidable
of any collection of holy relics in Christendom. That you
knew.' Baldwin nodded. 'And so …' He held up his hands in
a gesture of helplessness. 'There: my professional opinion. I
am speechless. Now let us come to the point. Money is easier
to talk about.'

Baldwin puffed his cheeks and blew out. 'You are every bit

73

as direct as Louis described you,' he said. 'But that is good.' He cleared his throat, which set off a small fit of coughing.

'How much? How much is it all worth?' he said at last.

'All of it?'

'All of it. Every thorn, every stitch, every bone. I will lose my throne, sir, and all my vassals shall be cast out if I do not act now, this instant. So, how much?'

'To whom?' the Captain asked, as calm as ever.

'To whoever wants it,' said Baldwin. He was smiling, but shaking his head in exasperation.

The Captain brought his fingertips together and regarded them for a long moment. A death-bed hush had abruptly descended on the room. I watched the dust motes dance in a golden swarm through the sunlight from which Baldwin had withdrawn himself. Then the Captain stood up, a great black shadow that loomed over the emperor. The boy flinched.

'You ask me to put a price on what is priceless,' he said, and his voice was as hard and sharp as flint. 'I am not a pawnbroker. These relics, things that have touched Our Lord, that have rent His flesh, have no worth at all. They are truly valueless, as prayer is valueless. The prayer itself is nothing more than air. But what price the prayer that reaches the ear of the Almighty? I will not value these things of yours. If someone wishes to buy them, take what is offered. I can give you no more advice.' He gestured to me and I too rose to my feet, watching the man at my side for any sign as to what might happen next.

'We thank you for your hospitality,' the Captain went on at last. 'It is one of my dearest wishes to set foot inside the Pharos Chapel, and I am relieved to hear that it did not suffer the hideous fate that befell the rest of your city when Doge Dandolo and Baldwin of Flanders took it for themselves. But I cannot help you. I am no usurer, nor am I a banker. If you wish to raise a loan, there are many here in this city to whom you can turn. And there are many more, scrupulous and not, in Christendom and beyond. And now, by your leave.' He took a step towards the door, and I made as if to follow.

Baldwin let out a great cry, and instantly the two knights rushed into the room. When they saw the Captain and I standing there so solemnly they stopped and looked to their master. Baldwin had risen too. He turned impatiently to his men and shooed them out again. Then he turned to us, and flung out his arms beseechingly.

'Please, sir, please! Do not leave!' he cried.

'Why should we not?' asked the Captain bluntly.

'Because you have misconstrued me! You have taken offence where none was intended, but I clearly see my error. I beg you to reconsider,' the poor boy pleaded.

'Your Majesty,' said the Captain, to my surprise, as I had never heard him honour anyone with their title, no matter how illustrious. 'I am a businessman, and as such a very hard person to offend. You have not offended me in the slightest, but I fear you have wasted my time and yours. I wish you every good fortune, and now I must be on my way.'

'Jean de Sol, I command you … oh, fuck it,' said Baldwin, sinking down on his chair. 'I just want you to talk to the King of France on my behalf,' he went on. 'That is all. I have nothing, do you hear? Nothing!' His voice was pinched, shrill. 'You would not fix a price on a prayer, you say? Well, Louis would! For one of Christ's farts in a bottle he would pay enough for me to build a wall around my whole empire! These things are all I have, and you tell me they are nothing? Is this my punishment for trying to sell what should not be sold? Dear God, I am a Christian king!' His last words were shouted at the ceiling.

'I am sure that no one doubts your piety,' said the Captain in a softer tone. 'But if you put the Crown of Thorns up for sale as if it were a bale of silk or a sausage hanging on a butcher's stall, you will be reviled. Canon law is not specific on this subject,' he went on, sitting down again and arranging his sleeves like a schoolmaster. 'But I can assure you that the Holy See would accuse you of the sin of simony, *simonia realis* in this case, although to some even considering such an action makes you guilty. And simony is a grievous sin.'

'But simony is merely the buying and selling of benefices and indulgences,' protested Baldwin. He too seemed a little calmer, and had taken his seat once more. I was the only one standing, so I refilled my cup and sat down. 'It goes on all the time. I would guess every bishopric in my empire was bought, and who has not given a few coins for an indulgence? I know many who would not go into battle without one.'

'It is all a matter of scale,' said the Captain patiently. 'The Church turns a blind eye to many simoniac benefices because it is simply too troublesome to do anything about them, and too easy to bribe one's way out of trouble. It likes to sell indulgences because it is a simple way to raise coin. In my estimation, however, putting the relics of the Passion on the open market would be akin to buying the papacy. You would be excommunicated.'

'Really?'

The Captain shrugged. 'Perhaps. Who knows what the Church will do? How are your relations with the Holy Father?'

'His Holiness Pope Gregory has been kind enough to take a ... a keen interest in our affairs,' said Baldwin. For once he sounded like a courtier, and I understood that this was a speech he had made many times in the last two years. 'He has preached a crusade against John Asen, he ...'

'Concrete assistance? Forgive my interruption, but has he opened Saint Peter's purse for you?'

'Not yet, but ...'

'He was quick to excommunicate your cousin Frederick,' the Captain pointed out.

'Frederick Hohenstaufen is a godless, pitiless voluptuary,' squeaked Baldwin primly.

'But Gregory excommunicated him merely for not being quick enough to set off on crusade,' said the Captain. 'For all your protestations, Frederick too is a Christian king – your pardon, an *emperor*. No, I think you might find that old Gregory would swiftly show you his whip-hand if you attempted to sell the relics.'

'Then what am I to do? I cannot risk Gregory's anger. He is our one true friend in all Christendom.'

Strange, I thought, that young Baldwin had spent his life in thrall to old men. His Regent, John de Brienne, had been approaching his ninetieth year when death took him, and Pope Gregory was already ninety. This boy, who fancied himself a lion, was no more than a gelded ram at the mercy of prodigiously ancient shepherds. I shuddered: there was nothing in Baldwin's lot that I envied.

'We are here, sir, because you have a buyer for these things you cannot sell,' said the Captain. It was a statement, and Baldwin stiffened. 'But there is a difficulty,' he continued. 'Louis desires your relics, but he cannot buy them. And he would not: Louis, of all men, would not risk his mortal soul thus, nor would he be so vulgar.'

'That is it!' cried Baldwin, slapping his knees. 'You have cut to the very quick. My empire is saved, but for the scruples of my saintly cousin! He would give anything for the Crown alone, let alone the ... the rest of it, but he cannot. I am like

77

Taranto in Hades: I approach water to slake my thirst, and it turns to dust!'

'I think you mean Tantalus,' I said, before I could stop myself. Fortunately my remark went unnoticed.

'What does the empire require?' asked the Captain. 'I mean to say, what price had you intended to place on your treasures?'

'I – that is, the empire ... we require money, and men. Fifty thousand men at least, and the money to keep them victualled and armed. More money to pay our debtors.' He shook his head. 'We have nothing,' he said again.

The Captain was looking at me as if he wished me to contribute something sensible to the proceedings, so I steepled my fingers as well and leaned forward.

'Have you discussed the relics with Louis?' I asked.

I had expected Baldwin to be surprised and affronted, but he seemed to take me for an important confederate of the Captain, and answered willingly.

'Of course! Many times,' he said. 'It is a subject very dear to his heart – not, perhaps, as dear as the welfare of his kingdom, but ...' He closed his eyes for a moment as if remembering something. 'One day he took me to his private chapel at Vincennes and showed me his collection of holy relics. It was marvellous, I was duly impressed, and after we had prayed together we walked through the fields, as is his custom. He was greatly animated, and spoke of all the great treasures in his realm: the Milk-tooth of Christ, the two abbeys that claim to possess His ...' he coughed delicately, ' ... His Foreskin; the Robe of Our Lady, of course, in the Cathedral of Chartres. But none of these compared, he insisted, to the treasures of my house. How he envied me! That made me feel altogether dreadful, I can assure you, being all but overcome with envy for my dear cousin at that moment. The king seems to regard me as little more than a boy ...' he sniffed disapprovingly, and we did our best to look sympathetic. 'But in this matter alone he pays me some small deference.'

'Forgive me, but I must know: you have requested aid from the king?' I enquired delicately.

'I have. He is most sympathetic: one Christian monarch to another, you know. He has made me some promises and offered a little money. A very little money, although more than Henry, that ... no matter. His promises and gifts so far would barely pay for my passage home.'

'And why do you not simply approach the Venetian banks? One hears that their purses are practically bottomless. We assumed that was why you were here.' This last was pure inspiration, but I could tell by the way the Captain cocked his head that I had asked the right question. And indeed Baldwin puffed out his cheeks and expelled the air noisily.

'The Regent John has already placed my empire very solidly in the Serene Republic's debt,' he said ruefully. 'Indeed, until I return to Constantinople I will not know the true extent of it. And I am quite anxious that the Republic does not discover that I am here. I have placed myself in the lion's mouth – the *winged* lion as it were – to seek you out, sirs.'

The Captain nodded slowly. Reaching for a honey cake, he nibbled the edge, studied it for a moment as if it were of great worth, then popped it into his mouth. He chewed thoughtfully, washed the remains down with a sip of wine, and sat back.

'You will give the Crown of Thorns to Louis Capet as a gift,' he pronounced.

'I beg your pardon?' spluttered Baldwin.

79

'You will make a gift of the Crown of Thorns to your cousin.'

'But why? No, certainly not!'

'You will make him a gift of the most precious thing in your kingdom. I will ensure that Louis makes you an equally precious gift in return.'

'You? How?' said Baldwin. He was beginning to lose his patience, I saw.

The Captain stood up and Baldwin recoiled once more, but he merely brushed the cake crumbs from his clothing and sat down again.

'Do you actually know who I am?' he asked, a little pointedly.

'A dealer,' said the boy. He was trying to be flippant, but the Captain had him once again.

'You are right. I am a dealer. I am *the* dealer. Every important relic that is bought and sold in Christendom has passed or will pass through my hands in one way or another. Not the little vials of martyrs' blood or poor bits of sacking that have touched some saint's tomb: my business is the relic over which a cathedral will be built, a town founded, a cardinal's hat bought. I do not *buy* and *sell*: I arrange for the invention and translation of these things.'

Baldwin looked blank, so I explained: 'Church dogma has it that invention is the discovery of a relic. Translation is its transfer to a new home.'

'So I conduct my affairs under the mantle of dogma,' said the Captain. 'Thus souls can remain spotless. I have taken wine with popes, and taken their money. I am known to the greater number of your royal cousins, including Frederick Hohenstaufen, whom I count as a friend.' Baldwin looked surprised at that, and I was taken off guard as well: this was the first I had heard of such a friendship.

'Louis Capet, as I have said, is a man I know well. He will not *buy* the Crown, or any other thing, from you. He certainly would not buy them from me, and I would not offer them to him: as I have said, they have no worth. But a gift, an imperial gift: that, I will guarantee, will bring you a mighty reward. We have spoken of this very thing, sitting beneath his oak tree at Vincennes. "My dear Jean," I remember him saying, "Think of all the treasures yet behind the walls of Constantinople, the things that bore witness to the suffering of Our dear Lord."'

I had never heard the Captain talk so much like a common huckster, but then I saw that Baldwin was rapt, and that tears were welling in his eyes.

'"Would that it were in my remit to bring them to you, my lord," I answered,' the Captain went on. '"But I fear the Venetian wolves stole everything at the time of the fatal Crusade." "Ah, not so," he replied, "for I have read an account, *The Story of Those Who Conquered Constantinople*, by a noble knight of Picardy, one Robert de Clari. He lists the things the Venetians took, but the Crown remains in Constantine's palace, alongside all these others." And he listed to me the things that this Robert claimed had been saved from pillage. He believes you have in your possession the Crown, the Nails, the Burial Cloths, the Spear, Sponge, Tunic, Cane; the Stone of the Tomb, and the Cross itself, or parts thereof. "If," I said then, "if these things were indeed still owned by the emperor it is a great wonder, for I thought them lost." "No, no," he said, "They are there, and I tell you, I would give every coin in my kingdom to bring them here to France."'

'You heard those very words?' said Baldwin, faintly.

'And many more on the subject, over the years.'

The emperor opened his mouth, then closed it again. He

reached for the wine jug and filled his cup to the rim, drank most of it off and set the cup down again. His hand was trembling slightly.

'Can you help me?' he said.

Chapter Five

After the two knights had shown us out of the inn we strolled in silence across the square. The Captain was frowning slightly.

'Did that meet your expectations?' I asked, insanely curious.

He paused and bought us each a peach from an old woman. It was early for peaches and it was a little woody, but the sweet flesh was welcome after Baldwin's tart wine.

'It could hardly have gone better,' he said, a little distantly.

'What, then?'

'I do not know, Patch,' he said. 'It was all so simple, was it not?'

'Certainly,' I agreed. 'Young Baldwin is desperate. He will do anything you say.'

'"Young" Baldwin, is it? He is older than you, I think. No, that is right. This is a moment I have thought about for many years: as I told you, the ultimate of prizes. And it appears the boy has placed everything in my hands. I suppose that I cannot quite believe it.'

And he said no more, leaving me fairly boiling with excitement. So wrapped up was I in the complexities of what I had heard, and what I was now imagining, that I barely noticed the streets we were passing through, and even the squatting menace of the Castel Sant'Angelo failed to make me look up from the cobblestones. It was not until we were upon the marble pavement of Saint Peter's Bridge that my reverie was broken, and that was only because the Captain had caught me by the arm.

'Um?' I muttered.

'Hold up, lad,' said the Captain. He sounded tense.

Then I saw why. A small company of soldiers – I hurriedly counted eight of them – were strung out across our path. They did not loll, like most soldiers do when they wish to be menacing, but stood like statues. Five of them held short, broad-bladed spears, and all wore both swords and knives over surcoats of red and yellow. They all wore kettle-helms, brightly polished and gleaming, except for one man, the tallest, who was bareheaded.

'What is this?' I hissed.

'They wear the livery of the pope,' the Captain answered under his breath. 'Keep still, Patch. And on your life, do not touch your blade.'

The tall man stepped towards us, hand raised imperiously.

'In the name of the Holy Father, halt!' he proclaimed, somewhat unnecessarily, for we were rooted to the spot.

'Signor Michel de Montalhac?' he asked.

'At your service,' the Captain answered levelly.

'You will accompany me immediately. You too,' he added, with a haughty jerk of his chin in my direction. Without turning, he snapped his fingers, and his men started towards us. I noted, with more than a little unease, that they marched in perfect step with each other.

'Please walk ahead,' said the officer, for so I assumed him to be, with perfect politeness.

'Well, well. This day grows ever more interesting,' said the Captain calmly.

'My God, sir, what do you mean? What is happening?' I hissed.

'We have just received an invitation from the pope himself. Do not worry, lad: all this nonsense is merely a bit of mummery, meant to impress us. You are thinking of the poor flitches hanging from the tower over there, are you not?' I nodded, biting my lip. 'Well, do not fear. Those to whom the pope wishes harm are visited in the dead of night. You would do well to fear a knock at your door, but polished helmets at midday? Mere Roman nonsense. And besides, His Holiness is in Viterbo, I believe.'

'So what is all this about, then?'

The Captain gave one of his French shrugs. 'A diversion,' he said, carelessly.

And so we walked – calmly, for despite their order, our escort was polite enough not to hurry us – across the bridge, past the Tor di Nona and into the narrow streets beyond. Mummery it may have been, but the crowds parted before us as water divides around the prow of a ship. Through the broad ways we passed, through squares where marketing wives gawped at us, under beetling towers hung with flags, past knots of urchins who mocked us with great skill, for mockery was their stock-in-trade and they took pride in it. I did not notice much of this, for despite the Captain's easy words I did not feel at ease, and kept my eyes on the ground, watching my feet pace out the flagstones that lay between me and God knew what fate. The towers of the noble families loomed over us on all sides like a sinister forest of branchless trees: columns of brick all emblazoned and battlemented with the furious pride of their makers. Then we were in that quarter where the ancient ruins are more plentiful than the works of modern man, but even these are piled up with more brick towers and strange little fortlets that perch upon the ancient marble like the daubed nests of swallows.

And then a great shape rose before us, squatting, heavy as

the sins of the world, upon the earth. The Coliseum, almost domestic at this time of day: as we skirted it, I noticed that here and there a face peered out of a window in a crudely bricked-up arch, or a flag of newly washed clothing flapped pathetically.

Our escort whisked us past and into a quarter I had never entered. We had left the city behind – or so it seemed, for past the Coliseum the buildings thinned out and suddenly we were in farmland. Or rather, it was like entering a vast garden, for in the distance, all along the skyline, the jagged walls of Rome stood guard. We were climbing a hill, walking past churches and here and there a lone tower that threatened the poor farmers' huts that stood amongst the vineyards and fields of vegetables that were just now sprouting shoots and fronds of exultant green. Olives and figs grew on either side, and the din of human tongues was supplanted by the chit-chat of starlings and finches. Away to our right our path – in truth it was a rather grand road, paved with cut stone – was flanked by a high brick bridge, which began down near the Coliseum but which ran away out of sight over the crest of the nearest hill, upon which stood a great church rising amidst a village of smaller churches and cloisters. The strange bridge seemed to be purposeless, for it forded no stream and carried no road, but where it led was no mystery, for though I had never seen it, like every Christian man I knew what church stood upon a hill just within the city walls of Rome: Saint John Lateran, the pope's church, and next to it his palace.

At our swift pace we were there in the broad square before the church much faster than I would have liked, and our escort ushered us past the broad rise of steps that led to the church and through a gate into a courtyard. I fully expected to be strung up on the spot, but instead the officer gave us a courteous bow and led us inside the palace.

We were met, in some inner state chamber, by a cardinal, a sick-looking man in late middle age, who nonetheless was the first cardinal I had ever met and who therefore set my knees atremble with awe until I remembered that I had long since left the Church, and that I need not fear its lords, at least in principle: for as our current predicament showed, in practice any lord was dangerous whether he wore purple or cloth-of-gold. This cardinal was not especially happy to see us, and I suspected we had disturbed either prayer or breakfast, for he sniffed at us impatiently, and informed us that His Holiness desired to speak with one Michel de Montalhac, whom he presumed one of us to be. His Holiness was currently residing in Viterbo whilst the populace of Rome overcame its troubles and ceased to act like feral children – this last delivered with a sniff of extra severity – and so he regretted, et cetera et cetera, but we would have to take horse. This very moment. No delay possible. And out he swept in a petulant fuss of purple silk.

So it was out to another yard with us, where our escort – the same officer, but different men – waited with a pair of horses for us. Now here was mortification indeed, for I was forced to admit I had not ridden a horse since I was a lad, and then only Dartmoor ponies and mules. The soldiers exchanged looks of amused disbelief, and even the Captain permitted himself a little smile as he scribbled a message for Gilles on a hastily procured scrap of parchment, but at last a kindly guard took pity upon me and offered to lead my mount until I felt at ease on her back, and so we set off. It was strange to see the Captain swing himself up on to his horse as if he rode every day of his life, when in truth I had never, in two years, seen him mount so much as a dog-cart. I myself was very frightened, up there upon the back of my mare, but it was a fear based upon concrete circumstances

– the danger of a broken limb or at least humiliation – and so allowed me to forget, for a few miles, what fate must have in store for us. And although I sat stiff with fear for a mile or so, after I saw that I was not to be thrown or devoured by the great creature I began to grow more confident, and after an hour I was trotting along unaided.

Of the journey to Viterbo there is little to tell, save that it began to rain as we left the city and poured the rest of that day and the second too, and the sky was so low that the skirts of the clouds trailed upon the sodden ground. My world shrank to that portion of grey misery that was framed by the dripping window of my hood. We rode all day, and my arse, besieged by hard saddle and sodden britches, was chafed raw. That night we took our rest at Sutri, in a rich pilgrims' way station where our status as guests of His Holiness brought us abundant food and a comfortable bed, but we were not at ease, despite our escort's attempts to draw us out. For the Captain was polite but distant, and I was so caught between indignation and terror that I could muster up nothing but the sorriest parlour-talk.

There were not sufficient beds, it being a busy time on the Pilgrims' Way, and so while the Captain was invited to bed down with the captain of our guards – Captain with captain: there would be a song about that, I vowed, should I ever make it back to the *Cormaran* – I had to make do with a straw pallet in the corridor, along with the other soldiers and a heap of pilgrims, all snoring, farting and reeking of wet clothes and feet. It was no worse than sleeping below decks on a ship, though, and once I had overcome my damp shivers and made myself a little warmth, it occurred to me that, if the pope intended us any harm, his men would hardly be allowing us this casual freedom on the way to his lair. So I did sleep, after a fashion, and awoke with a stiff neck and a sleeping pilgrim hugging my legs as if they were his wife.

We set out again into the weather, and reached the town of Viterbo midway between lunch and dinner – or so we guessed, for we had seen neither glimpse nor glimmer of the sun's face the whole long, wet day. I was not cheered by the town, for it hid behind forbidding walls of some ominous grey stone, and the houses within those walls were all of a kind: grey and dour. There was no one about, and the rain poured from roofs and made brooks of the streets. Up these our party splashed, up to the walls of a building, half church, half fortress, that hunkered down amongst the grey houses like a defeated titan.

'The palace of the pope!' exclaimed our officer, trying to sound haughty, no doubt, but merely seeming wet and out of sorts.

'Mayhap they have lit a fire for us,' muttered the Captain, and seeing my expression, he added: 'Not that kind of fire, Petroc! We are safe, I promise.'

The gates thudded wetly behind us. I looked around and saw a large open space that looked something like a builder's yard: some grand project had got under way, and blocks and carved pieces of that depressing grey stone lay scattered about everywhere amongst wooden scaffolding, winches and buckets. We parted with our horses, I with great joy, for I could hardly walk, so chafed was my crotch. The grand doorway of the palace was guarded by men in shining mail coats who did not so much as glance at us as we entered.

Inside the palace it was gloomier than out, for no one had yet lit the torches that jutted from the wall, but at least it was dry: so dry, in fact, that I caught the stony astringency in the back of my throat and almost coughed. The air smelled faintly of incense, of beeswax and of dust. But before I could take stock, we were called to one side, into a sort of guardroom, and there up a plain flight of spiral stairs, along an unadorned corridor of stone and into a room, quite large and as austere as everything else I had so far seen. On the bed, which was large and of a dark wood, two sets of clothing were set out, and when I saw them my heart thumped, for they seemed to be priests' robes: simple things of black and white. What dreadful mockery was this? But while I quavered, the Captain had shucked off his wet clothes and pulled on the dry ones, and I saw that they were not vestments after all, but ordinary tunic and breeches, somewhat old-fashioned but made of fine cloth.

'How considerate,' said the Captain. 'Mine fit rather well. And yours?'

'Not too bad,' I admitted. It was somewhat delicious to draw on the clean, dry things after two days of sodden misery. 'I thought they were clerical robes, actually. Some sort of jest.' I swallowed. 'Or worse. I have heard that the heretic-finders dress their victims in such things before ...'

'Petroc! Your imagination is a rich and wonderful thing, to be sure, but calm yourself, I pray you! You and I would be hanging from the Tor di Nona by now if our host meant us ill. That I promise you.' The Captain combed out his lank hair with his fingers as he spoke. 'We are to be fed, not cooked. Sit down.' He pointed to the bed. I plopped down upon it obediently. He stood before me, arms crossed.

'Now then. I have not spoken of this since we were ... invited upon this journey, for although our hosts seem pleasant enough, I'll wager their ears are sharper than their swords. And besides, I have been sunk deep in my thoughts, for which I apologise. But here is something that will cheer you. Do you remember our conversation with Baldwin?' I nodded. 'Of course you do. Then you will remember that I told that foolish young man that I had supped with popes and emperors. That, Patch, was no idle boast. The truth is that I know old Ugolino de Segni, who now delights in the name of Gregory, ninth of that name, Pontifex Maximus, et cetera, et cetera ... I know Pope Gregory rather well.'

'You know the *pope*?' I was aghast.

'Extraordinary, isn't it? But in fact, not really that extra-ordinary. I knew him long before he took up Peter's keys. He was a diplomat, you know, roaming about the lands of the Church drumming up alliances against the German emperors. What better way to seal an alliance amongst clerics than with the gift of a relic? I became a trusted purveyor, and in time an occasional dinner companion. He is a very learned man, our Ugolino. I tend to keep off ecclesiastical topics, however, and fortunately we share an interest in philosophy. I can talk a little – and he a great deal – upon the subject of Aristotle, and things that branch off from there, and so we count each other as friends. There is no real foundation for it, but then again, he is the pope and, by definition, friendless in the earthly sense. You might find him a little *un*earthly, Patch. He is uncommonly ancient, but sharp as a pin. Be calm and close-lipped. I will handle the conversation.'

And that was the end of our talk, for at that moment a rap came at the door and a cleric in the robes of some important office entered. It was time for our audience.

Later, I realised it was a shame that I could not remember more about the pope's palace. I dimly recalled heavily armed guards in the papal livery – many of them, guarding a great many doors that stood at the end of a great many stone corri-dors. Although the place was not unlike a monastery, in that it was cold, austere and very old, I felt as if we were descend-ing into the earth, and that the successor of Saint Peter must dwell in some cavern in the depths like a lonely old spider. So I had little but an impression of gloom and disquiet, although

I also knew that for the privilege I had been accorded the armies of pilgrims who came to Rome every year would have paid almost any price. But those pilgrims would be bringing home tales to tell to their families and friends, and I had no home, no family. Another pair of halberds clanged in front of us, and I winced. Then the final door swung open, and we walked on into the light of a thousand candles.

Pope Gregory the Ninth was truly ancient. The wizened man who hardly filled his robes – let alone the great throne, raised on a red-draped dais, in which he slumped, looking unnervingly like a child's doll – did not, on first inspection, seem to be living at all. Less like a doll, I thought, imitating the Captain's reverent shuffle along the carpet that led to the throne, than a well-preserved relic. But as we grew closer I saw that I was very much mistaken if I thought that life had deserted this creature. For, although his eyes drooped and wept thin trickles of rheum down his leathery cheeks, they burned like pale embers. I noticed that the Captain was being deferential only to a point. He performed the bare minimum of obeisances, drawing – or so I perhaps fancied – disapproving glares from the clerics who surrounded us. But I did not have the Captain's strength of will, and scraped and simpered my way along behind him until all of a sudden the Captain came to a halt and I all but slammed into his back. The pope was holding up a ring-festooned hand – a claw, really: no more than a simulacrum of a living hand – and was glaring at us with what seemed to be unrestrained fury. I glanced nervously at the Captain, but he was smiling broadly, and now I saw that what I had mistaken for rage on the face of the Holy Father was in fact a fond smile, or as much of one as those moribund features could form. There was another wave of the claw, and two priests came forward with chairs and planted them on the carpet behind us. The claw bade us sit.

'Welcome, Signor de Montalhac. And welcome, Petrus Zennorius.' The pope's voice belied his necrotic form. It was deep and rich. If I had not seen the body from which it issued, I would have said it came from a man at the height of his powers.

'I am overjoyed that you have ceased your endless peregrinations long enough to pay our city a visit, but I understand my simple invitation to luncheon somehow translated into your good selves being frogmarched here by a squadron of my troops! So sorry, so sorry.' Try as I might, I could not discern a speck of sincerity in the pope's apology. 'You will forgive me, of course,' he went on. It was not a suggestion. 'I have always enjoyed our meetings.'

'As have I, Your Holiness,' replied the Captain, with complete sincerity. I was astonished. Here was Captain Jean de Montalhac, whom I respected and admired above all other living men, but who made his living from – I shall not be reticent, as the Captain never was – from thievery, deception, usury and sacrilege, talking to God's representative on earth as if to a favourite uncle.

'We are old friends, are we not?' said Gregory, as if to confirm what I had been thinking.

'I hope so,' said the Captain, simply.

'I was sure of it. And because of our long friendship, and my appreciation – nay, I will say admiration – for your knowledge and experience in certain areas close to both our hearts, I would talk with you about a matter that has come to my attention. It is a matter that concerns me very deeply in one area, and it should, I hope, concern you just as deeply in another. And now, while it was a pleasure to meet your young colleague, I think perhaps ...'

'Your Holiness, Master Petrus should stay, if you will permit him to do so. He has my fullest confidence, both as

93

to his integrity and his discretion, and besides, I intend to tell him word for word of our conversation in any case.'

The pope tipped his head back on its skinny neck and laughed, somewhat raggedly. 'Your candour, Montalhac: so shocking.' He stopped laughing abruptly, and leaned forward, fixing me with his eyes. I flinched.

'Master Zennorius. I hold a million or more souls in the palm of this hand.' He held it out to me, and suddenly balled it into a knobbed, bony fist. 'If Signor de Montalhac has given you his confidence, then so shall I. Do you know what that means?' I nodded my head.

'The emperor himself does not have my confidence, my child. Almost all of those present in this room do not. And you know of what I am speaking?' Gregory's eyes burned into me.

'Your Holiness, I only meant that I understood the stupendous honour you bestow upon me,' I stammered. So much for keeping my mouth shut. I had the sensation that my bowels were about to let go.

'Ah. There is more than that. Tell me what you are thinking, boy.' I believe I could actually feel his gaze scalding me. Having no idea how to reply, and suddenly in immediate fear for my life, I closed my eyes. My thoughts whirled, but suddenly, in broad Devon tones, my mind provided the answer. It is the pope, you numbskull, I told myself. Tell him the fucking truth. I opened my eyes. Something like a smirk was playing upon Gregory's desiccated lips.

'This morning I stood on the Pons San Petri, Your Holiness, from where I could see your prison, your fortress and your church. Your trust is to be found somewhere between those three points.' I bowed my head, and waited for the gaudy men-at-arms to drag me away.

There was a noise like dry twigs being snapped, and I

looked up. The pope had slapped his hands together, and now pointed a skeletal finger at the Captain.

'How do you teach your pupils, de Montalhac? What power do you hold over them, that they will put their head into the lion's mouth? Your young man is truthful, and bold, and he sees the way of things. And in that I see you. Well done, my child,' he said to me. 'But do you fear me?'

'Very much, Your Holiness,' I said emphatically.

'That is good. I have had word of you, boy. Of your bereavement.' I blinked at him, and he smiled, thinly. 'You may stay,' he said, and sat back with a sound like old brambles dragged across a windowpane.

At a signal from the pope, an official-looking man came up to receive his whispered orders. There was a slight commotion as the room was cleared. A band of serving-men brought us wine and sweet cakes, and the Captain gestured that I should take a little of each, although I was almost too nervous to move my hands. Meanwhile the pope and the Captain chatted easily, of which discourse I can recall only that their words were utterly inconsequential.

'Now, to business,' said the pope, after he too had taken a few sips of wine. 'How fared you with the boy de Courtenay? Did he entertain you well?'

The Captain set down his goblet very carefully, and examined his thumbnail for a long moment.

'Tolerably well, Your Holiness,' he replied. 'His table is somewhat meagre in comparison to your own, but he served something rather appetising nonetheless.'

'Of course he did. That is the matter in hand. It is of great import to me, and it can be made of equal import to you, de Montalhac. I will be brief, as I grow a little weary. You would be well advised not to grow old, young man,' he told me, drolly – or at least, I hoped he was being droll, as he had just made it very plain that he could prevent any further ageing on my part with a twitch of his eyebrow. I attempted an obsequious laugh, but instead made a sound like a costive raven.

'Now,' said the pope, appearing not to have noticed. 'You have met the new Emperor of Romania, so-called. Having met him, you will perhaps understand why he is something of a worry to me. My uncle – Pope Innocent, boy – caused nothing but trouble when he allowed the Venetians to take Constantinople. Each sovereign has been a disaster, each worse than the last. And the present one, this Baldwin, shows no sign of being any better. His own family regard him as a simpleton. However, I have met him, and now so have you. He is no simpleton, but he is in a great deal of trouble, and he knows it. His *empire*,' he curled his lips derisively, 'is bankrupt and under siege from Greeks, Slavs, Turks. It cannot stand without outside help.'

'He was abroad when he inherited the throne, was he not?' asked the Captain.

'He was – in fact he was here in Rome, begging me for money.' The pope sighed. 'He has many relations here in the West, and he has begged from all of them. And of course, because my uncle made the installation of those Frankish buffoons – those *Latins* – on the throne of Constantine a sort of holy enterprise, I have been under some pressure to contribute something myself.'

'Fascinating,' said the Captain. His face was a bland mask.

'No, it is not. It is exceedingly tiresome,' snapped Gregory. 'I have had to make appeals, much against my better judgement. I preached a crusade against the Bulgars. I have called upon the Catholic monarchs to send men and money, but they have not. Of course not! Why on earth should they? The enterprise is doomed, and all those with sense know it. I have opened the strongbox of Saint Peter and given him some small tokens, but Baldwin's hunger is born of desperation, and it is boundless.'

'I, for one, would not be in his shoes,' said the Captain.

The pope sighed again. 'I am lecturing. There is a reason for this, however. I …' He straightened up and looked around him, and in that instant the years seemed to fall away and he seemed, for a brief moment, young, vital and even more dangerous. Then he slumped once more. 'The execrable Baldwin stooped low – very low indeed. He sought to bribe me – *me*, Christ's Vicar on earth!'

'What with?' asked the Captain, as if on cue, leaning forward intently.

'The contents of the Pharos Chapel in Constantine's palace!' hissed Gregory.

'My word,' said the Captain, both eyebrows up now, but no more than that hint of emotion on his face. 'What did Your Holiness do?'

'I refused, naturally!' said Gregory, slapping his knees angrily. 'I could not but refuse.'

'Of course not. But even so …' the Captain began.

'Do you think I turned down de Courtenay's offer happily?' asked the pope. 'We have, you and I, talked of the Pharos Chapel many times. There is no doubt in my mind that its riches belong here, in Rome. But for Baldwin to buy me with …' he shook his head. 'If I had accepted, I would have been a greater sinner than Simon Magus. Good God,' he went on, 'I have accumulated a great store of regrets in my long life, but this may be one of the greatest.'

'You could take no other course, and it is a mark of your strength and wisdom, Your Holiness.' The Captain paused, as if a little surprised at his own words. 'And what do you believe Baldwin will do now?' he went on.

'He will tout his treasures around Christendom like a common peddler,' spat Gregory. 'That is what you discussed, is it not?'

I prayed for the ground to swallow me up, but the Captain merely chuckled. 'Naturally,' he said.

'It is most vexing. I was tempted to excommunicate Baldwin on the spot for his temerity, but I need him. There is some indication that the thorn who presently festers most painfully in my flesh – I mean Frederick von Hohenstaufen, boy, who carries the title of Holy Roman Emperor as if he were biting his thumb at Our Lord Jesu himself – some hint that Frederick may be thinking of an alliance with Baldwin's enemy John Vatatzes, who is a true monarch, by all accounts, and would dearly like his throne in Constantinople back. That I cannot allow. I have to prop up the Latins like so many stuffed corpses, if only to stop Frederick's canker from spreading eastwards.'

'But meanwhile, Your Holiness, you will be all too aware that I can do nothing for Baldwin, much as it would profit me so to do,' said the Captain, coolly. 'Unless . . .' I held my breath.

'Pardon, your pardon, de Montalhac,' said the Pope, chuckling. 'There is, of course, something I require, as always.' Apparently distracted, he stuck a finger into one white-tufted earhole and searched intently. Then he signalled for more wine.

'I have been thinking of what fate I would prefer for Baldwin's treasure if I cannot possess it myself,' he said at last. 'The worst possible thing would be for it to be divided up, scattered like so much plunder. The worth of each individual piece is incalculable, of course – spiritual worth as well as monetary. But how much greater is that spiritual worth when the treasure is intact!'

'Are you asking me to act as broker?' said the Captain.

'Perhaps. Yes. Yes, I am.'

'You honour me. I accept. And does Your Holiness wish to discuss the details now? We can ...'

'No, no,' snapped Gregory. He pressed his knuckles to his forehead for a moment, and took a deep breath. 'Baldwin has a benefactor in mind. If I might risk a guess as to whom ... But no, dear Michel, perhaps you would save me the bother. Tell me.'

'Louis Capet.'

The pope let out a gasp. He slapped the arm of his throne. 'God be praised!' he croaked.

'Might I ask why?' asked the Captain delicately.

'Because Louis is a good and holy man. Because he is a great friend to the Church. And I will soon need him against that horse-fly Frederick Hohenstaufen. I want you to arrange it. Make no mistake, though: this has been my wish all along. It is merely convenient that Baldwin has reached the same conclusion. So! It will be simple. Louis is a great collector, of course, and conveniently, he desires the things of which we speak.'

'I am aware of that,' said the Captain.

'But of course, how simple I am being. You are a close acquaintance of the king, are you not?'

The Captain shrugged modestly. 'I have had the pleasure of his conversation – and his patronage – more than once,' he murmured. 'Indeed, we have touched upon this very subject – the Pharos Chapel, that is.'

'So much the better, dear de Montalhac! It will be an easy matter for you. You must discover a way for Baldwin's treasure to be translated to France, and for Baldwin to receive, ah, *gratitude* from Louis, commensurate to his needs. To that end, I desire that you set out no later than tomorrow for Paris.' He gripped the sides of his throne and struggled to his feet. It was clear that our audience was at an end. I surreptitiously brushed cake crumbs from my tunic and stood up alongside the Captain.

'It has been a great pleasure, as it ever is,' said the pope. 'I pray that the Almighty will grant us more such meetings before I am taken.'

The Captain bowed deeply, and I followed suit. Gregory held out his wizened hand, and first the Captain, then I, bent to kiss the great ring that glimmered against the deathly pale flesh. I made ready to leave, but the Captain paused.

'Your Holiness, if I am to be broker, who, then, is my client?' he asked. The pope drew himself up to his full height on the dais: he was far taller than I had expected, and he towered over us.

'Our Lord Jesus Christ!' he thundered, pointing up towards the shadowed ceiling.

The Captain gave a French shrug, a flick of his chin.

'Who, then, will be paying my commission?' he asked, levelly.

Gregory the ninth blinked owlishly for a moment, and then began to cackle. Reaching into his robes, he brought out two slim rolls of parchment sealed with great gobs of red wax and handed them to the Captain.

'I am certain that Our Lord will provide,' he said, and at that point his cackle was overtaken by a fit of coughing. He sat down again heavily and waved us away. The Captain took me gently by the arm and together we walked carefully back down the carpet. Halberds were drawn aside, the door groaned on its hinges, and we were out, into the cold grey halls of Viterbo stone.

Chapter Six

As soon as we had left the audience hall I had to trot along behind the Captain, whose strides seemed to lengthen until we had reached our chamber. Once the door was latched behind us, he went over to the window and beckoned to me. We leaned on the broad windowsill, gazing out at the flickering curtain of rain turned the colour of pewter in the failing light.

'You have a keen mind, Patch,' he told me. 'I could have come up with no better answer to old Gregory's bullying.'

'Would he have ...' I let my words trail off.

'No. At least, probably not. He and I are, as we have both told you, old friends. He was probably expecting you to faint, but instead you came up with something intelligent.'

'Damn me!' I said. 'I should have thanked him for the loan of his physician. What a thoughtless wretch I am!'

'Do not worry. It is probably better that you did not. Gregory is old and difficult. You might have given him some obscure offence if you had. And now, let us look at these things, eh?' And he pulled out the documents that Gregory had given him. One was adorned with a great, heavy disc of lead – the *bulla* of Saint Peter. The Captain squinted at it.

'This is for Baldwin,' he said. 'It is a bull: my guess is that it commands him to submit to the pope's authority in the matter of the relics, and most probably further commands him to give me the power to act for him and the Latin empire.

You will have to deliver it to him, I am afraid, for it seems I must away to France. But now, what is this? It is addressed to me.'

The second document was thicker than the first, but sealed only with red wax. Very patiently he worked the seal free of the vellum and opened what proved to be a single sheet, folded many times. He frowned for a moment, then a slow, stunned smile crept over his face.

'As I did not dare to hope,' he said softly. And then he passed me the vellum. I plucked it from his grasp and, holding it carefully in somewhat tremulous fingers, I peered at it. It was a plain, unadorned list, written in a clerk's austere hand. The ink was black, save for a scattering of viridian periods. I squinted at the title.

INVENTARIUM *of the Holy Chapel of the Virgin of the Pharos in the Palace of Bucoleon, Constantinople*

'The Pharos Chapel,' I murmured. I let my eyes run lightly over the script. And then stared. In simple Church Latin, itemised like any marketing list, I saw:

The Crown of Thorns
The Swaddling Bands of Christ
Of John the Baptist his arm, and a part of his head
A piece of the True Cross, and another such
The holy Spear
The Sponge
The Chain
Milk of Our Lady
The Reed
Our Lord's Blood
The purple Tunic of Our Lord
Blood of Our Lord as expressed by a holy picture

A victorious Cross
A Stone from the Sepulchre
The Shrouds
The **Sudarium**
Towel that dried the feet of the Holy Apostles
Head of Saint Blas
Head of Saint Clement
Head of Saint Simeon
Rod of Moses

Perhaps I was staring for a long time, for when I looked up the Captain had turned away and was leaning on the parapet, staring down into the dun-coloured waters below. I cleared my throat and he looked around.

'I thought you had turned to stone. What do you make of it?' I could only shake my head in answer.

'The *Inventarium* has a powerful effect on most who read it,' he said, reaching for the vellum, which he refolded and tucked away in his bosom. 'The credulous, the pious, the merely curious, and of course those of us who have a professional involvement.' I was glad to listen to him, for I discovered – indeed, for a superstitious moment, actually feared – that I had been struck dumb. But the Captain's eyes bored into me, and at last I found my tongue.

'All those things: all those holy things.'

'You are thinking like a Benedictine,' the Captain said, not unkindly.

'Forgive me, but ... but I *was* a monk once: the things on this list were the pillars of my faith, and my faith was every moment of my day. And to see them itemised thus and thus, like stuff in a tithe-barn ...'

'... is shocking?'

'Yes. I am shocked. Truly.'

'Itemised like stock-in-trade. That is precisely what they are: to Gregory, to Baldwin de Courtenay, to me and, my dear Petroc, to you. And to a thousand others.'

I sat in silence. He was right: I knew that. Had I not broken into a church to steal the body of a saint? Had I not seen a man butchered before my eyes so that another might possess the hand of Saint Euphemia, a saint with no importance outside one little English city?

'I cannot believe what I have read,' I whispered.

The Captain nodded. 'Two days ago, you heard me speak of the Philosopher's Stone. Well, these things were what I meant. They have the power to convert the base metal of credulity – let us call it *faith*, if you prefer, my Benedictine – into the purest gold. Well,' he exclaimed, rising and clapping his hands together. 'This has been a fine morning's work. I feel as if I have dozed off beneath a tree and awoken to find a golden apple in my lap.'

'So you will accept this commission?'

'Accept? My dear boy, this is …' He threw back his head and laughed at the ceiling beams. 'There is no greater prize in all the world for a man in my trade. I believe I will indeed accept.'

'Gregory seems to think that it is a difficult proposition, though, sir.'

'I do not share his anxiety. And,' he dropped his voice to a whisper, 'it will bring us a river of gold, all of it *honest*. I … to be frank with you, Patch, this is quite beyond belief, and I am not at all sure what it will mean for you, for me – any of us.'

The Captain's distant mood vanished after that, and we fell to the kind of plotting and scheming that is the fruit of an excited mind, but that is forgotten once calm returns. And our surroundings began to seem more pleasant. We were not prisoners, that was clear enough. But we were not free, if only because we had nowhere to go. In the event, we were summoned to dinner before our gentle captivity grew too onerous, and followed a major-domo through the outskirts of the palace and into a long refectory that would not have been out of place in a monastery back home in England. It did not seem to belong to the palace itself, although some attempt had been made to make it seem grand with hangings and gleaming fittings of silver and gold. An altar stood at one end, upon which a great and ancient-looking crucifix stood. But the golden candlesticks seemed out of place on the plain, monkish tables, and for the first time in two days I began to feel a little at home. We were evidently not to dine with His Holiness, for I guessed these were not the state dining halls. And indeed we filed in with the lowlier sort of cleric – that is, given the circumstances, for I had never in my life thought of bishops and abbots as lowly, but today I had seen cardinals swarm like sparrows. Many of these worthy souls knew their place and took their seats in groups of friends or compatriots, I supposed. I was casting around for a spare couple of places when the major-domo gravely nodded towards three empty settings towards the end of the table nearest the altar. I glanced at the Captain, who shrugged and followed the man.

No sooner were we seated than another man appeared at my shoulder. He was slim of build and he would have had a rather jolly face had his eyes not been hooded and shrewd. His black hair was tonsured. He wore robes of pure white, unadorned, which lent him a certain ghostly gravity, but this was dispelled when he tapped the Captain lightly upon the shoulder and smiled down at him.

'I believe we are ordained to be companions at dinner,' he said. 'Or at least this worthy fellow tells me so.' The major-domo bowed stiffly and turned back to the throng.

The white-clad man sat down next to the Captain, reached for a nearby bread basket and offered it to us.

'I am Peter of Verona,' he said. 'Here, have some bread. It is a rarity for a mendicant to be offering food, though, is it not?'

I laughed politely, and the Captain did too, although his laughter was a little forced.

'Well met, Brother Peter,' I said. 'My name is Peter too: Petrus Zennorius, late of Cornwall.'

'And I am Michel Corvus Marinus,' said the Captain.

'Cormorant! A mendicant and a cormorant at the same table – the kitchens will be in turmoil to keep this table stocked,' smiled Peter. I laughed again: it was rather a good jest, for a cleric. At that moment the food began to come out, and it was excellent. We fell to, and I had spilled much gravy down my chin before any of us were ready to converse again. Indeed I was so busy chewing an exceedingly tasty but stringy piece of roast kid that I did not even notice that we were being addressed.

'Well, that explains it,' Brother Peter was saying.

'Indeed it must,' agreed the Captain.

'Explains what?' I asked, no doubt rudely.

'The reason for our being thrust together at this worthy table,' said Brother Peter. 'The Lord has seen fit to provide me with a travelling companion – well, to be precise, the Lord's Vicar – for I am setting out tomorrow for the town of my birth, and your friend is turning his head towards France. His Holiness told me I would not be travelling alone, and now there will be two upon the road, for a day or two at least.'

'An unlooked-for blessing,' said the Captain, with very uncharacteristic piety.

'The finest blessings are always those that come unasked,' returned Peter.

'Amen,' I agreed. 'And what is the nature of your journey, if I may humbly ask, Brother?'

The friar threw up his hands. Something about the vigour of the gesture made me flinch. 'To preach, of course!' he said, as happy as a child. 'Three years past – we were speaking of unsought blessings, were we not? – when our beloved Gregory began his attack on the plague of heresy I was given, by His Holiness in person, the honour of being his Inquisitor General in the northerly part of the Italian lands, and alas! my official duties bring me south too often, for I love my homeland, flat and marshy though I will admit it is, and even more I love preaching the word of the Lord to my own people.'

We were dining with an inquisitor. No wonder the Captain seemed a trifle stiff. I tried to catch his eye, but his whole attention was upon the friar, who was tapping a goat bone upon the table top to make his point.

'And that is what I mean,' he was saying. 'These unhappy souls will gladly let their errors lead them to the fire if we do not save them! And if we cannot? Well, burn they must!'

To my enormous relief, the Captain soon turned the conversation aside from heretics and their ordained fate, and we fell to empty bantering before parting as bosom friends, Peter arranging to meet with Master Corvus after breakfast for a leisurely start upon the road. But as soon as we had gone our own way, the Captain's mouth froze in a grim line and we marched in stony silence back to our room. Once we had shut and latched the door, I was amazed to see my companion blow life into the embers that lay in the hearth, for the evening had grown warm and much of the dampness had left the chamber. But he fanned them into a blaze and laid on more wood, until he had made a pyre fit for a phoenix, that leaped, crackling and roaring, up the chimney. Then he leaned back in his seat. It was uncomfortably hot now, and sweat was beginning to bead on my temples.

'How pleasant it is to warm my old bones,' said the Captain loudly. Then he turned to me, and I saw that he too was red-faced and sweating. 'A little excessive, perhaps,' he said in a lower voice, and gestured. 'Come closer,' he said. I pulled my chair up next to his, and he poured me some wine, which was white and beginning to grow unpleasantly warm.

'I do not think that this is entirely necessary,' he began, waving at the fire. 'But we are in the pope's house, and the walls may be listening. Oh, yes,' he said, seeing my shock. 'It is a simple thing to build hollow pipes into the walls of a room, that carry sound down to waiting ears. And perhaps there is a black-robed brother kneeling before our keyhole. Would you care to find out?' I shook my head. 'Sensible. The crackling of our fire will mask our words, I hope, and I am sorry I could not think of a better way. Needs must.'

'But I thought the pope was your friend!' I told him.

'Popes have no friends. That is how they become popes,' said the Captain. 'He is a customer, an acquaintance and someone who finds my profession a source of great fascination – that is, what he believes to be my profession. If he knew the truth, he would be fascinated in quite a different way.'

'That at least I can believe,' I said, choking back a mouthful of the hot, sour-sweet wine.

'Ah, Patch,' said my companion, with a sigh of such unguarded melancholy that I turned to him, startled. His face was grim, set, as if he were about to open a door and step out into a snowstorm. Instead he reached out his hand for mine, and grasped it tightly.

'This is something of which we have spoken very briefly,' he said, sadly. 'I should have talked of it sooner, but when one is so much out in the world, as we have been, it is hard to talk about things that belong within. We both have much to forget, you and I, but now, alas, it is time to remember. There would have been a better time and place than here in the lion's den, but so be it.' He paused, and threw another twiggy branch of olive on to the blaze. The dead leaves flew up in a sizzle.

'You know all the secrets of our ... of the company of the *Cormaran*, let us say. And the chief secret, to those who care about such things, is that some of us – Gilles, myself, Roussel, the other men of Toulouse – are Good Christians. That is, we are what the people call Cathars, worshippers of cats, for the Church considers no slander too vile for us. To the world at large, heretics. Now, I should add that most of us, most particularly myself, are not very diligent in pursuit of our faith. We are outcasts, and most of us still feel the anger and pain that attended our casting-out. We carry horrible things here,' he touched his breast, 'and here.' And he held his fingers against his brow. 'Because those we left behind us have been destroyed, by the French and by the creatures of the pope: aye, this one as much as any, and perhaps he will prove to be the worst of all.'

'This I knew,' I said quietly.

'I am glad,' said the Captain. 'Then you may or may not know that, within our faith, there are two sorts of believer. The greater part of us have always been what we call *credenti* or croyants: those who believe the tenets of the faith but are not constrained by all its practices. I am a croyant, as is Gilles. We all are. But the second ... they are the pinnacle of our faith, if you like. We call them *perfecti*. They are the ones who have given themselves in body and in soul to the Lord.'

I blinked: it was utterly strange to hear the Captain talk of the Lord in this way.

'The *perfecti* are those who take the *Consolamentum*, which is our only sacrament. In doing so they renounce the world and all its temptations. It is all a little complicated for such casual talk,' he said apologetically. 'But I can explain the essence thus: God is perfect; nothing in the world is perfect; therefore nothing in the world was created by God. The Evil One – whom most call the Devil – made this visible, tangible world, and indeed he is that which is called "God" in the book you know as the Old Testament, for who but the Devil could use his creations so cruelly? God made the *invisible* world. So you see it is all very simple,' he smiled thinly. 'That is why we are so suited to our vocation: to us, no relic can be holy, for all matter is evil.'

'And the Saviour?' I breathed, for here it was at last, the question I had longed to ask but dared not, for although I had lost my faith I still quailed at the bald fact of heresy, though it drew me on.

'Jesus Christ was the Holy Spirit.'

'Not a man?'

'How could he be, when all flesh is the Devil? Christ was spirit, and any man who takes the spirit within himself will become Christ.'

'But the Crucifixion …' I began.

' … Was a sham, a mummery. A trick to deceive mankind. The Holy Spirit cannot die.'

'So this world is nothing?' I pressed. 'But what of the scriptures?'

'The New Testament is also our testament,' he said. 'The Old tells of nothing but the Devil, for no God would treat his people thus.'

'So God – my God, I mean, the God of Christendom …'

'Is the Devil himself,' said the Captain, flatly. I gasped.

'So you have not taken this sacrament, this consolation?' I

asked, after a long pause. Perhaps I had not understood any of this aright.

'No. I could not live the life …' he paused, and ran his fingers through his hair. He had removed his coif, and in the torchlight I noticed that his hair was beginning to tarnish into silvery-grey. I had never given it much thought, but now I began to wonder exactly how old Michel de Montalhac really was. Certainly I had never seen him so weary. Meanwhile he took a draught of wine and held his glass cup aloft. 'I could not do this, for example. I could not eat flesh, nor milk, nor eggs; nor could I seek fine lodgings. I would have to go about always in the company of another of the *perfecti*. It is a hard road to choose – deliberately, of course. Most of us, most *credenti* only take the sacrament on our deathbeds, or when we know …'

The Captain was looking quite stricken. His hands busied themselves with his goblet. For a while he fussed with the poker, stirring the blazing coals until the heat grew almost intolerable. Finally he heaved a great sigh and slumped back in his chair.

'My dear Petroc. We have known each other for two years now, and I know, it is certain, a good deal more about you than you know of me. You have never asked, and that was good. I do not care to speak of the past – I who make the past my own special affair – but tonight matters have come to a sudden and unexpected point. If you will favour me with your patience, I will tell you of my past, or that … that event in the past that now bears very heavily upon our present. Can I do so?'

I nodded. He squeezed my hand and placed it gently upon the wood of the table. Then he took a sip of wine, pushed his plate away to the side and began.

'Patch, I think I told you where I was born, did I not? That night in Gardar? In any event, I came into this world as the heir to the seigneury of Aupilhac, which lies an easy day's ride to the north and east of Toulouse. To pare a long night's tale down into that of a moment, my people, and most of the folk who dwelt in those lands, were Good Christians. I ... No matter, it is all gone, all burned long ago. My dear friend Gregory's uncle and predecessor Lotario de' Conti, who you will know as Pope Innocent but who was as innocent as a ferret in a rabbit warren, declared a crusade against our liege lord, the Count of Toulouse. In the course of this most holy war, the French jackals came down upon us and destroyed all that they could. What they did not ruin, they stole. My parents died when the French chief, Simon de Montfort, burned our castle. I was young and bold, and I escaped the fire, as ... as you will have gathered.' He paused, and placed the tips of his forefingers gently against his closed eyelids. Thus he sat for a long while, and I waited, not hearing the hiss and pop of the fire, but imagining the grey stone walls of our chamber straining to catch his next words. At last he opened his eyes and blinked wearily.

'The fury of the Church of Rome died down a little after Avignon fell to Louis of France,' he said. 'That Louis in whose company I have sat, and who is a kind and gentle man, but who has sent a legion of my folk down to death. No matter: there is a stain upon all of us, even those who call themselves innocent. But here is the burden of my story: there is a new danger lately risen, worse in a sense than the crusaders because it creeps through the land like fingers of rot in an old house. When Simon de Montfort sacked my home, there was a priest in his company: one Dominic Guzman, a Castilian. This Dominic had a special hatred for the Good Christians, for whatever reasons men are driven to such passions. He was de Montfort's pet – he would watch the sieges and butchery from his master's side. And he was at Lavaur, of course, and Béziers … all great slaughters. I can hardly bear to tell you that this man was declared a saint two years ago, although the world has been rid of him for longer than that – he died in his bed, make no mistake. But not before he had founded his own order of preachers …'

'The Dominicans, yes: who in England we call the Black Friars. And our new friend Peter of Verona is …'

'One of Gregory's black-robed devils.'

'There was a Black Friar in Balecester for a while,' I said, remembering. 'He came and stirred things up – I remember him preaching in the market and outside the cathedral. He was thin and white-faced, and a bit sweaty. Folk would have fits and roll about in the mud at his feet. Not at all like our friend from Verona.'

'And yet that jolly man is filled with hatred, do not doubt it,' said the Captain, bitterly. 'And no doubt it is a hatred very specifically of my people. The *domini canes*, as they call themselves: the hounds of God – they are darkness manifest. I cannot look upon their black cloaks without my gorge rising, for they wear them to mock our *perfecti*. They mock the living and the dead without distinction. Patch, had Pope Gregory ordered the Inquisition while you were still a cleric?'

'Word had just reached us,' I replied. 'Although it did not mean very much to me then, I confess. But sitting here …'

'It makes the crackle of the flames a little less friendly,' finished the Captain.

'Master, are you saying that His Holiness placed you at the right hand of this Peter deliberately? How much does he know about you?'

'He does not know I am a … a *credente*,' said the Captain, all but swallowing the word. 'I am certain of it. Only my company knows that secret, and not all of them. We are all bound to each other by secrets, as you know. I believe – I *think* I believe – that it was a meaningless act. But the Dominicans themselves have much to say on the nature of belief.'

'No man less like a devil could ever be imagined,' I said. 'I have never liked friars, but I would gladly have ridden a few days in Peter's company. That is …'

'I cannot abide them,' said the Captain. 'That they mock my faith, that is one thing. But they roam the country, begging and pretending that they live the life of the Christ, when all they are about is prying and sniffing and stirring up hatred in the breasts of ordinary folk. But …' He dragged his fingers across his brow. 'I should not have spoken so hotly.'

'But they killed your people!'

'Loathe them as I do, I have always striven not to be drugged by hate's poison,' he sighed, and bowed his head wearily.

'I suppose it makes no difference,' I muttered. 'Hate will not raise the dead. But it is as strong as love, is it not? It makes a wondrous armour, I think.'

'But my dear Petroc, it gets in the way of business,' said the Captain. I had never heard a man utter a sadder thing, nor heard such a note of desolation in a human voice.

'If it were me, I would wish them all in hell,' I said, bitterly.

'Have you not heard what I have been telling you?' said Michel de Montalhac, softly. 'My poor friend, this is hell.'

We talked a little, after that, of lighter matters, and the fire died down, but a pall had been cast over the evening and I took myself off to bed before long, although I could not sleep at first. Then I dozed, and when I opened my eyes again I saw the Captain hunched over in front of the embers, writing. The scratch of the quill and the low hiss and spit of the fire sounded like the breathing of a dying man. The quill was scraping as I went off to sleep, and was scratching still as I woke the next morning.

'There: it is all set down,' said the Captain, turning to me, his eyes bagged with netted shadows. 'There are instructions for Gilles, and an account of what has passed here. Take these back to Rome, and wait for your orders – for orders there will be, Patch! Will it not feel good to be about things again?'

'Indeed, sir,' I said politely, stretching, and noting that an ecclesiastical flea had left a trail of bites up my leg.

'Well, I am looking forward to the off,' he said. 'Even though I ride with the Devil himself.'

'Be on your guard,' I said, then bit my tongue at my presumption.

'I shall. Nay, do not fear. Yon Peter is no devil – not *the* Devil, at least. He believes he does good. Though I think I will find his goodness more insufferable, in the long run, than plain evil. Besides, he and I will part company at Fidenza, which is only a few days from here.'

'Be that as it may, I will be fearful for your safety until I hear you have reached France safely,' I said.

'Oh, I have supped with bigger wolves than he,' said the Captain. The dark mood of last night seemed to have left him, and he shook out his grey locks like a happy dog before tying on his travelling coif. There was not much else to say, and after he had handed me a thick parcel of letters and embraced me, he left me to my own packing and was gone. I heard his strong, confident stride ringing along the corridor. I went to the window to look for him, but the view was of some inner yard where an old woman sat plucking a goose. It began to rain, and soon Viterbo was wrapped in a wet, grey shroud once again.

Chapter Seven

I arrived back in Rome two days later, having spent the night once more in Sutri, although this time I had at least found a pallet before the fire, and so had not woken feeling like a drowned sheep. Nevertheless the weather had not broken, and when at last I dragged myself up the stairs of the Palazzo Frangipani I was feeling more like a selkie – that faery seal that can take a human form – than a man. Trailing puddles behind me – for since I had crossed the Tiber and entered the gates of Rome the rain had turned into the kind of torrential deluge I had only ever encountered out on the deep ocean – I staggered into the kitchens, shedding clothes frantically.

'Good Petroc, what cheer?' called Roussel.

'None whatsoever,' I shot back, grumpily. 'I have water in my ears and mayhap I am growing fish scales beneath my tunic. For the love of God, find me something hot to drink!'

'Nothing easier,' said my friend, pouring a big cup of red wine into which he thrust a poker that had been resting in the fire. A cloud of fragrant steam boiled up. 'Is Captain de Montalhac close behind?'

'No,' I said, curtly. I was naked now, and freezing, and realising what a mistake this was I ran out and across the hall to my chambers, where I grabbed a blanket and an old tunic I had left flung across the bed. I returned to laughter, for

Gilles had heard me, and Horst, and I had to smile in turn as I crouched before the fire, warming my gooseflesh.

It took several long, gut-warming swallows of the hot wine before I felt inclined towards conversation, but meanwhile my comrades had gathered around me and were waiting expectantly. It was Gilles who broke the silence.

'What happened, Patch? Where is the Captain? Where … where have you been?'

'To see the pope,' I replied as casually as I could.

'That we know,' Roussel chimed in. 'We had a visit from the Lateran guard, who came looking for the pair of you and to inform us that you were to be guests of His Holiness. We rather took that to mean you had been arrested, but then the Captain's note arrived, which put us at our ease.'

'So where was old Gregory?' asked Gilles. 'Rieti? Trevi?'

'Viterbo,' I said. And I told them of our journey, a tale short in the telling, for I had nothing to relate of the road nor the city save endless rain. 'But as to what befell us there,' I finished, 'you must read this. The Captain stayed up all night writing it. I hope it is dry.' I fished the bundle of letters from my sodden valise, and found, to my relief, that the thick oiled leather of the bag had indeed kept out the deluge.

'But, Patch,' said Horst, through clenched teeth, 'where is Captain de Montalhac?'

'Ah. He is making haste northwards as we speak, and I hope he has found fair weather. Gregory … I mean to say, His Holiness commanded him to meet with the King of France as soon as possible. It is all in the letter,' I added, hopefully.

'France?' cried Roussel in disbelief.

'Indeed,' said Gilles. 'It is all here. And there are orders for us. The quiet life is over, boys.'

'I'm not going back to France, that is for fucking

certain,' said Roussel. Horst said nothing, but his shoulders slumped.

'Nothing like that,' said Gilles consolingly. 'We would be leaving Rome in any case within the month. You did not wish to stay for the summer, did you? For the agues? Watching the dead pilgrims being stacked one upon the other, and wondering if you will be next to go? I think not.'

''Tis true that the poison creeps from the river when the hot weather comes,' muttered Horst, reluctantly.

'When Orion calls his dog to heel,' added Roussel. I nodded my head. When the Dog Days came, every sane man left Rome. And I knew full well that the bestial vapours and poisons were particularly deadly to Englishmen.

'Well then, do not fret. You are bound for Venice and the Ca' Kanzir – not you, though, Patch. Does that not cheer you?'

The others nodded, mollified, but I jumped up, dislodging my blanket. 'It does not cheer me!' I exclaimed. 'Why must I be left to face the ague?'

'Peace, man. And put your bare bum away. You are being left nowhere.'

'What, then?' I said, tucking the blanket back about me while the others chuckled.

'Give me a little time to ... to arrange things in my mind, if you would,' said Gilles. 'Let us discuss things over dinner, you and I. Roussel, I should like you to ride down to Ostia Antica post haste, and begin putting the *Cormaran* in readiness. The Captain wishes us to sail within the week.'

After Roussel had gone off to pack his valise and Horst to instruct the kitchen, Gilles began to pace, head deep in the letter.

'What is the Ca' Kanzir?' I asked him.

'The Captain's palazzo. Home, on land, to the company of

the *Cormaran*. Your pardon, Petroc: the captain's writing is atrocious. I need to concentrate.'

I took myself off to my room to get dressed and mull things over. I had heard that the Captain owned a house in Venice, but it had not occurred to me that our company – which I had always likened to that bird, the petrel, whose fate it is to fly endlessly across the wild ocean, alighting only in death – could have a permanent home on terra firma. It was then that I realised that I had not been paying attention, that my world had been filled with my own desires and fears and with Anna, and that no doubt my employers found me an exasperating, if not dull young fellow. Chastened, I found a bottle of Isaac's foul but potent tonic and forced some down. It warmed me, and I got ready for dinner feeling very young and unworthy.

I gave Gilles all my news in the greatest detail. I noticed that he stiffened when I related our meal with Peter the Dominican, and that the poor Captain must perforce be suffering his company at this moment, and at least until they had reached the plains of Lombardia, but pressed on, for I assumed that the details of this must be in the long letter he had read. Still, our gentle abduction made a jolly story now that it was over, and Gilles pressed me for every minute detail of our audience with the pope.

'That reminds me: shall we examine our gift from His Holiness?' said Gilles at last, when I had all but run out of words. He drew out a square of vellum, which I recognised with a start as the one that Gregory had entrusted to the Captain. His eyes raced across the page, and in his excitement his face became quite red. Finally he looked up, and his eyes shone.

'By ... by Origen's ballocks! I am amazed. This is the *Inventarium* of Bucoleon!'

'That it is,' I agreed.

'How did His Holiness get his hands on this wonder?' breathed Gilles, studying it again. 'I have heard of such a list, but ...'

'Baldwin de Courtenay gave it to him,' I said.

'Why on earth would he do such a thing?'

'The emperor tried to bribe the pope,' I told him.

'And...'

'He failed. Now Gregory is trying to arrange for Baldwin to bribe – forgive me, to freely give as a *gift* – Louis Capet of France with these treasures, in return for aid to prop up his tottering empire,' I explained.

'With your humble servants as intermediary?' asked Gilles, grinning like a child.

'God wills it,' I said piously, and we woke the spiders in the ceiling with our amazed laughter.

I slept fitfully that night, sleep eluding me in the way it does when one is utterly exhausted: another of nature's merry jests. So I was up and about early, and just about to set out for Baldwin de Courtenay's lodgings to deliver the papal bull, when Gilles found me as I was helping myself to some bread and bacon. I told him what I was about, and he shook his head, smiling.

'No, no. This is a high, *high* matter of state. It wouldn't look right for you to just trundle up to Baldwin's door and hand that thing over as if it were a tradesman's receipt. No, send Piero to announce your intentions. Request an audience. Tweak the man's pride a little. He is worth it to us.'

So Piero was sent off in his most respectable clothes, only to return within the hour with the annoying news that Baldwin and his retinue – if two men may be called such – had departed on a hunting trip with the Count of Tivoli.

They would be gone for at least ten days.

'So what shall I do with this thing, then?' I asked Gilles, brandishing the letter with its absurdly heavy seal. 'Leave it with his landlady? I jest, by the way.'

Gilles puffed out his cheeks in exasperation. 'You are right: it is exceedingly vexatious,' he said. 'Sit with me: I have made my plans according to Captain de Montalhac's instructions.'

'Then tell me, please, for I wish to know if I must expose my tender English flesh to Rome's summer poison.'

Gilles laughed. 'No. Listen. I am being sent to Byzantium to open negotiations with Baldwin's new Regent, one Anseau de Cayeux. Meanwhile we shall dissolve the present company for the time being. I plan to set out as soon as I can – tomorrow, I hope – for Brundisium, to find a fast ship bound for Greece. I am sending the *Cormaran* to Venice as per Captain de Montalhac's instructions, where Roussel will set up our winter lodgings. Now then. Patch, you have been at loose ends these past weeks, yes?'

I nodded ruefully.

'Then perhaps you would like to make yourself useful?' I nodded again, eagerly this time. 'Excellent. I would like you to go ahead to Venice and make things ready for the *Cormaran*. There will be much to occupy you, and many vital things to learn. Indeed, this has been my task until now, so it bears a deal of responsibility. Are you equal to it?'

'Of course I am,' I said proudly. 'I thank you all for your confidence, and I promise to reward it, many times over.' Flowery words, perhaps, but I was overjoyed. I had become a supernumerary to the *Cormaran*'s affairs, and now I was being offered a chance to get back into the heart of things. 'I am at your service, sir!'

Gilles nodded gravely. 'I – neither the Captain or myself – have never doubted that. That is why I have more to tell you. We would like to establish a permanent base here, Patch,' he said. 'Rome is the very heart of our trade, as you must understand. It would be valuable to us if we had a representative here. After Venice, we – this has been in our thoughts for some time, you might like to know – would like you to look into that matter for us.' I must have been gaping like a codfish, for he laid a hand on my shoulder and squeezed companionably.

'Everything in time, Petroc. These sound like mighty affairs, but they are not, necessarily. We want you to stretch your legs, see a little of the world, and hopefully divine your place in it. Still as sanguine?'

I pulled on an earlobe. 'He is considering!' cried Gilles, merrily. I slapped my hands on the table.

'No, sir, I have considered. I am your man, whatever the task. I owe you and Captain de Montalhac my life, and it is at your service.'

'Done,' said Gilles. 'Very well. We are leaving this place. Horst is finding you a room in the English Borgo, where you will stay for the next few days.'

'But I thought I was leaving at once?' I said, confused.

'Ah. You must deliver Gregory's decree to young Baldwin de Courtenay, or have you forgotten already? And as for Venice, do you know the way?' I shook my head. 'Easily remedied. The Captain has a map, of course. And there is the small matter of transport,' he went on. 'You can, of course, ride?'

I felt my ears redden. 'Only mules,' I muttered, mortified. 'Mules, and the horse I rode up to Viterbo and back,' I added hastily, hoping to salvage a little dignity.

'Yes, that is rather what I meant. Michel mentions in his letter that you were a little … gingerly, he put it, upon your mount. Well, with your new-found rank we will not send you out into the world on an ancient mule, lad,' said Gilles. 'You will ride a horse, like a gentleman – for that is what you are, make no mistake – and you will ride it well. Horst will teach you, I think.'

'Horst?'

'He was once a knight in his own land,' Gilles said, 'and a warrior who rode out to battle many times. He will teach you, all right, probably far more than you will ever need to know. And now, let us find that map.'

Thus the day settled into the more comforting and familiar rituals of route-planning, timetables, and all those other ways in which men seek to impose form and order on the trackless future. At last I had a purpose. And more: I was to be the Captain's agent in Rome, perhaps – and that, at last, was purpose indeed, and although the Captain and his lieutenant had seemingly tossed it my way like a scrap to a dog, it was a scrap that I kept returning to, each time finding it more savoury.

My new quarters turned out to be two plain rooms two flights up above a narrow street in the English Borgo. I loved this quarter, with its ancient, crumbling buildings and teeming, polyglot inhabitants. Like all of Rome it seemed to have stood forever, quietly wearing away like a great stone outcrop, while men came and went, leaving no more impression than ants. But of course the reverse was also true, sometimes in spectacular ways. Buildings seemingly disappeared overnight, collapsing in dusty mounds, their stones pillaged instantly for new buildings that sprang up as if conjured out of the ground. Everywhere was noise, hubbub, commotion, bustle, laughter, strife, argument, song. I call it the English Borgo, and indeed there were others – Frankish, Frisian, Langobard and more – but in truth the northerners mixed promiscuously, or at least as promiscuously as pilgrims and clerics may.

All this delighted me. I loved to hear the voices of my homeland, of course, for I was an exile, and exile is a sickness for which there is no cure, only balms to assuage the worst pangs. I had, perforce, to assume a false name, for – as I had discovered during my short time in London, and much to my horror – the crime of which I had been accused had given me the sort of notoriety that has maids all a-flutter, their dads growling about nooses and their mothers loosening their stays. I had not, thank the Lord, been accorded the honour of a ballad, but I had a new name, the Gurt Dog of Balecester, a beast who ripped out the throat of the bishop on the altar of his own cathedral and then ran, naked and bloody, through the streets of the city, killing and maiming as he went, before vanishing into the night. The Gurt Dog is what we Dartmoor folk call the Yes Hound, the Devil's own hunting-hound, a sight of which is a sure foreteller of death.

I was a little amused at how my legend had grown, and a great deal more distressed that I had become a beast and a devil in the minds of my erstwhile countrymen. I wondered, of course, how the memory of Hugh de Kervezey was honoured in Balecester. For it had been Kervezey, the bastard son of the Bishop of Balecester and a cold, demon-hearted schemer and murderer, whom I had met, as I believed by chance, one night in a tavern in the city where I was a scholar, and who had cut the throat of deacon Jean de Nointot before my horrified eyes. I had fled, painted with the deacon's steaming blood, and Kervezey, feigning the innocent, had led the hue and cry that had driven me, after long and miserable wanderings, to seek the protection of Captain de Montalhac. Only much later had I learned that I had merely been a very minor pawn in Kervezey's long and cunning game to ensnare the Captain and usurp his business and his power. Fate – I will call it fate, although it is long since I believed in fate, and could as well call it destiny, or chance, or a flaw at the heart of a madman's flawless plan – led Kervezey and me to a distant beach, where, beyond all hope, he died at my hand, slain by his own knife. Thus I saved myself, and avenged my dear friend William of Morpeth, who had been drawn into Kervezey's net alongside me but who had not survived. Now I wore that knife, that was called Thorn, to remind me of William, and so that I could remember the young novice monk who, coming back from a piss, met a pale-eyed man who, with a wave of this same narrow blade of washed steel, had transformed him into what I now was: the Gurt Dog, Petrus Zennorius, Patch to those who knew me well, and Petroc of Auneford never more in this life.

So it was as Petrus Zennorius that I made my way about the Borgo and the greater city around it. It served its purpose, and Patch was as likely a nickname for Peter as for Petroc, so I would not easily be caught out from that quarter. My habitual roaming and prowling about the place, poking into the oldest nooks and seeking out all that was ancient and odd, led me into many chance conversations with other Englishmen, and while I was delighted to fret the air with the usual useless but irresistible discourse on the weather back home (worse than Rome) and the food (far better than all this foreign poison), what I really desired was to ask about Balecester and its grisly hound. I knew better, rest assured, and contented myself with seeking out men from Devon or Cornwall, for simply to hear their homely voices was more refreshing to me than a draught from Jacob's Well. I spent more than one evening in the taverns and cook-shops of the Borgo, keeping myself to myself for the most part, listening and avoiding trouble, for even amongst pilgrims there is conflict, and it was not rare to find blood in the cobbles come morning-time.

Alas for me, although I was simply waiting for the return of Baldwin de Courtenay, my days were not entirely without purpose. Gilles stayed true to his intentions and left the day after our conversation. And I moved the day after that, for the company was leaving the Palazzo Frangipani. Horst, my Brandenburger friend, came for me before I had even unpacked my few belongings. I thought of making some excuse and dodging my obligations, but one look at his set jaw was enough to tell me that my first riding lesson was about to take place, whether I was willing or not. And I was not, for I was, frankly, terrified. It was one thing to ride a corpulent old abbey donkey, quite another to climb aboard a proper horse like the one Horst was holding by the bridle as he stood in the street and shouted for me to come down. Even from three storeys up the beast looked vast and dangerous. I pulled on my travelling boots, buckled on a stout belt – in my panic I believed this was crucial – and descended the stairs with infinite reluctance.

'His name is Iblis,' said Horst, sidestepping the usual niceties and shoving the reins at me. I took them, gingerly. 'He is a Saracen horse, very beautiful. Aren't you?' he enquired of the horse, who nodded and bared massive teeth. 'Fit for a prince, Patch, so do not disappoint him. He is smaller than our Frankish war-mounts, but he is a warrior nonetheless. You will ride him with pride.' It was a command, delivered with Pomeranian finality.

'Iblis ... What, pray, does his name signify?' I asked, patting the beast experimentally on the muzzle, which was soft and slightly moist. Then it nodded again, and I snatched my hand away.

'I believe it is what the Mussulmen call the Devil,' said Horst, absently. 'Don't do that, Patch. He'll bite you.'

'What, don't pat him? But you were ...'

'No! No, do not treat him as if he were a lion, or red-hot, or whatever ridiculous fancy you have concocted. He is a horse, a kindly, gentle beast who wishes to be your friend. Think of him as a dog, if you like.'

'A gurt dog,' I muttered.

'What?'

'Nothing. So now must I clamber up on his back, for God's sake?'

'Not here. I do not want you falling on cobbles.' And with that hopeful remark he set off down the street and I followed, leading the horse. He was undeniably cooperative, although I suspected he was saving his energy for some appalling savagery later on.

We left the Borgo and ascended the Janiculum hill past the crumbling remains of the ancient wall and into an area of gardens and meadows – meadows in the Roman sense of a wide expanse of sun-killed grass, thistles, dust and stones, haunted by feral goats – where we halted, and my riding lesson commenced.

I will draw a veil over these proceedings, and those that came after, for the sake of brevity and to preserve that which I laughably call my dignity. For the arse-bruised, thistle-pricked and, if memory serves, goat-nibbled fool who limped back to his quarters that evening was as broken in spirit as any newly mastered horse. It was with dread that I greeted Horst's implacable summons the next morning and the morning after that, and on and on for an entire week of torment. I fell, more than once. I sobbed into the beast's rough and pungent mane. I was ignored, and then obeyed far too vigorously. He stepped on my foot and ate a fistful of my hair. Finally, late on the seventh day, as I guided Iblis around an improvised course of boulders and dead olive branches, Horst clapped his hands loudly. Iblis started and reared, and instead of flying off and landing on some unsuspecting goat I dug in my knees, shortened the reins and told him, in no uncertain terms, to settle himself down at once. Then I trotted over to where Horst stood, grinning.

'What the fuck, Herr von Tantow, was that?' I enquired. I had had enough: of Iblis, of goats and the hard and thistly Roman ground, and above all of the unbending, tyrannical Horst.

'That was you finally learning how to ride a fucking horse,' he told me. 'Now let us go and get very drunk.'

'Amen,' I breathed. And so Horst von Tantow walked at my side as I rode Iblis, the Devil's horse, back down the Janiculum and through the Borgo to the stable, where we left him to his oats and barley mash. Horst knew a drinking-house run by a Saxon who brewed fine beer, and so we took ourselves off to it and dived headlong into the beer.

We had supped a brace of mugs apiece when Horst, wiping the foam from his lips, said, almost absently, 'Does it pain you to ride Iblis?'

'Do you mean my ballocks?' I asked. 'Yes, but it has got better.'

'No, no! I meant … after London.'

'You mean Anna …' I paused, considering. 'Perhaps at first, but I do not fear Iblis very much now, and … and what happened to Anna could have happened to anybody.'

'Hmm. This has been troubling me since that day, Patch. Do you remember, this afternoon, how I made Iblis rear up?' I was about to give him a friendly cursing for it, but he shook his head. 'Listen. If I had been under his hooves he would not have come down upon me. He would have thrown himself sideways, or … the point is, he is a trained riding horse. If you were lying upon the ground and I galloped at you, he would jump or swerve. Riding horses will not hurt a man if they can avoid it.'

'What are you saying?' I asked, for I could not make him out at all.

'I am saying that a horse that rears up, strikes a human being and does it again is either a wild animal, in which case it could not be ridden out in the street, or it is a destrier, a warhorse. Such a beast is a weapon, as much as a sword or a lance.'

'Then it was a knight's horse, my friend,' I told him, growing impatient, for his words were beginning to trouble me.

'But such a horse will not strike unless his rider tells him to. Once, perhaps, but he will not go on until he has … Listen, Patch: forgive me. I should not have dragged this out. But I used to ride such horses, and I know them well …'

'It was an accident,' I said, for my friend had clearly been torturing himself. 'It was fate.' And although I did not believe in fate I said it eagerly, desperately, willing it to be so.

'Oh well, you may be right,' said Horst gently, although he had turned quite pale and seemed to be searching for something in my face as he snapped his fingers for more beer.

It came, and kept coming, and I sucked it down to wash away the thoughts that my friend had seeded in my mind. We supped so freely that only the haziest memory of that evening remains: Horst, deep in his cups, telling of a battle fought against the idol-worshipping Letts on the borders of his country. And of that, all I have is an image: of fresh bright blood flung across snow. It haunted my sodden dreams that night, the snow turning to London mud streaked with black hair, and I woke up the next morning wrapped tight in my bed linens, although the day was already sweltering.

Chapter Eight

When I awoke the next day and made to rise, I found that while I slept I had been bludgeoned by a great fatigue which clung to my limbs like leaden chain mail. I felt as if I had walked a hundred miles, and I had neither the strength nor the will to get out of bed. My landlady, a widow endowed with a kindlier heart than most boarding-house owners, decided that I had caught a cold, and took it upon herself to keep me fed after Isaac the physician had called around that first day and found me fretting and foul of temper. So I lay, looking at the cracks in the ceiling, drinking the widow's excellent soup, which tasted no better than Tiber water to me, and trying to predict the movements of the little sticky-footed lizards who roamed the walls in search of flies. Finally Isaac thought to bring me something to read, to whit, extracts from Pliny the Elder and the same map that we had pored over that day back at the Palazzo Frangipani.

'Pliny is for your amusement, but he will teach you about the country you will be riding through,' he told me. 'But this –' and he waved the map – 'is work. The *Cormaran* is leaving Ostia tomorrow, and you should think of leaving for Venice as soon as you have got your strength back.'

'Has Baldwin returned?' I asked, weakly.

'He was not there this morning,' said Isaac. 'But he may be now. Why don't you see for yourself?'

I sat up. In truth I did not feel particularly ill, but my

130

strength, as Isaac had noticed, had ebbed a little more than my sickness merited. I thought it was the lingering effect of my fall, but Isaac shook his head and tutted.

'You are still pining, my friend,' he said gently.

'I am not! I am ill,' I protested.

'Nonsense,' he said, kindly. 'I can see it in your eyes.' I snorted. 'No, no,' he went on. 'I can tell if it is the body or the soul which suffers. In your case it is the latter, far more than the former.'

I muttered churlishly but, as ever, he had struck home. I had been following the cracks in the ceiling, as I have said, but every one of them had become a road that led to Anna, wherever she might be. I could think of her a little these days, and they were happy thoughts, at least until the spectre of her ruined eye rose, as it always did, like a moon whose light turned everything in my heart to ice. Now I remembered her as she had been in London, in the inn where we had lodged. I had never tired of exploring that face, although I knew it better than the landscape of my home. So that last morning I had no need to search it so carefully, but had I known I was taking my final leave I would have taken note of every tiny hair, every freckle.

Lying there in Rome I found I could remember no single word she had spoken that day. Instead, my somewhat fevered mind returned again and again to the fine dark down that, in certain lights, could be found on her upper lip. I travelled up the single wrinkle that lay between her eyebrows, and along the two frown lines upon her forehead, and dwelt for long hours in the place where the gold wire of a jewelled pendant pierced her earlobe.

Now, on the fourth day of this agonised lethargy, I lay and made this journey again and again, but by then I was barely ill, in truth, and my lassitude was more of an indulgence than an affliction. Ill thoughts prey upon idle minds, and Horst's words came back to me. Why had such a dangerous animal been ridden down one of London's busiest streets? And what of the rider? He had never come forward, and the coroner's men had not found him. But these thoughts were unbearable. That would mean that Anna had been murdered. Was that what Horst had been trying to tell me? Of course – and he believed it too, it was plain. But it made no sense, for who would wish such a thing, and plan it so neatly? Neat it had been, but crude and bloody, not like something planned. So I began to brood and fret, and at last I began to toss and turn and finally to pace about the room, which tired me so that I returned to bed, to begin the miserable process over again. I had paid the landlady's little nephew to keep a watch for Baldwin, and to run and tell me should he arrive, but no word had come. The day became a fevered round of pacings and a kind of stunned lassitude, until night fell and I finally, gratefully, began to grow weary enough to sleep. I was beginning the feathery drift down into oblivion when a sharp rapping came at my door. I thought I had dreamed it, for it had the quality of those strange sounds that jolt one awake but come from within one's own head. But the rapping came again, insistent, commanding. Puzzled, I reasoned that it must be the landlady, for all my friends had left the city by now, but the raps, when they came again, were so commanding that, unnerved, I snatched up Thorn. Pulling my cloak around me I lurched up to open the door a crack, and peered out.

I was met by the grey gaze of Michael Scotus.

'Hello, lad. Did I not say I would see you again? Get dressed. Come with me.'

'To where? Good Master Scotus, what hour is it?'

'You are sick. I have come to heal you for good and all. Physicians keep odd hours, and this is one of those. Come.'

Never in my right mind would I have gone out into the streets of Rome with a stranger in the dead of night, but as before, the words of Michael Scot brooked no refusal. I found myself pulling on clothes, and tying up my boots.

'You will not need your knife,' said the Scot.

And I left it under my pillow, and followed him out, meek as a calf. He led me up my street, while I cursed silently for giving up my weapon so easily. I was about to plead sickness or some other more transparent excuse when I heard a snort and, turning a corner, saw a knot of men waiting, dressed in black cloaks like Michael Scot, and grasping halberds. My heart clenched like a fist but my companion shushed me peremptorily. 'Our escort,' he said. 'Vatican guards. And here: our mounts.'

The guards stepped aside to reveal two mules. Their coats glinted like pewter in the light of the young moon. Mules are the least sinister of creatures, and these two, the colour of spiderwebs and thistledown, held so little threat that I almost laughed with relief.

'Come away,' said the Scot. 'We have a distance to go, and the night will soon be waning.'

He climbed nimbly on to one of the mules, again belying his threescore and more years, and I mounted the other. It was odd being astride such a small beast after a week of Iblis, but I was soon bouncing along behind Michael Scot, who without another word had kicked his mule into a quick trot. Strange to say, I felt none of the fevered torpor that had dogged me all that day. The guards fell in around us and began to jog silently, keeping pace with us, although we were not slow. Their boots seemed muffled, for they made hardly any sound. Soon we had crossed the Tiber and were clip-clopping through the quiet streets on the other side. We passed through the Campo dei Fiori, threaded through some alleyways and emerged under the sudden bulk of the Capitoline Hill. This we skirted, keeping it to our right. Then we were in the valley that lies, a confusion of ancient ruins and newer but no less ruinous slums, between the Capitoline and the Quirinal, and there, in the distance, squatting and monstrous, the Coliseum. Feeling an unbidden stab of dread I turned to my companion. The moon shone full in his face and made of it a mask.

'What are we about, and ... where exactly are we going, sir?' I asked, trying not to sound querulous and, I realised, not succeeding.

'Why, there, of course,' he said, casually. 'Have you never visited the Coliseum at night?'

'No, and nor does any sane man!' I blurted. 'What folly is this, sir? It is no place for the living – every Roman knows it!'

'Are you a Roman? No, and neither am I. As for the why of it, here I shall complete your cure.'

'But am I not cured of ... of what afflicted me before?' I squeaked, for my illness was so far behind me that I barely recalled it. 'I have a mere cold now.'

'Hardly. The flesh fares well, my good lad, but the soul, I perceive, yet has need of medicine. That is what we seek tonight.'

His Scottish brogue seemed a little thicker, somehow, and strangely I found it calming, for my heart, which had started to knock with anxiety, fell back into its quieter rhythm. Nevertheless I shot a look around me at our escort. But all had pulled up their cowls and their faces were hidden in shadow. The hooves of our mules clacked emptily against the stones of the street. We might have been a procession of the dead.

In the daytime the Coliseum is a brutish place. Its stones

bask in the sunshine with a kind of stolid self-satisfaction, and it dwarfs with ease the sightseers who dare to poke about in its cat-haunted mazes. On my wanderings I had learned that, only a few years before, the place had been a fortress until an earthquake had driven out the occupiers, and left it at the mercy of stone-thieves who picked away at the marble to burn in their lime-kilns. But as all men knew, it had been built in pagan times as a temple to all the old gods of Rome, and when Mother Church had ended their rule on earth they lingered on here as demonic shades, lappers of blood, who were known to issue forth and spread plague and misfortune through the city. They took the shape of beasts, and there were many who had seen them emerge from the great arches led by a phantom bull, mighty in size and red as blood, bellowing forth fire and smoke.

Nowadays the Romans themselves keep away from the stones, although they will picnic in its shade and make assignations – although, unlike any other ruin or alleyway, couples do not rut in its cool halls and caves, for the place has an atmosphere, an air as heavy as its vast round mass, that does not tempt one to linger there. It is the pilgrims from the northern lands who enter, rivalling the pigeons with their chatter, and who clamber over the walls and through the galleries, weaving excited, fatuous speculations as to past glories and horrors. But even they are oppressed by the place, and eventually seek ever more desperately for the way out, and one sees them regrouping – pale and over-sated, like guests at an over-rich meal at which the meat has spoiled – out in the sunshine, while the Romans regard them with superior contempt.

At night, though, it might be a different place altogether. While the merciless Roman sun makes the mighty circle of arches seem heavy with slothful menace, the moon, if it is bright, turns it into a many-eyed phantom. If in the daytime it squats, at night it appears to hover and shimmer, and if in the sun it is unquestionably the work of men who exercised all their brutal skill to draw it out of the base earth, at night it is unearthly, its myriad arches and windows giving it the mottled, silvery aspect of the moon's face. Tonight there was not a living soul anywhere to be seen or heard as we rode out on to the dead grass of the field which surrounds it. We skirted the building, riding through the moon-shadow and out again into light, until at a signal from Michael we halted and dismounted. Our escort gathered up our reins and tied the mules up to a slender marble column that stood nearby. Then Michael took my upper arm gently but firmly and nodded his head once, solemnly. I saw that in his other hand he held a long, slender staff of dark wood that was finished in such a way that it did not catch the light. He inclined it very slightly, pointing towards an archway in which an immense door of studded wood hung askew off its hinges. It was very black beyond the door, as black as Michael's staff, which now led us onward under the mighty keystone of the entrance.

'Do you know Bede's words on this place?' Michael asked. His voice came from next to my ear. He was leading me through the thick darkness, through which I could see nothing, although his footfalls sounded as sure as if he were strolling about in broad daylight. In truth I had read the venerable monk's writings on Rome, but at that moment I was too full of confusion to recall them, for I had given myself over to the trust of this man whom I did not know in any real sense, and of whom I knew only the vaguest and most unpromising rumours. Nevertheless here I was, being drawn through the belly of this most cursed of all buildings in this whole haunted city, and I was not at all certain how I had allowed this to happen, and why I was not tempted, even now, to escape. So I shook my head, knowing that the gesture was invisible.

'I cannot remember,' I breathed, suddenly terrified lest my words disturb whatever horrible legions might be hiding in the almost palpable dark.

'"*Quandiu stabit coliseus, stabit et Roma,*"' Michael intoned. '"*Quando cadit coliseus, cadet et Roma. Quando cadet Roma, cadet et mundus.*"'

'"While the Coliseum stands, Rome stands,"' I said, re-membering words I had read long ago, in the light of a spring morning in Devon, when my life still stretched before me, secure in the promise of its safety and blissful uneventful-ness.

'Very good,' said Michael, approvingly. '"When falls the Coliseum, Rome shall fall; when Rome falls the world shall fall." I take that to mean that this place is the very centre of the world – where all roads converge: *all* roads, the seen and the unseen.' With those words we stepped out into the moonlight once more.

We were on the lip of a vast pit which, with the play of the silver light over a confusion of trees and ruins, appeared to be full of boiling quicksilver. I could make out no order, for there seemed to be newer buildings here and there, and even the crooked belltower of a little church that lurched at a dangerous angle. I let out a small squeak of breath, more of relief than anything else, for I was still in a place, a location on the face of the earth, although as Michael had guided me through the darkness I had felt the growing fear that I was being led to no-place, a way station on the unseen roads of which he had spoken. But I had no time to gather myself, for my escort was beckoning. He had begun to pick his way through a sloping maze of truncated walls and roofless pass-ages down towards the centre of the Coliseum, which seemed to be a sort of oval field of flat earth or grass on which had been built a rough cluster of sheds or huts, most of which had burned down or collapsed. There were trees growing there too: olives, a stunted pine and the spiny billows of gorse. I followed, keeping my gaze fixed uneasily on Michael's staff, which he held up in front of him, a line of blackness, as if the door to an even more absolute night were opened just a hair's breadth. There was an urgent scrabbling to my right and I started and turned to see a cat clambering up a mound of scree. Another was already there, regarding me with slit-eyed contempt, and I realised that if I had thought this place was deserted I was mistaken, for there were cats everywhere. At first I was relieved to find only cats and not flame-mouthed bulls and demons, but before I had even reached the level ground where Michael now stood waiting my fancy had begun to work upon me, for the gaze of a cat is powerful, and when that power is multiplied a thousandfold it becomes something quite frightful.

I strode quickly to where Michael awaited me, trying to appear brisk and not terrified. He had found the very centre of the oval field. I looked about me: now I was in the midst of the seething cauldron, and the black rim, sometimes perfectly regular, sometimes jagged, sometimes adorned with crude battlements, framed an oval window of sky.

'At the centre of all things,' Michael said, startling me. His voice was low and calm – priest-like, in fact. It was hard for me to picture him as the priest I knew him to be. But what manner of priest would seek out such a place as this?

'Do you see how we are in a kind of bowl?' he asked. 'And have you seen how the water in a trough, when the bung is removed, forms a spinning vortex as it drains, or how a child's marble, dropped into a dish, will circle around, spiralling ever downwards until it finds the still centre? So it is here, at the world's heart. All things that travel the invisible roads of the earth and of the heavens, can be brought to rest here. We have only to call them.'

'Call what?' I asked, feeling as if a tiny clawed hand, cold as ice, had just settled on my belly and was seeking a way inside.

'Whom, lad: whom,' said the man who had almost been Archbishop of Canterbury.

He bid me wait there while he vanished into a nearby hovel. Emerging with a bundle of firewood – it was tied, and did not look like a chance find – he placed it carefully, turning to the four points of the compass and adjusting it according to some hidden purpose. Then he drew me back and, with the end of his staff, drew a circle in the sandy earth around the sticks. Turning his face to the sky, he muttered something at the stars and drew four symbols that I did not recognise into the earth at the cardinal points. They seemed a little like Arabic letters but also like sinuous little pictures of something indiscernible. Then he stooped over the wood. There was a loud sigh, as sleepers make when they are in the throes of a dream, and fire blossomed under his hands. He stepped back, and flames flew up higher than his head, sparks hurtling towards the moon.

'Stand here,' he told me, taking my shoulders and positioning me, as if I were a mannequin, in front of one of his symbols – and indeed, from the moment I had been awakened by Michael's knocking I had been no more in command of myself than a puppet. I believe I was facing west. 'Now look into the flames. Look!'

Wordlessly I obeyed, for I had no choice. The wood was burning fiercely, and gave off a rich and sharp smell. Michael Scot muttered something and waved a hand at the fire, which crackled into a storm of violet sparks. Then there was a roiling of oily black smoke, and when this cleared I was staring into a sheet of pure, golden flame. It was as if I were a child again, newly woken in summer and opening the door on a perfect day's morning. There was utter calm. I felt myself sway, and then Michael's hand was across my shoulders, steadying me. Then something disturbed the golden peace: at first it seemed as if the smoke had returned, for an ugly stain had formed amongst the flames, but as I watched it resolved itself into an image.

Have you ever seen a piece of amber in which the corpse of some insect, an ant or a fly, hangs suspended? One looks as if through a hole in time at the creature whose tiny limbs are still but seemingly not dead, for there is no corruption. It is not a picture but a real thing, held just out of reach and magnified by the lens of its glassy tomb. Thus did I look into the flames and see, hanging a little way from the searing bed of embers, a swirl of black hair, billowing as if in water. I gasped, and felt – or imagined that I felt – Michael Scot's hand taking hold of the back of my skull, for I tried to turn my head and could not. And I very much wanted to turn away, for I knew what I would see next.

Anna's good eye stared into my own, unblinking. Down her cheek, livid and incongruous as a poached egg, hung her other eye. With the unbearable clarity that sometimes comes in dreams I saw every detail of her face, as if through a reading stone: every pore, every tiny hair on her upper lip, the pock-mark that lay in the curve of her nostril, the smile lines at the corners of her mouth. And always the awful, the intolerable presence of the eye, as dead as this creature of flame, this fetch of my dearest Anna, was surely alive. As I stared – for now I could not have torn my gaze away even had I tried – I saw her hands rise from the embers. They seemed to reach for me, and although they did not leave the nimbus of flame I seemed to feel them grasp my own wrists, although their touch was cool, and to see my hands – for now I was, or seemed to be, both standing on the earth and also within that world of fire – as she guided them to her face. She pressed my palms to her cheek and my left hand felt the yielding orb of the dangling eye. I tried to scream, but I felt her fingers pressing mine, drawing them upward. So we stood, half in this world, half in another, for how long I cannot tell, for there was nothing in my head but the soft whisper of the flames and the almost-warmth of the flesh that held my own. Then I felt her grasp loosen, and what I thought had been my hands fell from view. I felt them, back in this world, hanging at my sides, but only dimly, for Anna had lowered her own hands to show her face once more, and now two brown eyes, almond-shaped and perfect, regarded me. She blinked once, and smiled, and I saw the gap between her front teeth for the last time, for she was dissolving, pure as a blessing, into the shimmer of flame.

Chapter Nine

I awoke from a black and dreamless sleep that had brought true rest for the first time in many weeks. The day was gone, and the shadows were gathering outside my window. As soon as I beheld the cobwebbed beams of my room I sat upright with a gasp of shock, for my last clear memory was of standing in the Coliseum at night, while someone lit a fire. Then, as with shaking hands I found a flask of water and drained it, I remembered that Michael Scot had called on me and led me through the streets to that terrible place, and what he had caused to appear. But the apparition he had conjured, for I knew now that I had witnessed some manner of necromancy, was not altogether clear in my mind, and after it everything faded into the haze of a dream. I recalled, with the effort with which one pieces together the events of a night when one has drunk oneself near-insensible, that Michael had led me back through the pitch-dark tunnel and out into the city where our mules and escort awaited, and that I had ridden in silence back to my lodgings, where I had allowed myself to be laid in bed. I thought perhaps that Michael Scot had sat at my bedside for a time before I had fallen asleep, but nothing was clear. But it was not, I found, a worry to me that I had all but lost the events of the night, for then, as indeed now, when I try to summon their memory, what had seemed ominous and then frightening had shed its fearfulness. Michael seemed a wise friend, our excursion a great adventure. And what I had seen in the flames – whom, rather – had not been a spirit or demon. Strange as it may seem, it was clear then, as it is even now, that a window was opened for me, and I was given the great gift of being able to look beyond this world, and in doing so to be healed of a dolorous wound. And when I try to discern the taint of magic or the hand of Satan I cannot, for it left me feeling as clean and whole as a bathe in a Dartmoor brook, and I knew with utter certainty that Anna was gone from me as a wounded ghost, but had returned, whole once more, to my heart.

I wandered over to the window. Evening was turning the shadows blue outside, and the air was cool, although the stone of the windowsill still held the sun's warmth. I looked down into the street. People ambled and scuttled, lounged and slumped. I took a deep breath and stretched, and found to my surprise that I was better. Where there had been searing pain there was only a dull ache upon my spirit, and the tight, fickle rawness of a new-healed scar. And there was the prospect of a journey ahead. It was time to leave this city, at least for a while. The landlady knocked on the door to tell me that the parties I had been waiting for had returned to the White Hound. That news put the final touch to my spirits. I called for some fresh water, and the landlady fetched it, beaming at my recovery, as if I had shaken off some mortal illness, and took my sweat-fouled clothes away to wash. I sluiced the staleness from my body, dressed in clean clothes and went out to find some supper. As I was opening the street door, the landlady startled me when she all but leaped from her own doorway.

'I entirely forgot!' she exclaimed. 'Your friend the Frenchman left this for you.' From the upland of her bosom she produced a fat letter. 'Oh, and some money; rather a lot ... it is all there!' she added hastily.

'I am sure it is,' I told her, and waited for her to retreat into her chambers before I hefted the little purse. It was stuffed full of coin, which proved to be all of gold, and I doubted she had robbed me of very much. I was tucking the letter into my wallet when I felt the crackle of something already there. I pulled it out: a piece of parchment, quite old and mellowing into the colour of autumn oak leaves. Curious, I unfolded it. It was nothing but a few lines of Greek, a crabbed, hurried scrawl. I frowned at it for a full minute before the words began to come into focus. As they did so I gasped, for what I read there was this:

The **Mandylion** of Edessa
The **Keramion**
The Crown of Thorns
The Swaddling Bands
Sandals of Our Lord
The Cross of **Basileus** Constantine
A portion of the Cross
Another part of the True Cross
The miraculous Reed
The Spear of Longinus
A Chain, that bound Our Lord
The Sponge, from which he drank
A Stone, that came from the holy Sepulchre
The Shrouds
Holy Cloth in a sacred icon
The Grave-Clothes of Our Lord
The **Syndon** of Christ
The miraculous Tunic of Our Lord
A Towel from the washing of the Apostles' feet
Blood of Our Lord
Milk of the **Theotokos**

Maphorion of the Theotokos
Saint Blas, his head
Saint Clement, his head
Saint Simeon, his head
The Baptist, his arm, and also a portion of his head
Moses, his Staff

Baffled, I stared at the paper. I seemed to be holding a copy of the *Inventarium* of the Pharos Chapel, but it was not Baldwin's, not the one given to us by Pope Gregory. This had not come from Gilles, and it certainly had not come from the landlady. I remembered Michael Scotus standing over me as I fell off the high cliff of sleep: of course. It must have been Michael, but why should he give me such a gift?

I studied the list again. Some words I understood: *Theotokos* was the Virgin, the *Syndon* was, I guessed, something like the *Sudarium*, the cloth placed over the face of the dead Christ, that I remembered from the Gospel of St John, and that was on Baldwin's inventory. But what of *Keramion*? What was this *Mandylion*? Like a sleepwalker I stepped out into the cool Roman night. I found food and walked for a while through the noisy crowds, my mind on the baffling list, and on the journey ahead. When I returned to my lodgings I stayed up, the map spread out on the bed, until the bells of the city chimed out the third hour of the night. I counted the Captain's money – there was a princely amount of it, as the landlady had guessed. I thought to read his letter, but as I was about to, sleep began to creep over me at last. At last I laid my head upon the pillow, but my dreams were shallow and fretted with disturbing visitors: horse-teeth, the gibbets of the Tor di Nona, and the smoke from a greasy, raging fire, which grew until it overhung Rome like a storm cloud.

Chapter Ten

When I rose the next day I was as fresh as an adder who has left his old skin lying upon a rock. I would be leaving tomorrow, I thought, for my clothes were still being washed; so I had better deliver the pope's letter to the cursed, annoying Baldwin de Courtenay.

This time there were no guards at the door of the White Hound. Without the angry presence of my lords of Grez and Bussac, the place seemed defiantly ordinary, and I wondered how a man who called himself an emperor could bring himself to accept such lodgings. The serving-maid whom I recognised from my last visit blushed in a comely way when she saw me, but a fat older woman who I took to be the mistress of the inn shoved her aside, looked me up and down and waved her hand impatiently towards the stairs.

'They're up there,' she said shortly. I assumed she recognised me, for I was wearing my outlandish Venetian clothes again, so I said nothing; yet I wondered again at the grim circumstances that had befallen the young emperor. I climbed the stairs and, when I reached the landing, pulled out the pope's letter, the better to make a grand entrance – for I winced at the thought of fumbling in my satchel while Baldwin and his two gladiators smirked. So I stood before the emperor's closed door, arranging the letter in my hand so that the *bulla* hung majestically – or so I hoped – over my forearm, before giving the door a sharp, efficient rap.

The wood sounded hollow, and I realised that the door was unlatched. It opened slightly. To my surprise, I heard no one within: no answer to my knock, no summons to enter. Feeling like a jackanapes, I hesitated. Then I thought to myself how odd it was that the Emperor of Romania should leave his door unlocked. Perhaps, I reasoned, it was deliberate. Christ, now I suddenly wished to get this business over with straight away.

'Your Majesty,' I said, very loudly, banging on the door again, hard enough to swing it a good way open, as I had intended. A somewhat unseemly accident it would seem, but at least I would have announced myself.

But as soon as I crossed the threshold I saw that something was amiss. The chambers were empty: no, not empty, for the plain furniture was still there, but the shield with the black lion was gone, along with the tapestries. There was no chest against the wall. I blinked in the sunlight that was streaming in through unshuttered windows, and cocked my head. A sound was coming from the room where Baldwin had slept: a hissing, harsh and regular. In the confusion that still filled my brain-pan I could not place it at first, but it was not threatening, and I walked softly to the doorway and peered in.

A blonde-haired chambermaid, her long braids dragging in the rushes, was down on her knees, scrubbing the floor tiles under the window. She had already filled a sack with rushes, I saw, and now she was bent to her task, holding the brush with both hands as she scoured the tiles, here dark and stained, there clean and red-orange. But her hands were not the hands of a servant, red and swollen with water and lye: no, they were pale and long-fingered, and the nails were long and shapely. As I noticed this odd fact she looked up and saw me staring at her.

She had a long nose, not quite straight but with a delicate inward curve. Pale eyebrows were arched in surprise above wide, narrow eyes, forget-me-not blue. Her mouth was wide also, although drawn back with the effort of scrubbing, and she had a pouting upper lip. Her skin was almost milk-white and her hair was as yellow as new butter. It was a strange face, lean and yet fleshy and sensual, almost animal. I felt myself blushing. Then I recognised her: the woman from the market, who had been knocked down by her brutish man. Without taking her eyes from mine, the woman raised one long finger and flicked distractedly at a bead of sweat that was running down her temple. There was a pimple just breaking out beside her nose. Slowly she straightened up, until she was squatting on her haunches. Her feet were bare. Unaccountably I felt my loins tighten.

She was not dressed as a servant either: her tunic was of fine silvery linen that shimmered faintly in the light, like cobwebs in a pasture at dawn. As I realised this, there was a rustle of reed-stems to my left, behind the bed. I tore my eyes from the woman on the floor. A man was standing in the shadows behind a great beam of light that angled in through the windows, fogged with a confusion of freshly disturbed dust motes. I could not see his face, but I saw he was of medium height and stocky build, with the wide shoulders of someone used to heavy work. I did not have to see his pugilist's nose or florid skin to know who he was.

'What have you there, boy?' he demanded: the flat tones of a northern Italian. Zianni's voice, only full of mastery, of command.

'I seek His Majesty the Emperor Baldwin,' I told him, standing up straight and trying to look like a papal envoy, whatever that meant.

'Well, he is gone. I ask again: what have you there?'

'A communication from His Holiness Pope Gregory,' I replied. I did not care to be treated like a servant, and I did not like this bullying man one bit, whoever he might be. 'Where, if I might enquire, sir, is His Majesty?'

'He has decided to return to Venice – urgent news summoned him. I am his Majesty's agent: I have full authority to treat for him in his absence, and to conclude any outstanding matters.' There was nothing but disdain in his voice.

'This is not a grocer's bill,' I snapped, and immediately regretted it.

'No matter. You will leave it with me,' said the man calmly. He stepped into the shaft of light, and there was the flattened nose, the narrow eyes, the gleaming, freshly-shaved skin. His mouth was strangely delicate, as neat and sculpted as the lips of a tomb effigy, but petulant and cruel. I took an involuntary step backwards.

'Your pardon, good sir, but I will not,' I said doggedly. 'My orders were to put this thing in the emperor's hands, and his alone. If you will supply your name, I am certain all shall be amended.'

'Who are you, boy? No Lateran flunky, unless His Holiness is pulling bum-boys off the streets to do his errands.' He chose his words carefully, and when he spoke each one was like the prick of an assassin's knife. The icy delicacy of his voice was a strange match for his bulk and power, and I realised with a lurch of my guts that I had mistaken him, as an unwary ape might mistake the cold intent of a stalking tiger for dumb, bestial swagger. I began to sweat. 'My name is Nicholas Querini,' he told me. 'There: is all *amended*, my fine little fellow?'

'I ...' Glancing down, I saw that the woman on the floor was still studying me intensely, a look of faint amusement playing around the corners of her mouth. 'I am myself bound for Venice,' I said doggedly, and felt myself blush under the woman's gaze despite my growing fear.

'Oh, yes? Save yourself a long and hazardous journey, boy, and give me the letter. The roads are not safe for a lonely messenger.'

'But safe enough for His Majesty Baldwin? My dear sir, you confuse me,' I said, regretting my feeble jibe as soon as it had fled my lips.

'That, boy, was most assuredly *not my intent*,' he said, the last words hissed through clenched teeth. He took another step forward, and the air in the room suddenly felt alive, as if a thundercloud had thrust an arm in at the window.

'Begging your pardon, sir, but I will take my leave,' I stammered. I spun on my heel, conscious of two pairs of eyes flaying my back, and stalked out, propelled on a wave of ruffled dignity and embarrassment, but also fear, for although that man had claimed to be a royal agent, I could have sworn he had been about to knock me down. Send a boy to do a man's job, I told myself, and this is your reward. I ducked back into the teeming alleys of the Borgo, cursing Baldwin furiously under my breath. How could such a fool, such a flighty, inconsequential fool style himself Emperor of a chamber pot, let alone of *Romania*, whatever that meant? I felt the heft of the pope's seal in my satchel. It was a burden in every sense, this thing: now more than ever. I was going to have to chase Baldwin de Courtenay, it seemed. I would have to restrain myself mightily if I were not to slap his silly face when I caught up with him.

But as I strode through the warm, noisy streets I found it quite easy to keep my chin up and my mood, if not sunny, then at least a light shade of grey. I listened to the many tongues all raised in excited chatter, all bickering and haggling over gimcrack souvenirs. And as I noticed more and more strange and wonderful things about me I began to enjoy myself. A pretty girl selling oranges smiled at me; I found myself laughing at two dogs caught arse to ballocks in the midst of a fuck and dragging each other, yapping and squealing hither and yon across the street; and the simple sounds of people about their daily lives began to warm me inside. Baldwin was a fool: fiddle-de-dee to him and his ridiculous empire. I was bound for Venice myself anyway. Doubtless I would pass him on the road within a day or so, for he would surely be wandering along like a butterfly in a breeze. No matter. In fact, so much the better: a whole day in Rome with nothing to do but look forward to a journey on the morrow. Suddenly the world seemed suffused with the purest bliss. The dogs suddenly popped apart and fell to madly licking their privy parts in the midst of the street, and I laughed so hard that a brace of passing monks squinted at me in sour reproof and crossed themselves. Scowl away, good fellows, I thought. For I, sinner, reprobate and outcast that I am, am about the pope's business, and you, pious wax-faces, are not.

I crossed the Campo dei Fiori and headed towards the Jewish Quarter, for I was in the mood for the good fried fish that I knew could be found there. And I loved this part of the city, with its different sights and smells, and its sense of otherness, which reminded me of the *Cormaran*. I found a cook-shop selling red-hot fillets of some firm white fish and ambled through the streets, nibbling carefully on the searing morsels and looking idly at the life around me. It was thus that my feet led me to one of my favourite sights, the fish market on the steps of the Church of Sant'Angelo which stands in the shadow of the palace of the Savelli, everything in turn overhung by the ruinous, marble-tumbled bulk of the Capitoline Hill. The worthy canons of the church rented out their stone steps to the fishmongers of Rome, and it made for the oddest scene imaginable, at least to my eyes. I had come down here before just to watch the fun: the fish of all shapes and sizes, laid out on the worn marble; mounds of shells, buckets of writhing eels and seething elvers; crates and baskets of the oddest creatures from the deep pastures of the sea. In the air a stench of fish-guts and a babel of voices, greeting, haggling, arguing, protesting. It seemed to me an eminently sensible use of church steps. This morning the mêlée was in full swing, and I sat down on a piece of old column to watch.

The spectacle did not disappoint. A ruinously fat woman in the clothes of a wealthy dowager was engaged in a mighty tongue-lashing contest with a small, swarthy fishmonger. Both stood, hands on hips, and excoriated each other on some subject I could not hear, but which I assumed was piscatorial in nature. And indeed, growing tired of words, the woman hitched up her sleeves to reveal great doughy arms, bent down, and came up grasping a vast and grotesque creature, a spider-crab whose body was as big as the fishmonger's head and whose claw-tipped, hairy arms splayed out, waving feebly, like the rays of a blasphemous halo. For an instant I thought she was going to drop the thing on to the man's head, but instead the merchant threw up his arms, they both laughed, and in another instant the man was tying the poor crab's weakly protesting legs together with a length of twine and placing it carefully in the woman's basket.

This was better than a puppet show. I went over to examine the wares on display. Here was a crock full of cuttlefish, all nacreous ooze and popping, ink-teared eyes. A pan full of eel-like creatures with long, sword-like beaks looked naked, visceral. I admired the golden bream and the night-striped mackerel. Enough, then: I was hungry again, and I had it in mind to take a last stroll around the ruins of the Campo Vaccino as well. There was a smell of grilling fish in the air, and I located its source: a stall behind me, over by the Palazzo Savelli. I went to investigate. Sardines: fresh and succulent, the man informed me. I was just handing over my coin when, over the grill-man's shoulder, I happened to glance over at the shadowy arches of the palazzo. A gang of urchins, cruel and noisy, were hunting fat fish-market cats in the shade, and their hoots and halloos were echoing off the stones. I was idly following the proceedings when my eye caught sight of a face in the shadows, for a spear of sunlight lay across it, catching the yellow hair and an oblique slash of face: a hint of an eye, the tip of that unmistakable nose. It was the woman from the White Hound, from Baldwin's chambers.

My heart jumped, and several thoughts flew up at once: what happenstance; she followed me; she has come to buy fish, of course. I blinked and set down my coin, and in the time it took for me to grab my leaf-plate of fish, she had vanished. Ah, then it had been an illusion. Rome, I was finding, was apt to play tricks upon the mind, especially those fevered with a newly resurgent lust. I shook my head ruefully and walked over to the palazzo, just to make sure. And indeed the curved, cloister-like space behind the arches was empty of blonde women. But it was full of screeching children with the scent of cat blood in their noses, so I moved on.

I spent the next hour clambering over the ruins in the Campo Vaccino, the very heart of the world when Caesar ruled it, but which was now half weed-choked desolation and half cattle market. It was also a crucible of the sun's scorching heat, and so I tired of poking through the bramble-carpeted motley of foundation walls and collapsed pillars. With nothing to occupy them, my thoughts had begun to turn again and again to the wench in Baldwin's chambers. I rolled her image around in my head, toying with it as a kitten plays with a vole: first touching, then patting, then batting, then licking, and then devouring it, until it had become such a vivid daydream that only when I tripped over a half-buried column and and scraped my hands did I come to my senses. So I said farewell to the ruins and climbed the hill to the Campidoglio, and thence down into the familiar tangle of the Campus Martius.

I wanted to visit my favourite place in the city once more before I left, and so a little before None I arrived before the Church of Santa Maria of the Martyrs. From the *Mirabilia*, I knew its true name to be the Pantheon, and indeed the great portico, with its inscription to Agrippa, seemed like the entrance to no church I had ever known, even in this city of confounding discoveries. But it was not the outside that had drawn me here again and again in the past weeks, but what lay within, through the mighty bronze doors.

It was almost empty inside, save for a nun sweeping the floor and a verger talking with two monks against the far wall. As I always did, I paused on the threshold before setting out into the great well of dusty light, padding across the marble and feeling the round walls rise around me, letting my head fall back as I walked until I was in the centre of the floor and gazing straight up at the sky through the perfect circle of the oculus. There I stood, seeing nothing but that disc of purest blue hanging at the apex of the domed roof, and all around it the squares within squares that made up the dome, carved from stone but seemingly weightless. A pigeon fluttered to and fro across the shaft of sunlight that angled down towards me. Sparrows twittered faintly out in the portico. I breathed in the cool air, and felt the hair on my head rise ever so slightly, as it always did in this spot. For here, I was sure, was the centre of the world, the point on which everything turned. Here was stillness, utter calm, the axis: around me, the seas, the countries at war and peace, the fretful seas, the clouds, the stars in their spheres spun and danced.

The nun began coughing horribly behind me, wet, wracking spasms. I sighed and looked down. The marble walls in all their colours glimmered. I rubbed my eyes: I had walked far today, and I realised I was tired. The nun coughed again. I glanced over. There she was, hunched over her broom, shoulders heaving. The verger was also regarding her with irritation. And further around the curving walls, a woman in a tunic of silvery linen, whose yellow hair fell straight behind her back. This time she was no illusion: the monks were watching her too. She caught my gaze, and began to edge along the wall towards the door. She walked, step by cautious step, and I turned in place, still the axis, still caught under the eye of heaven. Through the golden half-light she slipped, past empty niches and tombs, past the nun, recovered now; I turned, and she reached the door and darted outside.

Released by the oculus, I took to my heels after her, ignoring the throaty admonitions of the nun. But out in the piazza I found only the dun-coloured flocks of pilgrims circled by sharp-eyed Roman wolves. I looked about me in a frenzy: where had she gone? I chose an alleyway at random, and ran up it until I reached a little church, around which the streets diverged in three directions. It was hopeless: she had probably not even come this way, I told myself. But she had followed me after all, for happenstance does not strike the same two people twice in as many hours. Why? I leaned against the church wall, panting.

Slowly as pitch trickling down the planking of a ship, comprehension dawned and I realised what I had to do. I must hide the pope's decree at once. The yellow-haired woman was no scullery maid, and what she had been scrubbing from the emperor's floor had been blood. I had not liked the voice of the man in the shadows. I had not liked that he did not show his face, and the way his flat Venetian voice had drilled into me, full of command and condescension. If they were following me it was not for myself, for I was nothing. It was for what I carried.

I had a fairly good idea where I was, so I made my way, through back alleys and the narrowest passages, west to the piazza in Agona. The long, broad field of the piazza I skirted to the north, through alleys overhung with towers snarling across the air at one another. I thought to slip across the bridge to my lodgings in the Borgo, but that would be too obvious, for that man in the White Hound was used to command – he would have more than a wench at his call, that was certain – and no doubt he was watching the bridges.

Who could I go to for help? I was starting to feel exhausted, for I had been on my feet in the heat all day and had eaten and drunk but little. A cup of cool wine would surely clear my head. I thought of a comfortable cellar and a friendly barrel of white wine from the Alban hills, and then it struck me: Marcho Antonio Marso, the Captain's old companion-in-arms.

I found the covered passage with a little difficulty, for I was coming at it from the wrong direction, but at last I was in the piss-soaked gloom and walking past the crooked windows and the midden heap to the door of Marcho's inn. To my dismay I was not the only customer at that early hour, for a couple of carters, already drunk, were mock-arguing in the corner and a whore was flirting mechanically with the pot-boy in hopes, no doubt, of a scrap of free food. I beckoned him over, slipped him a silver coin and asked for wine and meat. When the wine came I enquired, casually as I could, if the master was about. I got a look, sharp and curious, but before I had taken my second mouthful, the ominous form of the innkeeper appeared at my side.

'I am busy,' he said, shortly. He was radiating annoyance like a brazier.

'Good Marcho Antonio, I am a companion of Captain de Montalhac. Do you not recognise me? I have enjoyed your hospitality often.'

'So what?' growled the man, although his countenance seemed to soften imperceptibly.

I was wasting time, and I wished to get things over with one way or another, so I stood up and placed my arm around his shoulder. Ignoring his palpable irritation, I leaned close in and muttered in his scarred ear:

'Marcho Antonio Marso, are you a Good Christian? I mean, are you a *credente*?'

He stiffened as if I had driven a knife between his ribs. I pressed home.

'I am guessing, Signor Marcho. But you have my master's trust, and I am giving you mine. Listen to me: I am about Captain de Montalhac's business, and the enterprise is in danger. I need your help.'

Marcho let out a ragged breath. He glared at me, but he had gone rather white, and there was a bead of sweat working its way out of one eyebrow. Then he gave a twitch of his head, half nod, half spasm.

'In the back,' he hissed. Then, raising his chin, he bellowed over to the pot-boy: 'Eh, Lodovico! I'll be in the back. Do not bother us, understand?'

I followed him through the door in the back of the room, which opened on to a short flight of stairs. We descended into a low-beamed cellar, earthen-floored, with walls of narrow bricks and hunks of marble. There were barrels everywhere, hams and sausages hung from the beams, and a soft light shone over all from a brace of fat candles that were melting slowly over a battered table at the far end. Marcho halted in the middle of the floor and faced me, arms crossed stolidly across his chest.

'What do you mean by all this, boy?' he asked. His voice was cold, and suddenly I wondered if I had made an awful mistake. Nevertheless I bit my lip and pressed on, heart fluttering.

'I have sailed with Michel de Montalhac for two years,' I said determinedly, although I was all too aware of how hollow my voice sounded in this cave of a place. 'He saved my life. That is what he does, is it not? Save people, the unwanted, the persecuted? I am not a Good Christian. I ... am nothing, an outcast from my own church, an exile from my home. I meant no offence, and I did not mean to alarm you, for I know ...'

'Ah, boy, enough.' All of a sudden, Marcho looked bone-tired. He pointed to a barrel. 'Sit yourself down. You look ready to fall.' There was kindness in his voice now, at least a tinge. 'Yes, I am what the people of Toulouse call a Good Christian. My brothers and sisters call ourselves Patarani. There: you have the power to burn me now, as my brothers were burned six years ago in front of Santa Maria Maggiore. You see, they still make human sacrifice in Rome.'

'I am sorry for it,' I said, sinking down on the barrel.

'Do not be: they made a good end, despite the baying of the mob.' He shrugged, that fatalistic shrug that I had seen Gilles and the Captain give a thousand times. 'Now, what is your trouble?'

'Captain de Montalhac has been in negotiation for a ...'

'No! I do not need to know the details. It is business, yes?' I nodded. 'Then tell me the trouble that afflicts you now.'

'I am being followed. I have something that the men ...' I

closed my eyes for a moment, and saw yellow hair and sharp eyes. 'They are Venetians, I believe. I am carrying something they want. They will probably kill for it. It would be better if they killed me and lost this, than the alternative. As far as business goes, that is,' I added. He did not laugh, and I could not.

'In the valise?' I nodded again. 'Give it to me.'

I made to open the satchel, but Marcho shook his head. 'Do not. Again, I do not need to know. I will not open it. What will you do?'

'I need to give this to the man it is intended for, but failing that, to the Captain himself,' I said. 'I will ride north to Venice, for that is where the *Cormaran* is headed. But Rome is deadly to me now.'

'And you cannot leave today?'

I explained, as briefly as I could, that my lodgings lay in the Borgo, together with my horse and the money that Gilles had entrusted to me. They would be sure to have the Pons San Petri watched, and perhaps my rooms as well, though I doubted they knew where those lay. I would have to grab my belongings and my horse, and make a dash for it.

Marcho grunted when he had heard it all. 'You will have to cross to the south,' he said. 'Take the Jews' Bridge or Saint Mary's. Then work your way through the gardens under the Janiculum and round the back of Saint Peter's. They'll be watching the city side, not the country.'

'But I'll have to come back for ...' I nodded at the valise.

'No. I doubt you will be safe coming back over here, even on a horse.' He squinted at me, as if worrying a broken tooth. 'I will bring it to you,' he said finally. 'Ride north along the river. I will meet you at a place called Saxa Rubra, just beyond the Milvian Bridge.' He must have seen my look of shock, for he smiled for the first time. 'I owe Michel a turn or two. Do not concern yourself about me: I will amble up the Via Lata with the rest of the bumpkins, as I do whenever I go to look over my vineyards. I've got a nice little farm picked out for myself when I leave this game, away over in Tolfa. No one will blink if they see me leaving town.'

This was beyond hope, and I was so moved that I doubt I could have found enough words to thank him with had he not bustled me out of the cellar and walked with me to the door of the inn.

'You are armed: know how to use it?'

'A bit,' I said.

'My advice? Do not. If they catch you, they'll be wanting this.' He tapped the bag. 'They will not harm you unless you give them reason. I know ... and you must know, boy, that there are men who are glad enough for a reason to spill blood. Right then. Tomorrow, the Saxa Rubra, around eight bells.'

'What manner of place is that, Marcho?' I asked.

'Just some red rocks beyond the bridge. Don't you know your history, boy? *In hoc signo vinces*. Let us hope that they will mean victory for you. One more thing. Do you know what is in there?' He nodded at my valise. I hesitated, and shook my head.

'A ... a letter, for someone else,' I said.

'If you are risking your liver for it, I would read what it says, if I were you,' he said. 'Might not be worth it.' With a gruff nod he left me there and shut the door behind me.

I thought for a while, and then drew out the letter with the great leaden bull. It was sealed with wax, and I opened it carefully with Thorn, taking care to keep the seal intact. The candles threw their yellow light over illuminations and letters in a beautiful, snaking hand. There was much courtly and legal stuff, and I searched impatiently for the meat. It was a decree all right, a *mandamentum*, and it had to do with

Baldwin. But it was not addressed to him. It appeared – I could not entirely make sense of the legal curlicues – to be made out to the Captain himself, or to the company of the *Cormaran*.

> *It is the business of the pope to look after the interests of the Latin empire of Constantinople,* I read, *since it was taken from the schismatic Greeks with the approval of the papacy, and since it is the papacy's bulwark in the East against the Greeks and the Infidel.*

There were more niceties, and then:

> *In support of the eastern province, in addition to the forgiveness of sins which we promise to those who, at their own expense, set out thither, and beside the papal protection which we give to those who aid that land, we hereby decree by the paternal love which we have for you that whosoever offers for sale, sells, seeks to purchase or does purchase any and all of the holy relics of Our Lord and of His saints yet remaining in the city of Constantinople and its territories under the aegis of this decree shall have, by the power vested in us, dispensation to make any such transactions and absolution from simony, that the eastern province may accrue such riches as will shore up its defences and so carry out God's will.*

And there was the signature of Pope Gregory. I leaned back against the cobwebby bricks, my heart pounding. No wonder they were after me. I found an awl and heated its tip in the lantern flame, melted the wax and resealed the letter. Marso was waiting for me at the top of the stairs. He studied my face, but took the valise without a word and stood aside to let me pass.

*

As I crept south through the narrowest, stench-plagued alleys I could find, I sent up a thousand wordless prayers – to whom I knew not, for the god of the Cathars was a puzzle to me, and the god I had once served had ceased to listen to my prayers some time ago – for Marcho Antonio Marso. I had no doubt that he would be waiting for me in the morning with my valise and the papal bull. But whether or not I would make our rendezvous was another matter entirely. My predicament was now beginning to reveal itself to me, although I was still guessing as to the details. It was plain that something bad had befallen the hapless Baldwin de Courtenay. I doubted that he was dead: one did not kill an emperor, however petty, and stay to clear up the blood. So he might have been taken, against his will: hence the blood.

The man in the shadows had been Venetian. What had Baldwin said that day? I racked my brains, and fought my way down through hazy memories of the Captain aloof in his chair while Baldwin squirmed, and how young the emperor had looked, young and frantic. There: I had it. 'Very solidly in debt to Venice,' he had told us. Very anxious that the Republic did not know he was in Rome – or perhaps he had meant Italy. So the man was a creditor. But why abduct Baldwin, unless … I sighed. He meant to hold the emperor as security, or ransom him. Christ's foreskin: Venice had repossessed Baldwin de Courtenay.

By this time I was drawing near to the fish market again, for I was back in the Jewish quarter. It was a good place to hide, for there was much to and fro of people, much noise and commerce. I found a rag-pickers' market set up in a little piazza and let myself fade into the corner. I needed to think. There was a stone bench on which two old men were sleeping, spittle crusting on their bristly chins. I sat down next to them and leaned back against the brick wall behind me.

The bull: there was no reason to believe that the Venetian knew anything about it. Baldwin had not been expecting any such thing, and the Captain had not known of it until Gregory had entrusted it to us. But to Baldwin's captor, any document from the pope might signify money, and that was why he had sent his creatures to pursue me. Or perhaps he believed I was a witness to his crime, whatever it had been, and had decided to silence me. If so, I was in mortal danger, for they would kill me out of hand. I preferred to believe that the document was drawing them on, if only to quell the icy fear that had settled in the pit of my belly.

It was late in the afternoon, and the little square had fallen into shadow. I had been keeping watch on the main entrance, but no one worrisome had come in or out. The rag-sellers were packing up now, but I realised that in my bright Venetian costume I was an easy mark and so I bought a ragged old traveller's cloak for a few pennies and threw it about my shoulders, much to the amusement of the gimlet-eyed merchant, who offered me silver for my cycladibus and tunic, and more if I would strip off my hose into the bargain. I hesitated, though, for they were Anna's gift, and left the man shaking his head in disappointment.

So I lurked in my cloak, which carried the whiff of night-soil in its folds and made me feel somewhat unlike myself: a true disguise, I suppose, for as I slunk about, stinking, I began to feel as if I were sinking down into the understorey of the city: the human detritus that lies, like leaf mould in a wood, unnoticed underfoot as the better sort of folk go about their business with their noses turned up. I wandered the streets, keeping to the shadows, pausing once to take a cup of wine at a fisherman's tavern near the river, but not yet daring to step out on to the open ground that lay between the buildings and the water. I had already decided that I would take the Jews' Bridge, for the bridges over to the Tiber Island were less crowded, and I did not like the look of the towers that guarded them. I found another tavern, barely worthy of the name and haunted only by broken-down folk to whom my vile cloak no doubt seemed like a king's ermine. It stank of unwashed tripe and forgotten fish-heads. I was served wine, of a sort, by a young wench with limp whitish hair and a double chin who made sheep's eyes at me and dangled her tits in my face as she poured out my vinegary drink. But I could, by craning my neck, see the end of the Jews' Bridge and the traffic going to and fro upon it, still busy as dusk came on with folk going back to their houses in Trastevere. I thought I would cross with the crowds, but as I watched I knew I had missed my chance for that. Courage would have seized the moment, but instead I had skulked in a dead man's cloak. Tra-la. I would have to wait until dark, then.

I pretended to drink my wine, but then bought myself some more time by draining my cup of its foul contents and suffering a second helping. The wine was scouring my insides, and as my guts were already roiling in fear and anticipation I was starting to feel quite horrible. But the sun was setting at last behind the Janiculum and now the shadows on the banks of the Tiber were growing. Another cup of infernal wine and I could leave.

My stomach was beginning to feel as if it were filled with burning coals, and the pain was making me wince. A wave of it struck me and I screwed my eyes shut against the raw agony. When I looked up I was staring into the face of the woman from the White Hound.

'You going to finish that?' she enquired, nodding at the cup which I was gripping with pale knuckles.

'What?' I said, surprise making a mooncalf of me.

'Because I wouldn't. Finish it. Honest.' To my mangled wits came the information that she was speaking English, London English.

'Why not?' I stammered

'It'll kill you. Now then, time to go. Come on, love.'

I looked at her, bereft of words.

'Has this stuff burned your tongue out? Because you don't say much. I took you for a clever one.' With cool fingers she prised my own from the cup. 'Makes no odds. Time to go outside.'

I stood up, for it struck me that one woman could be overpowered, or merely run from. But she followed me with those eyes. 'Where is the bag?' she asked, mildly curious, or so it sounded. I watched her for an instant.

'I took it back to the Lateran,' I said. 'After the Pantheon. I thought you meant to rob me, and it was not enough of my affair to . . .'

'Have I put you to any bother?' she asked, sweetly. 'Come on. You are not in the pay of the Curia. You are Jean de Sol's man.'

'What makes you think so? And who is this Jean de Sol?' I added hurriedly.

'The man in whose company you visited His Majesty Baldwin of Romania a couple of weeks ago.'

'I don't know—'

'Please. Put a stopper in it. Innkeepers talk. Servants never stop talking. And surly Frenchies, even, if you ask them nice enough. We know, all right?'

'You don't. You cannot. And what have you done with Baldwin, for God's sake? What was that blood you were scrubbing away?'

'Not that you care, of course, for you know nothing, do

you? Someone had a nosebleed, my sweet. Do not worry: Baldwin is our guest. And now, out. We are upsetting these nice people.'

I saw no evidence of that, save for the looks that the serving girl was giving us, enough to curdle milk. I stood up. We would walk to the door, and I would run. This girl would not catch me in her skirts. And I still had my knife.

'Well done – oh, don't forget to pay!' she scolded, blue eyes flaying me. Flustered again, I threw a handful of pennies on to the table, turned on my heel and made for the door. I heard her chair scrape behind me, but I was pushing past the fat serving maid, now positively squinting with displeasure, and lifting the latch I stepped out into the warm dusk. Except that it was not dusk. While I had sat there in the tavern the sun had departed and night had fallen. I hesitated, confused, trying to get my bearings. A fisherman's fire burned on the river bank to my left, and torches flickered in the street. I took off, heading for the river, thinking to sprint for the bridge, but as I rounded the corner of the tavern wall I slammed into something and fell back hard on to my arse.

'Pick him up, Dardi,' called the blue-eyed woman in broad Venetian. I looked up into a broad, bearded face, smiling nastily. Hands like farriers' tongs grabbed me under the armpits and hoisted me upright.

'*Salve*,' said Dardi, not letting go. A hand snaked round my waist, fingers just brushing the top of my groin, and relieved me of Thorn. The woman took the knife and admired it.

'Ooh, how pretty,' she exclaimed. 'Thank you, gentle sir!'

'Don't cut yourself,' I said in English, through gritted teeth.

'I'll try not to,' she whispered back. She stepped in front of me. I saw that she had two companions: the man called Dardi, who released me, and another man, tall and slim, who in the same moment produced a long, slim, double-edged dagger.

'Please give us the pope's document,' he said pleasantly. 'We have no quarrel with you, boy.'

'I don't have it,' I told him, hoarsely. 'Ask her.'

'Well, Signora Letitia?'

'He claims he took it back to the Lateran. I don't believe him. In any event he does not have it now,' said the fair woman.

'Then you will fetch it,' said the man with the knife, his voice tighter.

'I will not. I cannot,' I muttered.

At that, Dardi drew back and punched me hard in the stomach. I bent double, meeting his knee with my chin. Quicksilver flooded into my eye sockets as I reeled, fighting to keep on my feet.

'You will fetch it,' Dardi grunted.

'Fetch it yourself,' I told him. I reasoned, very foggily, that if they were beating me up they probably would not kill me, at least right now. If I could just stay upright ...

'Stop it, Dardi,' said the woman, impatiently. 'Listen, boy. You are wasting our time. No, actually,' she said, shifting her feet and crossing her arms resignedly across her chest, 'you are wasting our master's time. Much worse.'

'Who is your master, then? Not that blustering coxcomb Querini?' I gasped.

'Nicholas Querini of Venice. Hardly a coxcomb: an extremely wealthy and reputable gentleman. Ask anyone about him. Jean de Sol, for instance.'

'Wasn't he the one who knocked you down in the street the other day?' I shot back. 'I felt sorrow for you then, fair maid, all sprawled out in the market square.' I straightened up carefully. She was scowling. 'I would have offered you my hand.'

'I didn't need it,' she hissed.

'Letitia's not your real name,' I went on, babbling to stay alive a minute longer. 'You're no Venetian. You hail from London, I'd wager, and I'll further wager that your tongue got its edge somewhere lovely like New Gate.'

'Aha! And under your Venetian silks *you* are a little Wessex sheep-shagger,' she told me. Perhaps I imagined the hint of amusement in her voice.

'Devon, ma'am,' I told her, as proudly as I could. 'I know of no man called Sol. I am clerk to a lazy swine at the Curia who promised me a silver coin if I delivered that letter while he went off and fucked his mistress. Now I have no coin, and you are about to remove my giblets. A very poor bargain all round.'

'What is your wish, Signora Letitia?' asked the one called Facio. He raised his blade and pointed it at my throat.

'Listen, you,' she said. 'My master is a great friend of little Baldwin de Courtenay – his very best friend, I would dare say. The emperor needs to be protected from scum like de Sol. Last chance. The letter – tell us where it is.' I shook my head, feigning ignorance but not desperation. She leaned forward, until her chin almost touched my shoulder. '*This* is your last chance,' she whispered in her London drawl. 'I did see you in the market: 'twas a kind thought you had. And you had me nearly right: it was Smooth Field, not New Gate.' Her breath smelled of fennel seeds. She stepped back and scratched thoughtfully at her nose, where this morning I had seen a spot breaking out – this morning, an eternity ago. Then she smiled.

'Well then. Nice to meet you, Master Devonshire,' she said briskly. 'You must have been the best-dressed suitor a sheep ever had. Pity you ever left your bog, though, innit?' She brushed past me, cupped her hand around Facio's ear and whispered something. Then she took to her heels, and in a moment she was gone, lost amongst the pools of light and dark between the city and its river.

'*Allora*,' said Facio, pleasantly. He tapped Dardi on the shoulder and gave some guttural command in Venetian, and in the next instant Dardi's booted foot had caught me squarely between the fork of my legs and I was retching on my hands and knees, aware of nothing but churning agony and bile scaring my nose and throat. Then those tong-like hands had hoisted me up again and I was half-walking, half being dragged towards the river. I dimly felt my legs snag in some low brambles. Then Dardi stepped back and Facio was standing there. I could barely see his face, but he might have been smiling. Then he nodded briskly, placed the palm of his left hand square upon my breast-bone, and drew back his knife hand. I barely had time to draw in a rasping gulp of air when I felt a terrible blow on my left breast and a splinter of frigid pain. Then my head burst into stars and I was falling down, down, blows striking me from left and right. But I could not feel my body, for I was no longer the tenant of that destroyed shell of flesh. I was dissolving into the night, the fetid, marsh-stinking night.

Chapter Eleven

It was a smell that brought me to my senses. Nay, not a smell: a stench, a miasma. I opened my eyes, or at least fancied that I had, for it was pitch dark. For an awful moment I was struck by the horrifying, juddering fear that I was smelling my own long-dead and rotten flesh. I could not move, not a sinew, and that dreadful reek was all about me, smothering me like cuckoo-spit on a leaf. I could not even move the tiniest breath of air through my throat, could not utter a sound. As slow as judgement I sank, choking, into the darkness once more.

When I awoke again I was lying stretched out upon something hard. In a flash I fancied that it was the bottom of my coffin that I felt, but then I opened my eyes and saw, not the solid black of a grave, but whitewashed plaster arches, dimly flickering with lamplight. I shut my eyes again, disbelieving what they told me. But when I opened them again, I saw a tonsured head above me, and a face that, save for a pair of kindly eyes, was all nose and fleshy lips. I gave a small cry, for this was worse: surely now I was beginning my atonement for all my vile past, for why else would a monk be here with me? He was still there when I dared look again, though, and this time he spoke, not with the voice of a demon or a judge, but in the rough, reassuring tones of a Roman.

'Are you awake, my son? What is your name?'

'Is this hell?' I asked.

The monk chuckled. 'Only when the Abbot is in his cups,' he whispered. 'But I did not say that. No, you are in the Hospice of Saint Bartholomew.'

'In London?' I croaked, sitting up with a jerk.

'No, no!' said the monk, eyebrows signalling amusement on one side and concern on the other. 'On the Tiber Island. Is there one in London?'

I nodded, not wishing to explain how I knew. 'A fisherman found you and we brought you here, for you were lying no more than a few yards from our bridge,' he continued.

I lay back, trying to remember any of that, and failing. Then I remembered something after all. 'I was stabbed in the heart! How …'

'Stabbed, you say? Well, well. No, you were not stabbed, my son.'

'No, I saw …' I looked down, and realised that I was naked under a rough flaxen sheet, and that I stank, although not of the corpse-fetor I was expecting, but of vinegar. Despite a stiff neck I searched for the wound I was sure I would find in my chest, but instead saw only a great bruise, two or three small grazes and a long scratch, fine as a hair, under my arm. 'But truly, I saw the knife! I felt him stab me,' I protested.

'Him?'

'The … the footpad,' I stammered. 'There were two of them.'

'Yes, they did rob you,' said the monk, frowning. 'We found no purse with you. We had to wash your clothes in vinegar, and swab you, too, for you were lying in a great dead fish, all slime and maggots.' He mimed being assailed by a ghastly stink.

'I must go,' I said. 'Please bring my clothes, Brother. I am unhurt, it seems, and I must …'

171

'No, no,' said the monk, grasping my shoulders. 'You took a blow to the head, for one thing.'

But I protested, vehemently if politely, and at last the poor, confused soul shuffled off to fetch my clothes, much scrubbed and free of the horror of dead fish, but practically glowing with the fumes of vinegar. They were still wet, and the vinegar made my various scrapes and bruises sting. I guessed that the doughty fishermen had taken my purse, and I considered the money well spent. I knew who had my knife. But it was not until I was limping out of the building, the monk fussing at my side and I making haste, for I did not want the Watch to be called, or to have questions put to me, that he sighed and said, 'A sorry night for guests in our city. You at least are leaving us on foot.'

'What do you mean?' I said, half listening.

'Well, we pulled a Frank out of the river at sundown,' he said. 'A Frenchman. You were lucky, my son. That one was dead.'

I stopped in my tracks. 'Dead?' I asked. 'A Frenchman? How do you know?'

'He carried a promissory note from the Margrave of Namur. Namur is in France, I think?'

'You are right. Was he short, with grey hair and no front teeth?' The monk shook his head, humouring me. 'Then was he tall – taller than you, anyway, with a broken nose and an old scar on his face?' I drew my finger from my left temple down to the corner of my mouth.

'He was. He was! Lord in Heaven, did you know him?' The good brother was aghast. I shook my head hastily.

'No,' I lied. 'But a companion of mine, another Frenchman, was looking for his friend, a knight of Namur, who seemed to have disappeared this morning. Shall I send him down here to see if it is the right fellow?' I added guilelessly.

'Oh, please do so,' said the monk, crossing himself. 'What an ill fortune follows you, my son! Why not stay awhile, and I will hear your confession? Or you may pray in the church ...'

But I was already gone, walking as fast as I could across the bridge to Trastevere, where I ducked into the narrow streets and left the hospice, and the kindly, confused monk behind me. And behind me also, the corpse of Fulk de Grez, late companion to the Emperor of Constantinople. Like a spirit summoned up from the mist on the river, I remembered something my father had told me many years ago on a wet Dartmoor afternoon. We were watching his dogs herd a flock of bedraggled sheep into a pen of hurdles, and I had exclaimed, worried that the dogs were going to harm the sheep, for they snapped at their heels with great fury. But no, said my father. Think of your hands and fingers, all the things you can do with them: tie knots, pick your nose. A dog has no hands, and perforce he must do everything with his mouth. A dog's teeth are his fingers, and he knows exactly what to do with them. He will not bite the sheep. When a dog snaps at your hand and misses, we think he tried to bite and failed, but no, it was a warning. If a dog wishes to bite you, bite he will. And now I thought: as dogs with their teeth, so Venetians with their knives. If a Venetian bravo wished to cut out your sweetbreads with a flick of his wrist, he would do it. These folk did not miss. I had been spared – spared, and warned.

It was easy enough to get back to the Borgo, though it took what remained of the night. I found a path that ran between the high ground of the Janiculum hill and the river, where the folk of Trastevere have their gardens, and crept past sprouting cabbages and new beans, dozing chickens and rabbits shut up in their hutches. I saw nothing and nobody save a fox, which did not bother to run from me but glared from beside an artichoke bed, and a polecat, surprised atop a henhouse, that fled silently. The gate into the Borgo was not guarded – or at least there was a guard, but he was at muffled rut behind a tree and I slipped past as the woman begged the guard to stab her with his great big sword.

I made my way home, squinting through a raging headache at the skinny cats who, by night, filled the doorways of the quarter. On my own doorstep, a fat, red-faced priest gaped at me with alarm and I stepped back, for he seemed to have four feet, two sandalled ones planted on the stone step, two bare ones reversed and facing me, soles out. Shaking my fuddled head, I realised that the bare feet belonged to a tart kneeling before him, his cassock providing a sort of confessional that covered her from the knees up, and indeed there were muffled sounds coming from under the cloth.

'She's making a full confession, I see,' I said. The man's eyes were bulging out of his face, and still he made an effort to avoid mine. 'And I believe that's worth a three-year penance,' I added, slipping past him and closing the door on his quivering back. This city was starting to bother me: I thanked the stars I was leaving in the morning.

I was sure that my lodgings would be watched, but they were not, or at least I saw nothing to make me suspicious. And I had been certain that they would at least have searched my rooms, but again all was safe and in its place. So I hastily pulled on my clean clothes, neatly folded on the bed, and stuffed the vinegary ones into a saddlebag. The gold was where I had left it, up in an old mortise-hole in one of the ceiling beams. The excitement I always felt before beginning a journey was offset by a sharp foreboding that, on top of my sleepless night and the blow to my head, began to make my limbs twitch as though Saint Vitus's dance were creeping over me.

Eventually I could bear my own nerves no longer and drank off a pint of the landlady's strong, sweet wine I kept for emergencies, but which I heartily disliked. But it did the trick, settling my stomach and curing me of the urge to scuttle away to the jakes every five minutes. At last I saw that I was ready for the off, and allowed myself a moment to lean on the cold marble of the windowsill. There was no one about down in the street. The air was cool and sharp, not the usual rich swirl of the sun-baked kennel, but astringent, dry: the breath of Rome's ancient stone. There was a pallor in the east, and the red flowers that cascaded from roofs and windows all around were beginning to glow with the first hint of sunrise. Time to go. I buckled on my sword and slung my bags across my shoulder.

Dawn was unfolding its petals far above the city as I looked up and down the street from the doorway. It was still night down here, and I saw nobody, heard nothing, until my own footfalls rapped – too loud, surely – along the dirty stones. I tried not to hurry around the corner, through the passageway beside the Frisian hostel, and as I saw that only the bony grey cats kept watch my heart began to grow calm and I slowed down. There was a lamp lit at the livery stables and a bleared and surly boy in a leather apron greeted me with an uncivil leer. My horse was deep in his nose-bag and bared his great teeth at us when we put an end to his breakfast, but when he saw it was me he had the grace to nod his head and even whinny a little. I raised an eyebrow to the stable-boy, who ignored my natural mastery of all creatures and instead presented me with his master's well-padded bill, which I paid with what was, by Roman standards, quite good grace. He watched me critically as I made my packs fast to the saddle and fiddled unconvincingly with the bridle and girth. I tossed him another farthing to get lost, and when I was sure no one was watching I patted the horse on the nose and muttered into one ear: 'Don't fuck me about, please, beast.'

The horse – I could not bring myself to think of him as Iblis, a far too exotic and mysterious name for a pretty grey nag – regarded me with a jaundiced eye. I had never noticed how long horse eyelashes are, and seeing Iblis bat his girlish lashes at me, I began to feel much less afraid of him. I swung myself up into the saddle. This was the moment of truth; I made sure the stable-lad was not looking, and urged the horse on with a gentle rub of my heels. Earning my eternal gratitude, he snorted purposefully and headed for the door.

Horst, I realised, had taught me well. Now I was on my own, I found that riding held no terrors for me after all. Indeed, by the time we had wound our way through the tangled lanes of the Borgo, keeping the grim bulk of the Castel Sant'Angelo to our right, I felt, if not quite a centaur, at least almost normal. The guards outside the fortress gate regarded us with baleful disinterest. Dawn was soaking fast into the sky, and on the other side of the river the mouldering corpses that hung from the gibbets of the Tor di Nona were tinged a lovely shade of rose. I spat, and urged Iblis into a trot.

There were no straight roads in Rome, I knew, and so I plunged into the chaos of streets and alleys, always keeping the rising sun on my right hand. The great city was waking up, and as I rode deeper into the maze I found myself pushing through a growing crowd of people, some friendly, some not, but all of them as loud and vehement as a flock of magpies. Cooking smells filled the air, doing battle with the fetid reek of night-soil, and I was tempted by more than one food-seller. But I was in a hurry, and keeping my rumbling guts under control I pressed on. Now I found myself in a river of men and women pushing barrows, driving carts or bent under packs, all on their way to the Pons San Petri. They carried vegetables, fruit, flowers, all still with the morning's dew upon them. I passed what seemed to be a walking rose-bush, and looking down, saw a little girl staggering along under the weight of a huge bunch of roses, all pink petals and gold stamens and so fresh and fragrant that a few sleepy city bees were taking breakfast there. The girl looked up at me and for a moment I caught her eye and she stuck out her tongue at me and cackled. She was the happiest creature I had seen that morning, and I would have dropped her a coin or two if I had not seen that she needed both hands and all her strength to carry her gorgeous burden. And I noticed, as I rode on, that the thorny stems had scratched her bare arms so that blood had begun to drip from the cut ends. I shuddered. As usual, Rome was making me feel slightly sick, but if it was with disgust or joy I had still not quite decided.

At last – it seemed as if I had been riding for an eternity, and I had begun to fear that I had missed my way – the dark, narrow alleyway down which I had been forcing Iblis, and which had seemed like the only even vaguely northward-leading route, suddenly gave out on to open country. Just like that, I had left Rome. The buildings thinned out abruptly until I was riding through a curious landscape of poor huts, vegetable plots, wasteground through which jutted odd, decayed blocks of travertine, and everywhere the low, toadstool-shaped pine trees that grew wherever men had abandoned even the tiniest patch of Roman ground.

On my side of the river I was in a landscape of little hills, all terraced and planted with olives and vines, and crowned, every one, with a thicket of Roman pines. From every bush and tree, insects battered and clattered out their songs. Here and there, great clumps of butcher's broom were flowering, and the scent filled the dry air. It was already getting hot, although I found I had made good time so far. Leaving the city had been much easier than I had expected. And the day seemed to be going well for my fellow travellers as well, for I was riding against a flowing stream of country folk all hurrying towards the city. They were seemingly all in good humour, singing and laughing to one another, exchanging loud greetings with others passing in the opposite direction. It was impossible not to get caught up in the jollity, and soon I was beaming to myself as I rode along. And what was there to be sour about? The blue heavens stretched flawlessly above. A light breeze stirred the olive trees, and their silvery grey leaves danced against the sky. I was alone with nothing more daunting than this road before me, and – this above all else – I was friends with my horse.

And he, it appeared, was determined to be friends with me. He clopped along at a sprightly walk that had us overtaking most of the other traffic, but he did so with a supple grace that caused my arse, unused as it was to the hard contours of a saddle, no undue discomfort. Such was our progress that in what I judged to be an hour and a half we came up to the river Tiber – for I had asked the way to the Saxa Rubra from a couple pushing a handcart of pinioned geese – and to a disreputable, crumbling bridge that had undoubtedly stood there a very long time. I heard the words 'Ponte Milvio' uttered several times by those preparing to cross, and then I realised that this was the Milvian Bridge I had read of in Eusebius, years ago in the college library of Balecester. This was where Constantine had seen the fiery cross and the words of the Lord before his battle with Maxentius that had won him the Roman Empire. I glanced up, but the sky was innocent of either cross or writing. *In hoc signo vinces*, the emperor had been told: 'In this sign you shall conquer.' But time appeared to have conquered here, and human frailty, judging by the party of lepers who squatted off to the side of the road, waiting for a break in the traffic so that they could cross without disturbing those of sound body. I looked down at the Tiber as it rippled below, hoping to catch some hint of the Divine, perhaps, or at least of something vaguely mysterious. But here, as at the ancient, holy monuments I had visited in Rome, there was nothing but decay and the exuberant intrusion of the present. I shrugged, scratched Iblis behind the ears, and rode on, looking out for Marcho Antonio Marso.

The Rubra Saxa were not the landmark I had expected, just an outcropping of reddish stone that reminded me of the red earth around Totnes, far away in Devon. Marcho Antonio appeared from a spinney of holm oaks, seated, to my amazement, upon an ass that supported his angry bulk with the detached look of a martyr in extremis.

'Who goes there: Maxentius or Constantine?' he boomed.

'At this point I'm the disembodied fucking voice,' I told him. 'There's not much else left.' He laughed and handed me my valise.

'I resisted the temptations of the Dark Lord and did not break the seal of Antichrist,' he said. 'Very sorely tempted I was, too. If you get the chance, ask Michel to explain it all to me one day, will you?'

I assured him that I would, and to my surprise he leaned across and embraced me. It was like being hugged by a bear that had bathed in wine and rubbed its pelt with garlic, and I was so moved that I began to weep.

I halted for the night at the village of Rignano, that lies under the mountain called Soracte. It had been an easy ride but a long one, and the stars were beginning to shine and bats to whirr above my head as I guided my weary but uncomplaining horse up the narrow street to the inn, which a countryman, baffled at first by my request for directions in execrable Roman dialect, had kindly pointed me towards from the now almost deserted Ravenna Road. Dog-tired, I ignored the travellers' chatter around me in the common room as I hurriedly ate a chicken and bean stew, drank a jar of thin wine and took myself off to bed, but not before giving my vinegar-soaked clothes to a maid for the best wash she could manage. Iblis I left in the stable, face deep in a bag of oats. As a brand-new horseman who had just completed his first day in the saddle without mishap, I can perhaps be forgiven for the grateful kiss I planted on his bony forehead, and the silver coin I gave to the astonished stable-lad to buy the best possible care for my friend.

I secured the door to my room, and dropped on to the bed. It was time to examine the letter that Gilles had left me, and suddenly I hoped that it had not contained instructions for any task I should have performed before leaving Rome. I broke the seal with anxious fingers. The bulk of the letter – what had made it seem so fat – was merely another map, a simple copy of the one I already had, which dispensed with all except the line of the road and the towns and landmarks along it. I was pleased to see Rignano appear as a tiny tur-reted building, then squinted to see the word 'bedbugs', much underlined, scrawled beside it. Plainly, I should have opened the letter last night. I looked closer, and saw that the map was heavily annotated in many different hands. I recognised Gilles' letters, but there were others that were strange to me. Nevertheless they offered good advice, these absent guides: 'sweet water'; 'brigands'; 'dishonest landlord'; 'horrible wine'. Beside one village much farther up the line, someone who I took to be the Captain had scribbled 'Try the sheep's feet!'. In other places the only admonition was a stark 'AVOID'. I turned to the other part of the letter.

To Petrus Zennorius, traveller, vanguard and agent of the ship Cormaran, *greetings!*

I trust this finds you recovered from your sickness. I trust you will pardon our precipitate departure, but I received word of a ship to be had at Brindisi, and I have already delayed long enough. My hope is that this crude map will be of use and comfort. I assure you, though, that I, and the others whose scrawl you will find upon your map, have trod those roads, and slept in those beds, more recently than Pliny.

One thing: I would have you perform a small service for us on your way. Take the branch of the Ravenna Road which passes through Spoleto – that is the right branch that comes soon after Narni – and in that interesting city put up at the White Lion. I have sent Horst there. He will have left some documents for you, letters of credit from some business contracted in Florence that Captain de M wishes you to deposit at our bank in Venice. If he is still there, make him buy you dinner, for he will have received a fat commission (but please do not tell him that you know this!). That is all. Then hurry to Venice. Your destination, in case you do not remember, is the Palazzo Centranico on the Rio Morto, hard by the Church of San Cassan in the sestriere of Santa Croce. You are expected, and more detailed instructions will await you there.

With any luck at all, you will also find some fresh communication from myself and perhaps Captain de M as to the progress of our affairs. If all goes well I shall see you there myself before next spring has passed. But we will discuss this in more detail, for, good Patch, I will require you to be a more diligent writer of letters than you have so far proved.

So, until we meet again, good luck and fine weather!

Gilles de Peyrolles

Chapter Twelve

The next morning I awoke to bedbugs and drizzle. The tiny swine had pecked a tracery of red into my shins and arms, and one of my ears felt hot and swollen. I cursed them volubly in broad Devon. Tired as I had been last night, I had made sure to tuck my sword beneath my bolster in case the inn was less friendly than it seemed. I had been attacked, all right, but the villains had been rather smaller than I had thought to guard against. But my clothes were clean and had dried by the fire, and to my surprise the hideous cloak, now freed of the filth of ages, seemed to have once been a rich man's garment, for there was silver thread in the hem, and the cloth was fine. I grudgingly paid my bill and managed to be back on the Ravenna Road while the air was still cool.

I had hoped to spend the night at Narni, but it was further than I had thought, and instead we stopped at Vigne, where I took the precaution of sleeping on the floor of my room. Rising early next day with no fresh bedbug bites, I set off for Narni. It was late afternoon before we topped a ridge and saw the town before us, perched on a steep stone hill above the Tiber. There was not much left of the day, and I should have halted there, but I thought it looked sinister perched up there on its crag, and so I urged Iblis down the slope to the bridge. The country on the other side of the river looked rich and friendly, and I guessed I would find a pleasant bed there without too much difficulty. The guards – the first soldiers I had seen on my journey – regarded me sourly but gave me no trouble, and I paid my toll and rode across. It was indeed pleasant on the other side, and with the anticipation of supper giving me confidence, I nudged Iblis into a trot, then a canter. Down the road we swept, kicking up dust and earning curses and cheers in equal measure from the people on foot, for the road was busy again here.

But strangely, as we topped the nearest ridge, the people thinned out to nothing and we were alone again. And there before us, painted a sombre crimson by the setting sun, was a great slab of mountain which cut off the view to the north and east. It was like a wave of stone rearing up over the gentle landscape, menacing it with a savage face of cliff and tumbled rocks. The road descended to pass beneath this frightful monster, and down there it looked dark and sinister. I scanned the way ahead for any sign of an inn or even a farmstead where Iblis and I might buy a place to sleep, but there seemed to be nothing but olive trees and the occasional hovel. So reluctantly we passed the night in a grove of ancient olive trees a little way back from, and above, the road. It was clear that the trees were ancient, for they were little more than gnarled tangles of wooden tracery that still supported branches heavy with leaves and unripe fruit, and their roots reared up out of the ground, forming little hollows filled with dry leaves, natural beds that looked almost inviting. Fortunately I had bought bread, hard cheese, some onions and more leathery sausage at Vigne, and I had topped off my wineskin too, so supper was no great hardship. And to sleep on the bare earth was nothing new to me, so after making sure that Iblis had plenty of green stuff on which to graze, I arranged my packs to make a pillow and laid my sword down beside me, and tried to fall asleep.

If you are bone weary you will fall asleep under a tree as

readily as you would in a feather bed. If you fear the wild world, you will lie, saucer-eyed, and try in vain to see through the black night which your fancy has peopled with imps, ghosts, wolves and murderers. But if, like I was then, you are neither tired nor afraid of the world beyond your walls and doors, you will stay awake for hours listening to the sounds of the night and gazing up at the stars. Tonight the Via Lactea leaped across the sky and all the star-creatures blazed down: bears, dragons, long-dead gods and heroes made immortal as solemn, silvery points of light. A nightingale started up in a thicket nearby, then moved further and further away until I could hear her no longer. Owls hissed and shrieked, and everywhere, from every rock and blade of grass, the insects poured out their song, as implacable as waves hissing on a pebble shore. So there I lay, idly sipping from my wineskin and thinking of the last time I had slept on the ground: a far less happy night that I had passed under a rain-drenched yew tree in one of Dartmouth's churchyards. I had been a frightened boy then, nothing but death behind me and less than a glimmer of hope in front. I had woken up starving and robbed some poor gravediggers for my breakfast, but that night I had come aboard the *Cormaran* for the first time.

As I say, I was indulging myself in these thoughts, full of wine and pleasant fatigue and beginning to sink drowsily into my nest of crackling leaves, when Iblis gave a snort, and then a quiet whinny. Startled, I sat up, but there was nothing but the cicadas and the shrilling of bats and so I settled back down. He has probably scented a fox or a badger, I mused. And what a fine guard-dog he makes into the bargain. Feeling drowsy again, and pleased with my good fortune, my eyes began to droop and my head to nod, when from below me on the road came a loud drumming of hooves. More than one horse – three or four, by the clamour of them – were racing up from Narni at breakneck speed. Iblis whinnied again, then neighed in earnest, but if the riders heard him they did not stop, and I doubted they could hear anything above the din of their mounts. But I was surprised enough to grab the pommel of my sword and throw my blanket off, and in the few moments it took me to do so the riders had passed and the sound of them was fading away northwards, soon to sink beneath the chorus of cicadas.

I sat for a while, waiting for my heart to still, and listening for more travellers below. But everything was still on the road, and before long – and with the aid of the last of the wine – I laid my head down again, this time to sleep in earnest. By the time I woke early the next morning, thick-headed and with a mouth full of tiny ants, I had all but forgotten the riders. I found a little stream nearby and led Iblis to drink there, and bathed my own grimy face. Then we set out again.

After I had ridden for a couple of hours, the Ravenna Road began to amble through soft, rolling country again. It was a little like Devon, I mused, but with olives instead of apples. And then, to confound me even more, orchards began to spring up on either side of the road. There were mountains not too far away, brown backs dotted with trees, and every hilltop hereabouts seemed to have a castle or a fortified village perched upon it. I took an excellent lunch of grilled sausages in one of these villages before pressing on to Spoleto which, despite the innkeeper's gloomy assessment, I drew near to well before the sun began to sink behind yet another ridge of high mountains.

If I had found Narni a little sinister, it was nothing compared to my first view of the city of Spoleto. I crested a hill, and the road – little more than a track, in truth – dropped steeply down into a wide basin between the ridge of mountains I had been riding towards, and the hills over which I had just ridden. A river ran coolly through the darkening land, past a crude round fortress; and away to my left a broad, flat, marshy valley stretched away almost to the horizon, only to be blocked by a high, round-topped peak that seemed to rise vertically from the valley floor. But ahead of me was a town built on a hill that rose from the centre of the basin – I say a hill, but it seemed no less than a tiny mountain in itself, so steep and craggy was it. Down this crag seemed to pour – or rather ooze, like golden resin from a pine-tree – a confusion of honey-coloured stone, which, as I stared, resolved itself into churches, spires, houses and streets, all clinging to the sides of the mountain and springing up in tighter clusters wherever there was a hint of flat land on which to gain a purchase. In the fading light it looked unbelievably ancient, or indeed other-worldly, as if not made by the hands of men at all. With a growing sense of foreboding I rode down the hill towards the gate.

The sun was not quite down, and the guardsmen, decked in livery the colour of old blood, let me through with suspicious glances but no trouble. I was to meet Horst at the White Lion, near the cathedral. I asked an old woman leaning in a doorway where that might be, and she wordlessly pointed straight up. I took this to mean that I had to ride to the very top of the hill, and indeed I thought I remembered seeing at least one belltower up there, so with a sincere apology to Iblis I guided him up the horribly steep roadway.

The arms of Spoleto proved to be a white lion, so I guessed that Horst was lodged at the city's chief hostelry. I was looking forward to some supper and a wash, so I fell to imagining what the kitchen might be offering, while Iblis plodded up, climbing the cobbled street with his head lowered purposefully. After a while I took pity on him and dismounted, and together we laboured along our zigzag course, for the road wound up the hillside like clumsy stitching. But despite my misgivings this seemed like a pleasant city after all. The streets, most of which, apart from the one we had chosen, seemed to be nothing more than staircases cut into the face of the hill, were full of people taking their ease, and children playing noisily with tops and hoops. Food was being prepared, and folk were bellowing at each other companionably from windows and doorways. Nevertheless I was beginning to grow weary by the time I led Iblis under a great, mossy archway and on to a patch of mercifully flat ground where, judging from the rotting fruit and vegetables being fought over by a swarm of bone-thin dogs, a market had recently held sway. There was a large church in front of me, and I hoped this was the cathedral, but a cowled monk, scurrying across the marketplace on some errand, told me that the place I sought was beyond, and to the right. As I suspected, that meant heaving our exhausted carcasses up another almost sheer street, and I was cursing the whole world when suddenly the buildings opened up on my left and I found myself looking down a wide course of steps and on to a wide piazza of golden brick, beyond which a marble church rose, blushing faintly pink with the last rays of the sun. This, plainly, was the cathedral. But where was the inn? I was sinking down on the topmost step to get my breath back, Iblis breathing hotly down my neck, when there was a loud flurry of voices behind me. I turned, and saw that a party of young men were trotting down the street towards me, chattering loudly. Behind them, at the top of the hill, a loud argument was being played out between a very fat man with a bald head and another younger fellow, who with a final angry wave of his arms, took off after his friends. The fat man watched him go, hands on fleshy hips, before shaking his head and stepping back through a doorway, above which hung a sign emblazoned with the image of a white lion rampant against a blood-red field. I had found my inn.

The proprietor of the White Lion – the fat gentleman I had seen arguing outside – was evidently used to his guests arriving in the last stages of fatigue, and he raised not so much as an eyebrow hair as I stood before him panting, sweat pattering down on to my tunic from the tip of my nose. He had a bed for me, but of course. Please to leave my beautiful horse with Giovanni the groom. Of course, Signor Horst of the *Cormaran* had arrived four days ago; and come in, come in.

'He left this for you,' said the innkeeper, opening a drawer in his table and passing me a letter. I glanced at it, and saw that 'Petrus Zennorius' was written there. I was about to ask for Horst's whereabouts, but at that moment a serving girl passed with a flagon of something cold enough to make the earthenware beady with dew. I must have looked desperate, for the innkeeper signed discreetly to another girl, who was placing a beaker of icy white wine in my hand so speedily I thought for a moment that I had conjured it up myself by sheer force of desire. I took a deep draught as the fat man watched me indulgently.

'It is good, yes?' he asked. I nodded, although the cold liquor was making my teeth ache and my eyes throb. 'Our cellars are deep, the deepest in Spoleto. The Romans dug them down into the cold heart of the earth. Now, you may eat when you wish, but I would like you to take a jug of this wine to your room and lie down for a little. You look – forgive me, sir – but you look as if you passed last night in an unfriendly ditch.'

'Under a tree, actually,' I gasped through frozen teeth.

'Sir! My remark was made in jest! Where was this tree? I am overjoyed that you made it alive to stand beneath my roof, for the roads hereabouts are not safe at night. Not safe at all, sir.'

'I was molested by nothing worse than ants and mosquitoes,' I said, tipping the last of the wine down my gullet. 'I thought it a friendly country, to tell you the truth.'

'That, my dear, exceptionally fortunate young sir, it is not. No, not by any means. Now, if you will not lie down I surely will, from the shock of what you have just told me. Druda!' He beckoned over the girl who had brought my wine. 'Take the young master to his room – the good one with the red awning. Bring him more wine, and tell him to drink, and sleep.'

I did not, it seemed, have any choice in the matter. Druda, a solid girl with thick brown hair gathered into a purposeful bun, showed me to my room and returned a minute later with a bedewed flagon. She regarded me, a stern look on her freckled face, until I gave up fiddling with my pack and lay down on the pallet.

'Good,' she said, and set the flagon, and a beaker, down next to me. Then, with a final glance to make sure I was obeying orders, she left me. I had to admit the bed – it was a real bed, a massive thing of black oak with four pillars and a canopy of somewhat threadbare red velvet – was comfortable. The hay that filled the mattress was fresh, and the linen smelt of flowers. I obediently drank a beaker of wine, then another, and settled back against the bolster.

The innkeeper had been right. When I opened my eyes again it was pitch dark in the room. Wondering how long I had slept, I sprang up and hurried to the window. It was late: the waxing moon which had kept me company last night was nowhere to be seen, and the stars shone very brightly. But there was still noise drifting up from the town, and I hoped I had not missed dinner. My head was clear, and all the fatigue of the day had drained from me. I stretched happily.

Then I remembered. Horst must be waiting for me. I hurried out into the hall, felt an absence at my waist and, patting myself, realised I had left my knife on the pillow. I buckled it on, along with my purse, which I had also, improvidently, forgotten. Shutting the door, I was surprised to find a large, gnarled key in the lock, so I turned it and tucked it away in my purse. I clattered down the stairs and was met by the raised eyebrows and indulgent smile of the innkeeper. Lamps were flickering from many sconces in the stone walls, and tired-looking servants scurried about.

'So you did sleep, signor!' he said. 'You have all but missed dinner,' he went on, with a kindly wag of his finger, 'but certainly we can find something tasty for you.'

'Oh. That would be wonderful,' I said. 'By the way, did my friend Horst return?'

The innkeeper looked puzzled. 'Why, no!' he replied. 'Were you expecting him?'

'Of course. He is lodging here.'

'No. No, sir, he is not. He stayed one night only, then left very early the next day. If I might risk an opinion, he seemed in a mighty hurry.' He frowned. 'I did give you his letter, did I not?'

'Yes, you did, but I have not …' I drew it out, and the innkeeper's eyes fell on the unbroken seal. He brightened.

'I knew I had not forgotten! But, signor, I see you are confused. Why not open the letter? Perhaps things will be clearer.'

I was frowning now, and I suddenly did not want to read Horst's message under the eyes of this stranger. But an odd sense of urgency set me to work on the seal, which broke easily. I unfolded the parchment and found it held another folded note, this one on fine white paper. The open letter was signed Horst and was near illegible. I tilted it towards the light of a rush lamp and glanced at the innkeeper, who was obviously burning with curiosity, and who was leaning his fat frame closer. He caught my eye, coughed respectfully and withdrew, reluctantly, behind his table. I peered at Horst's words. They were hastily written with a badly cut quill, and I guessed that Horst was a poor scribe at the best of times. But with a little more light and a deal of squinting, sense began to emerge from the tangle of scratches and inky splatterings.

> To ~~Petroc~~ Petrus Zennorius, in haste!!!
>
> I missed you on the road, friend, though I sought you day and night. A letter from Captain de Montalhac found me in Florence: business gone awry, says he. And he bid me turn you from Venice to Ancona, whence M. de Peyrolles awaits with a ship – by God's grace he has not yet found one! I thought I would wait for you here in Spoleto, but cannot wait. I will be two days in Foligno, up the road. If this finds you, meet me there! I am away myself to said Ancona before dawn tomorrow. Follow with as much speed as you can muster. Enclosed a message from the Captain. I have no more news than this. Hurry, friend, and take care, for it is not SAFE for us now. We will await you at the Three Dolphins. HURRY!!
>
> (Sweet Christ, the wenches in this place, and NO TIME) Horst von Tantow ex Cormaranus

I folded the letter back around the Captain's note and slipped both inside my tunic. I must have had surprise writ boldly on my face, for the innkeeper was almost fizzing with interest, but I hastily feigned what I hoped looked like bored irritation.

'He could not wait for me, the wretch!' I sighed. 'No matter. Good sir, I will take up your offer of supper, even if it be table scraps, for it seems I must rise at an ungodly hour. My foolish friend believes he missed me here and is hurrying to catch up with me ...' I hurriedly racked my brains for Gilles' map, and for the name of the next town on the Ravenna Road. 'Foligno,' I said finally. 'He waits for me in Foligno, now. That is not far, I do not think?'

'A pleasant morning's ride,' said my host, his face showing genuine relief at so easy an explanation to my troubles. 'You may sleep late and enjoy the day, signor.'

'And yet I must make haste,' I said quickly, echoing Horst's words. 'He is a fool, alas, and will not tarry. I would not have us chase each other all the way to Ultima Thule, so I had best put an end to this nonsense. I will leave at sunrise, although I would greatly prefer to stay and enjoy your excellent hospitality.'

And there was an end to it. I went off to dine on an endless procession of wonderfully savoury dishes which, if they were table scraps, came from the leavings of Mount Olympus. I took care not to drink too deeply of the wines, both white and richly dark, with which the servants were most solicitous. Nevertheless it was with a groaning belly and slightly numb limbs that I at last dragged myself back to my room, having left strict instructions that I was to be woken before dawn. I locked myself in, stretched out on the bed and, remembering Horst's warning, tucked my knife under the bolster. Then I drew out the letters, threw Horst's scrawl to one side, and examined the smaller document.

Even in the weak candlelight I could read the Captain's bold, educated hand. I was about to break the seal when there came a discreet tap at the door.

Chapter Thirteen

Sighing, for I was quite full, I rose lazily and unlatched the door, which opened to reveal the freckled face of Druda. I believe I blushed, for during my supper I had been having thoughts of a somewhat speculative nature about this serving-wench, the speculation directed mainly at what she might look like without her very proper clothing. And indeed she lowered her eyes most fetchingly, but then broke the spell by giving me a message from the innkeeper: namely, that my friend had arrived and was waiting for me. Puzzled, I followed her downstairs. There was the innkeeper, somewhat the worse for food and drink at this late hour, scratching his head groggily.

'Ah, my dear sir! Your friend has returned ... no, no, that is not it. He has *not* returned, but sent a message back for you with a gentleman.'

'A gentleman? Is he here?'

'No. He waits outside. Apparently he had made prior arrangements for his accommodation ...' he shook his head, as if such a thing were completely unthinkable. 'He has yet to settle his horse, and would not let my groom near it. These northerners! Oh, I beg your pardon sir: this gentleman is from the north of these lands, not your own brave and magnificent country,' he went on, regaining some of his unctuousness.

'How vexing,' I muttered. I did not wish to go out again. But I supposed that I must, so I opened the heavy door and was about to step out when the innkeeper exclaimed behind me: 'Good God, your honour! Do not go out in the night air without your cloak! The draught will kill you! The man who was looking for you: Christ's blood, but his tunic was so short you could see his knees!'

I waved him off, for what could be more ridiculous than a Devon man laid low by cold air, and stepped out, leaving consternation behind me. The street was dark, of course, and empty. I was about to go back inside when I heard a snort and the unmistakable clack of a shod hoof on stone, coming from further down the hill. The gentleman, whoever he was – and I half-thought it might be a friend from the *Cormaran*, perhaps Zianni, for who else would be wearing a cycladibus out here in the country – must have grown tired of waiting, and set off to find his own lodgings. Feeling that to retreat back into the warmth of the inn would be something of a defeat, and not wishing to prove that fussing old woman of an innkeeper right, I set off after him. If the message he bore was urgent, I would save time and, besides, it was a fine night for a stroll, and I had a large supper to walk off.

The hill was steep and the dew had already begun to wet the cobbles, so I went slowly, confident that I would soon catch a man leading a horse. But when I reached the point at which the street gave out upon the stairway that led down to the cathedral I still could see no one, and there were no more noises to guide me. Well, I had missed him. Apparently whatever message he bore could wait until tomorrow. Feeling rather glad that I could still enjoy what was left of the evening, and suddenly quite happy to be outdoors, I decided to stroll down and look at the cathedral, for doubtless I would have no time on the morrow.

I wandered down the wide steps and across the square. The stars gave enough faint light to show the carvings on the pillars and the cathedral walls: beasts and birds, carved in the strong, strange manner of a century before. I stared up at the towering campanile, patted the head of a stone lion, and – finally admitting to myself that the air was a trifle chilly – decided to start back to the inn. I had traversed the square and had just set foot on the bottom step when two things happened at once. I heard the clash of hooves pounding on cobbles, and looked up to see a figure standing at the top of the steps. I raised my hand, hoping it was not the Watch – and perhaps he had summoned help, for why else would anyone be riding at breakneck speed up that infernally steep hill? And at that moment, hurling sparks to left and right, the horse came into view. The watchman, if so he was, turned and threw up a hand, there was a flash of cold light and the horse sped on, clambering more than running up the hill, the memory of sparks staining my vision. The clatter was barely fading when I heard another sound: a hollow thud, thunk, thud, and saw the watchman collapse into shadow. But still that noise came, like old winter turnips thrown into a barrel, and as I started to run up the steps I understood what was making it. For down the stairs towards me rolled a ball, and as it bounced and juddered to a halt above me I saw that it was a human head.

Half disbelieving my eyes, I squatted down to make sure, and felt the bile burning its way up my throat, for sure enough I beheld a tangle of wet hair and a pale ear. With infinite reluctance I stood and turned it a little with my foot. The face of Giovanni the groom grinned up at me, teeth clenched, a black bubble swelling and bursting as I watched. I turned aside and puked, then swallowing hot bile and curses, I ran up the remaining steps to where the rest of Giovanni lay in an unseemly tangle of misarranged limbs. There was no sign of his murderer, although the cobbles of the street were scarred with livid marks where the horseshoes had gouged them, and the smell of metal against stone still hung in the air, mingling with the darker scent of blood and fresh shit. I felt very tired all of a sudden and sank down next to the corpse, and noticed that before he died, Giovanni had put on my lovely blue riding-cape.

I raised the alarm, of course, although no alarm had needed to be sounded, for the horseman had awoken everyone in the street and perhaps in the whole town. The innkeeper was beside himself, and the inn filled with wails and groans as four watchmen bore the groom's corpse in upon a trestle, his head perched grotesquely upon his chest. It was explained, first to the watchman and then to me – and then, over and over again, to the whole congregation – that the innkeeper, fearing for my safety and seeking to protect me from the deadly air, had sent Giovanni after me with my cape – hanging by the door, sir – which the poor boy must have put on, for the night was cold and he must have thought he would catch his death without it, poor boy – may the saints and the Holy Mother clasp him to their breasts – and so the robber or bandit, or whoever had done this terrible thing – may devils chew upon his liver for eternity – had caught him out in the empty street.

For some reason the fact that he had been wearing my cape seemed to escape the quick minds of the Watch. And I myself, and indeed the other guests, were all but forgotten in the chaos that had descended upon the inn. The messenger who had come looking for me – this detail too was brushed aside. Still I lingered, half-expecting to be arrested by the Watch, but when a parcel of old, black-clad crones arrived, silent but grimly excited, to lay out the body, I slipped away unnoticed. Back in my room, I secured the latch and pushed the room's one chair, a vast and hideous affair carved from oak, but fortunately for my purposes as heavy as granite, against the door. Then, my hands trembling in earnest now, I pulled the Captain's letter from my tunic.

The front was blazoned with a large **P** and sealed with black wax into which the image of a flying, sharp-winged bird had been pressed. I took out my knife and used it to prise up the seal without breaking it. Then I opened the letter. At first I thought it had been dropped in water and the ink all run together, so dark was the page. But looking closer I realised that the Captain had covered every fraction of the vellum with script. I cursed gently. I could not wait for daylight, and yet surely I would be able to read nothing in this paltry light. Looking around the room I saw three other little rush lights dusty and unlit in a corner. Lighting these, I arranged all four flames in a crescent on the floor and, stretching out on the cold tiles, I found I could more or less make out the writing.

Petroc of Auneford, from Michel de Montalhac, greetings!

The letter began conventionally enough, and this I took to be a hopeful sign. And it was not in cipher, Saint Lucy's rolling eyeballs be praised. The Captain disdained such things, though, for as he said, in ignorant times such as ours, plain script is cipher enough. My own eyeballs watering in protest, I read on:

I am hopeful that this letter will reach you in Rome. If it does not, the bearer must perforce chase you the length of Italy, for you must have this news. I am at Imperia, a week's ride from Venice. The letter is entrusted to the swiftest horsemen, but it may be that I will be not so far behind it. No matter. There is reason for my haste, and great need for haste on your part as well.

There is no time for lavish explanation. My journey was short, for I heard Louis Capet was near Marseilles, and so had no need to cross the Alps. Louis C was eager – nay, ravenous – for that item of which I bore tidings. It was the work of an hour, sitting under an olive tree as per his custom, to negotiate a transfer: aid to Baldwin de Courtenay in the form of funds, in return for said item. The next day the king let fly the great bow of state, and sent me speeding into the east in the company of two Dominican brothers who have the power to offer a great portion of the French treasury in return for – I repeat myself – said item. So far, most satisfactory, but as we made ready to depart I discovered that the banks there were abuzz with rumour: the French king calling on his reserves and credit, and suing for more credit, to raise a gigantic sum, reason unknown. Excellent, thought I. But bankers' news flies fast as greed, for now this came to my ears.

It is not by chance that I share a banking house with the Republic of Venice. In that infinitely malleable place, everything has its price, especially information, and the bank's agent in Marseilles had some for me, namely this: young Baldwin de Courtenay is up to his eyebrows in debt to Venice, and the Doge is getting impatient. He is about to make the strongest demand upon Baldwin's Regents in Constantinople for collateral – or he perhaps already has, for matters are not clear. In a bankrupt kingdom, what can collateral mean? Olive oil? I rather think not.

Petroc, I fear our nice, easy coup is in the process of going badly awry. I require you in Constantinople with Gilles now, not in Venice. Horst will go with you. I can all but hear you ask, why must it be me? I trust Gilles had a talk with you about the greater trust we would like to place on your shoulders. Well, we are calling upon you sooner than we had thought. As Gilles perhaps also told you, I wish to bring you into the heart of our *business. Well then, at this moment there is no place more vital to that business than the Pharos Chapel in Constantinople. Gilles needs a strong companion. Do not tremble, Patch: it is for your quick wit that he needs you, and for your excellent Greek which the Vassileia Anna drilled into you. This affair will be words, not daggers.*

A hundred pardons for wrenching you from what I hope has been a pleasant tour of pleasant lands, but you will see wonders, my friend. I will require a full report of them, you may be sure! Until then, I wish you speed and safety. Gilles will instruct you, do not fear.

Farewell!

Michel de Montalhac, in Lyons

Patch: Pay Attention!

Jesus. My stomach cramped suddenly with anxiety, and I dragged myself up off the floor and staggered to the window. I thought I might puke the rest of my rich dinner out into the night, but the warm and resin-scented air calmed me at once, and I found that my turmoil had given way to a strange, buoyant calm. It seemed that Venetians were all around me. The Captain had made no mention of danger: *This affair will be words, not daggers*, he had said. Well, that was rather obviously no longer true. I was ahead of him with the news. Venice had taken Baldwin himself as collateral. And I held a papal decree that gave Baldwin absolution from simony. With this instrument, whoever controlled Baldwin could strip his empire of every holy relic it possessed and sell them for hard cash. *Business gone awry*, Horst? I should say so. I should very definitely say so.

With a clarity I had not felt since arriving in London – nay, since the time, long ago it seemed now, that I had set out in the dark of night to steal the bones of Saint Cordula from her island shrine – I turned my head to the east. A half moon was hanging above the turrets of the fortress. It was waxing, and shone so brightly it dazzled my eyes to look upon its face. All was quiet save for the whirr of insects and the piping of the bats. I would leave immediately, I decided all at once. I would ride through the end of the night, and feel the dew gather on my horse's mane. I would see the sun rise before me, and I would take my course down to the sea. I held up my hand. It glowed softly in the light of the waning moon, just risen over the roofs of the town, and cast a crisp shadow on the windowsill. I closed my eyes and imagined the moon working on my blood as it worked upon the waters of the ocean, pulling me ever to the East. I saw a sea of white, dancing light, and beyond, the long walls and strange spires of Byzantium.

I pulled out my old rag-pickers'-market cloak and tied it around my waist with my sword belt. The cloak was black, which was good: patched and faded as it was, it would attract no attention. Nevertheless I cursed Giovanni for denying me my new cape, then cursed myself for my ingratitude, for the poor fellow had undoubtedly saved my life with the surrender of his own. I was pretty sure that Iblis would be unguarded in the stable, for everyone would be downstairs, gawping at the body; but how to leave unseen? I pondered this for a moment. It would be good to slip away, and to put a distance between me and the Venetian, whoever he was, before he discovered his mistake. Peering out of the window I considered jumping down on to a lower roof that jutted out below me, but it looked slippery with lichen and the tiles were crumbling to boot. So there was nothing else for it. I unhooked my sword from its belt and tied it against the saddlebag, which I slung over my shoulder. The bed, so comfortable and clean, mocked me as I laid a gold piece on the bolster, more than ample payment for my stay. Then I heaved the chair out of the way and peered out into the hallway.

There was no one there, and the rush lights had almost burned out. A great commotion came from downstairs, grief-filled wailing, but also the excited chatter of men. I tiptoed down the stairs, and craned my neck over the banisters. The entry hall was empty. All the noise was coming from the back of the inn, for they had laid Giovanni out in the dining room. Sending up a prayer of thanks, I was about to let myself out of the front door when it struck me that the place was probably being watched. Or perhaps not, I thought, hand beginning to sweat on the latch-ring. The murderer must surely have fled? Yes, but what if he had not? Biting my lip in vexation at my own wariness, I turned back. The kitchens were this way. Had I not seen the groom disappear that way, a coin in his hand, with orders to lavish the finest bran upon my horse? I thought perhaps I had.

The kitchen was empty too, and I snatched up a flitch of bacon from the table and a bottle of wine from the floor. From behind a door in the far wall came the sound of dreaming horses. It was dark in the stables, and I had to light a lamp with my tinderbox, taking care not to spill any sparks on the straw. Iblis was not best pleased to see me advancing upon him with his saddle, but let me belt it on, snicking his teeth and shaking his head.

'You have no idea,' I assured him. By way of apology I waved a full nosebag in front of his eyes. 'This for later, good beast. Now we must hurry.'

I guessed it was still not quite midnight by the time I led Iblis out into the night. There was no sign of a watcher with a horse, thankfully; but I had no wish to attract attention, and indeed I knew full well that I was far too poor a rider to canter, or even trot, down these almost sheer streets. First, thinking to find a back way out of the town, I climbed to the very top of the hill, past a little church standing at the end of its own square, and beyond to an open space filled with ruins and sleeping goats. Then the land dropped off into a sheer, wooded ravine so deep that I could barely hear the rush of water below. So I led Iblis back, and we walked slowly down a quiet street that seemed to run parallel to the one we had come up that evening. Sure enough we soon came to an ancient-looking archway I remembered, and then I took both our lives in my hands and plunged down a stepped alleyway. But the wide way coiled about the hillside and after a few agonising minutes of tripping and slipping on dewy stone only to find we had again fetched up on the main street I gave up and swung myself on Iblis. The gate was not far now. I tried to remember if I had heard a curfew bell, and thought perhaps I hadn't, and indeed the gate was open, although a knot of men-at-arms lounged around a glowing brazier. I had buckled my sword back on by then, and was wondering if I would have to charge the guards when one of them, scratching his arse and leaving his halberd leaning against the wall, wandered into my path, hand held up more in greeting than warning.

'What cheer, friend?' He asked. There was no edge to his voice, only wine and the lateness of the hour.

'Not much, friend,' I answered in my thickest Roman accent, hoping that it would disguise my poor Italian. 'I must be in Assisi by dawn, and it is a ways away, right?'

'That it is. But why travel by night? You should be by the fire.'

'Ah, I *was*,' I told him, leaning down with what I trusted was an easy smile on my face. 'Fell asleep, didn't I? In company, if you get my meaning. Should have set out this morning, but ...' I threw in a leer for good measure. 'Now, my master's a churchman, and an important one, and he'll have my skin for a book-binding if he finds I've killed a day in the arms of a wench. So I'm happy to risk a ride under the stars,' I finished with a wink. To my relief the man winked back, a conniving grin spreading across his bristly chops.

'Wouldn't want a flaying on my conscience,' he said. 'All right, be off with you.'

'Thank you, friend,' I said. 'By the bye, I'm not from these parts, in case you hadn't noticed. I take the north road, yes? How far do I have to go?'

'You'll make it by sunrise if you hurry,' said the guard. 'The road takes you up the valley. It's not yet midnight, and you should be in Foligno by the fourth vigil. If you aren't, ride like the Devil, my friend! Leave the road at Foligno, keep Spello on your right and you'll keep your skin.'

I bid him farewell, and even waved at the other guards, who ignored me. Beyond the gate the road stretched out into the plain between two mountain ranges, one low, one high and steep. I trotted for a few yards until the gate had fallen far enough behind, then kicked Iblis into a gallop. Away we sped amongst the willows. My plan was to catch up with Horst at Foligno, if indeed he was still there, for two would travel more safely than one, and Horst would know better than I how to deal with the nasty turn things had taken. So I hurried on, giving Iblis his head for a mile or so and then walking for a bit, then racing on again. I was keeping an ear cocked for pursuers, but nobody seemed to have followed me, and the road was utterly deserted.

Not a friendly country. No, not by any means. The innkeeper's words fluttered around my head and I tried to keep my nerves at bay, though my path led through land that, while it was no doubt pretty in the light of day, was decidedly sinister under the moon. It was flat, and criss-crossed with streams and ditches. Shadowy willows and poplars lurked on either side. But on my right, on the dark mountainside, white villages gleamed, and that made me feel less alone. I did not tarry, though, and saw the towers of Foligno rise before me well before the stars had begun to fade. Now at last I decided to rest, for if the Spoleto watch had been careless, the gates ahead might be more vigilant, and I did not think a night-traveller would be welcomed. So I found an ivy-swarmed ruin a little way off the road, gave Iblis his long-promised nosebag at last, drank some wine and stretched out before the remains of the fireplace, my sword unsheathed at my side.

I did not sleep long, for a pair of doves fell into conversation in the ivy above my head just after dawn. I arose and looked out of the one remaining window on to a lake of fog, above which the mountains rose, glowing pink. I breakfasted on cold bacon and set off for Foligno. It must have been market day, for the country folk were crowding through the gate, pushing carts, riding on wagons or simply lugging great bags and baskets. I fell in line behind a peasant family pulling a trolley piled with baskets that held fat white geese, hissing and cackling in fury. This town, I was glad to see, was flat, and I headed straight for its centre, steering by the tallest campanile.

It was the habit of the company of the *Cormaran* to take the best lodgings in whatever town they found themselves, and so I asked my way to the Golden Fleece, which everyone seemed to think was the fanciest inn, and which I found in a narrow street lined with the grand houses of rich merchants, just behind the main square. It was indeed a comfortable place by the looks of it. I went in, and I was wondering if I might dare risk a sleep in one of its no doubt luxurious beds, when a plump and pretty woman emerged from a side room. She saw me and began wringing her hands.

'No rooms, dear sir, no rooms today, and I beg your pardon for it!' she exclaimed.

'Nay, I do not wish for a room,' I told her, noting that she was ashen and that the skin under her eyes looked almost bruised. 'I am seeking a friend of mine. He might have stayed here last night or the night before – Horst of the *Cormaran*? Tall, half an ear, German?'

'Oh, dear God!' sighed the woman, and sagged against a table. She began to fan herself with a hand, and I thought she would faint. I too suddenly felt dizzy.

'Good lady, what ails you?' I asked, tremulously, for perhaps I knew.

'Your poor friend!' she burst out. 'Oh, for pity's sake . . .'

Just then a younger man hurried down the hall and took her shoulders. He gave me a slit-eyed look.

'Good wife, who is this?' he demanded.

'Petrus Zennorius, at your service,' I informed him, bowing politely. 'I merely enquired after a friend whom I hoped to meet here, one Horst, but I appear to have given grave offence.'

'Friend, you say?'

'Friend, comrade, associate.'

'He's dead,' snapped the man.

'I . . .' I reached for the wall, feeling the powdery whitewash rubbing against my palm. Horst could not be dead. The bacon turned to rottenness in my stomach.

'Listen, sir, I do not wish to seem unmannerly, but I have passed this morning and the greater balance of yesterday scrubbing his blood from bed linen and floor, which is all in the way of an innkeeper's trade, no doubt, but the thing of it is, your . . . your friend had no coin with him that we could find, and so there has been a tragedy, my poor wife is undone with the horror of it, and we are out of purse. There you have it.'

'Good master innkeeper, do not trouble yourself over payment. I will cover it,' I said briskly, straightening up. I wished I could be sick, but there would be time enough for that. The man brightened, and so I pressed on: 'What happened? Where is he?'

'The holy brothers took him to the charnel house,' said the innkeeper. He was still furious, it seemed, although with me or with fate I could not tell. So I pulled out my purse and found an appropriate coin.

'Will that allay your trouble?' I asked, tersely. But the two of them brightened, and the woman took the coin and vanished with it into the side room. 'And now, please: what happened to my friend?' I demanded.

'It was not last night, but the night before,' the innkeeper told me at last. He had led me into a dining room and poured me a mug of cool wine and one for himself. 'Master Horst had arrived from Spoleto and took one of our best rooms. A fine-looking gentleman, and very well mannered ...'

'That he was,' I agreed, thinking how fitting it was that tall, stern Horst, knight of Prussia, should leave this final impression.

'He ate here, and stayed up late, for he appreciated our wine ...' I nodded again. I'm sure he did, I thought. Just as I had enjoyed my own dinner in Spoleto, which ought to have been my last. As grief wrapped its tatters about me, I saw, in the merciless glare of hindsight, the trap that had been laid for us both. Chance, blind chance that I had escaped, and my friend had not. '... and took himself off to bed after midnight,' the man continued. 'He told us he thought a friend might join him that day or the next, so when the other gentleman arrived we thought nothing of it, and sent him up to your friend's room.'

'He was expecting me,' I put in. 'He left me a message in

Spoleto, where I had planned to meet him. And there ...'
I stopped myself. 'No matter. Who was this other gentleman?'

'A Venetian,' he said, as I knew he would.

'How did you know that?'

'Oh, by his voice – talked through his nose. And by his
ridiculous, foppish dress,' said the innkeeper scornfully.
'Showing his knees, if you can believe it.'

'I can indeed,' I muttered.

'And then there came a crashing and banging, which we
tried to ignore, as we pride ourselves, sir, on our discretion.
But then came laughter and then nothing, and we forgot
about the noise until next morning, when the chambermaid
found him.'

'Found Horst ...' I said, an image forming in my mind. I
tried to drive it out, but it would not go.

'Found your friend dead on the bed, all cut up. I have
never seen the like. There was blood *everywhere* – oh, sir, I do
beg your pardon,' he said quickly, and poured me more wine.
'In our business one does endure the occasional death on the
premises, but from apoplexies or fevers. Never—'

'And the Venetian?' I broke in.

'Vanished. Gone out the window, most likely. It would
not have been hard.'

'And everything was gone? All Horst's belongings?'

'His bag was emptied and there were clothes strewn all
over. But we only found clothes. No other effects, no papers,
no ...'

'No money.'

'Quite. And so we did not know what to do. The holy
brothers minister to the dead in our city, and they were
called. He will be lying in their house.'

'Oh, Christ,' I said, rubbing my hot but tearless eyes. 'He

would have been buried in a nameless pit, would he not?'

'And so thank the merciful Lord that his friend has come to save him from that,' said the innkeeper hurriedly.

He took me up to the room, but I saw nothing but a bare bed-frame and clean flagstones that reeked of lye. The walls had been freshly whitewashed, and the place had nothing to tell me. I looked at Horst's clothes, but indeed that was all that had been left. In a daze, I picked out a tunic and some leggings, things that I remembered him wearing, to clothe his corpse for burial, and told the innkeeper to give the rest to the poor. Then he led me through the noise and life of market day to the monastery of the black monks who had taken care of my friend. A friendly, ruddy-faced brother – not at all what I had expected, in truth, for to work with the dead has always seemed to me a dark and lonely vocation – met us at the door and led us through white cloisters to a long room lined with marble-topped plinths, perhaps ten or twelve of them. All were empty save one, and on that one lay a long shape draped with a sheet of white linen.

Horst was dead all right, although as one so often finds oneself doing when confronted with such an obvious fact, I found myself checking for signs of life. But his skin was waxen and his lips were already drawing back into the yellow grin of death. His throat had been cut, which must have been the fatal blow, but I supposed he must have fought his murderer, for he bore many other wounds: a long slash across his brow, and punctures next to his breast-bone and in his belly. His hands were also cut, and the bones were showing through the butchered skin of his palms.

'You are merchants?' the brother was asking. I nodded, swallowing down my rising gorge. 'So many robberies, I am afraid,' he said almost apologetically. 'These are troubled times.'

'Many robberies, good brother, but murders?' I asked. The monk stroked his tonsured scalp absently.

'Murders, yes, of course. Those who love His Holiness are assassinated by the followers of the emperor, and, one has to admit, vice versa.'

'This is the emperor's city,' put in the innkeeper, with a certain pride.

'As I said, troubled times,' the monk said diplomatically. 'But a killing like this, for the sake of robbery?' He scratched his head again. 'I will admit, I was surprised.'

'And yet you see many corpses,' I said, curious despite the confusion of my grief.

'Such is the calling of this house,' he replied, bowing his head. It was a show of piety, but I thought that the monk was a practical more than a holy man, and a good one, at that. 'Yes, indeed we see the dead. I said these were troubled times, but, my son, look about you! I have seen every table in use, and more poor souls stretched out on the floor. Wars, and plague – the Lord sees fit to keep us busy. But, come to that, I have not often seen a thief go at his victim in this manner. He fought back, your friend: one can see from the hands.'

I nodded, sickened. Well, there was nothing more to be done. I thanked the brother, paid for a handsome burial for poor Horst and left a donation for the house and, for the sake of appearances, bought a mass for Horst's soul, although I was sure the beneficiary would not have approved. Then, business being done, I turned back to the corpse. He had been my friend, this man. Nay, we had been companions. We had drunk together, worked side by side and shared our tales and hopes through long watches at sea. With what patience he had taught me, his clumsy, clay-footed friend, how to ride! And now I must remember him thus, laid out like meat upon a butcher's stall. For the sake of propriety I crossed myself, then, in the manner of the *Cormaran*, I bent to kiss his cold lips goodbye. And as I leaned down I saw, in the corner of his mouth, pasted to the grey skin by a dab of dried spittle, a scrap of parchment. I made to smooth his face and picked it off with my thumbnail, gave my kiss and walked out past carven skulls and murals of dancing bones.

So I did not tarry in Foligno – not even long enough for lunch, for I could not have faced it – and set off instead up the Ravenna Road, up into the high mountains. Night found me bedding down in a verminous hostelry in some nameless hamlet, feeling alone and with a chill upon my soul, for I had planned to have Horst for company, and now I would never see him again. Then – and only then, by the light of a stinking tallow candle – could I bring myself to look at whatever I had taken from my friend's dead lips. It was not parchment, but paper, white paper, a piece no bigger than a fingernail, but on it there still remained a few strokes of ink, and though these had run, I could make out a 'c' and an 'o'. An idea flared in my confused mind, and with a tremble of excitement I pulled out the Captain's letter to me. If truth be told, I could not say yea or nay that the characters matched, for Horst's were all but washed away. But they were similar enough to my eye to set my hand a-tremble. Horst had died in the act of destroying a letter from the Captain.

And so I read my own letter again. There was the warning against Venetians, of which Horst must have been well aware. There again the order to join Gilles at Ancona. I rubbed my eyes in frustration, for I had not slept properly for two days and my head was pounding. What should I do? It seemed to me that the value of this commission was negated by Horst's death, and in that case I should hurry to Venice, to warn the Captain. But that would be to disobey his command. I wondered if Horst had kept his attacker from reading his letter, and what papers the Venetian had taken from his body. I thought about this as hard as I could, although my skull felt as though it were caught in the pincers of a huge crab.

In his scribble to me Horst had said only that he had been sent to divert me to Ancona, whence he too was speeding. Would he have had papers from the Captain to Gilles? Most likely, and now the enemy, whoever he might be, must have them, for Horst could not have bolted the lot. But again, Horst's last meal: surely, *in extremis*, he would have sought to destroy the most important letter? I had to hope so. Christ. Everything was turning to stink and ruin beneath my feet, treacherous as a Dartmoor quagmire. Two men dead in as many nights, and all for what? For the enrichment of a ridiculous boy-king? Or for ... I thought of the list Michael Scotus had given me. *Valueless*, the Captain had called the things that were named there. And yet how many men had died since I had first heard them spoken of? Fulk and Gautier, Giovanni, and now Horst. I could place a value upon them.

But Horst's murder had opened another wound, for I had not forgotten our last conversation, and his doubts about Anna's death. Horst had believed it was murder, that some-one had used a destrier's hooves as a weapon. I had kept my own thoughts at bay, but now that my friend had himself been murdered, I could hold them off no longer. Someone had wanted Anna dead. Who that might be I did not know, but the strange letter had seemed to speak of Greece. Could it have been her own uncle? But there was no reason for that. Someone from her past? That was more promising. The Captain had rescued her from exile in Greenland, where she had been sent when the mad Norse prince she had been given to as a child bride had turned upon her. Did the prince still live? I had no doubt that, from the tales that Anna had told of her life in Trondheim, he was mad enough. But where was the profit in this? She was dead, and I was yet alive and mired to the ears in some business that was threatening to devour the only world I had known these past two years.

I laid my head down at last, after I had barred the door with a chair and balanced upon that a pitcher of water, so that it would overturn if the door opened and wake me – in theory, at least. I did not dare undress, but lay like a knight on a tomb, hands clasped on the hilt of my sword. I was bound for Ancona, then. At least I knew the way, for the Ravenna Road passed through that city – indeed, that was where I would have turned north towards Venice. And then the solution slapped me across the face: Gilles was in Ancona. He would know what to do. All I had to do was find the Three Dolphins.

I slept, finally, for with my decision – or rather, my decision to leave any and all decisions to someone else, one of the most satisfying choices one is ever given the luxury to make – the crab had at last released my skull, and I passed the night unmolested save for bedbugs. Dawn found me on the road in the crisp air of the mountains, and alone. The stone-faced widow who had been my ungracious hostess had seen and heard nobody upon the road at night, and neither had the wall-eyed groom. I began to believe that I was not being followed after all, for I had seen no other riders behind me, even with the long views granted by my swooping route across the mountains, and I had not tarried long in one place since leaving Spoleto. And so I took myself over the Apennine Mountains and filled myself with their glorious solitude, as summer came to its peak around me, bleaching the grass in the valleys, drying up the stream-beds and making the very air shiver. And by the time I had passed over their spine and had dropped down into the rolling land between the peaks and the sea, the leaves were almost turning.

PART THREE

Constantinople

Chapter Fourteen

The waters of the Hellespont were turbulent and confused. They seemed to unravel around the galley's beak of a prow. There was a sharp and steady breeze blowing down the channel into our faces, making the oarsmen sweat and curse, and crusting our skins with a fine, stinging film of salt. There was plenty of other traffic around us. The coves and beaches that shone like white bite-marks at the base of the lowering mountains on either side each had its little shoal of fishing boats, and out here in the deep water a steady procession of big vessels struggled up under oars or ran down swiftly under straining sails. There were many galleys like ours, sword-like and scuttling, flying the gonfalons of Venice, Genoa, Pisa, Valencia and a confusion of others. There were squat trading vessels from northern waters, ugly as beetles among their southern cousins. And there were Moorish ships too, with their swooping sails and crescent-blazoned pennants. But what I saw most of were the little slipper-shaped boats of the Greeks, busily criss-crossing the channel laden with all manner of cargo. The men who sailed them were sun-scorched and friendly, and more than once one such boat dashed cheekily across our bows, to the delight of its crew and the fury of ours. But I, lounging idly where the rail met the bowsprit, always waved, and once was rewarded by a golden missile shied at me by a boy crouched atop a pile of baskets, which I caught, only to find I held a large, pock-marked orange.

I peeled and ate it gratefully, although the juice stung my salt-split lips.

We had been at sea the best part of a month, and although the weather had been fair – clear, hot days and warm nights – we had struggled against the wind since rounding Cerigo and entering the Aegean Sea. Our ship was a mid-sized galley chartered at Brundisium, Venice-built but now the property of a cartel of Apulian merchants, and as such flying the imperial standard. Perhaps because of this we had an easy time of it: in any case no corsairs came close to us, and the Venetians, not having quite picked sides in the gathering storm, left us alone as we skirted their Greek possessions. It was odd being a passenger, and at first I was irked by the strangeness of it, and kept offering my services to mend the sail or scrub the decks. But my offers were always rebuffed with a kindly, embarrassed firmness: we were paying our way, and paying handsomely, and it would not look right for rich passengers to be monkeying about in the rigging or down in the stench of the rowing deck. My companion was likewise affected, and, exiled like me to a life of wandering the deck and gazing at distant sails and shorelines, he sought my company and I his.

I had arrived in Ancona somewhat bedraggled and extremely saddle-sore. I had pushed Iblis much farther than I should have, and I hoped the poor beast had forgiven me. It had been an easy enough journey, although I had been caught in an early snow squall as I descended the western slope of the mountains. I followed the easy, straight road through the gentle country of the Marches: oak woods and vineyards, golden corn in the valleys and eagles above the high hillsides. And then, after a week and more, I crested an olive-crowned ridge to find the sea twinkling below. Ancona is not a large place, though tightly packed within its walls, and it was not hard to find the Three Dolphins, a good sort of sailors' hostelry near a mighty Roman arch that stood out on the promontory that formed the harbour's mole, its crumbling marble span framing nothing but the odd fishing dinghy. I gave my spent but uncomplaining Iblis to the stables with gold and instructions that his every need was to be met – the finest oats, spring water, a mare if necessary – and stalked on stiff horseman's legs into the inn. To my surprise and relief Gilles was there, poring over a pile of dog-eared pages. When he saw me his mouth fell open in surprise. Then he hurried over to embrace me, despite the road-dust that cloaked my clothes, skin and hair.

'Patch! How astounding!' he exclaimed, then broke into a dust-induced coughing fit. 'Christ, did you tunnel here? You are filthy,' he added, when he had caught his breath. 'But why are you in Ancona? We are not meant to be here either. I am waiting for Horst, in fact.' Then an explanation appeared to seize him. 'You met with Horst upon the road, it is obvious! Where is he?'

'Gilles, he is dead,' I said. I had had plenty of time to rehearse this moment, but when the time came I could only blurt out the news, and drop down on to the bench, there to sink my head in my hands.

'Dead? I do not understand. Was there an accident?' said Gilles, after a horrible pause.

'Horst is dead? Patch, what happened?' It was another voice, another familiar voice. The Captain was looking down at me, the lines at the corners of his eyes alive with worry.

'Master? What are you doing here?' I gasped. I was so weary and sad that I was not so sure, at that moment, that what I beheld was not some phantom conjured by my beleaguered mind.

'I am going to Constantinople instead of Gilles,' said the Captain. 'I left Louis' friars in Venice and wore out three horses to get here before he left. Gilles can manage whatever nest of snakes has been stirred up against us in Venice, and I know Constantinople a little better, so ... but Patch, what has happened to Horst? I must know quickly.'

So I told them my whole tale there and then, before taking off my cloak, before slaking my thirst. From the morning in Rome when I had found Baldwin gone, to finding Horst stretched out upon cold stone. I gave him my suspicions as to what Horst had succeeded in concealing from the Venetians, and what he perhaps had not. When all was said I was exhausted, and would have laid down my head upon the table and slept there and then, had not the Captain's furious excitement kept my eyelids trembling, but open. If Baldwin was taken by the Venetians, then there was no reason for us to continue our mission, he said. But then again, if we reached Constantinople before the news from Venice, we might conclude some business there and salvage a little from the wreckage. I told him I thought it likely that we would be ahead of any message from the Republic. And then I remembered something. 'You must see this,' I said, taking the *Inventarium* of Michael Scotus from my valise and holding it out for the Captain. He frowned as he took it, but his eyes widened and widened until he was gawping like a shocked barn owl.

'Where ... where did you get this, Patch, for God's sake?' he stuttered at last. So I told him that, too.

'I am ... I do not know what to think,' said the Captain after a long pause. He had gone pale. 'This is an *Inventarium* of relics that reside in the Pharos Chapel, et cetera, et cetera. That you know already. But *whose* inventory is it?'

'Baldwin's?' I said, uncertainly. 'Are there others?'

'What we know of the relics of Constantinople come from old texts, but these are useless, for the city was plundered down to the roof-nails by the crusaders,' he replied. 'For what remained in the Bucoleon Palace, we have the words of Robert de Clari. This might be his list, but it is in Greek, so …'

'Wait. Robert who?'

'De Clari – a knight of Amiens. One of the crusaders who sacked Byzantium. Another Frankish plunderer, but at least he kept his eyes open and wrote down what he saw. His book is called *The Story of Those Who Conquered Constantinople*. I have it in my pack. Strangely enough, I received it as a gift from young Baldwin's cousin Louis Capet himself. But I do not think this is de Clari's list.'

'Whose, then?'

'For myself, I am almost certain it was made by one Nicholas Mesarites, a priest who before the sack was *Skeuphylax* – store-keeper – of the imperial palaces. He stayed on to negotiate between the Greeks and their conquerors and ended up, I believe, as Bishop of Ephesus.'

My mind was racing. The names meant nothing to me. And this list: why was it different? I tried to remember if Scotus had told me anything, for it seemed odd that he had not. Straining my memory, I could see nothing but flames, and the sour face of Pope Gregory.

'I do not see,' I muttered at last, 'how this can be important. It is ancient. And if it pre-dates the sack, the bulk of these things may well be gone.'

'My dear Patch, that is why I hope it was compiled by Mesarites, as he knew the chapel well after the pillaging had ceased. And there are more items on this list than de Clari mentions in his book. *Ergo* …'

'*Ergo*? You believe this to be demonstrated, then, Michel?' asked Gilles with a cautious smile.

'Um, probably, yes,' said the Captain, finally. The three of us laughed nervously.

'But what is this *Mandylion*?' I persisted. 'And *Keramion*? That sounds like something made of clay – a brick. The *Mandylion*: something "in a holy picture". Is it a relic lodged in an icon? That is common amongst the Greeks.'

'No, no. I am not actually sure *what* it is, if you want the truth,' said the Captain, ruefully. 'It is certainly a relic of incredible age, for it was known in Edessa – the city in Outremer,' he added, while I nodded my head impatiently. 'The *Mandylion* was supposedly a piece of cloth brought to a king of Edessa during the lifetime of the Christ. It cured him of an illness. The cloth was supposed to bear the imprint of the Christ's wet face.'

'Oh, it is the Veronica!' I put in again. 'But that is back in Rome.'

'No, no – the Veronica is something else: perhaps the *other* True Image, so called,' put in Gilles. '*This Mandylion* is a painting, I suppose, although in all the writings – and there are many on the subject – it is described quite strangely. The impression I have is that the face appears to be picked out in water, as though the cloth were still wet.'

'It seems as if you both know quite a lot about the thing after all,' I pointed out.

'Yes, well … no. You see, the thing has disappeared and reappeared again and again over the years. It came to Constantinople about three centuries ago, and when it did, a couple of people wrote about the occasion, for it was a very mighty one. I do not remember the exact words, but they do not describe a picture of a face. They describe a folded cloth bearing the full imprint of a crucified man, wounds and blood and all.'

'A painting of Christ's whole body?'

'As large as life. And not a painting, remember: a miraculous image. An imprint.'

'I have never heard of any such,' I said, astounded.

'And yet it was in Constantinople before the Franks came,' said the Captain. 'The same Mesarites who had charge of the Pharos Chapel describes a ceremony held every week in the city – "the naked Lord rises again," he says. And a few crusaders saw it too, including de Clari. Except the *Mandylion* was meant to have resided in the Church of Blachernae, which was sacked completely.'

'Then ...'

'Then nothing. It disappeared.'

'Someone stole it. That's not so astonishing. They seem to have stolen everything else, at least that is what Anna used to say.'

'That is what I believed. But ...' He tapped the list again. 'A *Mandylion* is here. And here: the holy Tile.'

'Tile!' I scoffed, feeling a little more confident about this. 'Another bit of old plaster from Mary and Joseph's palace, that if it were reassembled would dwarf the Tower of London.'

'It isn't,' said Gilles, shaking his head. I peered at him. He seemed to be quite serious. 'Nothing like that. Legend again, but it seems that the *Mandylion* was walled up somewhere in Edessa, leaning against a tiled wall. And the tile it leaned on received the image of the face of Christ.'

'But ...' I began to feel the ground beneath my feet, so secure for the past two years, begin to tremble.

'These are the True Images, Petroc,' he was saying, 'the ...'

'Yes, I know all that,' I said, worried now. 'The Veronica, the *vera icon*: True Image. The holiest relics of all. These are things supposed lost, and yet someone – a very strange person, to be precise – has let us know they still exist. And, in fact, where to find them.'

'And the most important thing of all: that their owner may not even know he owns them,' said the Captain. He folded the parchment and handed it back to me.

'Keep it,' I said. But he shook his head.

'I will take a copy,' he said, 'but you should keep it. It was entrusted to you for some reason – something to do with old Gregory, plainly, for it came from his physician. But ...'

'It makes a difference, does it not?' I said, brightly.

'A difference?' he cried, then he mastered himself. 'A difference, yes. Certainly. Ah ... perhaps, my lad, things are not as undone as they seem.' He kept rubbing his temples and staring at the little sheet of parchment.

'We will leave at once,' he decided. The ship was fitted up and ready, and it was the purest accident – a crewman had lost his hand while loading the cargo and a replacement had just been found – that he was here at all. If I would care to bathe and change my clothes, perhaps we could set off directly?

And so we left the shores of Italy. I embraced Gilles, and bid farewell to Iblis the horse, and to the surprise of us both I wet his soft snout with a couple of hot tears. I had grown extremely fond of the beast during the last few weeks. Poor Iblis! It is an onerous task to bear a man's weight at the best of times, but I had added to his burden with my incessant prattle, for I had not been alone and beyond human company for nigh on two years and found the solitude maddening. The horse suffered my life's tale a score times and more, not to mention my ramblings on birds, beasts, food, theology and, relentlessly, Anna's death. If a horse can feel relief, no doubt Iblis did when he learned he would be making his slow way back to Rome in the company of other horses, with no bereaved, raving madman bouncing atop his patient back.

The sweep of the oars and the cracking of the sail was strange music to me that afternoon, for I had barely drawn breath before we were aboard the ship *Stella Maris* and the master had ordered all lines let go. Galleys can be quick when the wind and tide favour them, and soon the white beacon of the Roman arch had slipped away behind and we were striking out across the ruffled waters towards Dalmatia. In a few days we were running south past Zadar and the Captain was pointing out the nameless little isle where Sir Hugh de Kervezey had undergone his strange transfiguration into Saint Exuperius of blessed memory, and a week later we passed the hog's back of Hrinos and came close enough to the high peak of Koskino Island that we could hear the cicadas and smell the sage and thyme of her hillsides. There was the horseshoe bay guarded by its three windmills, and there the tiny white huddle of the village, sleeping beneath its lemon trees. I felt a little strange, and fancied that the scars on my thigh, where a crossbow bolt had pierced me the night I had been hunted across those barren hills, were aching in some kind of sympathy with the place, but later I decided I had imagined it. But nonetheless I felt better when Koskino's mountain had sunk, in its turn, into our wake, and back into my past.

'I fear to tell you anything of Constantinople,' said the Captain, when I pressed him. He had been there, he said, but would not tell me more. 'If you find it one way, you will think I embroidered my account and be angry, and if another, you will say I was too mean and sparing and again I will be blamed,' he laughed. 'It is a very great city, as great or greater than Rome itself, for it is her sister. But time has used her very harshly, and ...' He shook his head and sighed. 'Perhaps her fortunes have changed,' he said, 'although all news that comes from there says otherwise. I have no expectations, so that I will not be confused and diverted from our task when we arrive and things are not as I thought they would be.'

It was all very mysterious, but I could extract no more from him. Instead he laid out our mission. We were required to secure the Crown relic and also to verify it, negotiate the transfer with Emperor Baldwin's Regent, and await the arrival of the French King's emissaries. Our key to the Chapel of Pharos was Pope Gregory's decree, which I handed over to the Captain with huge relief. Not for the first time, I pondered the strangeness of our lives. How could it be that we, who practised nothing but deception, find such willing accomplices amongst the great of this world, and how could it be that we now had the complicity of the Holy Father himself? And our business now was with an emperor, no less, or at least his Regent. No matter that the empire was a sham, an old sheep with its throat already in the wolf's jaws. What cared I for such distinctions? I was still, at heart, a shepherd's son, and my fortune was becoming such a thing that I would never have dared imagine in my deepest summer daydream. But the Captain was expecting trouble. What had been a simple job had become not so simple, for now we would have to persuade the emperor's barons that King Louis' offer would be worth the waiting, and that they should not be sniffing around in their treasure house yet.

So I burned with anticipation as we inched our way across the Aegean into the teeth of those Greek breezes that blow clean and steady, driving salt into the skin and making every piece of rigging hiss like a nest of snakes, but which barely ruffle the surface of the water. Our oarsmen sweated and groaned, but I tucked myself into the bows each day and dreamed of Constantinople. I had heard so much of the city from Anna that I could all but walk a maze of her streets in my mind, which was a little strange in that Anna herself had never set foot there, for her family had gone into exile long before her birth. Nevertheless, for her – as for all Greeks – it was the navel, the lodestone of her world, the true Rome, of which the great city I had just left was a pale, barbarian, and heretical counterfeit. But further, I still clung to the notion that I might find some answer there to the riddle of her death, though I had no idea how that might come about. So I burned to see Constantinople for myself, and as we at last put Samothrace behind us and inched into the great passage of the Hellespont, and when we burst out into the Sea of Marmara beyond, even my dreams had become infected with the place. My night-self inhabited a landscape of vast buildings: gigantic cathedrals shimmering with gold and gems, statues and monuments of pure marble rearing like great phantoms from amongst palaces sheltered by gilded roofs. And the people of this dream city were giants too: Constantines and Justinians, grave and terrible; white-clad empresses; warriors in the image of the Angel Michael and Saint George with flaming swords and armour of golden scales. And around every corner, someone with Anna's face. Sometimes this sprite fled from me, sometimes she beckoned me into some dark and secret place, but always I awoke as my hand reached for her.

So I was in a ferment when the cry finally came from the top of the main mast: 'Constantinople!' Yesterday the *Stella Maris* had rounded the island of Marmara and sailed into a placid inland sea, and I knew that we were almost at our destination. But according to the crew we were still a good twenty sea leagues away, and all that day we sailed towards a bank of heat shimmer that revealed nothing. Now, straining my eyes through the golden haze of morning I saw nothing, then a line of low hills that seemed to close off the way ahead, still many leagues off.

'There is the Long Wall,' said the Captain, coming to my side. I followed his outstretched arm and saw a great fortification snaking down to the water's edge. It was high and strong, and punctuated by sturdy battlements and towers, but looking closer I saw it was all abandoned, and that vines and small trees had taken root in its cracks. The land on either side of it seemed deserted too. There was no one abroad, and the farms were empty of people and animals. The fields stood fallow and the vineyards were choked with weeds. A pack of wild dogs was just visible on the long white beach. This had been rich land once, a garden of men, for every slope was terraced and the olive trees grew thickly. As the rowers bent into their work and the breeze, our friend for once, fluttered out of the north-east and gave a breath of life to the sails, we began to make headway, and by midday I could make out a blackness on the skyline which, with agonising slowness, resolved itself into the shapes of buildings. We had passed a small town that had seemed populated, although much of it was clearly ruined. The wind blew steadily, and was heavy with the scent of rotten fruit, for it was the end of summer and there was no one to harvest the great garden. It soon became cloying, and I pictured swarms of wasps consuming the bounty that men now ignored. When I asked the Captain what had caused all this desolation, he scratched his nose wearily.

'The Franks,' he said simply.

'But this is their kingdom – I mean, their empire!' I said, amazed.

'Such are the Franks,' he said.

'But why destroy it all?'

'It was not the Franks alone who did this. There has been war here – incessantly, really, for many score years. But the Franks aided and abetted the wreckers then, when they did not help. And now they are poor and incompetent. The good people who farmed this land, and who held it, are dead or driven off. Some remain, and they are harried and repressed by their new Frankish masters, who have set themselves up here in the manner they were used to at home, over folk they despise and do not understand. So it was in my land also.' He fell silent.

'But we are Franks too – at least to the Greeks,' I said carefully.

'That is true. We wear Frankish skins,' the Captain replied, his mouth twisted in disgust. 'But underneath ...' He spat over the side. I understood. Michel de Montalhac, as he watched the desolated lands drift by, and smelled the scents of neglect and decay, was doubtless seeing his own country. A crusade had laid waste to it, as it had to this country, and his folk had been destroyed or enslaved. I thought of Anna and how her face would tighten with rage whenever she spoke of the crusaders who had taken Constantinople – 'Dandolo's wolves', she had called them, when she was feeling generous. More often she would begin to swear in dense, rich Greek which I could not – perhaps dared not – translate. At such times I felt she saw my Frankish skin and not the man beneath; but then, I was no Greek, after all. The gulf between East and West, barbarian and Roman, Latin and Greek would yawn darkly, but always to be bridged, in the end, with kind words and a lover's touch. But now, as I was slowly realising, I had crossed that gulf. I was in Anna's world now, and I was a stranger.

The sun was almost setting as the horizon finally resolved itself into shapes that revealed the hand of man. A low spit of land jutted down from the north. It seemed hunch-backed, but as we pulled closer I saw that the hump was a great building, and I knew at once that I beheld the Hagia Sophia.

229

Now we were passing more great fortifications on the banks of the sea, and these were manned in earnest, although they too were beginning to crumble. The water was growing busy: fishing boats were passing us, heading out to their night-time hunting grounds. I saw many great ships of trade: galleys like ours, and round-bottomed northern ships too. And here and there, prowling like slow but dangerous beasts, ships of war cruised or rode at anchor. A pilot had sailed out in a fast little Greek skiff, and now he and the Captain argued loudly over some complication wrought by the harbour-master. The oarsmen were cursing as they were told this instant to speed up, the next to slow down. I was enjoying the spectacle and turned my back on the approaching city for a while. But then a particularly loud cry from the pilot's mate, who had taken up his position in the bows and was cursing some unfortunate fisherman, made me turn back. Nothing – not Anna's talk, certainly not my own dreams – could have prepared me for what I saw.

The sun was setting behind us, and every brick, every roof-tile of the city before my eyes was bathed in honeyed light. It picked out towers, steeples, domes, turrets, balconies, columns, flying flags and gonfalons, proud standards. And everywhere the gorgeous light was swallowed by black hollows of ruin. The city, as I have said, stands upon a promontory, and we were sailing around it, out of the broad Sea of Marmara and into a narrower estuary, the Golden Horn. From Anna I had learned that, like Rome itself, Constantinople was built on seven hills, but they are low and the great mass of Hagia Sophia looms over everything. The waterfront I saw now stretched away seemingly for miles in either direction, and was studded with jetties and wharfs that in their turn were crowded with ships and boats of every size. But beyond the wharfs something was terribly amiss. As, puzzled, I let my eyes roam from left to right and back again, I saw a mighty wall, high and strengthened with towers and battlements. But it was the ghost of a wall, for it was much breached and here and there it had been smashed as if with a giant's hammer. Beyond it, where the ground began to slope upwards, I began to make out great buildings, or rather their shells. They stood, some roofed, some open to the skies, like the ruins of Rome; save here it was plain that these buildings had been in use until recently, and not abandoned in some remote antiquity. Gutted hulks stood at intervals, and between them lay open spaces, which by the way they lay in shadow and ate up any light that fell upon them I realised were nests of ruin, tumbled and burned wastes of stone and charred wood. The ruined buildings were large and monumental, still clad with the remnants of marble. Some were roofed like Roman temples of the old times and some were domed in the Greek manner. Closer to hand, and standing proud and clean, was an edifice that stood out from its fellows in its newness and the resounding strangeness of its architecture.

It was not so strange really, merely a large church of the sort one might find in any well-to-do country town in Italy. It was new-built, and the ashlar of its walls gleamed, as if to confirm that here was a building that truly deserved the attentions of the setting sun. But it appeared to have no relation whatsoever to the tottering piles of stone that surrounded it. For my first sight of Constantinople had reminded me of nothing less than a rotten old jawbone, detached from its skull and mouldering alone in some charnel house. And this Frankish church – for I suddenly had no doubt it was exactly that – seemed like a new tooth that, miraculously, obscenely, had sprung up amid the death and decay. Now that we were drawing closer, I saw more new buildings: here a campanile, there a strong-house with the fish-tail crenellations I had seen often in my crossing of Italy. The banners that flew everywhere were all Italian, too. I saw the lily of Florence, the white cross and red field of Pisa, and everywhere, seemingly vying for every high place, the lions of Venice and Saint George of the Genoese. Our own ship had run up a gonfalon which held a cross of gold on red, with crosses in the four corners, and I saw this device echoed here and there, on one great building away to the north, and another, huge and much knocked about, just to the south. I had been wishing with all my heart that Anna could have been with me, but all of a sudden I felt profoundly grateful that she had not lived to see this. For over the whole city, from a mast atop the titanic dome of the Hagia Sophia, the crossed keys of Saint Peter, blazoned on a huge white banner that flapped like an ogre's bedsheet, proclaimed their dominion.

Being an Apulian ship and therefore owned and manned by supporters of the emperor, the *Stella Maris* docked at a Pisan wharf, which the captain called a *skala*. The Pisans were in those times allied with the emperor, unlike the Genoese and Venetians, although I noticed that the various communities seemed to live all mixed together here. How strange it was that the poisonous division between supporters of emperor and pope, or Ghibellines and Guelfs as they called themselves, was causing war and murder back in Italy, but here in Greece it seemed to hold little weight. Probably, I told myself, they were all too busy making money to kill each other. It was getting dark, and rather than cast about for a suitable inn, the Captain decided to accept the harbour-master's offer of hospitality and put up for the night at the Pisan trading-house to which our wharf was attached. There were many of these houses, all with their *skalai*, packed tightly between the water and the walls, and as the dinner hour approached fires and lamps were being lit up and down the shore. I was impatient to enter the city itself, but as the Captain pointed out, we would be better served by good food and a peaceful sleep. Tomorrow we would find our own lodgings, and seek an audience at the palace. And the Pisans were so friendly, and their food smelled so inviting, that it was far easier not to resist. So we were shown to a room, plain but comfortable, and later shared a meal that, after five weeks of ship's food, could just as well have been manna. The dishes were so savoury, and the company so lively, that it almost seemed churlish to wonder why, after an evening spent at the very centre of the Greek world, I had yet to hear a single Greek voice. But I set these thoughts aside and let the food – richly spiced with pepper and other spices fit to ransom a prince – and the good Tuscan wine lull me, and as the Captain had hoped, we both slept like the dead. But before I laid down my head I put my head out of the small window and craned to look up at the great walls of the city. A little moonlight glanced off the cut stones and sank into the gashes and wounds of siege and time. They had not kept out the robbers, these walls, and perhaps it was their penance to be reduced to a home for ivy and pigeons. Well, tomorrow I too would be inside, yet one more Frankish robber. I let out a sigh, and it was echoed by the breeze stirring in the caper shrubs that hung, lax and abandoned, from the stones above. This city is no longer defended, it seemed to whisper: it bowed down long ago. Downcast, I took myself off to bed, and thought troubled thoughts of Anna before sleep took me.

Chapter Fifteen

The next morning brought fog. It was chilly, and the Captain and I, accustomed as we were to the sun, shivered as we broke our fast with our Pisan hosts. Then we set out for the palace. We had nothing but our packs, and the Pisans offered us a servant to carry those to the inn. To be polite we accepted, but not the offer of a guide. The Captain could find his way, he said, and we set out. The dour mood of last night had vanished with the morning's fog, which the sun had indeed chased away, and I was fairly skipping as I followed the Captain along the foot of the walls, winding through a maze of lodgings, warehouses, offices and churches, some of which were still being built, and all of which hummed and sometimes raged with Italian voices, the sing-song dialects of Genoa and Venice, Pisa, Florence, Siena and a babel of others I did not recognise. It was here I heard my first Greek spoken, though the speakers were labourers working on one of the new Frankish churches, whose campanile was beginning to rise above the level of the sea walls. Soon afterwards we came to a gate, much broken down and guarded by sleepy-looking men-at-arms in the imperial red and gold livery, leaning on their spears in the shade and gossiping with each other in French. They did not bat an eyelash at us. Thus I entered Constantinople.

The street we found ourselves walking down was almost empty save for a few ancient crones in dusty black clothes who regarded us with icy indifference. As soon as we had passed through the gate I knew I was inside the rotten jawbone I had imagined from the boat. The houses around us, once grand, were in a horrible state of disrepair. Some were roofless, the sun shining through their upper windows. Those that were intact looked half occupied, with some windows boarded up and others showing a ragged curtain or a drape of tattered laundry. Every wall showed evidence of fire. I have said the street was near empty, but only of people: stray dogs, emaciated and flayed by mange, scurried everywhere, and the air was rank with their piss and turds. We hurried on under the impassive eyes of the old women. Turning a corner, we entered a wider thoroughfare, but the same neglect and ruin was in evidence here also. The buildings were high and flat-fronted, in the main, with many tiers of round-arched windows. They stood side by side so that often the street was a seamless wall of stone. The effect was majestic even now, and more than a little sinister. This had not been a city like the ones back home, I knew now, with their ramshackle houses of wood and mud all leaning on each other's shoulders like a congregation of drunkards. And it had paid a terrible price for its superiority.

Thus we made our way, mostly in silence, although the Captain would every now and again point out some landmark, or what had once been such, for invariably it was now a gutted shell. I could not believe how empty the streets were. This had been a city of a million people, and now ... There were a few more old people here, and children with matted hair and dirty faces played in doorways and chased the dogs. I shook my head in dismay, but all of a sudden the Captain grabbed my shoulder and jerked me against the nearest wall. There was a cacophony of barking and curses, and a great pack of mangy dogs hurtled past us, driven by a company of men-at-arms who marched towards us up the street, swords and spears clinking against chain mail, jeering and swearing at the few people who were abroad. The old folk retreated into their houses, crossing themselves in the backwards Greek fashion, but some of the bolder children fell into step with the soldiers, tugging on their surcoats and holding out their hands. A couple of them were rewarded with small coins, but one, a cheeky boy with great brown eyes who was skipping about in front of the man who looked to be the company's leader and chanting 'Please! Please!' in Greek, came too close and the man suddenly lashed out, sending him sprawling over the flagstones. The others laughed and, to my horror, marched right over him, trampling his little body heedlessly with their boots. I was about to drag him out of the way, but the Captain stopped me, and indeed the little one picked himself up, dusted himself off and limped away to his fellows, who surrounded him, cackling. Meanwhile the soldiers had drawn abreast of us, and the one who had trampled the child glanced our way and saluted us, a twisted smile on his boozy face. I was about to tell him what was on my mind, but again the Captain stopped me, and replied to the soldier's greeting with a haughty lift of his chin. The soldiers clattered away towards the sea, and left the street to the dogs, the children, and ourselves.

We walked on, but the children, in search of fresh diversion, began to tag along behind us. We had gone a few paces when I felt a tug on the hem of my tunic.

'Lordos! Lordos!' The voice was a hoarse squeak. I turned and looked down into the dust-streaked face of the little boy. He was around nine years old, I judged, and his hair was thick with dust. A thin trickle of blood ran from each nostril, and he had wiped it crosswise across his cheek.

'What do you want, little one?' I asked him gently, in the

Greek Anna had taught me. He stepped back in amazement.

'Coin, Lordos?' he asked again in Venetian. I pulled out a silver florin and and held it out to him.

'I am no lord,' I told him in Greek. He looked me up and down in disbelief, and I realised I was dressed in my finest Venetian clothes: short, point-sleeved tunic of white and black-striped silk; bronze silk surcoat with broad blue stripes, scalloped at the neck and hem with bronze ribbon; red woollen hose; saffron-coloured coif. I had my sword buckled on, and the knife hung next to my red leather purse. The boy snatched the coin and took a couple of hasty steps backwards.

'Who are you, then?' he asked me in Greek.

'*Kakenas*,' I told him. Nobody. He cocked his head and regarded me for a moment with hooded eyes. Confusion and perhaps anger came from him like the heat of a fever: I could feel it. For a moment I thought he would spit at me, but instead he bit the florin and turned his blood-smeared face up to mine once more before turning on his heel and running back to his mates.

We walked on through one ruined street after another. The very air was suffused with an oppressive melancholy, as if the ruined buildings were breathing it out through their blackened skull-mouths.

'Where are all the people?' I asked quietly.

'They fled, some of them,' the Captain answered. 'Like Anna's people, to Anatolia, Epiros. Scattered. But many did not flee.' He pointed to an empty house. It had been quite grand once, red brick trimmed with marble that had been carved, around windows and door, into thick, leafy vines. Now fat stains of soot stretched up from each blank cavity where a fire had once raged. 'They died in their houses, or in the streets. Or they were herded into the churches and butchered like vermin.'

'Raped on the altars.' It was something that Anna always said, and I always thought it a bit of hyperbole. Now I saw it must have happened just as she had told it.

'Yes, then hacked to pieces. The crusaders hated the Greeks. Called them effete and soft, corrupted. Do they look effete now?'

'Indeed they do not.'

'This place ... thirty-three years ago, in my lifetime, this place, this Constantinople, was the centre of the world,' he went on. He was angry, I realised: very angry, though not with me. 'It was the greatest city man has ever known. Look! This street is empty, save for that beggar, those children. That woman – is she a whore, or simply a pauper? There used to be a million people teeming here. A million! These walls would have swallowed every soul in London, Rome, Paris, all of them at once without a trace. Doge Dandolo and his crusaders looted and burned until there was nothing left. I was born the year the crusaders came here, but I have talked to old men who remember the city that was—'

'And Anna, too,' I interrupted. 'To her it was a city of gold, a miracle.'

'And now it is a skeleton.' The Captain kicked a lump of charred brick, which clattered hollowly into an empty doorway.

'That is what I saw from the ship, as we came in last night,' I told him. 'A jawbone, all rotten. And the merchant churches like fat worms feasting on the decay.'

At last we found ourselves in another open space, a public space, surely, but one that now held no one who might be described as public. It did, however, contain a large number of armed men, who loafed about, polished weapons or fed horses. On the far side rose a vast wall of stone and brick. It rose in a series of arches, one row atop the other, to a tumult of domes, battlements and spires topped with Greek crosses, two-headed birds and other arcane devices. Many flags and pennants fluttered: the gold and red of the empire, of course, and others I did not recognise. As we walked closer I saw that we were approaching a gate in an outer wall, that was in itself as complex as the palace – for so it was – that it shielded. It extended out of sight on both sides, swallowed up in other buildings or in heaps of rubble, to which, in many places, it had itself been reduced. Now at last we were among crowds, and it became apparent that these men did not follow the practices of the effete Greeks they despised. For they stank. The square gave off a rancid stench of unwashed flesh, manure and horse-piss. It was almost as foul as the air on the rowing deck of the *Stella Maris*.

Around us, uncouth voices croaked and snarled in French, Flemish, Catalan, Piedmontese. I guessed it was some regular gathering – pay day, perhaps – for the soldiers were bored but restless. The bulk of them I took to be mercenaries – for what else would Catalans be doing in Greece? – but here and there I saw white surcoats stitched with the rough cross of the crusader. Old Pope Gregory had said a crusade had been preached, and evidently a few, at least, had heeded the call, but their fresh, younger faces were at odds with the scarred, scowling countenances of their fellows. Those men lolled about, many of them perched on plinths of stone that were dotted about regularly, and which I guessed had held statues or monuments that had been looted or destroyed. And indeed I glimpsed a headless marble figure that had evidently been part of a fountain or some such. Now it lacked, not only a head, but one arm and much of its upper torso. By way of compensation, though, it had been endowed with a gigantic, virile cock sketched crudely in charcoal. Horses were tethered to one of its legs. The streets we had walked to get here had been more or less clean, save for the detritus of ruin, for there was no one to foul them. Here, though, the ordure lay in heaps all around, and the stone pavement of the square was all but hidden by a thick layer of dung and other filth. It was a barnyard, a midden. The Franks had been here thirty-three years, and they had yet to find a broom.

The gate, in keeping with the gargantuan scale of the palace, was towering, and wide enough for a company of horsemen to ride through six abreast. It had been much hacked about lower down, and was charred and streaked with the memory of fire. Many of its iron fittings were bent and buckled. And yet it was still formidable, and at this hour it was shut fast.

A pair of smart-looking guards in leather hauberks, with gold crosses upon their red surcoats, came noisily to attention as we stepped out of the reeking throng and approached them. For the second time that morning I remembered that we were dressed like Frankish lords, and felt somewhat smug when the guards wiped the surliness from their faces. I allowed the Captain to take the lead, and when one of the guards stepped forward to ask our business, he flourished the letter with the gigantic papal bull under the man's nose. In the wink of an eye the gate was hauled open a crack by unseen hands, and we had been ushered through into an immense courtyard. The guard indicated a second gateway, and we set out across the yard. In a way this place was the exact opposite to the square outside. Here the marble flagstones were swept clean, and the statues still upon their plinths, although here again only a couple still retained their heads. It was clean and orderly, but I had the sense that, when once such a majestic yard would have had dozens of servants devoted to its upkeep, now it was maintained by one tired man. The trees

– for oranges, olives, bay laurels and even palms grew here and there – were dead or dying, although their fallen leaves had been removed. Swarms of brown sparrows and pigeons crowded the dry branches and filled the air with their shrill riot. It was as bright and cheerful a scene as I had yet found in Constantinople, and yet it was a ruin nonetheless, and here, as outside, there were phantoms.

'Well, gentlemen, greetings indeed!' said Narjot de Toucy, looking up in surprise from the pope's letter. He beckoned over a tall, thickset man who was standing against a nearby column. 'This is my lord Anseau de Cayeux, Regent of the Empire of Constantinople. Anseau, these chaps have a letter from the pope.'

It was our turn to be surprised, and we both backed away and made the lowest, courtliest bows in our repertoire.

'Jean de Sol, at your service, Excellency,' intoned my companion.

'Petrus Zennorius,' I echoed. The man laughed good-naturedly.

'Nay, nay, good people. You are most welcome here. We do not stand on a great deal of ceremony, as you have no doubt observed.' He laid a friendly arm across the shoulders of Narjot de Toucy, and the two barons regarded us amiably. They were quite unlike, these two: de Toucy was hollow-cheeked and crow-like, with coarse black hair and a short-cropped soldier's beard; de Cayeux was somewhat florid, with a lion's mane of golden curls. He appeared to be running to fat, but I saw that this was not the case. His jolly appearance was deceptive: what seemed to be fat was muscle, and his happy blue eyes were piercing.

We had arrived at this temporary throne room after much peregrination through the labyrinthine and decaying corridors of the Bucoleon Palace. Beyond the great doors we had entered another courtyard, this one shaded and smelling of cat-piss and wet moss, and through another gateway into a high hall that receded into shadow in a series of pillared archways. Here again the cats had been diligent, and although large Flemish tapestries were hung here and there on the walls they were dwarfed by the great height of the ceiling, and, when I cast my now expert eye over one as I passed by, I saw that it was old and not of any great quality: no more than would have graced the dining-chamber of an Antwerp burgomeister of the middle rank. The tapestries tried to mask the faded murals and damaged mosaics that covered the walls, but seemed crude and ugly in contrast. For though the plaster was crumbling, and the mosaics had been stripped, I guessed, of their gold, where they still existed they yet possessed a hint of dignity, like the shred of life that lingers on the faces of the dead until the flesh has grown cold. As we made our way down this hall we came upon small groups of men who turned their heads and regarded us suspiciously as we passed by. They were French nobles and priests, mainly, to judge from their dress. We came to the end of the corridor to find ourselves at a locked door and a crossways: seeing people to our left we chose that road, but only by asking a legion of slack-faced serving lads had we found ourselves in this far-flung corner of the palace. I had long since lost track of how we had come here, although, thinking back, we might have passed the ancient throne room, a lofty cavern whose walls were faced with purple stone but whose ceiling had indeed caved in. Nothing but spiderwebs here now: spiders and dust.

I was beginning to wonder if one of the thousand locked doors we had passed hid the Pharos Chapel, and if its wonders were not already buried under tons of ancient roofing.

When we had at last found the guarded door we sought, we were ushered in, only to find that there was no throne to speak of, only a round-walled chamber with marble columns supporting a mercifully strong-seeming roof, around which a gaggle of men stood, talking loudly and idly picking at a table laden with silver trenchers of food. Silence fell abruptly as we were announced by a man we took to be the chamberlain, and all heads turned towards us. It was strangely like walking into a country tavern where you are not known. Finally the man with the black hair had stepped forward, gestured for our letter, and blinked with amazement. At once the hubbub was restored, the chamberlain had wandered away, and the Regent had come over to meet us.

Anseau de Cayeux studied the letter in silence. Nothing disturbed his placid face save a little twitch of one eyebrow. Then he murmured something into de Toucy's proffered ear. Their eyes met for a brief moment, then the Regent turned back to us.

'Jean de Sol, Petrus Zennorius. Your visit was unlooked for, but it comes as the answer to our prayers,' he exclaimed. 'We are ... the empire is suffering a small upheaval, temporary of course, and we cannot welcome distinguished guests as we would wish. This ...' he swept his arms around the low-ceilinged room in which we stood. 'These are somewhat sorry-looking quarters, but the roof collapsed in the throne room – fearful builders, the Greeks! – and in a month or two we shall be moving the court to the Palace of Blachernae. Shocking, really. But soon remedied!' And he threw back his golden head and laughed, as if all this – the palace, Constantinople, the empire itself – were nothing but a good-natured prank at his expense.

'Now, come and share our meal,' he finished, and with a familiar hand on our shoulders he steered us over to the table. Taking my lead from the Captain, who appeared entirely at ease, I accepted a goblet of wine and tore the leg off a pea-hen. The room might be shabby, I thought, but the dinner service was quite impressive: ancient silver and gold carved and hammered into scenes of gambolling animals and humans. I wondered how long it would be before it was sold off. Although the Regent and de Toucy were solicitous, the other barons held back, ignoring us or studying us with hooded eyes. Nervous, I tried to ignore them, and instead watched a tendril of carved ivy as it strangled a marble pillar.

'Where are you lodging, may I ask?' The Regent was asking a question.

'We arrived but yesterday evening, and stayed at the house of some Pisan merchants,' said the Captain. 'We shall take rooms in an inn close by here, God willing – our hosts recommended it.'

'An inn around here? Good Christ!' the Regent guffawed, then belched. 'Your merry Pisans must think you have a taste for knocking shops! Nothing wrong with that, nothing at all,' he added. 'But you are the emissaries of the Holy Father, and the King of France, no less. I do not think our local inns can provide you with the *milieu* that befits your station. You shall be our guests.' He held up a finger, mock-stern, and I knew we had no choice. My heart sank.

We ate and drank quite companionably, despite our somewhat frosty audience. The Regent was a jolly host, indeed, so jolly that I was quite surprised when he abruptly laid down his cup, signalled for a salver of water and washed his greasy hands.

'Now, let us speak in private,' he said, wiping his hands on a linen towel. We were led through a low door at the back of the chamber into a smaller room lined entirely in snow-white marble. There were a number of curious fittings jutting from the wall, and I guessed that this had been a bathing place once. Now, chests covered with heavy tapestry covers were pushed against the walls, and in the centre a stone-topped table stood on graceful iron legs fashioned to look like the limbs of a beast of prey. We were offered folding stools cushioned in bronze silk. De Cayeux, de Toucy and the chamberlain, a silent man with close-cropped grey hair, a large nose and pendulous earlobes, seated themselves across from us.

'Now, gentlemen, welcome again,' said the Regent, fulsomely. 'I trust your voyage here was easy? And you came from ... where, by the bye?'

'From Rome,' said the Captain.

'Ah, how superfluous a question that was!' said the Regent hurriedly. 'But your journey?'

'Was easy, certainly,' said the Captain. 'Is that not so, Petrus?' He turned to me, eyes signalling me to be alert.

'Indeed, although we caught a damnable headwind that blew against us right across the Aegean,' I agreed, and swallowed, hoping the Franks did not notice my dry mouth.

'And how do you find our city?' asked de Toucy. To my horror, I realised the question was intended for me. I opened my mouth like a codfish, then shut it again. What, by the excised tongue of Saint Eusebius, was I to say? My lords, your programme of destruction has been admirably efficient?

'The streets are wonderfully clean,' I blurted out. The barons' eyebrows shot ceilingwards. 'And ... perhaps that is an outward manifestation –' I took a breath – 'of the cleansing of the schismatic churches, and the saving of heretic Greek souls.' There. I seemed to be finished.

But the barons were smiling, and the chamberlain leaned forward and regarded me keenly. I saw that those long earlobes were robed in silvery down.

'A cleric?' he asked. I had the odd sense that, had he been a hound, his snout would have been carefully sniffing my clothes.

'Would that I had such a calling,' I gushed. 'No, no, I …'

'Master Petrus is a scholar,' said the Captain, smoothly. 'He is too modest: his learning is equal to his piety. This young man could have served Mother Church faithfully from within. For now, he chooses to do her work out in the world.'

'Would that I were as modest as that – but Master Jean is too kind. I am a bookworm, no more.'

'And yet you both look like soldiers,' said the chamberlain. 'De Sol – a Toulousian name?'

'Aquitaine,' said the Captain, crisply. 'My father held estates in Les Landes.'

'And I am Cornish,' I interjected.

'Indeed. Zennor?' De Toucy rolled the word on his tongue as if it had a taste he was not sure about.

'Hard by Falmouth. The most beautiful place on God's earth – save the Golden Horn, of course.'

'Quite. But you have a soldierly air – Hughues is right,' said the Regent. So the chamberlain was named Hughues.

'One may serve the Church with the sword as well as the Word,' I said.

'Amen! Amen to that, young sir,' said the Regent. 'It that were not so, the poncing schismatics would be fouling this great city as we speak. Piety keeps our defenders on the ramparts, but steel keeps the enemy at bay.'

'As to armed men,' the Captain said delicately, 'we were given to understand that the emperor is at this moment seeking to raise a great army.'

'Which brings us to business!' said the Regent, slapping the table with a meaty hand. 'Now. You bring a letter from the Holy Father, and yet you are not priests. You serve the interests of the King of France, yet you bear no accreditations. Forgive me if I sound churlish, but who precisely do you serve?' For the first time, the jovial face had acquired a hardness, almost imperceptible.

The Captain presented our mission as our hosts studied us with mounting interest. 'And Louis Capet will be immensely grateful,' he finished.

'Immensely grateful? In what way?' asked the Regent, grudgingly. His face was flushed, and he rubbed the stubble on his jaw as if something had bitten him there.

'In the only way that could possibly matter to your empire,' said the Captain.

'He would put a price on ...' spluttered the Regent, incredulously.

'Oh for Christ's sake, Anseau,' barked de Toucy impatiently. 'This is no time for your piety. Yes, dear men,' he said, turning to us. 'The gift is freely given, if we have your guarantee of the *immensity* of Louis' gratitude. Now enough talk. I am sure our guests would like to see what they have come so far to ... what did you say? Facilitate? Hughues, the key to the Chapel of Pharos, if you please.'

The chamberlain disappeared into the outer room, and returned momentarily with a great iron hoop upon which dangled a small silver key. The effect was comical, but then, I reflected, here in miniature was the predicament of Constantinople: the delicacy of one race skewered upon the hard brutality of another. We followed the Franks – so I now thought of all these folk, forgetting yet not forgetting that I was one of them, for if I was their brother by what was writ in our blood, in my soul I was utterly different – out through the makeshift throne room and into the dead belly of the palace beyond. The two barons seemed almost as lost as the

Captain and I, but Hughues strode confidently ahead. We passed the wrecked chamber with the walls of purple stone and plunged down a wide flight of stairs, then another and another. The palace seemed to be built in tiers that spilled down the hillside towards the sea, and as we descended, so the structure became damper and more decayed. Finally Hughues put his shoulder to a fine wrought-iron gate which shrieked open and painted his white robe with rust. I smelled burning, and in another pace we rounded a corner and entered a high domed chamber. Four guards in imperial livery crouched, playing dice, under a guttering lantern which, although it was broad daylight outside, was the only light in that place. We might have been deep beneath the earth for all I could tell. The guards sprang up and the chamberlain seemed to be about to launch some harangue, but de Cayeux put them at their ease with a lordly wave. Hughues stooped to fit the little silver key into a plain door set into a narrow, round-topped arch. The lock snicked neatly, and the door swung inward on silent hinges. The three Franks crossed themselves and prayed silently, eyes screwed shut. The Captain and I hurriedly imitated them. I looked beyond the door, but there was nothing but a velvety darkness.

Chapter Sixteen

The air was thick and stale, but the clear scent of frank-incense cut through like a trickle of icy water. One of the guards had lit a taper for the chamberlain, and now he held it before him and stepped over the threshold. Anseau de Cayeux followed, head bowed reverently. The Captain and I hung back politely, but Narjot de Toucy stepped behind us, and we had no choice but to go on into that dead air.

Hughues was touching his flame to racks of candles that stood on either side of the door. Light sprang up, dim at first but growing like a bashful sunrise until the walls, the ceiling, the floor itself began to glow and to throw back the rich candlelight with the gleam of gold. For there was gold everywhere, save on the floor, which was all of dazzling white marble. At first I thought the walls were hammered sheets of the stuff, but as my eyes became accustomed to the light I saw that I beheld mosaics. Every inch of wall and of the columns that held up the domed roof was inlaid with tiny squares that my intelligence told me were glass but that my soul – for if ever a place called out to my soul, it was this chapel – saw as rubies, emeralds, precious metals, garnets. The walls were lined with portraits of standing figures, scores of them, all of them stern. Bearded prophets regarded us, shoulder to shoulder with warriors clad in ancient armour, angels wrapped in their wings or in fire, queens with tower-ing crowns, hollow-cheeked saints. I gasped, and backed into the Captain, who steadied me with a hand. Looking up, I saw that the little cupola in the ceiling bore the likeness of Our Lord, bearded, his face blankly serene, holding out his pierced hands. Either the air in that musty chamber had affected me, or the man who had made this image, far back in some unimaginably deep corner of time, had been possessed by some rare genius, for this Christ appeared, as I stared, to grow as vast as the sky, his arms stretching to embrace the horizon. I gasped.

'Rather extraordinary, isn't it?' said de Toucy blandly. 'Look at all that. The Greeks ... profligates, every one.'

At that moment I realised that this tiny chapel, with its encrustations of wealth and elaboration going back through long centuries to its birth at the hands of a Roman emperor, was a last clue to the tortured husk of the palace in which it lay. It must all have been like this once, I thought. Those halls would have been magnificent beyond imagining. The throne room ... I shook my head. It had been stripped, like crows and foxes strip a dead sheep. The big beasts had torn off the meat, and the little ones, the ants and maggots, had picked the bones until they gleamed. I remembered the words I had read in the history of the Sieur de Villehardouin: 'the lordly Palace of Bucoleon, a more magnificent building than had ever been seen before.' To my Anna, whose tales of this place came from folk who had known it well, it had been a wonder of the world. And in half a lifetime it had come to this. If raw stone had value, there would be nothing here at all. I wondered if the jolly Regent had already mortgaged it off to the lime-burners. I thought of the city outside. What legion of wonders had been sold off or wantonly destroyed? What glory had passed from the earth, never again to be seen by men's eyes? The air was growing heavy with the scent of beeswax, and my eyes wandered around the figures watching us from the walls, gazing at us through the windows of the past. The chapel itself seemed to be humming, as if we were inside a bell that had been struck a long, long time ago, but in whose metal the memory of the blow still resonated, a ghost of sound.

The chamberlain and the barons were picking their way through the columns towards a golden structure that loomed at the back of the room. I glanced at the Captain. He was watching them too, his eyes narrowed. I shook off my fancies. We were here on business. And without a doubt, every man who had set foot in here in the past thirty-four years had been on business too, like those three men now making a perfunctory genuflection before the altar.

'Here we are,' I muttered to the Captain, just to break the silence.

'And there, presumably, *it* is,' the Captain replied. 'Well, the hound sees the hare. Shall we go on?'

'View halloo,' I said faintly.

'That's the spirit,' said the Captain.

We walked forward, our feet clicking on the time-rounded marble tiles. In the Greek fashion, what I would have called a rood-screen – and doubtless Anna would have put me briskly to rights – formed a complete wall before the altar, pierced by three doors. This wall was populated by a host, nay, a regiment, of painted saints that thronged in tiers, row upon row. Here and there the panoply of age-darkened figures was interrupted by a patch of bare wood, where an icon had been pried out none too tenderly. But the Franks had gone through the central door into the well of darkness beyond, ignoring the paintings. A light flared, and first one candle, then a cluster of them began to flicker upon the altar. We passed through the narrow door in our turn, and stepped into a smaller space. It was a semicircle, and there were three small windows in the back wall, although two had been crudely bricked up and the third shuttered with a piece of slate behind an iron grille so that it admitted nothing but the most minute thread of daylight. There was no mosaic here. The plaster walls were painted black, purple, deep red, with here and there a gold line or band. But behind the altar the wall had been gilded, and from the floor to the apex of the ceiling rose a cross.

Our Lord hung there, His face fixed in as terrible and sorrowful an expression as paint and the hand of man has surely ever rendered. A crown circled His brow, an appalling thatch of murderous thorns that pierced and rent His flesh. The artist had known that blood would soak Our Lord's hair, and showed it limp and wet, clinging to temple and cheek. The body hung, the weight of death already dragging it earthwards, bones and sinews tearing where the nails had pierced the hands and meekly crossed feet. Christ's flesh was pale, almost snow-white, and seemed to hold its own faint luminescence. As the blood had flowed out, so light had crept in to fill the empty places.

Years of training in monastery and school had not prepared me for this. Nor had a lifetime of belief. And the utter loss of my faith, which had come upon me when I fled England, had left a great wound that, I now found, had not yet fully healed. For my first thoughtless impulse was to fall to my knees and cross myself, something I had not done in three long years, and my second was to puke. A burning gout of bile rose in my throat and I would have vomited at the foot of the altar had not some inner discipline, some strength I had not known lay in my possession, caused me to clamp my mouth tight shut and swallow. It was all over in an instant. The Franks doubtless approved my piety, and the Captain doubtless thought my acting skill worthy of emulation, for he too dropped to his knees and genuflected. I stood up and shook my head, trying to clear it. The oppressive stillness of the chapel was worse in this chamber, and the air was more dead. My head buzzed, and I shook it again. Then a loud clank brought me more or less to my senses. The chamberlain had dragged a large chest into the circle of candlelight, and was fiddling with the lock. Now I saw that the room was lined with such chests, some large, some very small. Some were ornate reliquaries dripping with gems, others plain wooden boxes. The one which Hughues was now working upon was black and banded around and about with many hoops of metal and studded with nails. It seemed to swallow the candlelight, for it had been coated with pitch long ago.

'Do we need a priest for this?' the Regent asked querulously. De Toucy shrugged, and Hughues shook his head.

'Not if we don't touch it.'

'Carry on then, man!' said de Toucy impatiently. The chamberlain went back to the lock, which finally opened with a sound like the snapping of bone. He scrabbled for a purchase on the smooth pitch-covered wood, and with a barely stifled oath managed to heave up the lid. As one we craned forward, like so many peasants at the summer fair, straining for a first look at some two-headed piglet.

There was nothing to see at first, nothing but a black cloth spangled with tiny golden stars. It was as if the chest contained the night itself, I thought, but then Hughues pulled it away to reveal the yellow shimmer of tarnished silver. With a grunt he set his feet like a wrestler, leaned forward, and heaved out a large box. It was evidently quite heavy, for he winced as he set it down on the floor. The Captain dropped reverently to his knees, and I did the same. The Frankish barons darted quick looks at each other, but followed suit, and de Cayeux crossed himself fervently. I regarded the box. It was a cube of silver, somewhat battered with age, its corners rounded and with a dent or two here and there. In fine gilded relief, figures with the delicate poise of ancient carvings I had seen in Rome acted out the Passion. On the lid, a calm Christ, looking young and unconcerned, hung from a slender cross. Hughues bent and kissed the metal, then carefully lifted the lid and handed it to the Regent, who accepted it reluctantly, as if it were burning hot. Then he stepped back, and gestured us over to the box. We rose, knelt again, crossed ourselves reverently, and peered in.

Something unfathomably old and horrible nestled down amongst the folds of stained linen. Jet black, a mass of thick and wickedly curved spines, it seemed to reach up towards the dim light like a crippled spider. The spines twisted about each other in a whorl. It was a blighted flower that had no centre. I thought of sea urchins and the teeth of night-terrors. At the same time I had the overwhelming urge to reach for it with my hand, which I resisted with difficulty. I looked at the Captain. He had gone very white, and had an odd half-smile on his lips that could as easily have signified pain as amusement. The barons and the chamberlain, I noted, had retreated and stood, backs pressed against the wall. The Regent fidgeted, his body twisted with unease. Again I had the urge to plunge my hand into the midst of the thorns, imagining them snag and burrow into my flesh, closing around my wrist like the jaws of a mantrap. I shuddered. The Captain must have felt it, for he stood up quickly and took two brisk steps backwards.

'My lords, I have no reason to doubt the authenticity of this holy thing,' he croaked.

I rose too. My legs felt weak, and I felt sick again. Christ in His agony loomed over us, and the ghastly Crown bristled at my feet, sucking the candlelight from the air. And then

I remembered the *Inventarium* I had first read that day in Viterbo. It had been nothing but a list then: how had the Captain referred to it? A stock-in-trade. And yet now I was in the storeroom, and I knew what the boxes that littered the floor held: the holy Lance, Christ's Shrouds and Burial Cloths, the vinegar-soaked Sponge, the Chain. That was what vibrated in the close air: it was torment, and death.

'Would you care to see more?' De Toucy had paced to the centre of the chamber and was peering at a stack of chests. 'Hughues, what have we here?'

'Narjot! In Our Lord's sweet name, please! This is not a larder, man!' It was the Regent, and his voice was full of pious indignation.

I could have sworn that the chamberlain and de Toucy rolled their eyes at one another. The baron shrugged, and Hughues busied himself with the lid of the silver box. De Cayeux made a small hiss of displeasure and came over to where the Captain and I stood. He gave the Crown a wide berth.

'You do not wish to see any more at this time, do you, gentlemen?' he asked. By the way he kept glancing over our shoulders I could tell he was anxious to leave. The Captain smiled and rubbed his jaw thoughtfully.

'It is no secret that the wonder we have just beheld is but one of many such in this chapel,' he said. The Regent's face fell. 'The Head of the Baptist, I believe?' the Captain went on. 'The Robe of the Virgin herself?'

'Yes, yes, and more, much more,' blurted de Cayeux. 'But surely you are both tired. Surely . . .'

'You have a list, of course,' said the Captain, implacably. 'His Majesty King Louis has an interest that does not necessarily end at the holy Crown.'

The Regent, well and truly impaled on the hook of

greed, writhed. Strong and vital as he was, he was plainly unmanned. This place seemed to have the same effect on him as on me, although where my discomfort stemmed from my loss of faith, I guessed that for the Regent, piety and a guilty conscience – both beasts with sharp teeth – were gnawing his insides. I felt a tiny prick of sympathy for the man, then stifled it.

'Yes, a list … I believe such a thing exists,' I said. De Cayeux gave a sort of whimper and ducked through the door. We followed. He stalked up the central aisle, then halted and turned to face us. He had mastered himself.

'There is an inventory, to be sure. I would be delighted for you to see it, and …' He dragged a sweaty hand through his curls. 'And I will order a copy made, for His Majesty the King.'

'That will be excellent,' said the Captain. He turned, genuflected a final time towards the altar, and strolled to the Regent's side. 'Such wonders,' he said, shaking his head in a fine parody of ecstatic disbelief. 'I never thought to see such a thing. That these unworthy eyes …'

'Indeed! It haunts me, this … that is to say, the responsibility of guarding the relics of Our Lord's Passion is an honour that I never thought would rest on my shoulders,' said de Cayeux. He had reverted to his blustering tone, but I knew he had revealed to us a glimmer of truth. What mortal man would not be haunted by that terrible thing? But those two men who still pottered around in the chamber behind us like pantrymen clearly were not, and many more like them had stripped a holy city of its wonders as one might skin a rabbit. The Regent was evidently cut from more delicate cloth, as far as his immortal soul was concerned, at least. Leaving them to their devices, he ushered us out to where the guards were waiting with their smoking lantern.

'Dear visitors, I must get back to my affairs. But I insist you shall be our guests tonight, and as long as you stay in this city.' He turned and barked through the chapel door: 'Hughues!'

The chamberlain's grey head popped up behind the altar, looking rather spectral in the dim light. He saw the Regent beckoning impatiently and disappeared, to emerge with de Toucy. The two men hurried about, blowing out candles, and finally left the chapel, their clothes reeking of soot. Hughues was commanded to show us to our new quarters, and the Regent, with a final bow, hurried away down the ruined hall, de Toucy following behind. There was anger there, if I was not mistaken. And now the chamberlain pocketed his key and regarded us, buzzard-like. He scratched his grey stubble with a yellowed nail and sniffed thoughtfully.

'Now. Where shall we put you?' he mused aloud. I looked around at the ravaged walls and shuddered. Where indeed?

In the event, our rooms were not so very horrible, which was fortunate, as we were to make them our home for the next two months. They were two flights up and faced south, out over the Bosphorus towards the shores of Asia. We were in another part of the palace from the Regent's throne room, and it took all our navigating skills to find our way to and from our lodgings to the state-rooms. There were other folk living around us, some in some style, others in more straitened circumstances. Perhaps it was the only section of the wrecked complex that was fit for habitation, for it had the air of a boarding-house, albeit a noble one. I did not know where the Regent had his rooms, but I recognised several of the barons from his court. They too lodged on our hallway, and every time I saw one of them, haughty or sometimes harried, toing and froing from the throne room, I could not help but reflect on the tenuous nature of this empire's heart.

Below us was another courtyard, clean-swept but mouldering, in which a party of stone statues held an eternal conference. Perhaps they were comparing their various dismemberments, or bemoaning the state of their home. In any event they were silent neighbours, although when the moon shone down upon them they seemed to gain some measure of life, an odd revenant tremble that made them kin to the fading, gouged faces of the frescoes and mosaics inside the palace. For although the Bucoleon was all but deserted in most of its vast area, its half-looted decorations kept watch. There were eyes everywhere, and if they were but paint and coloured glass, still they observed our mortal comings and goings, and judged them sternly.

The rooms themselves were pleasant. They were dry, their ceilings were firm, and the walls were painted gaily with flowering trees and vines, gambolling animals and happy birds. My chamber had three high-arched windows and slender stone columns that ended in carved thistle-leaves. I had a gigantic bed and linen that was changed tolerably often, from which I guessed that a Greek held sway at least over the running of the household; and indeed I was right in that, for the serving girls who made up our beds, the pot-boys who brought our food, and the major-domo who called in every so often to make sure all was in order – all these folk were Greek. It was clear that no Frank would sully themselves with such demeaning work, although most of those who were not soldiers appeared to have no function at all in the working of the palace, and indeed often seemed half-starved. But the Greek servants were cowed, and if they were not, perhaps, slaves, they were not free.

The days passed slowly. The Regent was distracted by the crumbling state of his borders and was often away from the palace for days at a time with his barons, and so there was no one to negotiate with. We did some business with the Italian merchants on the Golden Horn, and I went out sometimes to walk through the city, but I found it too ominous and sad, and all but empty of the Greeks, Anna's own people. Those that remained were wan and half-starved, and cringed from the swaggering Franks like beaten hounds. I saw more than one man set upon and dragged away by the Regent's men-at-arms, and the city's gibbets were always heavy with stinking fruit. Once I came upon a naked corpse, so bruised that at first I took it for a Moor, sprawled in an empty doorway, and two smiling Franks walking away from it, eyes chilly as fox-lights. So most often I stayed in my chambers, reading the old Greek books that I would find amongst the rubble in deserted rooms. Winter was creeping in, and I found that Constantinople grows bitterly cold when the wind begins to blow down from the land of the Russians. One day, after I had been wandering through the palace in search of wood to burn in my fireplace, I returned to find the Captain waiting for me in the doorway to his own chamber.

At last there was, all of a sudden, much to occupy us. The Captain was already packing his bag. He would be taking ship back to Italy as soon as one could be found, and he hoped it would be in the next two days. A fast ship from Venice had brought a letter from Gilles, and the Captain handed it to me after first locking the door of his chamber.

'Jean de Sol and Petrus Zennorius, from Gilles de Peyrolles, Greetings,' I read.

I am in Venice, dubbed the Serene, although serenity is not, at present, a commodity of which I have much stock. I arrived in time to meet the envoys of His Noble Majesty et cetera, et cetera, Louis Capet, the two Dominican friars. They will be taking ship for Constantinople early next week. If the vessel I have chosen to carry this letter is swift, it should arrive a good while before them.

I hope with all my heart that it does. For Baldwin is not here in Venice. I have been to the offices of the Doge, and have searched high and low, but he is nowhere. My friend, I fear that Petroc is right: Querini is holding him. This Querini is a power in the city and I fear it is not safe for our company here. I am leaving for Rome, and on the way I shall make further enquiries. The Cormaran *I have sent to Alexandria under the guise of trade, but perhaps it will draw Querini's spies.*

The brothers will be with you a few days after you receive this. They are good men, and you are right to trust them. Can you trust anyone else? Dear friend, my suspicious heart tells me that there is more rottenness in Constantinople than even you no doubt suspect. I recommend that, when you receive this news, you will make haste back to Paris with the brothers. Could Petroc remain behind, and use his excellent wit to divine the true nature of this looming disaster?

Michel, I hope I shall see you anon. Safe journey, my friend.

Petroc, to you our usual advice: Pay Attention!

Farewell!

Gilles de Peyrolles

'It makes perfect sense, does it not?' I asked the Captain.

'Alas: it proves – finally, I should say, although I did not ever doubt you – that Baldwin is no longer his own master. Why would he avoid those whose sole intent is to cover him with gold? Baldwin is a fool, but not that big a one. Now there is hardly any point in us being here at all, in this forsaken city, and this ridiculous heap of a palace.'

'But the emissaries, these friars, are on their way,' I

protested. 'They are ready to offer gold for the relics in the Pharos Chapel.'

'I do not believe anyone here is really in a position to negotiate,' said the Captain.

'No. But what if ...' I began.

'What?'

'Nothing,' I said, deflated. 'I was thinking that if Querini is holding Baldwin in lieu of a mortgage, there might be a way for us to parlay the negotiations with Louis into ... no, it does not make sense.'

'No, go on,' said the Captain. 'I had not been thinking in terms of a mortgage, simply of hostages.'

'Well, if Louis has money to spend on the Crown, could not he still buy it? Then the barons would have money to ... to ransom, or redeem, rather, their sovereign.'

'Yes! But why should they, though?' the Captain said, shoulders sagging.

'Because he is their ruler, and because the pope will be, I don't know. Very angry. Excommunicate Constantinople, not that it would make much difference.'

'You might be right,' said the Captain, not sounding very convinced. 'No, you might be.'

'And we would collect our commission whatever happened,' I pointed out. He raised his head at that.

'A fine point!' he said. 'If money changes hands between Louis and the empire, we stand to collect. The nature of the transaction need not concern us. Patch, you have it!'

'But I cannot do this alone,' I told him.

'Nonsense. It will be plain dealing. The friars will talk money and the Regent, sick with gold-greed as he is, will agree to anything. You have the pope's decree, which gives you the authority to make the transaction. Then you need merely witness the contract, and your work is done. That you

261

can do alone,' he added. 'So. It is agreed. Gilles' information cannot be ignored. I will leave on the morrow – I have found a ship already, a fast Venetian galley with a master happy to be bribed – and you will stay and conclude this ridiculous affair. I am sorry to leave you here, though: this city is detestable.'

'It is,' I agreed, although I was blinking with surprise at the speed of all this. I did not let the Captain see, but I was shaken at the prospect of being alone here, and in the rafters of my mind the ghosts had awoken. I made my excuses soon after and went off in search of drink strong enough to put me to sleep.

I thought it would be easy enough to fetch a servant, but no means existed that I could see. I wandered through the rotting halls, through the pools of shadow that stretched between the rush lights in the walls, thinking to hail someone. But I had navigated my way almost to the Regent's state chambers before I chanced upon a serving wench hurrying on someone else's errand, a linen-draped trencher in her hands. I stopped her and she stared at me, terrified, great black-ringed eyes searching my face for who knows what dreadful portent. It was the girl who sometimes came to clean my room, I found, but it plainly heralded terrible things for servant girls to be hailed by Frankish men in this place, for she did not seem to recognise me, and I hastily spoke to her in Greek.

'Wait, dear one. I wish nothing more than a jug of wine. Do you know how I might come by such a thing?' And to show her I had no ill intent, I stepped away and held my palms up before me. She quivered like a mouse stranded in the middle of a threshing floor.

'The tap-room?' I tried again.

Again she shook her head. Indeed she shook all over, so hard that I feared she would drop her trencher. I was so appalled by the terror I was inflicting upon her that I had backed up hard against the wall.

'*Sto kalo, despoinaki*,' I told her: Go to the good, little queen. She goggled, and as I edged away she scuttled off in the opposite direction and disappeared into the gloom. Feeling more unnerved than ever, I kept walking until I came to the zone of light and life, where servants were running to and fro and where I could at last follow my nose to the kitchens. There I procured myself a great clay jug of wine from a fat German cellarman, who was quite disturbed to be collared by one of the quality in his own domain, but who promised me the best of his supply. By the smell of it, his supply was poor indeed, but it was not vinegar, and gratefully enough I set off again into the purgatory of deserted hallways.

I had already climbed the stairs and was, I thought, quite close to my chambers when I heard a muffled squeak and a thump behind me. Those sour shadows were rich with suggested horrors, and so I whirled around, to find empty gloom. This was a desolate quarter of the palace, where the walls were flaking and the rush lights few and far between. Doorways appeared at odd intervals, and side passages opened unexpectedly, sometimes giving on to stairways going down and sometimes up, although as far as I knew the upper floors were unsafe and uninhabited. The little hairs on my neck were prickling, and I shrugged away the gooseflesh, shuddering. This place gave me terrors far worse than come upon folk who wander in open places. The sullen dead of a thousand years had left their essences to flitter and blunder about like grey and dusty moths, so thick in places that you could almost smell their grave-cloth wings. I began to step backwards towards the nearest pool of light. Then the sound came again.

It was no ghostly sound after all. A man's low growl, the

click of metal on stone, and a woman's moan, stifled. I listened again. My hairs were still prickling, but now they were telling me of a different kind of fear. Was it fear, though, or pleasure? A tiny, sharp voice in my skull told me this was none of my business. I agreed with myself wholeheartedly, but then came another moan, more desperate than before. That was no woman: it was a child. I set down the wine and made my way towards the sound. My feet made no sound in the thick dust, and it was obvious from the rustling ahead that I was undetected. Now I could tell that it was coming from one of those sinister side passages. Back to the wall, I slid along until I was close enough to peer around the corner. I hesitated, for I was fearful that I had heard nothing but an illicit but happy coupling, and that my intrusion might be taken for prurience or worse. But I was no prude, and knew what love sounded like, and lust as well; and this did not sound quite like either. So, gritting my teeth, I leaned slowly, silently, into the darkness of the passage.

Nothing was visible at first save two pale stains of light, and for an instant my heart lurched at the threat of the unearthly, but then they resolved themselves into a pair of naked legs, white and sun-starved. A man seemed to be crawling up a narrow flight of stone stairs on his hands and knees, but there, in the almost black shadows beneath the collapsed tent of his clothing, was another pale smear: no more than two black holes in a weak halo of light, a ghost skull which, as I blinked, uncomprehending, became the great, terrified eyes of the little Greek serving girl I had met in the corridors below. She mewed like a kitten, and no louder, for a thick hand was over her mouth. The ink-black circles of her eyes were as hollow as those of a corpse, yet she gave a feeble jerk and the man who lay upon her slapped her head hard with the hand which was not stopping her breath.

Black hair, pale skin, dying eyes. I did not think, I did not consider, until my hands were caught in the man's clothes and I was wrenching him backwards. He was big but surprised, and I threw him against the wall, grabbed him and spun him towards me. I glimpsed thick, sandy hair and a dull, drunken Frankish face. Then I broke his nose with my forehead, a sound like a walnut cracked between stones; and as his blood ran down my neck I kneed him in the cods and swung his slumped weight out into the corridor. He landed heavily on the stone floor. I ran at him and landed one good kick in his guts before he cringed away, stumbled to his feet and lurched off into the shadows. I heard his feet picking up speed and vanishing into the desolation.

I turned to find the girl cowering against the steps. Her long tunic of homespun was still tangled about her ankles, and I reckoned, my mind whirling to make a calculation of the unspeakable, that her attacker had not reached his goal. Making soothing noises as if to a frightened beast I reached out to her, but she gave an awful, feral cry and, gathering her tunic up to her knees, jumped up and darted past me. She sprinted away, pale legs scissoring, up the corridor towards my quarters. In another instant she was gone. Had I not had a ringing in my head, and another man's blood trickling down my front, I might have dreamed the whole thing for all the evidence that remained.

My jug of wine was where I had set it down, but later, as I lay upon my bed and drank, I knew that the sly palace ghosts had lapped at it like Aristotle tells us the shades of the dead heroes, feeble and squeaking, drank the warm blood of sacrifices. The haunted wine was suitable company, for if I had gone in search of wine to dull her memory and my grief, I had instead found Anna's fetch. For what else could that girl be? I knew it was not so, with my scholar's mind that shunned superstition and with the aching in my head, for I had butted a living man, and such oafs do not seek to violate spirits. But my bereaved heart had found a shred of relief, a piece of flotsam to cling to in the howling storm, and so I lay there and remembered how I had first found my love and saved her from a man who meant to kill her, how her black hair and white skin had pierced my soul. Only when the wine was all but gone, and I could taste clay from the jug in the dregs, did I banish such thoughts and tell myself that I had merely saved the virtue of an inconsequential servant, and made an enemy of Christ alone knew who. At last I slept, and the mothy ghosts of the palace swarmed about me, drawn to me, as to all who slept there, as if to flame. We draw them, we living souls, our hot blood and beating hearts as enticing as a lantern on a summer night, but the dead are never warm, and we cannot give them warmth; and they dash themselves against us as we dream our little, desperate dreams of life.

Chapter Seventeen

Two days later the Captain left on a Venetian galley that was guaranteed, by its eager master, to be the fastest in the port. The party made its way to the docks with all ceremony, and I trailed along, somewhat abjectly, for I was not relishing – nay, I am dissembling: I was frankly terrified of – the prospect of being left alone in this wretched city. I went down to the docks and waved the Captain off, feeling as if I were sawing through my lifeline with every wave. I watched his ship lose itself amongst the sun-shimmer and the teeming boats, then set off back to the palace. Before me stretched nothing but empty time to fill until the King of France's emissaries turned up, and who knew when that might be. So as I trudged back through the empty, hollow streets I trailed my spirits behind me in the gutter like a tattered cloak.

The palace was more gloomy and dispiriting – if such a thing were possible – without the Captain, and my days would have passed as though in a veritable purgatory of boredom and isolation had it not been for one thing. For after a morning spent wandering the empty halls, I returned to my chambers to find a maid turning down my bed linen. When she heard the door she jumped and turned to face me, shoulders clenched in anticipation of something – reprimand, or worse – and I saw that she was the girl I had rescued. When she realised it was me she blushed, more from consternation than embarrassement, bowed nervously and scuttled past me and out into the hall.

After this inauspicious start I saw her often, for – whether she had been assigned to me or had merely chosen the duty herself I could not discover – she was often in my chambers, bringing fresh linen and water, a jug of wine in the evening and a meal if I was in need of one. She was as light and pale as a ghost, and if I believed in such things I might have thought her a house-spirit of some kind. For she never spoke, no matter how I tried to draw her out. At first, when I addressed her, she would simply leave. But after some time had passed she decided that I merited a smile and a shy duck of the head, and sometimes I was honoured with a smile or a nod in answer to some question. I never even learned her name. I hoped, at least, that she knew how much I had come to treasure her silent ministrations.

Meantime I filled the next few days with wandering about Constantinople, finding its famous landmarks and finding each one in such horrible stages of ruin or neglect that each expedition left me more crestfallen than the last. It was after one such day that I was greeted, upon my return to the palace, by a summons to dinner at the high table. Someone had taken pity on me and, I guessed, wished to curry favour with the pope. Somewhat reluctantly I dressed in my finest Roman garb and made my way to the state rooms.

In truth, it was not a bad evening. As a stranger, I was somewhat left out of things, but that suited my mood and anyway, the food was excellent. Or rather, the dressings and accompaniments to the various dishes of meat were delicious, the joints themselves being of poor quality: old, ill-fed beasts had died to provide the barons' feast. And yet the Franks fell upon this meat with great joy and smacking of lips, all but ignoring the smaller dishes of greenstuff and vegetables which were cooked in the Greek style with plenty of oil, lemon and olives, and on which I fell greedily, to the surprise of my fellows. To fit in, I allowed them to serve me half a septuagenarian cockerel and a lump of mutton with all the appeal and texture of oakum. I choked this down with draughts of adequate wine, and, as I was enjoying its strengthening glow, I felt a dig in my ribs.

'Are you a priest, sir?' my neighbour asked me. He was a black-haired man a little older than myself, with a sharp nose and piercing eyes.

'God, no! I mean, no, sir, I am not. A lay brother only.'

'Hmm. D'you hunt?'

'Not habitually.' Not much of an answer, but better, I hoped, than a flat 'no'.

'And yet you are a man of action, I perceive. A soldier, I hear, yes? Would you care to hunt the wild boar with us tomorrow?' I saw the black eyebrows rise in challenge. Was this man trying to pick a fight or make a friend? I picked a steely mutton fibre from my teeth and considered quickly. I had never enjoyed hunting, and yet I was bored almost to the point of sickness. What possible harm could there be: another wasted day at worst.

'I should be delighted!' I said.

'Good, then: I was sure you would be. The Regent has charged me with entertaining you while you are a guest here, and I took the liberty of organising a little hunt in your honour – sure you would not be offended, and you were not! We will meet at dawn, by the fountain in the square before the gate. And now, let us be strangers no more. I am called Aimery de Lille Charpigny. My lands are to the south of here, in the Achaea, but I have been at court since the siege last year. Lord, this place is dull ...'

'Amen, sir,' I agreed with all my heart.

Thus commenced a pleasant few hours. Aimery had obviously appointed himself my host – or been so appointed, although I was glad of it either way. He kept my cup full and, with little prompting, told me much about court life, such as it was; the parlous state of the empire, and how much he detested Greeks. He grew positively rapturous, however, describing his barony in the far south of the empire, a land of crags, miraculous wine and endless hunting. In turn I told him a bit about my own homeland, embellishing it a little and inventing a past for myself that left out my humble birth and career as a novice monk, embroidering matters instead with tales I had heard from my long-lost friends at school in Balecester. By the time the fire had died down and people had begun to drift away I was almost looking forward to my first boar hunt, for it sounded like no more than a jolly excursion to the woods. So I bid Aimery a grateful farewell, and promised to make the arranged rendezvous at dawn. He had been diligent in making my evening a pleasant one, and I was truly thankful for that. In the way of these Franks he was not truly friendly, for a suspicion, a chill, seemed to lie behind the smiling face. But we were both a little drunk, and so we clasped hands warmly and I took myself off to my bed.

The next day was the boar hunt that Aimery de Lille Charpigny had organised in my honour. It was still barely light when I found the company gathered in the open space before Hagia Sophia, horses snorting plumes of white breath, men passing flasks between them and cackling hoarsely in early-morning voices. Aimery, clad in green fustian and with a great horn slung across his shoulders, greeted me as if I were an old companion-in-arms and not simply a chance dinner companion. He showed me to my borrowed mount, a lovely white and dappled mare, and introduced me to the others. They were Franks all, bearing sturdy French names like Eudes and Raymond, and they all had the loose-limbed confidence that rank and privilege confer. I did not doubt that this lot would have been as happy hunting Greeks as wild pigs. One of them, Rolant, introduced as Rollo, seemed to be Aimery's particular friend. He was a tow-headed, round-faced young man whose mouth seemed perpetually open in laughter. He slapped me hard on the shoulder and made some jolly comment about Englishmen that was obviously meant to be funny. I smiled dutifully, and was relieved when, as the company made ready to leave, Aimery chose to ride by my side.

We left the city by the Blachernae Gate, trotting out past unshaven guardsmen scratching their fundaments while the smoke from their breakfast fires seeped thickly from the arrow-slits in the guardhouse. The alaunt hounds sniffed them curiously and were driven away with boots and curses.

'The chimney's blocked,' I observed to my companion. He laughed.

'There's no chimney. Those are Catalans from the high mountains. They miss their stinking turf huts, and so they light their fires on the floor.'

'But they will burn themselves out of doors!'

'Good Christ, man, they do that with some regularity.'

Pondering upon the quality, or lack thereof, of the men who guarded the great city of Constantinople, I rode along in silence. The land began to slope upwards almost immediately. It was a patchy mix of houses, abandoned and fast tumbling down, fields that were reverting to wilderness, and scrubby copses of turkey oak and olive trees. We were on a wide paved road, which we had all to ourselves. It was becoming a jolly party now that we had left the city. The annoying young man with the long hood had pulled a rebec from his saddlebag and was sawing away at it, singing French love songs in a high, somewhat cracked voice. In truth he was not bad, and pulled some sweet tones from the strings, although his throat seemed in need of lubrication. However, when this was provided, in the form of wine, it had no effect save to turn his songs bawdy. The others began to join in one by one, until the whole party – save myself, who did not know the words – were singing lustily. Every so often a dog would give tongue, perhaps in protest, and his fellows would join in, to the merriment of all. I had to admit that this was not, perhaps, the worst use of a day, and by the time we came to a fork in the road and left the wide highway for a narrower track, I was in quite high spirits myself. I had not let my guard down, not quite; but I was beginning to feel loose-limbed and hot-blooded, and I was looking forward to the chase.

We had come no more than two miles, riding slowly, passing flasks of wine to and fro. The woods were thicker now. Plane trees, their leaves dead and dry, spread their great canopies for the starlings, and cypresses grew straight in deep green spinneys. We had seen almost no one since passing through the gate, and passed a very few mean habitations – hovels amidst patches of bare earth in which bald, mite-gnawed chickens scratched resignedly – but here we had entered a desert. No smoke rose, and no one seemed to use the road, which, although it too was paved with good Roman stone, had been left to the mud and colonising grass. But I began to notice that the beasts had found this lack of men much to their liking. Rabbits shot across our path, and I saw how well trained our hounds were, for they did not so much as twitch in their direction. A fox loped away and then sat on his haunches like a tame dog and regarded us from an outcropping of rock. Pheasants and partridges burst away from us in whirring explosions. Birds shrilled and gossiped everywhere. In all, this empty heath was a livelier place by far than the city of men we had left behind us.

At last we came upon evidence of man's presence. A great tangle of furze had been hacked down and burned, and beyond the black and ash-heaped circle left by the fire stood a wall into which a gateway had been let. Gateless now, the archway had been overrun with vines, and a thatch of caper plants grew from its apex like a badly made wig.

'Here is the Philopation,' said Aimery. 'Hunting park of the great Roman emperors. Fucking mess, isn't it?'

'It does not look very imperial,' I agreed.

'What does, eh? What does,' Aimery agreed. 'Too near the walls. We wrecked the place when we took the city. There are palaces in there, all fallen down. Terrible waste, really. But who would make their home out here? Not I.'

'Does anyone live here, then?'

'Vagabonds – nay, not vagabonds ...' It was one of the others, a tall man in green who wore a fine, old-looking horn over his shoulder. He had been riding at the front, and seemed to have some authority. Now he clicked his fingers in search of a word. 'Rollo, what do they call them? The conjuring folk?'

'Athingani,' answered Rollo, tucking away his rebec.

'Lori,' added another.

'Aigupti,' a man with a crossbow chimed in.

'There you have it,' said the man. 'They are wanderers, and have power over beasts, particularly snakes. The men have a snake tattooed across their chests, the savages! Their women are dark ...'

'And fuck like a basketful of vipers,' said Rollo.

'Into which I would sooner stick my cock,' Aimery said. 'But we will not see them. They do not like us, nor we them. In fact, a florin for any man who kills an Athingani! Eh?' He

273

winked at me, perhaps to signify that he did not mean it. Or perhaps that he did. In any event I thought no more of it. The park looked utterly deserted, and any conjurors would surely have sense enough to steer clear of a pack of buffoons such as us.

Beyond the walls the land began to roll away in a lazy ripple of knolls, little crags and shallow, wooded ravines. I could see that it had once been cared for, as it was overgrown but not wild. Not far away stood a little stone lodge, gutted by fire. There had been a group of marble fountains in front of it, and these were cracked and choked with moss. The ruin of Constantinople could not be contained, plainly, and must spread its tendrils outwards like dry rot to consume everything within its reach. I felt someone walk across my grave, as I often did in the city's smashed and fouled streets, but resolved not to let the day be spoiled by melancholic thoughts. I was free, at least for the day; in jolly company, and with the prospect of fine sport ahead.

'Well, lead on, boys!' I called. Aimery whooped and set spurs to his horse, and we crashed through the gate and into the park.

We had gone no more than two bow-shots from the gate when the land closed in around us. The gate and the lodge were invisible, swallowed up in a haze of cypresses and young oaks. Aimery declared that we would split up into pairs and hunt until lunchtime, but the tall man thought it would be better sport to divide into two groups. Thus we would have company as well as sport, and perhaps after lunch we could go off in pairs. We had dismounted in a clearing, and the servant had opened his oilskin bundle to reveal short spears with broad, leaf-shaped heads and stout iron cross-guards. There were bows too, short, curved Saracen ones with quivers full of red-fletched arrows. The alaunts sniffed about, cocking their legs and dropping huge, reeking turds wherever they pleased, while we hunters fortified ourselves with wine and dried sausage. To my chagrin, Rollo singled me out and cast his arm around my neck.

'Let us bring each other luck, friend Petrus,' he said. I agreed with what I hoped was good grace. His puppy-like quality grated upon me, as did his somewhat desperate need to be loved – unnecessary, for his companions seemed to love him to distraction – and the prospect of wandering through gulley and thicket while he jabbered and jested dampened my mood. But I put my best face upon the situation, for I was a guest and a gentleman (for all they knew) and must show my breeding.

'Will you sing the beasts out of their lairs for us?' I asked him, with my best grin.

'And on to the points of our spears!' he crowed.

'Aye, and who could blame them,' I told him. His eyebrows shot up, but then he treated me to another of his laughs. Aimery, who had heard my poor joke, joined in, and soon the whole party was cackling like a building of rooks. I joined in while making sure my wine flask was full, for I feared it would be a long time until lunch.

Our party chose to take a narrow goat-path that led off to the south, towards the river. The others decided to try their luck in the higher ground to the north, where the park rose to overlook the Golden Horn. But we had been riding no more than five minutes when Rollo signalled to me and dropped behind the others. Then, when we were a horse's length behind the last man, Rollo whistled out his four dogs from the pack, then wheeled his horse with a mad cry and set off into the trees to our left. My horse, whether scared or excited, took to her heels after him. We were off into the wild. I was intensely grateful to Horst, for my merciless riding instructor had made sure I could ride and use a weapon. Finally Rollo slowed his horse and let me catch up.

'What fun!' he cackled. 'For God's sake, man, did you want to hunt with all those old women? Thought not. My dear, lucky friend, I have my own secrets, and today I am going to share them with you.' He tapped his nose. 'We, and only we, will be bringing the prize home today.'

We set off again through the trees and scrub. It was not easy going. The worst part of it was the boar spear I carried in my right hand, and between making sure it did not snag in every low-hanging branch and keeping my horse on the path I soon grew quite hot and silent, although Rollo kept up an endless patter of self-regarding nonsense, mostly relating to wenches he had or intended to swive, and fine ladies who had or intended to swive him.

I found it easy to ignore him, for years spent aboard a ship had inured me to the vexing effects of idle chatter. And besides, it was a beautiful day. The dogs were putting up fat birds that looked like grouse to left and right. Even though we were long past the first frost, cicadas had dragged themselves out of hiding and were rattling half-heartedly from the olive trees. I interrupted Rollo to suggest we try our hands at shooting some of the grouse, but he waved me off.

'No, no, good Petrus. I know where the big beasts are. Let us not waste our time with birds. Do you not want to be the man who kills the finest boar?'

'I should be glad if it does not kill me,' I muttered. But Rollo took that for assent, and we trotted on.

The valley of the Lycus river is quite deep and wide, although the stream itself is small. Our path began to descend past ruined walls and odd grottoes scooped into the ground where it was steep.

'See those caves?' asked Rollo. 'When this was the royal

hunting-ground, there weren't any trees, not like now. No cover for beasts. So they dug caves for them, and ditches and the Lord knows what else. Lazy emperors would always know where to look, eh? Bloody Greeks!' He laughed. 'No, I am a liar. I have nothing against Greeks – in any case not their women. Although they do grow fine moustaches. But then again …' And thus, having imparted a morsel of interest, he began his prattle once more. So it went on. The track led us down through flowering gorse and thickets of broom, and into a wood of young oaks. Boars lived here, all right: the ground between the trunks was quite bare and churned up. Now I saw the river, a dark gleam through the trees.

'This is where they are,' said Rollo, dropping his voice at last. 'I saw a huge brute here once. Killed my best dog. Gored a servant too,' he added as an afterthought. 'Dogs! Here, you lovely beasts!' And raising his horn he blew three high, urgent notes. The four alaunt hounds, who were milling about around us, stopped and stared up at their master. Rollo blew again, and the dogs, as one animal, set off at a dead run towards the river. Signalling me to follow, Rollo kicked his horse into a trot and went after them.

All this talk of monstrous boars had made my mouth somewhat dry. I hefted my spear and wondered, not for the first time that day, how one actually used these things. Was I supposed to throw it? Or just try to skewer the boar while it tried to kill me? Throw it and run, I decided grimly. Rollo clearly felt no such misgivings. Winding his way through the oaks, he was singing a lively song, a rather beautiful one about hunting both stags and amorous ladies, and for the first time that morning I almost liked the man. Trotting in his wake, I kept a tight grip on the haft of my spear, and hoped, friend or not, that any hideous beasts would charge Rollo first. I was in the midst of these uncharitable thoughts when my companion reined in and held a finger to his lips.

'Do you hear that?' I shook my head. 'The dogs. Over there: they have picked up a scent. Or ... no! They see something!' And with a yell he dug in his heels and took off at a gallop. I had no time to admire the skill with which Rollo guided his horse around the tree trunks, for I had all my attention fixed upon my own spear and reins. So when he stopped suddenly in a clearing I nearly rode hard into him. He said nothing, but pointed to the far side of the open ground.

A stone wall ran down through the trees and ended at the river. Beyond, the turkey oaks spread green shadows. In the angle of the wall and the river stood a boar, hemmed in by the four hounds, who were barking madly but keeping their distance. In this they showed sound judgement, for the boar was a monster. Big as any pampered farm hog – big, indeed, as a bear – he wore a thick coat of dark-grey fur which stood up in a tall crest along his back. His ears were huge and pointed and his eyes were small and livid red. But it was his tusks that made the sweat start cold across my skin. They sprang from the black snarl of his lips in a tangle of dirty ivory, big as Moorish swords and all a-quiver with their owner's rage. Pearly spittle dangled in ropes, which flew and caught in the greenery like spiderwebs when the beast shook his great head.

'Mary's dugs,' whispered Rollo when I came up beside him. He had stopped his horse ten or so paces behind the dogs and was gripping his spear with white knuckles. 'That is the fiend I chased down before. God almighty – he has grown, I think.'

'Now what?' I asked, tersely.

'Now we kill it,' he said, simply. Then he turned to me, a warm smile on his lips. 'The honour is yours, good Petrus.'

I thought this must be another of his jests, but with a

bilious lurch of horrified realisation I saw that he was sincere. I gave him a wordless grimace of refusal, but he was watching the boar and did not see. What was I to do? I had a general idea of how these things were done. The dogs would hold the creature at bay while I rode in and stuck it with my spear. But it was plain that the dogs would not be able to hold this monster if he decided to break free, and it was just as plain that I had not the slightest idea how to spear a gigantic, enraged boar from horseback. I dithered, and my nerves were felt by my horse, who had been good enough with me all morning but now began to fret. She started to dance sideways on stiff legs, and I cursed and pulled on the reins. Rollo mistook this for eagerness on my part, and raised his horn to sound the charge, or whatever madness is the proper form at such times. But as he did so, and as I was about to drop my spear to devote both hands to my horse, there was a crescendo of barks and growling and I looked up in time to see one of the alaunts break the circle and leap upon the boar. The monster shrieked – a ghastly, almost human sound – and with a flick of his snout he opened the dog up from balls to chest. Guts spilled out in a livid jumble of blue and red, and as the dog tried to stand they tangled around his legs and held him fast as he kicked out his last seconds. This was too much for the other dogs. As one they rushed at the boar. One grabbed the bristling snout in its teeth and with one flick was sent flying. The others came at the boar's flanks and battened on. But the great dogs seemed like mere ticks compared to the muscled bulk of the pig. Spinning around, he shook one loose and, dragging the other dog, whose teeth were sunk in his shoulders and tearing deep, bloody furrows through the fur, he charged the stunned alaunt and gored it in a shrieking frenzy until its throat burst open and showered everything with bright blood. Then the boar, seemingly oblivious to the remaining dog hanging from his flesh, turned his fury upon us.

My horse pranced and snorted, for the stench of blood and swine was heavy in the air. She twitched, and suddenly I heard Horst's voice in my head: 'Take command,' he said. He had yelled those words to me countless times as I tortured poor Iblis with my clumsiness and stupidity. Now I saw very clearly that my mount was on the verge of panic. She would bolt or throw me off – either way, things would be grim. Beside me, Rollo's horn was poised before his lips but instead of blowing he stared, white-faced, at the ruin that had come to his dogs. I could not run away, I supposed, my mind whirling but time oddly stilled around me. So I did what Horst had taught me: I charged. All the horse's terror, the panic that quivered in her limbs like stretched bowstrings, found its release the moment my spurs met her flanks, and she sprang forward. The boar, who had no doubt been sizing us up for butchery, gave a falsetto screech of surprise.

I had been standing no more than four horse's lengths from the brute. Now, as I hurtled at full tilt towards him, my mind seemed to split itself into twain. On one side I could sense nothing but my grip on the reins and the smooth wood of the spear haft in my right fist. On the other, with agonising slowness and perfect clarity, I beheld the ground disappearing beneath the mare's hooves, the sunlight shafting through the dusty air, and the boar himself. He was doing a kind of stiff-legged dance, a jig of rage and indecision. Numbly I picked my target: the great, bristled hump behind those pointed ears. The hooves pounded down again. The boar shook his head and lowered it, tusks aimed at my poor mare's belly.

The part of me that was observing all this noted that I had miscalculated: the pig would eviscerate my horse before

I could stab it. Then everything happened very fast. The boar shook his head again, and the alaunt who still hung there, forgotten by events, must have bitten down, for the boar suddenly lurched and threw himself sideways, landing on top of the dog with his full weight, just as I lunged with my spear. The mare, seeing the great bulk of the swine rolling towards her, leaped blindly. The spear-point stabbed thin air and I nearly fell from the saddle. As the horse came down I shut my eyes and wrapped my left arm around her neck. My forehead slammed into her mane. The spear snagged on the ground and was torn from my hand. There was a great turmoil, then silence. My mouth was full of horsehair. I looked up. We were standing in the river. Brown water lapped around the mare's knees. She was steaming with sweat and quivering, but I could feel that her panic had departed. Overcome by my blind good fortune, I forgot about the boar for an instant while I stroked the mare's hot neck. Then a horrid noise brought me to my senses.

Rollo must have hesitated. Doubtless he had charged the boar in his turn, but the swine must have found his feet, for the fate he had intended for my horse had befallen Rollo's. It rolled in agony, white ribs and darker, softer things welling from a cavernous rent across its underside. The boar was nowhere to be seen, and I assumed that Rollo was pinned beneath the horse. Then the boar appeared from behind a tree and ran into the horse's belly once more, tearing another horrible wound. The poor animal shrieked for the last time, dropped its head and lay still. The boar commenced its stiff-legged dance again, and then I saw Rollo. He had dragged himself over to an olive tree and was propped against the trunk, spear out and wavering at the boar, who, having killed the horse, had now seen the man.

The pig had so far killed four dogs and a horse. Rollo quite plainly had no chance. He looked hurt as well as terrified. I would have to save him. That, or watch him be dismembered. Would I be able to face Aimery and the others if I did not help him? Quite easily, I thought. Oh yes, very easily indeed. I cursed loudly, and louder still when I realised I no longer had my spear. But I had no time now. With a whoop I kicked the mare forward. She lurched towards the bank, sending up sheets of water. Then her hooves were sliding in the mud and we were back on land. She was breathing hard again and showing the whites of her eyes, for the stench of the dead horse's guts was very strong, so I gave her no time to hesitate. Pointing her between dead horse and dead dogs I kicked again and she dashed across the clearing. I had planned to snatch Rollo up but when I reached him he shoved the spear at me.

'Kill it!' he rasped. 'Kill it, for God's sake!'

Fending off the spear, I grabbed it just under the cross-bar. 'Get up on the fucking horse,' I all but screamed at him. I saw my spittle land on his face, but I did not care. 'Get up!'

The mare was starting to prance in distress. I wrenched her head around to the left so that she could not see the boar, who was regarding us coolly, his tusks festooned in rags of horse guts. Meanwhile Rollo had let go of the spear. The boar's eyes flicked from Rollo, who had drawn his dagger, to me, and back again. He blinked and gave a snort, sending flecks of blood and meat in all directions. Then he began to saunter towards us. It was plain that he had decided to finish us off at his leisure. Rollo gave a deep sigh.

'Right then,' he said. 'You back up a bit. He'll go for me. I'll bring him on, and you come in from the side and stick him.' I looked down in surprise. What I had mistaken for fear had been nothing but shock and pain, which he had mastered. As if to prove the point, he winked at me.

'Yes?' he asked. I shrugged tightly.

'All right,' I said. The mare wheeled and I managed to get her feet set. The boar's head swung towards me, then back to Rollo.

'Come on, you fat cuckold!' Rollo yelled. 'Come *on*!'

The swine did his stiff-legged dance again, as if overcome by gleeful, murderous anticipation. Rollo waved his dagger. With a squeal, the pig made his decision and launched himself at Rollo. At that moment I yelled at the top of my lungs and charged. The boar saw the horse bearing down on him and paused. The horse saw the boar pause and hesitated in mid-stride. Still holding the spear and the reins I flew clean over the horse's head and before I could even blink, landed with a crash across the bloody shoulders of the boar. With a bellow he rolled over on top of me. I was aware of a hideous, crushing weight, and then the world vanished in a whirl of sparks chasing through my skull.

I opened my eyes a long instant later. There was bloody, matted pig bristle an inch from my face, and the sharp reek of slaughterhouse and sty burning my nose. I was sure my ribs were snapped like chicken bones. The boar gave a lurch. If he thinks I am dead, perhaps he will ignore me, I thought. Instead, I felt the boar's own ribs heave, and a mighty sniffing, like pease-porridge sucked in and out of a giant pair of bellows, came from somewhere near my right shoulder. Then, quick as lightning, the brute rolled away from me and came to his feet. I saw those seething eyes and the yellow bone of tusks, and I screwed my eyes shut and prepared to die. But instead of goring me, the boar gave a final, defiant sniff, pirouetted on his hooves and bolted for the trees. Before I had even released what had almost been my final breath he had vanished.

I lay, still as a carving, hardly daring to breathe lest my ribs crumble. The sun was almost overhead and was lancing down through clouds of dust. I heard laughter, and Rollo's face appeared above me, pale as milk but contorted with mirth. He still held his dagger.

'Petrus! Christ above, Petrus! What did you say to him, the beast? Christ's blood and bones, he took offence, all right! What did you whisper in his ear, eh?'

I could not even find the strength to reply. Instead I looked past his face at the swirling motes, and wondered vaguely if I had shit my breeches. Rollo was almost doubled over with laughter. He was prattling on, and every word seemed to make him laugh the harder.

'Something nasty about his old sow, what? Or his daughters, eh? Eh? How—'

The babble halted in mid-flow. As Rollo's face came into focus through the sun's glare, I saw that mirth had vanished. His eyes were very round and his lips had gone quite white. He dropped the dagger, which chinked into the ground an inch from my hip.

'What …?' I began, as he straightened up and swatted at something behind his back. Then there was a hiss and the grey feathers of an arrow appeared, like a grotesque sleight of hand, under his armpit. With a sound like the snapping of fingers another arrow transfixed his cheek, and two more struck his side. He scrabbled at the bright snakes' heads of metal that jutted from his belly, and our eyes met. They were full of the most intense concentration as though he sought for some answer in my own, and his face was grave and strangely noble, despite the horrible adornment it had received. Then a great belch of gore spewed from his pierced mouth and his eyes went blank. Slack-limbed, he toppled backwards. The arrows splintered loudly as he hit the ground and lay still.

Chapter Eighteen

I had still moved not so much as a muscle since coming to my senses, and although my first impulse was to leap to my feet, I did not. Through the shock of Rollo's sudden demise came filtering, like the dust motes that drifted above me, the realisation that whoever had shot my companion had not tried to shoot me. Therefore he – or they, for there must be at least two bowmen – supposed me dead. Was there the slightest chance that they might leave me alone, having killed Rollo? My mind was in a mad whirl. They must be robbers, I thought. That being the case, they would now move in to rob the dead bodies. If I moved now, they would shoot me from their hiding place. My only hope was to let them come up to me. I had my knife. If there were two men, and they both came out, I might have a small chance. If there were three or more, I was a dead man. Christ. Where was my horse? Could I draw my knife easily? Ah, holy Mother of God, I still held the boar spear, of course. My right arm was throbbing horribly. I fervently prayed it was not broken.

As these and a legion more thoughts gabbled inside my brainbox like a drunken conclave, I was struggling to keep still. All my reasoning could not blot out the very real chance that the bowmen might decide to put a couple of arrows into me, just to make sure. So I was almost relieved when I heard footsteps padding towards me. But now something was tickling my neck: a fat fly, drinking my fear-laced sweat. I must not twitch. Not now. The footsteps came closer, closer. More than one pair of shoes, I thought. There was whispering, hissed words I could not make out. Shoes were crunching on gravel very close to my head. Through slitted eyes I could see a man to my right, just a dark blur against the sun. He walked up to Rollo and kicked him. Then he bent quickly and slit his throat – or so I guessed, for it is a sound I have never been able to erase from my memory, and I recognised it all too well now. Straight away someone kicked me in turn, a hard blow to my left kidney. Knowing what would be next, I opened my eyes. A man's swarthy face, all hawk's nose and straggling eyebrows and framed with greasy black ringlets, was looking down at me. As he gave a start and began to bend towards me, I sat up, and in the same movement rammed the blunt end of the spear into his throat. It struck his Adam's apple with a jolt: not a terrible blow, but he was so startled that he lost his balance and sat down hard. As I tried to get my legs under me, an arm grabbed me around the neck. At once I threw my weight backwards, dropping the spear, and tried to stand; and if I had been able to feel astonishment at that moment I would have laughed aloud, for the man behind me was standing so firmly that I slid upright against the length of his body. I fumbled for my knife. There was an endless, infernal second during which my fingers felt only cloth, then they touched the cool steel ball of the pommel. Feeling his arm tighten and imagining the knife-hand that I could not see, I stamped down with all my might on the top of his feet and spun as his grip loosened minutely, my flesh cringing in expectation of the thrust of steel. My face came around into the hollow beneath his chin, all beard and garlic-sweat, and I shoved him away with both hands. He stepped back and raised his arm. He held a small sword, not a knife, and that had saved me, for he had not been able to bring the shorter blade to bear at close-quarters. His face was twisted horribly, and dumbly I realised I must have stabbed him as I fended him off. The sword came down and I stepped inside the arc of the blade and punched my blade into his guts again and again, perhaps five times, perhaps many more. He shrieked into my ear and dropped, writhing, to my feet.

I spun round. The other man had stood up, although he was stooped and was looking sour enough to let me know I had hurt him, however slightly. He leered evilly, his knife held straight out, point aimed unwaveringly at my face. I saw that he wore an odd sort of costume, something like a Saracen rag-picker: Moorish trousers, a loose-sleeved shirt and a waistcoat of filthy, painted leather. The shirt hung open to reveal a great black serpent tattooed on the man's dark chest. He smiled, revealing black and yellow teeth. Then he glanced to his left and held up his left hand. I had been about to run as fast as my feet could carry me, but now the logic of battle, all the training dinned into me over the past two years aboard the *Cormaran*, took over. There was another man, probably a bowman. He would not shoot me while I was so near his comrade. Or the snake-man was bluffing, and he had stupidly given me an opening. That was a better thought, and acting upon it I dropped my knife and lunged for the boar spear, which lay in a spreading pool of Rollo's blood. I came up with it as the snake-man turned back to me, and his smile vanished.

If you are extremely good at fighting, or just exceptionally lucky, you will very rarely find yourself with the upper hand and with the clarity of mind to choose your next move. I was no more than adequate in a fight but fickle luck had come over to my side and suddenly I was the master of an unequal struggle. The spear I held was a good six feet long, tipped with a long, razor-edged blade. My enemy held only a long dagger. Keeping my eyes fixed on his face I carefully stepped over Rollo's corpse and circled, forcing him to put himself between the bowman, if he even existed, and myself. I have said my mind was clear, but into that clarity anger now poured like burning tar. This man had meant to slaughter me, and I was suddenly disinclined to forgive him. My natural instinct, perhaps, would have been to let him run for it if he cared to, but I was so overcome with rage that instead of making my own bluff I began to jab at him, edging closer until he was parrying the spearhead with his knife. He did not look scared, however, in fact his smile had spread to reveal more rotten teeth. This merely fuelled my anger, and as rage makes a fair proxy for courage, I ignored what Dimitri my fearsome teacher had told me over and over again – keep your head – and lunged.

The man side-stepped and slashed. His blade slid down the haft of the spear and I parried it away. I lunged again, and again. He was still not afraid, still giving me his foul smile, but I was backing him up, keeping out of his reach but near enough that his friend with the bow – if he was real – would not shoot. I lunged, and he gave ground. Now we were picking our way among the corpses of Rollo's dogs, one of whom still kicked feebly. The man tripped slightly. We both glanced down. It was the spear I had dropped while charging the boar. Desperately I lunged again, but the man dodged, knocked my spear aside and flung his dagger at my face. His aim was perfect but I was too close, and the handle struck me crosswise across the bone of my nose. I heard it snap and felt blood begin to gush instantly. I staggered back, and through hot tears of pain I watched the snake-man snatch up the fallen spear.

'You bastard!' I yelled. I was still furious, but now I was frightened too, and barely able to breathe. In this confusion of rage and fear I leaped forward as the man was straightening up, and stuck my spear into his shoulder. It went deep, up to the cross-bar, and I yanked it out and thrust again. This time I missed, for he had lurched sideways. His own spear came up. I charged again: again my spearhead missed and I slammed into him. We stood for a moment, and then, overcome with blind panic I shoved him away and he shuffled backwards, grunting in pain. I pushed again and again, shoving him back. We were like two drunkards fighting in front of some tavern: both clumsy, both exhausted. But I was younger, and he was wounded, and in a turmoil of sweat and gasping breath I drove him across the clearing and into the river. His feet went backwards into the wet mud and his face went slack with horrified understanding as he slipped and fell.

There was a mighty splash, and the man vanished fulllength beneath the water. My own momentum carried me forward and my own heels struck mud. I landed hard on my bum and slipped down the little bank. As the man surfaced, spluttering, I levered myself up with my spear. I felt a moment of calm, a fragment of victory, for my enemy was down and unarmed, and perhaps this thing was over. But his arm came up with the spear and as he floundered, trying to find his feet, the long, wicked spearhead caught the sun. I swallowed blood, waded into the river and stabbed him full in the chest with all my might. I jerked it out and stabbed again, and again, until the man was meat and rags in the water.

I found myself sitting on the bank, head in my hands, which were filling with blood and snot like a chalice. There was a pounding in my ears, and I felt transparent, as if the sun were shining right through me. My legs were in the water, and dark ropes of blood were twisting like leeches about my calves. I retched: nothing came up, but I felt less incorporeal.

Raising my head at last, I saw the river, and standing in the middle of the stream, my mare, pale and grave. She dipped her head and delicately sipped the water that ran in crystal ropes around her knees. The man with the snake tattoo was nowhere to be seen.

Whether there had been other men in the trees waiting to finish me off, I will never know, for at that moment I heard the blast of a horn, and then another sounded in answer, not far off. Then, with an eruption of baying, the whole pack of alaunt hounds burst into the clearing behind me.

Feeling as if carved from ice, I wandered out into the river and took the mare's reins. We walked slowly back to the clearing. Rollo was still dead, the broken arrows making him look like a great seagull carcass, some strange flotsam thrown up on a beach. The man I had stabbed lay face up, eyes staring and filmed with dust. His tunic – the same Saracen rags as his comrade – was torn open and an alaunt hound was hungrily lapping the blood that pooled there. Sickened, I kicked it aside, but noticing something, I knelt down beside the corpse.

The dog's tongue, as it drank the man's blood, had dragged across the tattooed snake that writhed across his chest. Except it was not a tattoo, for it had smeared. I bent down and, despite my revulsion, took a corner of tunic and rubbed. The snake came away, leaving a faint, dark stain. Lampblack, or something like it. Thinking hard, I dipped my finger in more blood and rubbed it across the man's stubbled cheek. It left a lighter trail across the dark skin. What had they called them, these snake-men? Athingani. This man was no more Athingani than was I, on that I would wager the Crown of Thorns itself. There was a clatter of hooves and, on some impulse that was not entirely clear to me, I quickly rearranged the tunic to hide the man's chest. Staggering to my feet, I found Aimery and the rest of the hunt standing in a crescent around me, pale and gawping.

'This is a charnel house. Dear Jesus, is that Rollo?' Aimery rasped finally.

'Aye,' I said.

'Who …' another man began. I held up my hand to shut him up.

'I don't know,' I said. 'No. Those, you know. Those Egyptians. With the snakes.'

'Aigupti? You mean the Athingani attacked you? But they do not …' It was the man with the crossbow.

'Shut your mouth, Eudes,' snapped Aimery. 'They are savages and thieves. They despise us and now they have spilled good French blood.' He jumped down and knelt beside Rollo. 'Good Christ! Rollo, dear Rollo!'

'He did not suffer,' I said. 'Believe me when I say that he died laughing.'

Aimery gave me a cold look. 'But he killed this one?' He prodded the dead Athingani.

'Nay, it was I. Whether this man shot Rollo I cannot say. He had a companion.'

'There were two? Where is he?'

'Dead, in the river.'

'The Englishman killed two men?' one of the hunters said, admiringly. Aimery stared at me, his eyes even colder than before.

'But you could not save Rollo,' he said, bitterly. 'Why did they not shoot you?'

'I was down. There was a great boar …' Suddenly I felt weak, and sank to my knees. 'The boar did for the dogs and Rollo's horse. The boar, mark you, Monsieur Aimery, the boar had sense enough to fuck off. Men hunting boars, boars hunting men, men hunting other men …' Then everything went silver and black, and when I opened my eyes again I was lying on a pallet of folded cloaks under an olive tree. The man with the crossbow was holding a flask to my lips, and gratefully I slurped at the wine.

'Good man,' he said. 'We thought you were done for. But it's just your nose, eh? Took a knock to the head, did you not?'

'One or two,' I said, and tried to sit up. He restrained me gently but firmly with a hand on my chest.

'Stay there a while,' he said. 'The other chaps are putting Rollo on a horse. Poor bloody Rollo. Aimery and he were like brothers.'

'Aimery does not like me,' I said.

'Aimery can be a bastard, but we just found your other dead man, and he will give you some respect now, you can be sure. Why did you not tell us you were such a warrior?'

'Because I am not,' I said. But the man's face wore the sort of stupid grin that men wear when some act of bestiality or foolishness has impressed them. I could already see the day's carnage spun into some hero's golden tale. Sure enough, they handed my knife back to me as if it were Excalibur and I some vainglorious fool from the pages of Chrétien de Troyes; when later we rode back towards the city, Rollo's flopping corpse tied over a saddle, the company seemed more interested in the fight than in their dead friend. I was used to fighting men by now, but on the *Cormaran* we tended to rate survival above heroics. These men, though, were knights or sons of knights and they seemed to value life somewhat cheaply. Doubtless Rollo would be missed, but he was not mourned, not yet at least.

Save by Aimery, who alone amongst the merry huntsmen rode silent, pale and slit-eyed. He had been closest to Rollo, I understood that much. The tall man was as sombre as the others, and led our procession, head bowed. But I had not been stunned enough to miss the surprise with which he had greeted my survival. He had hidden it well, but the tall man had expected to find Rollo alive and me dead. I had received a thorough apprenticeship in the ways of deception and falsehood, and if I had not been able to read a lie like the one that had played over his face I should not have deserved my berth aboard the *Cormaran*. I was feeling sick in my flesh and in my heart, my nose throbbed horribly, and stars were still drifting across my vision, so I did not ponder these matters in any thorough way. But I reasoned that, if there was some plot against my life, it was known only to a few, or else I would have been slain by the company as soon as we had left Constantinople. It was easy to suspect the tall man, but now I began to wonder whether Rollo too had been a party to it. Why had we been paired together? And if Rollo were so dear to Aimery – for if there were a plot, surely they were all in on it – would he have been sent into danger so heedlessly? But then again, why had Rollo not killed me himself, and blamed the boar, or the Athingani, or whomever he pleased? Nothing was clear, save that three men were dead, and that I could very easily have been bumping along like Rollo, lashed to a horse's back, my head lolling against its flanks like a turnip. I ignored the excited chatter of the others as we rode through the lengthening shadows, the air starting to grow chill, towards the crumbling walls of the city, for my ears could hear nothing save the toc, toc, toc of Rollo's skull as it knocked against an empty stirrup.

Chapter Nineteen

Our sad party rode through the gates of the Bucoleon Palace a little before sunset. One of the guards who met us, gaping at the corpse we brought with us, was sent ahead, and so we were greeted, in the inner yard, by a party of men-at-arms and two noblemen. I found I was so stiff that I could not dismount on my own, and so I was helped down like an old man. A surgeon arrived, a Moorish gentleman, who gave me a draught of bitter herbs in strong wine and led me to a stone bench, the better to examine my wounds. I was grateful to him, for the group of hunters was telling their tale, and voices were being raised in excitement, disbelief, and now anger. I thought the nobles were glaring in my direction, but the surgeon was dabbing my lacerations with something that stung like Satan's pitchfork, and I could not tell if it was just my fancy. Aimery was shaking his head, and then he pointed at me. That I had not imagined. One of the nobles planted his fists on his hips and regarded Aimery belligerently, head cocked to one side. The huntsmen shuffled their feet, but Aimery uttered something I did not hear and pushed, with rude unconcern, past the angry nobleman. With that, the party dissolved. Rollo's corpse was led away, and that was the end of that. The hunters drifted off. The surgeon fussed about me with his diabolical unguents, and in the midst of his torture I looked up to find the other nobleman looking down at me, a concerned smile pinned to his florid face.

I do not remember the pleasantries and expressions of concern that were exchanged, for I was in too much pain, and too sick in my very soul to pay much attention. I nodded and smiled and told a rude outline of what had befallen Rollo and myself. I had enough sense to omit my discovery of the false tattoos, and I saw no need to voice my suspicions, for I felt far too weak and unsure of anything at all. The worthy Moor gave me another of his draughts and called for a litter, on which I was borne up to my chambers and put to bed – or at least I assume I was, for I remember almost nothing until I awoke late the next morning, feeling like something I had once seen a seabird vomit up on the deck of the *Cormaran*.

I lay there, feeling like meat on a butcher's slab and vaguely expecting to be sent for by my hosts, for the more I chewed over the horrible events of yesterday, the more strange they became. I did not suspect the Regent, for he was all but desperate that the business I had come to oversee go ahead, and indeed the future of his shoddy empire would seem to depend upon it. Perhaps, though, a plot had come to light and would be explained to me. I had some details that I was quite anxious to add, and surely there would be an inquest into Rollo's murder. But no one came, and at last I staggered up, found I was feeling far better than I expected, and so decided to take myself off for a walk, if only to get away from the palace, which I was beginning to find unbearably oppressive.

It was quite late when I made my way out into the rain: some time past noon, I guessed. I set off through the puddles and the freezing curtains of water, and had sloshed my way to one of the streets between the palace and the waterfront where I knew food was to be found, when I thought I heard someone call my name. Then it came again:

'Petrus!'

I whipped around, for my name had been called by a

Frankish voice, and it did not sound friendly. Indeed it was Aimery de Lillé Charpigny, who was striding towards me across the square. He was scowling. I drew myself up, limbs aching, and prepared for unpleasantness.

'Petrus Zennorius! Where are you going?' Not a hint of a smile, and no warmth in the voice.

'Nowhere in particular,' I told him.

'Then we will walk awhile,' he said, falling in beside me. I noticed he was wearing a huntsman's short sword. We strolled along in deep silence. Finally I could stand it no longer.

'Good Aimery, I owe you a debt of thanks,' I said. He grinned coldly.

'I doubt that,' he said. 'Why, though, do you say it?'

'Yesterday, when we returned from ... from the hunt, you took my part against one of the barons. If you will permit me, I will return your "why".'

He stopped and regarded me closely. His face, I noticed, was very white.

'I was tempted, sorely, to kill you yesterday when we found you and Rollo. I thought, and it seemed clear at first, that you had let my friend be slaughtered by those ... necromantic beasts. But I am a soldier, and have seen many battlefields; and even to my unwilling eyes it was plain that you had fought bravely and tried to save Rollo, and more, that you had made an end of his murderers. And so, when we returned and that fellow seemed more keen to prosecute you than to tend to the body of my friend, seemed, indeed, merely annoyed that Rollo was dead and that you lived, I took your side as a point of honour. And then I decided to find out exactly who you were, my friend.'

I studied his face as carefully as I could, and saw anger very plain there, and sorrow, but nothing else, I thought.

'Good Aimery, can I tell you the truth, as I perceive it?'

'As you see it? Ha! You churchmen and your words ...
Very well, I will make do with that, for the time being.'

'And could we, perhaps, sit down somewhere?'

'The palace ...'

'Not the palace, I think.'

To my surprise he gave a half-smile, a real one.

'No, not the palace. There is a place near here – a merchant's tavern.'

'Venetian?' I asked quickly.

'Pisan, I think. Why do you ask?'

'I am not sure. But Pisans will do at a pinch. Lead on.'

Aimery led me down towards the Golden Horn, where
the deserted streets had been colonised, ivy-like, by the life
and bustle of the Italian wharves. A ruined building had been
shored up and re-roofed and now bore a sign emblazoned
with a golden bunch of grapes being pecked at by a blackbird.
And sure enough, in the corners, the white cross of Pisa.
It was empty, and the proprietor had to be summoned. He
brought wine and bread, and left us alone.

'Now then,' I said, after we had both drunk. 'You do not
trust me, do you? Of course you do not. But listen to me: we
both have suspicions. Shall I tell you mine?' Without waiting for his assent I took the plunge. 'Those men were not
Athingani, nor Aigupti, nor any of the rest of it.'

That got his attention. He leaned forward like a falcon
who spies a vole in the weeds far below his perch.

'What do you mean?' he said, slowly.

'Did you examine the corpses?' He shook his head. 'I
did. One man drifted away down the river, but the other
one ... you saw the snake device upon his chest?' A nod.
'Lampblack. And their skin. It was dark brown, yet it had
been dyed – walnut shells, I would guess. They were no more
Athingani than you.'

'You are getting at something. What is it?' Aimery spat impatiently.

'I think, nay I believe, but I do not *know*, that they were Catalan mercenaries. They fought like mercenaries, anyway, and not like snake-charmers. In my opinion.'

'I do not believe you,' said Aimery. And yet, from his voice, I could tell that he did not believe himself.

'And when I had discovered that, I thought, why kill Rollo? Why bother to put on such an elaborate disguise, if they planned to leave no witnesses? So I will ask you: was it your plan – I mean the intent of the company – to split into twos and hunt far apart from each other?'

'No, it was not. Actually, that is how I prefer to hunt, and Rollo too. But Gervais – that is Gervais du Perchoi, the tall fellow – he insisted that we make two parties. Now I come to think of it, he mentioned the Athingani in the first place.'

'Who is this Gervais?' I asked.

'He is the son of Guillaume du Perchoi, one of the emperor's barons,' said Aimery. 'You will have seen him with the Regent. An old man, with a crippled hand.'

'But Gervais is your friend.'

'Not particularly. He is a little high and mighty. I am a mere knight, raised on the field. He will be a baron one day soon, and the Regent already looks kindly upon him.' I wondered if I detected a note of jealousy. If I did, it was but a hint. I pressed on.

'The false Athingani must have been told to attack the main party, to show themselves, but to only kill one man. And that man, I am certain, was to have been me.'

Aimery pressed the heel of his hand into one eye. Then he sighed resignedly. He looked tired.

'Why would that be, do you think?' he asked.

'First tell me this. Are there any Venetians at court now?

298

Are there any Venetians who have the confidence, the close ear, of the Regent and the barons?'

'No ... only lately, anyway,' he said. 'I mean to say, there are always Venetians, and Pisans, and Genoese coming and going, begging for favours, asking for this in return for that.' He looked disgusted.

'You do not have much love for Venetians.'

'Ach, there are so many useless mouths eating at the Regent's table!' he burst out. 'And so many useless tongues giving advice. We need men and arms, nothing more.'

'And money,' I put in.

'That too. But, forgive me, with the Venetians and their demands, and the Pisans squabbling with the Genoese and all of them seeking to take from us; and then strange emissaries like yourself who flatter us and make promises which are never kept – with all this going on, the Greeks and the fucking Bulgars are still creeping over our empire like a canker, and what are we supposed to do? Crush them with bolts of Venetian silk? Choke them with pepper, or shoot them with catechisms? It is nonsense, nonsense!'

'I ...'

'Your pardon,' he said, briskly. 'I meant no offence. At first I took you for one of those bloodless clerics who delight in telling us how holy is our cause, and how certainly we will prevail. But plainly you are not. What you are, I intend to find out ...'

'Well then, I will tell you. But first, who are you?' I filled his cup to show I meant no insult. 'You are French, I take it?'

'I am Burgundian,' said Aimery, with a proud curl of the lip.

'And how did you come here?' I asked.

'Is it not obvious, good Englishman?' he gave a mirthless

chuckle. 'I am a second son, and had to seek my fortune. I have an uncle who holds fiefs for the Duke of Athens, and my father sent me to serve him when I was a lad. When the last king, I mean the Regent John, called for aid, for the Emperor of Bulgaria and the Greek king, Lascaris, had attacked him, I led a company here in time for the siege. That was two years ago. It was the old man himself who knighted me, just a week before he died. A pox on these weak fools who govern us now, Petrus. Old John of Brienne was more of a man than any of them.'

He slumped and fixed his eyes upon the dwindling contents of his goblet. For the first time since arriving in this place I found myself feeling sympathy for a Frank.

'Listen to me,' I said. 'I have a question which I think you will find impertinent coming from my mouth, and perhaps worse. And yet if you will tell me yes or no, I can tell you what lies behind all this, so far as I can.'

He narrowed his eyes and pushed back from the table. There was a long pause. 'Ask away, then,' he said at last.

'My question is this,' I said, lowering my voice and leaning forward over the table. 'Do you love your Emperor Baldwin?'

For a moment I thought I had made a terrible mistake, for Aimery drew himself up and his lips went white. He seemed about to strike me, but then his shoulders slumped again and he shook his head.

'I love him, but I have never seen him,' he said at last. 'He had already gone abroad when I came to this place, and he has not returned. We expect him daily, but then we get word that he is in London, or Paris, or Rome – everywhere in Christendom save in his own domain. So if love means that I will lay down my life to keep this city in his name for one more worthless day, then I do love him; for on my honour, I will do my duty unto death.'

'I have seen him,' I said quietly. He looked at me, startled.

'*You?* Where?' He burst out.

'In Rome. I am here at his behest, or rather at that of my master.'

'The pope,' Aimery said.

'No, actually. My master, Jean de Sol – he was here until a week ago – has been commissioned by His Holiness to raise money for your emperor. Real money, mind, and a lot of it. I am here to effect a certain transaction ...'

'Transaction?' said Aimery sharply.

So I gave him the bitter tangle of what had befallen since that first meeting with Baldwin in Marcho Antonio Marso's tavern. When I came to Horst's death I fell silent. Aimery filled my cup.

'Then you have lost a friend to this as well.' I nodded. I was about to utter some maudlin sentiment on the subject of dead friends, for enough wine had been drunk for that, when Aimery snapped his fingers.

'Lately, there has been a nobleman – do they have noblemen in Venice? But he looks like one – who has been in and out. Ridiculous clothes on the man: all flaming silks, and he thinks we want to look at his knees, forsooth! They treat him like Prester John himself: quite the little monarch.' His voice dropped again. 'I do not care for the Regent and those who surround him, as perhaps you've gathered,' he whispered. 'There is something weak – no, not exactly that. They scheme when they should fight. I feel the foundations of our empire tremble these days, like a rotten old ship's hull shakes when the waves strike it.'

'My friend, I will not insult your empire, but, if you will permit me, I will not disagree with you. But this Venetian: how long has he been here, do you know?'

'I would say he arrived a little before your colleague left – a day, no more. Wait, wait – I have his name. It is Nicholas. Nicholas Querchetti ... Quirinale. No, of course it is Querini. How could I forget such a name: the house of Querini is one of the richest in Venice. Only the Dandolos and Morosinis – you've heard of them, of course – are more powerful. If you are talking about money, I would say that the Querini purse is pretty well bottomless.'

'Querini?' I stammered. 'A short man, thickset? A swaggerer with a broken nose?' Aimery nodded, curious. 'Dear God, Aimery. Your ...' I shut my mouth hurriedly.

'You know this man?' Aimery's brows furrowed in surprise.

'Of him. His reputation ... his influence, I mean, is farflung.'

'Saints' blood, but I thank God I am but a soldier. I could not find my way for one minute in the mazes of your world,' said Aimery. I thanked the Fates that he did not press me further on the matter of Nicholas Querini, for he would have wished for answers that I had just begun to quest for myself. The wine was gone, and he stood up.

'I must leave – I have duties at the palace. I am glad I found you, Master Petrus. I no longer wish to kill you.'

'Praise the Lord!' I uttered.

'But there will be an end to that nonsense, fellow,' he snapped. 'I am no fool, and you are no priest, nor churchman either. What you are I have not yet divined, but you avenged my friend Rollo, and you have scented out something rotten in my lord's court. For that you have my gratitude. You are very far from your home, as am I – but if I have no ken of your world of intrigues and companies, I understand this place, and you do not. Be very careful. I do not believe that you have any friends here.'

I could say nothing to that, so I stood and shook his hand.

'You should leave Constantinople,' he said, as we left the tavern.

'I cannot. I must wait for the French envoys,' I reminded him.

'Then I think you will die here,' said Aimery, bluntly. He shook my hand again, gave me a nod that was more of a soldier's salute, and strode off into the lengthening shadows.

Chapter Twenty

I went back to the Bucoleon, for where else could I go? Aimery was right: I was utterly friendless in this city. No one remarked upon my arrival, though, which I took as a good sign. Querini had plainly not been lodged in the palace, the lucky man. Soaking wet and feeling shot through with cold, I made my way to the dining hall, for a fire often burned there all day even though the place was empty. Sure enough, a big olive-wood log was smouldering on its bed of embers. I sat down on the hot stone of the hearth and shivered with gratitude as the heat soaked into me. I spread my cloak out beside me and sat like that for a while, gazing up at the ceiling of coffered plaster, trying to make sense of things. When that failed I fell to wondering, as I often did in this sad palace, what the room had been in its days of glory, and so engaged in this pleasant and useless reverie did I become that I was roused only when a company of serving boys came in and started banging things about on the tables. Cursing, for I could see that it was dusk outside, I grabbed my cloak – still damp – and crept away, for I was not in the mood for company, and I did not wish to pass the time of day with any more Frankish ruffians.

I was navigating the maze of hallways that lay between the dining hall and the state-rooms, beyond which lay the way up to my lodgings, when I heard voices up ahead. I had no wish to be seen, so without thinking I ducked into the nearest doorway. I found myself in the ruined throne room with its fallen beams and heaps of rubble, a place I had been meaning to poke around in, but which, at this hour, was almost pitch dark. I leaned against a pillar to wait for the Franks to pass in the corridor. They clattered by, and I heard the voice of the Regent. He was speaking urgently, and sounded excited. Then Narjot de Toucy answered, sounding worried. Suddenly curious, I peeped around the column, just in time to catch a glimpse of the Regent's back as he swept by. And next to him, strolling along as if he were the emperor himself, a figure in a Venetian tunic of saffron silk. It was Nicholas Querini.

My dampness and desire for solitude all forgotten, I peered out into the corridor. It was empty save for the Regent and his companions, and so I crept out and began to follow them, hugging the walls where the shadows were thick, and where I knew the thick carpet of dust and crumbled plaster would muffle my footsteps. The three men turned a corner, then another, but to my surprise I discovered I still knew where I was. I had been this way before, weeks ago. Then I passed a ruined piece of mosaic, a faceless emperor raising his hand to bless the cobwebs, and I realised where I was being led: this was the way to the Pharos Chapel.

The lamps were few and far between down in this far outpost of the Bucoleon. Most were guttering and some were out, and so I was picking my way through pools of darkness. I was not worried that I would be found out, for I had learned this craft from Gilles himself, and besides, there were plenty of places to hide. So when the final corner was turned I was able to hunker down in the shadows behind an archway and watch as the guards, who clearly had not expected visitors to their remote outpost and were busy playing knucklebones, leaped to their feet with a crash of rusty chain mail. The Regent barked at them impatiently and pulled out a key. I heard it snick inside the lock, and then the door opened. The Regent indicated, with a somewhat cursory show of deference, that the Venetian should go first, and so he stepped into the blackness, followed by de Toucy, who had taken a lighted torch from the guards. The Regent came last, and pulled the door shut behind him.

I squatted there in the near-dark, breathing in the cold smell of damp limestone and dead flies. But my mind was ablaze. What business could these men have in the chapel at this late hour? I chewed it over. The Regent had a right to be anywhere he wished, I supposed, for it was his palace as far as that went. De Toucy clearly had not wished to accompany him. And Querini? He looked happy enough. My calves were being chewed by cramp and I had all but resolved to creep back to my chambers when the lock of the chapel door scratched and clicked and the hinges gave a dry moan.

Narjot de Toucy stepped out. He beckoned to a guardsman, who bent to hear a muttered command. Then the guard barked at his company and they jumped to their feet, looking at one another in puzzlement. Then they shuffled together until they stood shoulder to shoulder, and on another bark from the man I took for their sergeant they turned and faced the wall. When every guard had his back to the chapel door, de Toucy went back through it, only to emerge a moment later closely followed by the Regent. They were carrying a large black chest between them, and from the Regent's strained look it was plainly quite heavy. Then the Venetian emerged, and it was he who took out the key and locked the chapel door. To my growing amazement, the Regent and de Toucy, red in the face and breathing hard, started towards me down the passage, the Venetian following them with his self-satisfied, considered walk, an amused look upon his visage. I just had time to slide along the wall and into a side-vault before they passed me. I had a clear look at the chest. It seemed as though the two Franks carried the night itself between them, for their burden was hooped about with iron and nails, and long ago it had been coated with pitch. It was the reliquary of the Crown itself.

Surely this was some official business? Were they taking the Crown to Louis already, even before Louis' friars had arrived? That must be it. These men were taking the Crown to the friars in Venice. These thoughts flew across my mind like swallows through a barn, but I could grasp none of them, and none of them rang true, save the the one that told me I was in terrible trouble.

I recalled the looks on the faces of the men as they had entered the chapel. It had been no state business. There was no doubt but that this was a robbery, if a man can steal his own possession: but was the Regent the man committing the theft? From the look I had seen upon the Venetian's face I thought I knew the answer to that. He was a thief, pure and simple. I had seen that look a hundred times, and felt it upon my own face.

Back through the dead palace I followed them, my heart knocking against my ribs now, for here was the end of all my hopes, and the hopes of every man who served the *Cormaran*. But what to do? This affair had been left in my care – mine! Feeling not at all like a man who had conversed with pope and emperor, but very much like a frightened Dartmoor shepherd boy I trailed the men back through the realms of spider and bat, past the smashed glory of a lost age, wondering how, in this world, I could make amends, and how I could, somehow, avenge my master.

Meanwhile, thievery had evidently loosened the tongues of the three men, for now the Regent had started to chatter nervously to the other two. I could not hear very much, for the walls either muffled sound or splintered it into a thousand twittering echoes. But as I crept along behind, at last I made out the words 'de Montalhac' and 'decree'. It was the Regent who had spoken, and in reply, Querini threw back his head and laughed. I skipped and shuffled as close as I dared, throwing myself behind an unravelling tapestry in time to hear Querini say: '... be dead by now, I should think ... paid the ship's master enough ...'

A chill descended upon me and I shrank against the wall, into its crust of rotten fresco and dead insects. The Captain was dead. No! Impossible: dear Jesus, it could not be possible. But he had left on a Venetian ship a day after Aimery had said Querini had landed. I closed my eyes, and there he was, hand raised to me against the muddy sky, the ship sliding out into the black water. 'I bribed the master.' I heard him speak the words, and saw, as I had done in Foligno, how clear had been the trap. Now ... now I was truly alone.

The footsteps in the passage were growing fainter. My quarry had not stopped at the state-rooms, but kept on towards the servants' quarters. Whimpering like an abandoned hound I forced myself to follow. They marched – more shuffled, in truth, for the two Frankish lords were plainly not in the flower of their manhood, and stopped more than once to set down their burden while they wrung their hands and panted. When they heard footsteps approaching they, like me, would duck into the first empty room, but as it was dinner time most of the Frankish folk were occupied, and I noticed that the Regent and his friends cared not that the Greek servants observed them. Finally they halted before a door I had not seen before, but which I judged must lead to one of the outer buildings of the palace. The Venetian knocked, and at once the door swung open to reveal a small company of soldiers. They were far better dressed and equipped than the imperial troops, for they wore new leather hauberks on which were sewn patches and bosses of shining metal, they were clean shaven and looked well-fed. I had seen such men on the deck of Querini's galley. The two lords had set down the chest gratefully, and at a signal from the Venetian it was at once scooped up by four soldiers and carried from my sight. The Venetian – even from my vantage point some way away I could see he was fairly quivering with pride – gave a jaunty bow to the Regent and offered his hand. The Regent offered his hand and winced when it was squeezed. Then, leaving nothing but a ghost of saffron light in his wake, the Venetian leaped after his men and was gone.

I did not wait to see what the Frankish lords did next, but rushed through a welter of grief and panic towards my chambers. I needed to make some sort of plan, I knew, but what, dear God, was the point? No! I must not fail my master and my company. As I forced myself up the long staircase, I thought I would write a letter to Gilles, which perhaps could be sent by fast ship tomorrow. But, no – a letter? What a feeble thought, what nonsense! It was far, far too late for that, I knew, for like words resolving themselves as the reading-stone is lowered on to them, the events of the last few days came into sharp and terrible focus. The Venetian, Querini or whoever he was, had killed Captain de Montalhac and bought the Crown. He had purchased it outright, I guessed, and the sight of real money had turned the heads of the Regent and his barons. The Captain had been too inconvenient; doubtless – how clear it all became now! – Querini planned to treat with Louis himself. And he had turned the court into a nest of simoniacs. Because ... because he thought the Captain still had the decree of absolution. How many were involved? Was it the whole court? But the three men had been furtive indeed, like thieves in their own house, so perchance this was a plot. So much the worse for me, then: Querini, or the Regent himself, had tried to have me put out of the way along with the Captain. I could not stay here an hour longer: Aimery was right. I was a dead man if I did not leave at once.

And then I understood, or rather surrendered myself to understanding, for it was not a path I wished to take. The discrepancies in the *Inventaria*: the sandals of Christ, the Robe of the Virgin Mary, and what had set Gilles and the Captain chattering: the *Mandylion* of Edessa. The spices, the Captain had called them: an added commission for us, priceless goods on top of the untold riches already guaranteed. They were to have disappeared into my luggage sometime during the leisurely negotiations and no one would have been the wiser. It was a plan almost banal in its simplicity. But now, suddenly, I had the means to offset disaster and the ruin of every one of our schemes. I still had the pope's decree, which perhaps was more valuable than everything else combined. But I would have to act fast. It should be easy to talk my way into the chapel, for the guards would not question the seal of Saint Peter. Nor would they question me, I hoped, if I removed certain things. For items were leaving already, and under the clear auspices of the Regent himself. It would be easy, if nerve-racking. I would do the thing now, at once, before I could change my mind. Then I would smuggle my loot out of the palace, make my way to a Genoese *skala* and buy my way on to the next ship back to Italy and the *Cormaran*.

I had reached my corridor, and all but ran the last steps to my chambers. I wanted nothing more than to lock the door behind me and curl up in a corner. But as I stepped inside I was grabbed from either side, pulled off my feet and dragged, at a run, over to the bed. I did not have time to cry out before someone grasped a handful of my hair, and then my face was being pressed into the sheets. I felt my knife being snatched from my belt, then my arms were tugged back much farther than nature had ever intended them to go. I shouted something – a protest, an oath – but a fierce blow to the ear silenced me. Then I was hauled up again by my arms, all but out of their sockets and flaying me with molten pain, and forced down on to my knees on the stone floor. I had time to see that the little iron-bound chest where the pope's decree had lain was open, the lock gouged and splintered. So Querini had it after all. Here is the end of everything, I thought. Then my hair was seized again – did I have any left? I felt tonsured anew – and my head jerked back so that I was looking up into the face of a man who had stepped in front of me. It was Hughues, the chamberlain.

'So: the murderer continues to enjoy our emperor's hospitality. How *practical* of him. Now then. Boy.' He snapped his fingers under my nose. Seeing how I flinched, he did it again, and when the others sniggered he slapped me across the face, hard. His fingers were loaded with heavy rings and I felt as if I had been punched by a mailed fist. Blood started to run down the back of my throat, and I coughed.

'All right, get him up, get him up. Take him to the scriptorium.' I tried to drink the blood that was pouring from my nose: I had a foggy idea that I could stop it staining my tunic.

'For God's sake, Hughues, can't we just slit his throat and drop him in the harbour? We know he killed young Rolant – don't we, Aimery?'

I tried to turn, but whoever had a hold of my hair gave it a twist and I bit my lip to keep from crying out.

'*I* know. He as much as told me. These churchmen, d'you see, they are so fond of their words. Condemned himself out of his own mouth. Shocking – absolutely shocking.'

The voice of Aimery was as cold and dull as the fog that drifted on the Golden Horn. Rage flared in my chest, but not surprise, for no betrayal, I thought bitterly, would surprise me again. But all I could do was writhe uselessly as my arms and scalp blazed with agony. But now I was pulled to my feet and my arms were released for a moment. The sudden absence of pain almost made me faint, but then my wrists were being tied in front of me and I was being pushed from the room.

My eyes had been watering so much from the pain in my scalp that I had not been able to look about me. Now I did, and saw that the chamber was full of men: Hughues the chamberlain, the baron who had argued with Aimery yesterday and another I had seen in the Regent's company; Gervais was there, and another huntsman, and a crowd of others whom I did not recognise but who all had the sneering cast of Frankish brutality about them. And, leaning on the door jamb, eyes narrowed, was Aimery himself.

When you are preparing for a fight – if you are lucky enough to be able to prepare – you can at least force yourself to believe that you will survive. And when you are fighting you do not think at all. But now, bound as I was and surrounded by hating strangers, I was visited by the certainty that I was about to die. Perhaps not instantly, no, but I knew, as sure as I knew my own name, that what was happening to me now was not part of my life: it was the very beginning of my death.

I had seen men die. It is horrible, always. They whine, they piss and shit themselves like helpless babies. They call on their god and they beg for their mothers. This was going to happen to me very soon. Strangely, I was not frightened. I was in pain, for my sinews were ripped across my shoulders and my cheek felt as if it were shattered; and perhaps that allayed the fear somewhat. But I also loathed these people with all my heart – with mine, and with Anna's, maybe – and I was furious beyond measure that my death was to come at their hands. I thought of Captain de Montalhac, and how relieved he had seemed to once more be aboard a ship, and of what had happened after that. So I drew myself up, stuck my chin in the air and paced as steadily as I could out into the passage. The huntsman and another courtier took me by the elbows and the others formed up in a mocking escort around us. They marched along quickly so that I kept stumbling, and as we went down the stairs I almost fell three or four times. Indeed, if they had not held me so tight I might have thrown myself down in search of a cleanly broken neck. But I reached the hall below and they dragged me along, making me trip and dance between them for the amusement of the company. What a merry gallows-crowd we must have made! But alas, only the Greek servants were there to see us, and they cast down their eyes.

The scriptorium turned out to be a room that gave on to the chamber where the Regent had received the Captain and me on that first day. It was small and lined with benches and tables, and felt a little like a study room in my abbey, far away in Devon. There were no monks here, however; just the Regent himself sitting in a high-backed chair. My escort took the other seats. I was left standing in the centre of the room. It took me a long instant to understand that my trial had begun. And at that moment my anger vanished and cold despair curled itself about me like smoke.

'Young man,' said the Regent. I wondered how he was feeling after his ordeal with the reliquary: he seemed to have recovered rather well, and with the aid of the silver jug and goblet at his elbow, no doubt. 'Young man, you have abused, *most horribly*, the friendship extended to you by His Majesty the Emperor Baldwin through his Regent.' He paused and scratched his throat, and I saw that he had succeeded in getting quite drunk in the few minutes since I had last seen him.

I drew myself up, damaged ribs shrieking within my breast. 'I am no murderer,' I said loudly. 'Where is Captain … Captain de Sol? I call Nicholas Qu—' A fist landed in my guts and I doubled over, retching iron-sour bile. Then I was jerked upright, and as I gasped for breath a wad of greasy cloth was forced into my mouth. I yelled into it, uselessly. Through watering eyes I saw that my wish had been obeyed, for there, against the far wall, leaned a heavyset man in Venetian silk. The Regent turned to him, and Nicholas Querini gave a curt nod.

'A young man – a *beloved* young man lies dead in this very palace, victim of a most cowardly and inhuman slaughter,' the Regent went on, as if I had not spoken. 'Rolant de la Rouche was the nephew of our gracious vassal the Duke of Athens. His death casts a pall over the empire itself, and dishonour to our court. Justice, we trust, will wash away that dishonour. Does anyone speak for the accused?'

There was silence, of course, except for some faint giggling. That unnerved me more than anything, and I felt my bowels turn to water.

'The court will note that the accused chose no representation, and has not spoken in his defence,' said the Regent. I was about to try to say something, but the echo of that giggle told me it was a waste of my breath. 'Witnesses! We have witnesses, do we, Hughues?'

'Certainly. I call Gervais de Perchoi,' said Hughues, lazily. The tall figure of Gervais stepped forward.

'Gervais de Perchoi, you were with the company that rode to the Philopation park yesterday.' Gervais nodded. 'What was your intent?'

'To hunt for boar,' said Gervais.

'And your further purpose?'

'To entertain an honoured guest of the emperor, sire.'

'Who was this guest?'

'The accused, sire.'

There was nothing more to it than that. Gervais was asked another four or so questions, the other huntsman stood up to confirm his answers. Then it was the turn of Aimery. He stood there fairly quivering with rage as he described what he had found at the scene of the fight: to whit, myself attempting to prop up an Athingani body so it might appear that Rollo and the Athingani had killed each other; my guilty countenance; and the plain impossibility that a young churchman such as myself could have done the deeds he boasted of. Plainly Rollo had killed both attackers and had then been murdered by the accused.

'And why?' The Regent was not curious. He knew the answer, apparently.

'The accused – a wretch without moral scruples – confessed rather proudly that he had murdered Rolant at the bidding of a Genoese interest.'

'That is so.' The voice of Nicholas Querini, fat with silken menace. He pushed himself lazily away from the wall where he leaned and ambled over to the Regent's table. 'We – that is, the forces of the Serene Republic of Venice, greatest friend to Constantinople and her Latins – intercepted this creature's master, one Michel de Montalhac, who styled himself Jean de Sol to ingratiate himself with Your Highness. He was en route to Genoa, swift – so he thought! – as a venomous serpent, gorged with vital intelligence of your empire's defences, treasury ... all that was necessary for Genoa to usurp the throne of Baldwin de Courtenay.'

There was consternation in the chamber, a clamour of

enraged voices, many of them buzzy with drink, singing like hounds for blood. I moaned into my gag. It was taking every ounce of my strength to stay on my feet.

'Fear not, brave souls!' Querini had to shout above the din. He held his arms aloft like a market preacher. 'The serpent is dead, and the worm will soon follow!' He scanned the room, a little smile curling his too-fine lips, and his eyes came to rest upon me. Unblinking, hard as iron nail-heads, his stare seemed to press itself into my eye sockets, until I flinched and looked away for an instant. And when I looked back, he had tilted his head a little to the side, and his smile was wider and more cruel. I was the worm, and he had crushed me.

'Extraordinary!' the Regent was blustering meanwhile. 'Hughues, order a sweep of the Genoese *skalai* immediately. Seigneur de Lille Charpigny, the court thanks you for your answers, and for your diligence in bringing your friend's assassin to justice. That,' he clapped his hands, and poured himself a little more wine, 'is that. The court finds the accused, Petrus Zennorius, to be guilty of the murder of Rolant de la Rouche, of conspiring with the Republic of Genoa against the Empire of Romania, and of passing himself off as the agent of His Holiness Pope Gregory. The punishment for any one of those acts is death.'

Querini laid his pugilist's hand, heavy and beringed, upon the Regent's shoulder. He bent and spoke into the older man's ear. Then he was gone, leaving nothing but the memory of his power, and the faint glow of golden silk. The rest of them let me stand there for a few minutes while they stared at me, muttering to each other and tittering. The Regent stood up and left in his turn, taking his wine with him. I tried to catch his eye as he passed me, but his face was sunk into a mask of something that resembled guilty delight. For my part I dared not move a muscle, lest it hasten my end. For now my thoughts had begun to turn, not to the fact of death itself, but the form it was to take. I feared that my audience was presently deciding that very thing. Finally Gervais rose to his feet and stretched.

'Come, fellows: we have a duty to perform.'

At once they swarmed about me. 'Come along, then,' said one of them, almost kindly. I felt a nudge in my back and followed Gervais from the room. I felt their eyes upon me. They were studying me closely, for to them I was no longer alive, but a mere curiosity: a ghost already.

'Take out the gag,' ordered Gervais. 'Perhaps he will beg us for his life.' The gag was yanked out, and I coughed and spat redly.

'Where are we going?' It was Aimery, and he alone sounded as full of rage as the others had earlier.

'To the courtyards, of course,' said Gervais. 'The gallows where they hang the commoners. I will send for the tanner: we shall flay him while he lives, and nail his skin to the gate of the Genoese quarter. Does that not seem fitting?'

We were walking through a plain, whitewashed passageway. It smelled of boiling food and boiled clothes. Doors led off here and there, and I glimpsed people bent over their work: mending, cooking, brewing, the things of life, the things I took for granted. And now they were going to flay me. I had seized my bottom lip between my teeth to keep from whimpering, and now my jaw so trembled that I bit clean through the skin. My mouth, though, was dry, and my throat was so parched that it felt like being choked. Yet everything about me had taken on a sort of luminous calm. The white walls shone like moonlight. I was feeling lighter: my feet no longer seemed to be touching the floor. So when Aimery halted in mid-stride and turned, I almost did not notice.

'No, Gervais! I cannot let you … it is for me to do! Rollo

was my dear friend, and now I must suffer the memory of this louse defiling his poor corpse for the rest of my days. Let me finish him.'

Gervais laughed sympathetically. 'I know, good Aimery. But consider, we are not exercising vengeance, but justice! We are mere instruments of His Majesty in this. Fear not: he'll linger.' And he turned and gave me a nod, as if to reassure me that I was in capable hands.

'No, by Jacob's ... No.' I wondered how I had not noticed before: Aimery de Lille Charpigny was plainly mad. He was shaking his head and twitching with fury. Finally, clenching his fists until I thought the bones would pop from his knuckles, he leaned towards Gervais with a forced smile on his lips. 'Well then, could you allow me a few moments? I'll ...' and the rest was whispered. Apparently Gervais found nothing objectionable, for he clapped Aimery on the back. 'Well then, go to, sirrah. We will await your call.'

Aimery strode up to me. He laid his hand on my shoulder and looked into my eyes. Then he brought his knee up smartly into my ballocks. The luminous calm of the world vanished into a whirlpool of nauseating pain. I bent forward and the Frank caught me by the neck and pulled me sideways. I heard the sound of a foot kicking wood, but dimly, because the blood was roaring in my ears and I had quite possibly just pissed in my britches. Then I was floating through the air, and just had time to wonder if the lovely pale calmness had returned when my chin struck a cobblestone floor. A hand grabbed my hair again and lifted my head. I found I was staring into the heart of a fire.

'Get up. Get up!' Aimery was almost shrieking now. He sounded almost like a woman. Was he a woman? I was not really sure what was happening. But I hauled myself up until I was kneeling, body propped on my bound hands.

'Now then, you Cornish maggot, I'm going to cut off your balls and make you eat them.' There was the neat little hiss of a well-oiled blade being drawn. Then the hand let go of my hair.

'For God's sake!' Aimery screeched again. 'Cannot a man be alone in this fucking place for one moment? Let me have my due!' And a door crashed shut behind me. I blinked, but all I could see was fire. Then through the fire I saw a dark blur. Flames and tentacles of black hair whirled and melded, and there, at the centre of that halo, a white face, a skull: only the eternal insignia of eye sockets, nose and mouth. The calm had returned. So this was what Michael Scotus had meant me to see: my death. I gave a little sob of relief, and felt tears begin to sting the gash on my cheek. Then Aimery seized me under the arms and pulled me upright.

'I am sorry, Petrus,' he hissed.

'No, it is all right now. I am ready,' I said.

'I am not,' he said, and I felt a brush of cold against my wrists. Suddenly my hands were free, and the blood began to rush back into them, agonisingly.

'Zoe! Take our friend, and hurry.' From behind the fire – it burned on a kind of plinth, and I saw we were in a brew-house, for huge copper kettles stood all about us – stepped the little Greek serving girl.

'Ah, fuck,' said Aimery. 'You will have to hit me. Wait …' and he pulled off his tunic and waved it over the fire until the hem and one sleeve caught fire. He hastily trod them out and drew the charred thing back on. 'Now, hit me.' He stood before me, palms up, impatient.

'Why are you …?' I asked him.

'Because to take an innocent life is a sin. And because to butcher you would dishonour Rollo. For fuck's sake, hit me!'

I could no more have hit a man at that moment than I could have laid a golden egg, but fortunately Zoe stepped smartly around me and before I could stop her, she raised a huge wooden pestle above her head and brought it down on Aimery's skull.

Chapter Twenty-One

Zoe seized my hand and tugged at it. 'Come,' she said. I looked down at Aimery. He was still and his mouth was open, though he still breathed.

'I think you broke his skull,' I said, stupidly.

'No. If his skull was broken he would be dead, or snoring like a pig as he died.' She gave an ugly snort. 'He is asleep. Come. Now. The rest of them are just behind us.'

So I followed her. There was a narrow doorway at the back of the brew-house, and the door had a bolt. Zoe struggled with the heavy, rusted iron, so I slammed it home and looked about me. We were in another corridor, this one much decayed. There was moss on the floor and rubble in heaps. Zoe bent down to snatch up a small bundle that lay just outside the door, and then, without waiting for me, she took to her heels, and I hobbled after as fast as I could go, for my ballocks felt like burning coals and I thought that a rib was surely broken, for there was a burning in my side worse than any stitch. And besides, I had not the faintest idea what had just happened. How did Aimery and this Zoe know each other? The girl, lean and dark as a shadow, darted around the fallen beams and turned a corner, then another. Growling through clenched teeth against the pain, I found her standing next to a door which she opened for me.

'Go in there,' she said. She followed me in and shut the door.

We were in a small, high-walled room with no roof. Rags of cloud were scudding past the stars high overhead. On two sides, the room was lined with stone benches into which round holes had been cut.

'A privy?' I asked Zoe, puzzled.

'Yes. Unlike you Franks, we do not shit in the corridors,' she said, haughtily. 'Wait.' She stepped over to the nearest bench, grabbed the edge of one of the holes and heaved. With a dull scraping, the whole stone top moved, until a gap had appeared between it and the wall.

'Climb down there,' said Zoe, folding her arms and fixing me with her dark glare.

'What? Into the …'

'There's nothing down there!' she hissed, exasperated. 'No one has used this place for forty years – more. No one knows it is even here. In another year or so, it will not be,' she added, glancing up at the ragged tops of the walls. 'This is how the palace folk come in and out when there is trouble. Climb down – you will find a tunnel. It goes straight and does not divide. Follow it. You will come out in an old cistern outside the palace. It is under a chapel to which no one goes. There is a trap-door up to the crypt. And take this.'

She thrust her bundle at me. It unravelled in my hands: my old travelling cloak, and a dagger – no, not a dagger, a cook's knife. I looked at it, stupidly. A single edge, pitted grey steel, and a much worn handle of whittled wood. But its single edge was sharp, and it had a point, of sorts. In that way it was as good as Thorn, as good as any blade. And there, heavy and officious, the leaden disc of the pope's decree. I opened my mouth to yell out with relief, but a small foot kicked me hard on the shin. When I looked up, Zoe was pointing, imperiously, to the latrine. Under her gaze I had no choice but to clamber up on to the teetering slab and sit down where countless ancient bums had sat, legs dangling down into the unpromising hole beneath. I tucked the knife into my belt so that the handle lay against the small of my back. Zoe came up behind me and placed her hands on my shoulders. I flinched, but she did not move.

'My debt is paid. I thank you, Master Frank. Find your way to Hagia Sophia tomorrow evening and go up to the south gallery. Wait by the mosaic of the *Deesis* – O Frankish dog, Christ with the *Theotokos* and the Baptist at his side. Someone will come for you.'

I turned, mouth forming a question, but she put her finger to her lips. I suddenly wondered how old she was, for in that instant she could have been a child or some ancient spirit of this cursed city. Then she smiled, and pushed me in.

It was a short drop, only my body's length and a little more, and I did not have time to protest. I landed on what felt like old turf but I knew was not. There was a grinding above me and I looked up in time to see a hand, framed against the stars by the rim of a latrine hole. It waved once and was gone. I heard the door clank shut. For a moment I considered hoisting myself out of this ghastly place and finding another way out, but then I reasoned that I might as well die on my own terms in a quiet jakes than be flayed in front of a gang of laughing fools. So I dropped on to all fours and felt about me. I soon found the mouth of the tunnel, and indeed a faint breeze came from within, so, wincing, I crawled in.

Immediately there was utter darkness. I was in a space perhaps a hand's span wider than my body on each side and above. The floor was dry and spongy, and felt like peat. I tried not to think about it, but in truth it smelled somewhat like a peat-bog: raw and ripe, but not fetid. I crawled on, keeping a hand outstretched before me, barking my elbows against the sides at first and once, when my hand found a thick skein of cobweb, banging my head when I raised it, startled. Like a badger or some other plodding, subterranean beast I blundered, losing all sense of time and distance, until my hand came down and found nothing. I almost pitched forward but stopped myself. I had reached the cistern.

It was utterly dark in here as well, and I did not wish to discover by touch what might be lurking around me, so I decided to stay in the tunnel. I hoped that the light of day would show me at least a glimmer of where the trap-door might be. Meanwhile, I had decided that the encrusted shit of millennia was as comfortable a bed as I could hope for this night. I curled up, hugging myself for warmth, and fell, suddenly, into a deep, stunned sleep.

When I awoke it was still nothing but heavy, silky darkness all about me, so I lay there, fretting and giving thanks by turns – for I did not feel so badly hurt and the rib was not, I thought, broken after all, only cracked – until, indeed, a faint outline showed, like four long golden hairs suspended in the blackness. It was the trap-door, and it was unlocked, and in a few moments I stood in the crypt that Zoe had described. Daylight does not belong in a crypt, but half of the roof had fallen in upon the grave-slabs and the stacks of rotted wooden chairs. I climbed cautiously into the chapel above: it was deserted and cold, and smelled of piss. The rood-screen had been desecrated, and yet someone had recently been here, for fresh candle-stubs stood in a little bowl of clean sand that had been placed before a mosaic of some armoured saint-warrior. I opened the door and peeped out into clear, early sunshine.

The chapel was halfway along a street of shuttered houses. There was a walled garden to the right, fig trees and un-pruned vines spilling over the stones. At the end of the street to my left I saw the sea, blue and serene. So I was facing west. I had done some thinking down there in the sewer. Go to Hagia Sophia, the girl had said. Someone will come for you. But who? It had slowly come to me that my best hope would be to reach a Pisan or Genoese *skala* and try to talk my way on to a ship bound for Italy, or indeed anywhere. They might even remember me at the place the Captain and I had spent our first night. They would feed me. And perhaps there would be news of the French envoys: surely they could not be far off now, and they would vouch for me, for I would tell them of the captain, and of the pope ... It was an excellent plan, made all the more tempting by the mild, hopeful air of morning. But no, Querini would be looking to meet the envoys at sea, and turn them back to Venice. Ach, I would promise them money from the *Cormaran*'s funds, and I could work my passage. What else could I do? There was no point leaving my bones in this sewer for want of strong nerves. So I set out towards the Golden Horn.

At the end of the street I turned a corner and found myself up against the outer wall of the Bucoleon Palace. Of course: I had not crawled very far, although it had seemed like a league or more in the dark. I backtracked, and found a street that seemed to be going in the direction of Hagia Sophia, and sure enough the great dome soon showed where a line of buildings had collapsed. There were few people about, just Greeks heading towards the palace and a few children up early to plan their mischief. I kept to the shadow-side of the streets, but had started to feel almost confident when a rattle of hooves sounded from behind. I had time to vault into a garden, from where I watched a Catalan mounted on a pony crash past, scattering the cats and calling down curses from the few tenanted windows. It was the sort of bullying nonsense that the occupiers did to pass the time, and so I started on my way again. But I had only gone a few more yards when another pony dashed across the way ahead of me. Soon I heard hooves everywhere. I edged along, looking around each corner. One alley led to the square before Hagia Sophia, and even from where I stood I could see that there were armed men milling about. I pressed on, but then a group of frightened people appeared, herded by two mounted Catalans. They protested, and one of the soldiers leaned down and whipped a woman across the face with his crop. Then they rode off, leaving the Greeks waving their arms in consternation. I turned aside and started down another street, towards the sea this time, thinking to work my way back to the chapel and hide there until nightfall, for clearly something was amiss in the city.

I heard a shout behind me. I turned around to find a Catalan standing at the top of the street. He beckoned to me. I turned and ran, only to run full tilt into the flank of a pony which was walking out from a side street. The beast flinched and I looked up into the bearded face of a soldier, a swarthy mercenary from the north or east. He leered and before I could move, grabbed a fistful of my hair. In a frenzy I seized his boot and pulled with my full weight. For a horrible moment I hung suspended by the hair, but I had put the man off balance and with a shout of anger he crashed down on top of me. I was up first, and kicked him in the face, but missed my aim and caught him on the ear. The pony was whinnying and so I got hold of the reins and tried to get my foot into a stirrup. The beast was frightened, though, and kept dancing, sending the mercenary scrabbling away from its hooves. At the last second I saw that I was about to be crushed between pony and wall and dropped to the ground, squirmed beneath the shaggy belly and took to my heels up the empty alleyway. Behind me I heard a bellowed curse and then the winding of a hunting-horn. Immediately the sound was taken up from somewhere all too near at hand, then another horn rang, then another. Booted feet pounded on cobblestones. I looked behind me one last time, to see a company of men-at-arms spilling out into the street. They had seen me. I tripped, got my balance and saw a narrow stepped way to one side, leading uphill.

I ran up the shallow steps, feet falling uncertainly upon crumbling plaster and slimy moss. A dying cat watched me through incurious, crusting eyes. Reaching the top I burst into open space and blazing sun: a little open square, ancient, sunken church at one end, windowless houses all around. A contorted olive tree wrestled in the strangling grasp of ivy as it guarded a broken marble well. And in front of the well, a naked man sprawled, headless. His skin was the creamy hue of a plucked chicken, made more yellow by the scarlet insult of the severed neck. I stopped in my tracks. A pair of women were making their way, crab-like, from the direction of the church, edging sideways, their heads twitching with apprehension. They wrung their hands and tore at their clothing in a way that seemed strangely inhuman, as if the conflict of grief and fear had reduced them to marionettes. I stepped back into the shade and squinted at the body. He had been tall and black-haired, and whoever had chopped off his head had subjected him to a long torment, judging by the bruises and slashes that were scattered over his chest and legs. This was the stock-in-trade of those men who were at this moment hunting me, and that thought sent me sprinting out from the shadows and across the square. The two women shrieked again when they saw me. I glanced at the corpse as I dashed past, and wished I had not done so, for I would not then have seen the pulpy void where the genitals should have been. Bile spiking the back of my throat I looked for the way out, saw an opening behind the church and bolted past the women, who fled away from me. Then I was back in the cat-scented shade again, and running down a level street. A wider thoroughfare crossed in front of me, and as I came out into the brightness again I heard the clicking of hooves. A company of soldiers were marching towards me, flanked by three men on horseback. In the moment it took me to take this in I saw that one of the horsemen wore palace livery and another was a beaky man who had often been in the Regent's company. I recognised him as he recognised me, and as the shadows swallowed me again the sudden tumult of spurred horses and shouted commands echoed from the walls.

Everything was ruined here. The great fires of thirty years ago had gutted every house and left the windows and doors blank. Soot stains ran down the walls like black tears, and weed trees were bursting from the ruins. The street ran straight, and I cursed the ancients, who had planned their city so well. My feet were crashing on the flagstones.

'There! There!' Excited voices behind me. I put my chin to my chest and hurtled on. The buildings on either side seemed to taper off into infinity before me like the landscape of a nightmare. I ran and ran, my breath growing shorter and tasting of blood. Oh Christ, where did this street lead? – to the Golden Horn, I prayed, but perhaps it just went on and on, to Novgorod or the barbarous wastes of the Tartars. I tripped and flailed, then recovered. The charred air was sour and damp. I gulped desperately. Then, like a blink of an eye, sunlight flashed to my right. I tried to stop, but tripped again and slapped into the wall, barking my hands, which came away sooty and grazed. But there was a tiny opening between two buildings, an alleyway. I fell into it.

The sun streamed down on to burned beams, tumbled marble and the tossing, yellowing leaves of an elderberry thicket. The bushes were heavy with the burden of black fruit, and a great cloud of sparrows, which had been feasting, flew up around me. I beat at them in a panic, crashing through the brittle twigs, ripe berries popping in my face like black raindrops. I was almost caught, for there were brambles with wickedly long thorns tangled all through the thicket. Then my foot hit something hard and in another moment I was scrambling up a heap of tumbled stones. My eyes were screwed shut for fear of the brambles, but my hands guided me up. Suddenly my fingers sunk into crumbling dampness and then thin air, and I tumbled forward into nothing.

I fell for an awful, belly-cramping instant, then landed on more wood – or so it must have been, for the rotten, chimney-tar stench of it scoured my nose and mouth – before pitching downward again on to something hard and angular. Stone steps, pale in the deep shadows. I rolled and jounced down and down, clawing for a handhold and finding none, before I reached the bottom and came to rest on mossy flagstones. There I lay, panting and battered, eyes shut, watching lights weave and pop behind my lids. When at long last I opened them, I beheld the stairway down which I had fallen reaching far up to a small, ragged patch of leaf-fretted daylight. Finding my neck and back were as yet unbroken, I sat up and looked about me.

I was in a large cellar, although it was the grandest cellar I had ever seen. An undulation of brick arches made up the ceiling, and although I could only make out one wall, that was of fine ashlar. I had narrowly avoided cracking my head on a stone pillar carved with vines and goggle-eyed birds, and many more of them grew up all around, a petrified, sunken forest.

'Here! He came this way!' Shouting came from high above me, and drifted down, thin and hollow. I could make out a Catalan snarling angrily, and the softer accent of some northerner. Then a crisp Frankish voice silenced them.

'He's gone down here. After him, you boys – terriers after a rat. Go on!'

I sprang up, bruised limbs objecting, set my back against the pillar and pulled out my butcher's knife. Much good it would do me. I swallowed, staring at the little square of daylight through which my killers would shortly come for me. I thought of the headless man I had seen, and my stomach lurched. Better to die now than to give such beasts their fun with me. I whimpered, and felt the blade's edge: sharp enough. Dear God. How best to do this? A thrust into my heart, or a slash across the throat? Not the throat, no! I would not drown in my own blood. The heart, then – it would be quick. I dropped down to my knees again and took the greasy old wooden handle in both my cold, damp hands. The blade quivered and I stilled the point against my chest. Do it now. Do it now! The little blue window of sky was so beautiful, blue as a jay's feather, as the summer sky over high Dartmoor. The tip of the blade jabbed my flesh and I flinched. I could not leave like this. The promise of that glorious blue was too strong. Let me at least sell my life dearly: let the last blood I spilled be that of those barbarous huntsmen. I lowered the knife and backed away into the shadows, keeping my eyes fixed to the top of the stairway. Another pillar. I slipped behind it, into the darkness, and crouched.

From up amongst the elderberries came a tumult of snapping branches and curses. A few dead leaves drifted down into the cellar. Boot-studs scraped on stone. Then the Frank's sharp voice rang out: 'Here! No, pigs, *here!*'

'Let him fuck his old mother,' said someone very loudly in Catalan. The man must be right by the cellar-hole. In the way that one's mind works in times of great danger or fear, I found myself wondering whether the Frankish lord understood the tongue of his mercenaries. It did not seem all that likely. I hunkered down: they were coming.

But they did not. The Frank's voice came again, further away now. When next the Catalans spoke, I could barely make out what they said: buggery, and sisters. They had not found the stairway. Of course: I had followed an alley, but the thicket had confused me and I must have strayed into a ruined house. My hunters had found where the alley continued on, and they would have assumed I had fled that way, and that I had a good lead on them by now. Hardly daring to hope, let alone to breathe, I leaned my forehead against the cold stone and watched the sky. One by one, then in twos and threes and finally in a swarm, the sparrows flew across the blue and soon the sound of their happily resumed feast told me that the ruin was once again abandoned by men. I breathed out, coughing, and put the knife away. There was a sharp pain under my left nipple where it had tickled my flesh. Would I really have killed myself? I wondered, feeling how shaky my legs were. My little wound stung me again, as if to remind me how thin was the border between being and not being. The hand thrusts the knife, the knife pierces the body and the soul flees. I rubbed at the cut and listened to the sparrows.

It would be folly to leave my hiding place in daylight, that was plain. Just because I was lost did not mean that my hunters were, and with so few people on the streets anyway, a marked man in nice Venetian clothes would stand out like a sore thumb. I settled down on the bottom step. Perhaps there was some food left in my purse. Rummaging, my fingers found, not the dry bread I had finished hours ago, but my tinderbox. I pulled it out, made a little torch from the litter of dead twigs that covered the stairway and struck a spark. The pithy elderberry twigs caught, but sullenly, and the pithy wood began to smoke. But as the flame grew hotter so the light grew. I held my torch up and looked about me.

Pillars stretched away out of sight, or at least beyond the reach of the weak flame. The flagstone floor was clear in places, but in others it was mounded with bat-droppings – only now did I hear the creatures cursing me from the roof – and piles of twigs and old rubbish that must have been dragged down here by rats. There was a wisp of red cloth sticking out from one of these rubbish nests, and, not having anything better to do, I went over and prodded at it with my foot. There was a dry rustle and the pile collapsed in on itself. Something large and pale rolled, clacking, at my shoe. Recoiling with an oath, thinking it was a cellar rat or monstrous, pale spider, for was I not sunk part-way into nightmare already, I drew back to kick it, but as I took aim I found myself staring at two great black eyes. Not eyes, though: shadows. It was a skull, a human skull, and what I had taken for a rat's nest was a huddled skeleton.

I yelped, then stifled it. Looking closer despite my growing horror, I saw that each bundle of rubbish was indeed a corpse. Feeling less bold with every step, but drawn on by that curiosity that forces men to stare, fascinated, at what repulses their every sense, I picked my way further into the shadows. Two skeletons, three, seven, a dozen … Christ! A score of them. And then I saw it.

The back wall of the cellar was not so far away, for the space was long but narrow. Piled there were the stores of whatever great house had stood above this pit: barrels, bales and bundles of fuel, stacks of those long clay vessels in which the Greeks store their wine and oil. All was caked in dust and soot, cobwebbed and blotched with bat-piss and mouse-dung. But amongst these things, and piled up against them like a frozen tide, lay bones. Hundreds upon hundreds of bones.

The close air of the cellar, foul as it was with thirty years of vermin and decay, became suddenly fouler still. Real or imagined, the stink of death stung my nostrils. I held up the torch to left and right: more skeletons stretching away into the shadows. The horror of it all descended upon my shoulders like a torturer's weight and I sank down, squatting on my heels. It was not simple horror that crushed me: each of those empty skulls exhaled sadness and desolation. The flame skipped over their yellowed domes, where patches of hair and tarry skin still clung. Near at hand, a ribcage held three little skulls and a puzzle of smaller bones. There were skulls of every size: families had died here, mothers sinking down across their children in a last, hopeless attempt to save them. Their bones were not charred or broken: I could see no shattered skulls. But, from the way they had huddled back here it was plain they had died in some single, appalling moment. I staggered back to the steps and looked up at the charred beams that framed the entrance. And then I understood what had happened. One of the *Cormaran*'s men – Dimitri, perhaps – had told me of a siege he had taken part in. A fortified town had held out for days until the besiegers had run out of patience and shot burning pitch over the walls. The town had burned like a pyre for a day and a half, and when the attackers marched in they took possession of a walled mound of ash. There were no people left: they found them when they dug out the foundations of the houses in search of loot. The townsfolk had taken to the cellars to escape the fire, but the raging storm of flames had sucked out the air and every last man, woman and child had suffocated. They had lain in twisted heaps, quite unhurt; but on every face – so remembered the storyteller – was the mark of agony and terror. To die down there in the dark ... we had all cursed and spat, and thanked our fortunes that we lived out in the wind and the salty spray.

Here were my Greeks. Here were Anna's people. How many other secret charnel houses were there in this great, empty city? Constantinople was a tomb. The flimsy little torch had burned down until it was singeing my fingers. I flung it away, and it guttered for a while on the floor next to a skull, casting its looming, billowing shadow large upon the wall. I had to escape from here, but to where? I could not leave until dark, but then ... I picked at a scab on my arm. Easy enough to climb out of this hole, but then I would have to leave the city. And perhaps I could slip past the guards: what then? I was a thousand leagues from anything I knew. Constantinople was ringed by enemies. I would fight or lie my way through, and then the whole of Greece was mine to cross on foot, penniless. And then the sea. To the north? Barbarian Cumans. To the east, Turks. To the south, the Greeks: the little empire of Anna's uncle. How far away were *their* lines? Then, subtle as a fly testing one's skin for signs of life or food, the tiny spark of a plan began to reveal itself.

It was a torture of high refinement just to wait out the rest of that day. I perched on the lower steps, too dispirited to light another torch, although it would have kept the shadows at a distance. I did not wish to gaze upon the carnage. The dead were best left in the darkness, and I wished I had never disturbed them. As it was, the darkness lapped at the foot of the stairway like a dismal tide. And so, as soon as the light above me had faded from gold to pink and purple and then a dull grey, for the fog was rising from the Golden Horn as dusk came on, I turned my back on the hidden people of Constantinople and fairly ran up the stairs, the hairs on my neck prickling until they hurt, for I imagined that, as soon as

I had turned my back, the shades that dwelt there had risen from their inky pool and were following me. I hurled myself over the rotten threshold and into the cold, taking a great gulp of the clean, sharp scent of elder-trees. I pushed my way urgently through the branches, feeling for brambles, and with every snag of their thorns in my leggings a nightmare bloomed in my mind: held fast in a dark thicket while the dead swarmed out of the grave-mouth behind me.

At last – how many hours were squeezed into those few seconds – I was free, and found myself gasping with relief in the tiny alleyway. The street beyond was deserted, as I knew it would be. The empty shells of the houses that overhung me on each side oppressed me horribly now that I had seen what had become of the folk who had dwelt in them and made this street and a thousand others bright and noisy with their lives. Soon enough I came to the square with the well and the old church. The body had gone, although it had left a dark, smeared trail. The two women must have dragged it off by the feet. I paused here to get my bearings: there was a faint glow in the west, despite the fog, whose tendrils were already exploring the square. Still retracing my morning's path, I jogged down the steps, turned a corner, and there, dark against the sky, were the mounded domes of Hagia Sophia, still a quarter-mile off.

Once I heard the clank of a patrol moving down a nearby street, but I saw not one soul. Only the cats turned the little lamps of their eyes to me as I crept past them. Soon I was cowering in the lee of the vast church, making sure that the square was empty. It towered above me, taller and more vast than anything in my experience. Arches looped and rolled, rising in tiers, sometimes supporting small domes. The front, before which I stood, resembled a gateway, with two mighty buttresses spanned by an arch, so enormous that a whole

335

cathedral of windows, columns and archways were contained within it. The whole assembly was in thrall to the great dome which it supported. So high that my neck bones creaked as I threw back my head to take it in, it loomed like some unimaginably vast celestial body broken loose from its mooring in the heavens and now rising over the horizon of our world.

Chapter Twenty-Two

I do not care for churches, and I like cathedrals even less. They are forever bound up in my mind with the bloody event which wrenched my quiet, unimpeachably mundane life from its pleasant, dull cage and sent it flying into the teeth of the world's storms, a homing pigeon who no longer possessed a home. I saw a man butchered like a hog inside the cathedral that stood in the little English city where I was a student, saw his blood splash and steam on the tiles and caught it in my nostrils as it overwhelmed the comfortable church smells: old stone, beeswax, incense, dust and piety (piety has a smell known to every cleric: a subtle distillation of clothes kept long in chests, boiled food, the hair of infants and the soiled breeches of the elderly; priests afflicted by a congregation of the very pious will always be profligate burners of incense). I had thought to find this one a miracle, for Anna had talked of it as the very navel of the world, but in reality it hunkered bleakly over the ruined city like a heap of giant skulls. So I had avoided the place until now, fearing that the city's melancholy decay would be unbearable here. But when I crept through the great doors, I was amazed.

English cathedrals are generally somewhat sombre. They amaze with their avenues of stone pillars that rear up and divide like tree trunks – so delicate and yet so deceiving – but their great vaults are shadowy and even when the day is bright outside the dust motes dance sombrely in the perpetual twilight within. And so I walked through the grand doors of Hagia Sophia expecting to enter such a night-in-day, to be greeted instead by light: candlelight and lamp light reflecting from the polished stone, gold, and twinkling glass of the mosaics that covered the walls. If from the outside the sheer mass of the church was terrifying, inside there was so much luminous space that I felt almost weightless, as if I were about to rise like a transfigured soul up into the embrace of the dome, where Christ waited with open arms, an indulgent young father perched on a rainbow.

I made my way up to the southern gallery and cast about for the mosaic Zoe had described, and found it easily, for it was quite new and dazzlingly bright even by candlelight. I sank down on a shadowed bench nearby and watched the candles flickering. Every so often a black-swathed crone would shuffle over to light another taper, but otherwise I was blissfully alone. After a time, my eyelids drooped and I fell into a sort of deep daydream, in which ravens circled over Dartmoor tors and little trout flicked through amber water while sedge waved against an empty sky.

There was a loud, wet sniff, and it came from very near by. I straightened up and looked about me. There was no one there, and I was about to lapse into my daydream, assuming my imagination had conjured an intruder, when the sniff came again, just by my left elbow. With a start I turned my head, and found myself looking at a grey head. A low marble sill ran around the base of the walls, and perched uncomfortably on this sat a man in the black robes of a cleric. The cloth was very dusty and full of rents and patches, and the man's hair was thinning and dirty. His scalp showed through here and there, angrily painted with ringworm, and drifts of scurf salted his shoulders. Feeling my gaze, he turned and looked up into my face. I beheld red-ringed eyes, a doughy boozer's nose and ashy skin. A long beard the colour of neglected silver spilled down his front. His neck was knobbed with scrofula, and he evidently had caught cold, for he sniffed again and wiped his nose with a sleeve that was already glistening with mucus. I gave a thoughtless shudder, then remembered myself and stood up. The man looked up at me, pulled at his nose and, using the smooth marble of the wall, slid himself upright. He regarded me with the intense gaze of a moth-eaten owl.

'My name is Walter,' he said.

'*Salve*, goodman Walter,' I replied, carefully. The man had spoken to me in English. Walter's red and rheumy eyes explored my face with great care.

'What are you doing here?' he asked brusquely, after an uncomfortable pause.

'Taking comfort in your beautiful Hagia Sophia,' I said, as politely as I could.

'My Hagia Sophia? *Mine?*' he replied. I could not tell if he was amused or angry. And I could see that his robes were neither those of a Greek nor of a Latin priest, but seemed to be a somewhat disreputable confection of elements culled from both. An ordinary madman, I suddenly thought. Well, no peace here, then, and he might scare off whoever was coming to find me. Time to go. I was turning, when a gnarled hand shot out and caught my sleeve.

'Wait, Devon lad,' Walter said. I turned and stared at him, mouth open like a codfish.

'Devon?' I gasped.

'Certainly. Devon. Devon*shire*. Well, you are not from Dorset, are you? Or a bloody Cornishman, against whom God defend us all?'

'No, no – I am from Devon, right enough,' I said, shaking my head. 'But what ... what do you know of Devon, goodman Walter?'

339

'None of your "goodman",' he snapped. 'Walter will do well enough. Quite well enough, thank you kindly. I know of Devon because I *am* of Devon.'

'Ah. From whereabouts?' I enquired, knowing as I did so that entering into discourse with the mad can have many consequences, the commonest being deathly boredom. But I could not help myself, for the name of my homeland was a charm strong enough to loosen my tongue even in this strange circumstance. But instead of answering, Walter began to throw furtive glances about the vast cavern of the church. Then he turned back to me, eyes twinkling.

He laid a finger alongside his nose.

'Nothing is what it appears, boy,' he rasped. Then he snapped his fingers gently and pointed to the far side of the church. I looked over and saw nothing but a Frankish cleric peering up at the rainbow-perched Christ in the cupola. He was far enough away that, in the hazy golden light, I could make out nothing save that the man was poised and seemed to be concentrating very hard on whatever he was regarding. And he was very well dressed in dark robes, like a scholar or a man of law.

'Another sightseer,' I shrugged. 'Perhaps he would be happier to join you. As a matter of fact, I have things ...'

'What things?' asked Walter blandly. I shrugged.

'Business.'

'Oh. Business.' He sniffed damply. 'He knows about all kinds of business. Perhaps you'd care to talk to *him*.' I glanced down into the church again, but the man had gone. Only a priest, I thought, or a monk.

'Would you care to talk more?' asked Walter. Then, not waiting for a reply, he added, 'I must retrieve my hat. Wait here.' And he shuffled off with surprising speed, and disappeared through one of the many stone-framed doors.

His hat, for God's sake? Was I to lose my chance of escape, because of a madman's hat? Cursing my luck, or the ruins thereof, I stood up and padded over to the stairs. Descending into the lambent gloom I cast about for signs of danger, but the body of the church was empty save for a few tardy crones busy with their candles. It occurred to me that I was a fool, for I knew but one way in and out of this place, but there was no choice, and so, skirting the walls and colonnades, I gained the main door. Out of pure habit I glanced behind me before I stepped outside, and noticed a Greek priest watching me a few paces off, arms folded. I gave him a quick, respectful bow, another habit; and when I raised my head, I saw it was Walter. He had donned a priest's high, toadstool-shaped hat. So he truly was a madman. Without further ado I turned tail and trotted – for I did not want to attract any more attention – out into the dusk.

The square that lies before the Hagia Sophia is a dismal and deserted place dotted with ruins and missing huge areas of flagstones so that gorse and other wild trees and plants have pushed their way into the sunlight. That night it was even more desolate, although the fog was clearing, and the sky was fretted with rags of black cloud fleeing westward from a brisk wind out of Asia. There was not a soul about, and, wrapped in my black cloak, I felt little more than a ragged cloud myself, scudding, dissolving. It gave me an odd feeling of safety, but a slow, creeping dread also, as if I had stepped out of this world altogether into the kingdom of shadows.

I resolved to make my way back to the ruined chapel. Perhaps the serving girl would come to look for me there. Perhaps, though, the serving girl had been caught, or killed, or worse. I shuddered, the hoar frost of guilt settling upon me. The Golden Horn glittered under a bright sliver of moon to my left, so I turned right. Blocking my way was a thicket of scrubby elder bushes that had grown up around a broken pillar and I stepped into its shadow. There was, I remembered, an alleyway that gave off the square and led towards the sea, and through it – I had trailed around all these streets to fend off creeping boredom these past weeks – I could wind my way through ruins and dead houses to the wall of the palace, and there to the chapel.

Footsteps sounded behind me. A priest was leaving the church. I guessed it was Walter, and stepped back into the thicket, letting the thin, pithy trunks of the elder bend against my weight. A bird fluttered and scrabbled behind me. Do not sing, I begged it, silently. It did not, but flapped its way free and whirred away. 'Thank you,' I muttered. The priest had stopped twenty or more paces away, and seemed to be gazing up at the stars. I sank back a little further into the elder bushes, feeling a branch dig into my back. Then another, and then before I could flinch a hand wrapped itself around the handle of the knife that lay against my spine, and another was clamped over my mouth. I felt the knife being tugged out and I bellowed into the suffocating hand, waiting for the butcher's blade to enter my back. But instead a dry voice hissed into my ear.

'Keep silent, boy. Turn around,' it ordered, in English. I obeyed. As I turned, there was a crackle of twigs and the hand left my mouth, to land upon my shoulder, thumb digging into the soft flesh beneath the collarbone. I ... I did nothing. Perhaps I was too tired and hungry to resist. I do not – choose not, it may be – recall what I thought in those instants. Be done with me, mayhap: do it fast, and do not turn me over to the braying Franks for their sport. So I did not bolt or even raise my hands, but turned like a child turns to face its father. And found the grey eyes of Michael Scotus staring into mine.

'I have cut myself on your bloody knife,' he murmured, and held it up, handle foremost. I took it, as if in a dream, and he put the ball of his thumb to his lips and sucked.

'Did Walter not tell you to wait?' he asked, when he was done. It was too dark to be sure, but I fancied his lips were flecked with blood.

'You? I was waiting for you?' I managed to choke out the words, but I was so dazed that I could manage no more.

'Aye.' The Scot was inspecting his thumb again. 'And I for you. For some days. Come quick, now,' he said. 'Walter will lead us.'

The mention of Walter cut into my torpor a little, enough to rouse a pinprick of resistance. 'I will not!' I said, my voice no more than a strangled bleat.

'Do you perceive that you have a choice?' said Michael with a half-smile. 'You may think this is but a dream, or some horrid chance, but it is not. Come: I will explain.'

He clapped his hands twice, and the sharp reports echoed back and forth across the square until it seemed to me as if the air were full of a thousand wooden birds clacking their wings, and I cringed. But the square was still empty when I looked up and here came Walter, trotting over stiffly.

'Said you would wait for me,' he muttered, testily.

'Never mind, old friend,' said Michael Scot. 'Lead on now: we will not lose the night if we are quick.' And to my amazement I found myself walking between Walter, the lunatic Greek priest from Devon, and Michael Scotus, physician to the pope or perhaps imperial necromancer, and who could not possibly be here in Constantinople, down a steep, empty street towards the sea, which sparked and burned with reflected moonlight and with the lights of the fishing boats setting out for a night's work. We had almost reached what was left of the city wall when Walter made a sharp turn to his left, and we followed him, ducking under a low, tottering archway and through a passageway barely wider than myself, that was heavy with the soft, cloying smell of dead fig leaves, like sweetmeats left to moulder. At the end was blackness – or a door, for Walter had stopped and rapped upon it twice, then twice again, then once more. He stepped aside, and Michael nudged me on. There was a creak and a complaint of worm-eaten timber, and I went forward, for I had no choice. The darkness within was damp and silent. Then a tiny light flared very close to my face, and passed, like a firefly, across and around my head.

'*Ela*,' said an ancient voice. Come.

As Walter and Michael pressed in behind me, the flame moved away and, like the Easter miracle, touched into life first one candle, then another and another, until we were standing in a blaze of light. Stone walls rose around us to a great height, and far above a vault of stone curved over us like a cupped hand. 'We are inside the walls,' I thought, and then I saw the man who had let us in.

He was very old, and his body was twisted like a tree that has stood for many lifetimes in a merciless wind. He had a long beard of yellowish white, and he wore a black cowl. His eyes were sunk deep into his head, so deep that the sinews that held them in place showed through the withered flesh of his eyelids. He was watching me, his head cocked like a bird, and I realised that he could not straighten it. Nonetheless he smiled at me, and it was a warm and welcoming smile. He pointed at a chest that stood near the wall.

'*Katsi*,' he said. Sit. And I did, for I was tired as a plough-horse, and the man's smile had made me less afraid. Michael was busying himself over by the door, and Walter, after embracing the old man and shooting me a reproachful glance, slipped outside and shut the door behind him.

'We will eat,' said Michael, in Greek. 'Petroc, you speak the tongue of this city, do you not?' I nodded, thinking only of the food. The Scot carried a covered clay pot and a basket over to us, produced a rickety chair for the old man and a stool for himself, and sat down. The pot contained boiled beans and pig fat, tepid, bland and uncommonly good. There was bread in the basket, and some hard-boiled eggs, and an apple. We set to – or rather I set to, and my elders watched. When the beans were all but gone, and the eggs, and the bread as well, and I was taking the first sweet bite of the apple, Michael whispered something to the old Greek and nodded at me.

'Now I will talk, and you will listen. You are shocked to see me. I am not surprised. Why am I here in Constantinople? Simply told. I am on an embassy from the Emperor Frederick to John Vatatzes in Nicea. My route led me through this city. Or rather I planned it thus, for I wished to see you. Do not gawp, lad: we are not strangers, are we?'

I shook my head. Then I nodded it. 'I do not know you at all,' I told him. 'And ... you are in the employ of· the pope – of old Gregory. I mean ... thank you for the food.' Somewhat unnerved by this unchecked flow of words, I plugged my mouth with the apple and regarded Michael. He did not seem to be planning to kill me, at least – and the old man: he seemed friendly enough.

'Oh! Did the pope send you?' I burst out again, struck by this thought. 'Or ... or Baldwin?'

'No,' said Michael with a dry chuckle. 'No, and no. I am in no one's employ, as you put it: neither pope nor emperor – and I mean the Holy Roman Emperor Frederick, not that callow little kinglet, Baldwin. I am in the privileged and uncomfortable position of being a friend to both men, and I have acted on both their behalfs at times, as I am doing now for His Majesty Frederick. The good Captain does not know I am here either. It goes back to business,' he explained. 'I needed to gather some information about Genoese interests at the palace, for the Genoese are the emperor's allies and hate Venice like the devil. It so happened that the pro-Genoese faction – for there are more factions in that place than there are rats in its walls – is made up of those men who hail from the Duchy of Athens, and chief among them was the duke's nephew, the unfortunate Rolant de la Rouche.'

'So Rollo was killed on purpose? I thought it was I they intended ...'

'They wanted both of you dead,' said Michael, shaking his head. 'Or rather they required *your* death, and Rolant ... perhaps it was planned, perhaps a lucky accident.' He made a revolted face. 'They are little more than children, these impecunious tyrants. Now then, when I found out about Rolant's demise I went looking for whoever else might proffer me assistance, and found Aimery de Lille Charpigny. From him I learned about your ... your teetering position here, and indeed all about your impending arrest and execution.

'Aimery – he lives, do not fear, although he has a sore head – came to warn you of the Regent's intentions. He found Zoe cleaning your chambers.'

'Zoe? The chambermaid?'

'She is the daughter of a friend. You are reeling, my lad. Too much happenstance for you, I would guess. But rest assured: the only happenstance in the whole tale was that you rescued Zoe from a vile ... a detestable fate. But even then, she was near your room because I had instructed her to keep an eye on you.' I blinked at him, struck utterly mute, so he went on: 'Now Zoe, who is as keen of wit as any man or woman I have ever met, could have forfeited her life when Aimery chanced upon her, for she had the temerity

346

to question a strange Frank, in his own tongue, about the business he had with you. But it seems that your friend has goodness or sense, or perhaps both, for he told her what was to happen, and there and then they made their alliance – to save you, lad, for their different reasons.'

'Well then, Zoe ...' I tugged at my hair in confusion. 'And Walter ...'

'Ah, Walter. The poor man was a jolly crusader who came to sack this city thirty-and-more years ago. He has been trying to atone for what he saw and did ever since. Like a ghost, he has become invisible to his own people, but the Greeks have taken him in, and he is almost one of them now. Almost. He lives, sometimes, in Zoe's household, where I have taken my lodgings, by the way. But I have wandered from the answer to your first question. Yes, I came to find you. You see, I know why you are here, and I was wondering if ... if you might do me a favour.'

'What kind of favour? I mean, yes, of course. Anything,' I babbled. The apple was gone, and I had nothing now to hide behind.

'Would you break into the Pharos Chapel?' enquired Michael lightly, as if he were asking if I would like to go out to buy a few more eggs.

'Umm,' I began, and then my tongue ran out of words.

'Because you were planning to, were you not? Have I mistaken the situation? Querini the Venetian has taken the Crown of Thorns, and will doubtless take the rest...'

'Querini has killed Captain de Montalhac!' I burst out. 'I heard him say so! My master left on a Venetian galley the day before the hunt. The crew must have cut his throat the moment they were beyond the harbour!'

Michael Scot looked at me levelly. 'I know that also. De Montalhac dead? Very possibly. Probable, in fact – I am

347

heartily sorry for it, and for you, my son. Now I am sorry to deny you your grief, but please pay attention.' It was what the Captain would have said, I realised, so I shut my mouth.

'So. Querini has the Crown, you say. But you have an *Inventarium* of the chapel – I know, I have seen one, for Emperor Baldwin has been shopping it around every court in Christ's lands. Gregory has one, and Frederick, and God knows who else. Now the saintly King of France has nothing to ... I was about to say *buy*, but that is not the word – you would know better than I. He will receive nothing from Baldwin and will give nothing in gratitude. You and your companions will be denied your commission. And so, if I were in your place, I believe I would indeed rob the chapel.'

'But how did you ...' I began. 'I mean, I was planning no such thing. But yes, things are how you have described them otherwise,' I told him hurriedly.

'Very politic, lad,' smiled Michael. 'Very well. Let us say I have deduced that it would be a very good idea for someone standing in your boots to rob the Pharos Chapel of certain relics sequestered there, relics that you know of but which are unknown to the Regent and indeed to the emperor himself.'

'I have no idea what you mean,' I muttered.

'Ah. So you do not possess the *Inventarium* of Nicholas Mesarites,' said Michael, laying a finger against the pewter stubble on his cheek. 'I thought I gave it to you, but perhaps that was someone else.'

'I ...' My mind was not working fast enough. It was barely working at all. I stared past Michael's head, desperately searching for something, anything to say. Instead I saw that someone long ago had taken chalk and drawn a stick man fucking a stick woman. In another place reared a cock, gigantic and gushing, and a pair of gaping thighs. I shook my head, trying to clear it. 'It is too late,' I said at last. 'I am sorry, Sir Doctor. Do not give me back to the Franks, I beg you.'

'There is a window, quite high up.' It was the old man. He was leaning forward, hands gnarled and white-knuckled, gripping his knees, staring at me. 'Quite high up. A man could fit through it – a young man.'

I remembered the window, a square of iron grillework above the head of Christ crucified.

'It is bricked up,' I said without thinking.

'No, not bricked,' said the old man. 'There was a sheet of agate there, but it broke, and I had them put a piece of slate in its place, thinking I would find more agate. I never did.'

'Who are you, *kyrios*?' I said carefully, searching the seamed face. The sunken eyes glared back at me.

'The grandfather of Zoe,' he muttered.

'This is His Eminence Nicholas Mesarites, late Archbishop of Ephesus,' said Michael, standing up and walking to the old man's side. He laid his hand gently on the twisted shoulder, and the old man smiled. 'And indeed, grandfather to Zoe Argyrina Mesaritissa.'

'But I thought ...'

'That he was long dead. And you thought the same about me, no doubt, for the world seems to believe me mouldering in my grave while I walk around, hale as a lamb,' said Michael. 'Such is the fate of the old: we die by reputation long before our hearts are stilled.'

'But this makes no sense to me,' I protested. 'Your Excellency Nicholas, I am ashamed, for yes, the doctor is right: I had planned to rob the chapel of those things ... those holy relics which you detailed, but which Baldwin does not know he owns. I suppose I thought that King Louis might buy them – your pardon, it is simony, I know, but as you must know, in my profession we do not much bother with the niceties of canon law. I was attempting to salvage something from the ruins of my mission and of my life, and to avenge my beloved master. It seems I have failed.'

'Not yet,' said Nicholas Mesarites. 'Not if you can steal the *Mandylion* of Edessa.'

'So are you not the pope's doctor? ' I had asked Michael Scotus. We had studied a rough-drawn map of the Bucoleon Palace that Mesarites had produced, and he had told me how I might go about entering the Pharos Chapel from outside. It did not seem easy, or indeed possible, but as nothing seemed real any more, and indeed I had begun to wonder again if I might be dead and this some purgatory designed just for me, I went along with the plan, such as it was.

'No, although I have treated him. I live between two worlds, you see.' I looked at him. I knew what worlds he meant, but then again, perhaps I did not. The air seemed to swim faintly before his face, as if I beheld him from a very great distance. Then I blinked, and he was just an old man sitting at my side.

'But I thought you were His Holiness' doctor,' I said, confused. 'It is well known that you used to be the Emperor's ...' I was about to say *necromancer*, but prudence caught my tongue just in time. 'Astrologer,' I went on. 'But also that His Holiness recommended you for the Archbishopric of Canterbury. So ...'

A shadow flitted across Michael Scot's face. Then he smiled, wearily. 'Both true,' he said. 'I was with the pope these last few years, but when the Emperor Frederick came down into Italy this year he summoned me. I go where I may serve,' he added, piously.

'Really?' I asked, surprised. Michael laughed.

'No, not really. I no longer need to act out of duty. My

motive is love, alas, for I am a friend to both men, though they do not love each other.'

'I have heard that Frederick seeks an alliance with John Vatatzes in Nicea,' I said. 'He knows that this leaking tub of an empire will not last long.'

'Aha. There you have it. I should have expected no less, from the company you keep.'

'And Gregory seeks the opposite, for he would like Venice to be a staunch ally in the north against Frederick.'

'Right again. And why does Gregory wish to broker the translation of Byzantium's holy relics?'

'To buy the friendship of King Louis, most pious of monarchs,' I said. 'And to bolster up poor Baldwin.'

'Again right. And why should a man ride a skittish warhorse down a busy London street of a winter's morning?'

The silence was absolute. I saw Michael Scot, and yet I did not see him. I saw Anna dead in London. I saw flames dance, and then they became bobbing rafts of ice upon the Sea of Darkness. I was not here. I was a statue, yet uncarved, nothing but silent grains within a block of stone.

'Do you know that, Petroc of Auneford? You do not, and that is as it should be. Still, the answer is on your hand.'

I looked down, as if through a poppy trance, at Anna's ring where it circled my finger.

'But it was an accident. She was kicked by a horse, good Master Michael. Do not say such things. Please do not.'

'You do not believe that, lad.'

'I … No!' Shaking with fear of what I was about to learn, I looked up into Michael's steady eyes. 'I *cannot* believe it, and yet … I know it may be so.'

'Listen to me. When Gregory's interest is aroused, wondrous or terrible things happen. He heard that there was an unmarried – you were not married, were you? – relation of

John Vatatzes of Nicea at loose in the world, and thought what a fine match she would make for his poor, weak Baldwin. He would make John into Baldwin's ally, not his deadly foe. This is a terrible thing to tell you, lad, but ...'

'Baldwin is married,' I said, desperately, my head spinning.

'If the pope cannot annul a marriage, who can?'

'No! That cannot be! It is ... monstrous!'

'Querini found out, for he has eyes and ears in the pope's court. He could not allow Baldwin's fortunes to change. And so ...'

The man at the door of the Blue Falcon, a soldier with a scarred face. I closed my eyes and saw Fulk de Grez waiting for Anna at the noon hour with his message from a place dear to her heart. We had thought Fulk's letter had hinted at Nicea, but it had not: it had spoken of that city at the centre of every Greek's world: Constantinople. Then the great horse reared up in my mind's eye, and I clapped my hands to my head to drive out the image of Anna's hair, blue-black against the Cheapside mud.

'I could have been a corpse by now,' I told Michael at last. 'Nothing more than a skin drying on some door. I wish with all my heart that I was, and not alive to hear this.'

'But you have heard it, and you still live. Which is good. I have need of you.'

'I do not wish to be ... I wish to die,' I said.

'That is not allotted to you, not yet,' said Michael sadly. 'You have suffered much in the last few days. There has been a battle, an arrest. You have become another ghost in this terrible city. And you have seen your hopes dashed. Nicholas Querini carried off the Crown of Thorns under your very nose. Now I am offering you restitution.'

'There is no restitution.'

'Then what about revenge?'

'What manner of revenge do you mean? Stealing back a relic for this Mesarites, if that is who he really is? Anna would not care. She detested superstition and the worship of ... of icons and suchlike.'

'I am talking about money,' said Michael Scotus, giving me a grey stare. 'More money than one man has ever seen. For you alone, or for your Captain de Montalhac. And with it the ruin of Nicholas Querini.'

'Ruin? What good is ruin? He should be made to feel what Anna felt! He will ...'

'To lose his wealth and his power would be worse for him than death, and you can strip him of both. And here as well is the chance to snap your fingers under Gregory's nose. Do not mistake me: I am a churchman, but I have no illusions about one thing: the Lateran is a great beast with iron jaws and flaming lips, and a terrible thirst that can only be slaked with gold.'

'Gregory knew what he had caused,' I whispered. 'He made mention of something, that day in Viterbo, but I thought nothing of it. I thought ...'

'Even a pope cannot bring about the death of a princess without feeling some prick of guilt,' said Michael, gently. 'It was he who sent you the *Inventarium*. At my suggestion. Some little gesture to make amends: no doubt he has forgotten all about it by now. But you, my boy, can use that little gift against him, against Querini – nay, against the whole of Christendom, if your rage is hot enough.' He set his chin upon his finger-ends and regarded me.

I tried to make sense of what I had heard. What did I care for money, or any of it? I wanted to kill Nicholas Querini, nothing more. My rage, kindled more by despair than anger, was as simple as my desire to eat the last apple on the plate before me. Use the pope's gift? Christ, I was become more an animal than a man! There would never again be a time for gifts. And … and yet there was something in Michael's watchful stillness that calmed the turmoil in my head.

'As to that, why do you want the *Mandylion*?' I asked reluctantly, for misery had begun to curdle into anger, and with it a sullen trace of hope. 'Old Gregory is your friend – you said so yourself.'

'And I meant it. The war that is coming: Guelfs against Ghibellines, spiritual against temporal, brother against brother. It will consume the world, gobble it whole. It is the Apocalypse. I will not take sides.'

'But the *Mandylion*?' I insisted.

'There is yet a chance that the war can be averted, for the beast's jaws are not yet locked. The *Mandylion* is a thing beyond worth: the holiest of the holy. I intend to give it to Frederick, so that he may present it to Gregory as a peace offering. Although you will not have heard this in Rome, Frederick does not seek war in Italy. He wishes to rule, not to destroy.'

'But you, Your Eminence,' I protested, turning to Mesarites. 'You are robbing yourself. Why would you help us Franks to finish the ruin of your city?'

'Mikaili and I have known each other for half a lifetime,' he replied slowly. 'We met here, in this city, when I was sent to debate with the emissaries of Pope … I do not remember which pope. It was thought that the two Churches, Greek and Latin, might be reconciled, and this has always been my dearest wish. It was not Constantine's vision, nor Justinian's, that the Empire of the Romans should be divided for ever, or that Christian should revile Christian over matters of mere custom. Mikaili had come with the papal delegation, and we became friends over …'

'Over Aristotle,' Michael prompted.

'Just so. I have kept abreast of matters in Rome and at the imperial court these many years through my friend. And so I know that Gregory truly desires unity between the Churches, but on his own terms. Frederick desires the same thing, but he loves the Greeks, and he would have our rights upheld. If there could be peace between pope and prince, brokered by our greatest treasure, it is my hope that the schism might be healed, perhaps in my lifetime – although that I do not dare expect.'

'But what, then, is this *Mandylion*? I have heard it is something like the Veronica, with a painting of Christ's face. There are many such icons, though.'

'The *Mandylion* is not one of those!' snorted Mesarites. He seemed to straighten up a little. 'A painting? It is … *acheiropoietos*. Not made by human hands. And not just the face …' he paused, and crossed himself. 'The whole of Our Lord's precious body, laid out in death.'

'Or life,' said Michael.

'Ach. We disagree. The impression – it is a miraculous *imprint*, Frankish boy, not a painting – is of a dead man. There are the stains of blood, around the head, in the side, in the hands and feet.'

'And you have seen this?'

'Oh, many times,' he cried. 'Our Lord was revealed every Friday in the Church of Blachernae, rising as if from the tomb. Resurrected in glory.'

'But it is a face,' I persisted. 'In a picture. It says so in the inventories.'

'Oh dear, Petroc,' sighed Michael, shaking his head like an exasperated schoolmaster. 'It is folded. Folded so that only the face shows, and so that it fits into a picture frame. That was its secret, and until a few years before the sack, known only to the archbishops of Blachernae. And because it vanished when the Franks took the city, that secret is not known in the West. Imagine the revelation, the … the universal wonderment when it is revealed. The pope will declare a jubilee!'

I looked at these two men, so agog at the wonder of it all. It was not so strange in the Greek, perhaps, for he was a churchman; but Michael Scotus … I was surprised that his dark and shadowy person should be so suffused with superstitious joy. I felt, all at once, utterly different from them, a goat amongst sheep or an ape amongst men. What cared I for their jubilee? If men could kill a blameless woman on a whim, in the name of holy Mother Church, was it not equally unbelievable that a piece of old, stained cloth would stop the same men from destroying each other? I did not care. But, I realised as I watched the burning eyes of the two old men, if something could be salvaged, some scrap for Captain de Montalhac, for Gilles and for the rest of us who lived outside the world of both pope and emperor, then I would gladly die in the attempt.

There was another door, an old postern that let out on to the beach below the walls. Michael led me through it and out into the night. The sea lapped and gurgled very near us, and the air was sharp with the rot of weed and flotsam that had once been alive. I trudged after Michael, to where a huge old plane tree, half dead, was growing out of the wall and hanging its branches far out over the water.

'Help me,' he said, beckoning. He was tugging at a pile of driftwood. When I reached it I saw that the pile was disguising a small fishing boat, short, pointed fore and aft, with a pronounced rocker and two rowlocks. We heaved it over. It looked seaworthy enough in the moonlight, for the timbers were sound and the paint was not old. It had a mast, folded flat against the deck, and a tightly furled sail. Then Michael led me back to the postern. Just inside were two ladders, lying propped lengthwise against the wall.

'Scaling ladders from the siege,' said Mesarites, shuffling over with a light. 'There were legions of them, a forest. Afterwards, some who were left alive picked them up and saved them, thinking they might have a use when pruning time came. But it has never come. Here: these are not long enough, but you can lash them together.'

To my astonishment, he produced a coil of thin rope, thin as string, and gave it to me. It was black and oily.

'Eel skin,' he said. 'It will take your weight, never fear.' As I was pondering this, Michael Scotus handed me a pack, with two straps for the shoulders, roughly stitched from what looked like sailcloth. I hefted it and looked inside: it held a chipping hammer and a chisel.

'Come now: it is getting late,' muttered the doctor.

With the growing sense that I was no more in control of things than a ball launched down a hill, I found myself clambering into the boat. Michael shoved me off as I fumbled the oars into the rowlocks.

'Do not dally, lad,' hissed Michael. And then: 'Be careful, Petroc. Be very, very careful.'

I raised my hand in a half-hearted salute and began to row, clumsily at first, the blades biting too deep or jumping across the surface. But in a minute I found my rhythm, and the little boat began to surge eagerly, happily across the still water. Soon Michael was swallowed up in the tree-shadows, and I was alone. I bent my shoulders into the work of rowing, feeling my hands grow sore with the labour, my spirits rising with each little rush across the water. I was propelling myself, at last, beyond the reach of both persecutors and those who called themselves my friends, but whom I knew it would be madness to trust. A faint breeze was blowing from the west, from Greece and beyond, and catspaws hissed against the side of the boat. There was the crouched, crumbled mound of the Bucoleon Palace, over my right shoulder. No lights showed anywhere to seawards. The home of emperors lay humped upon the shore like a great, dead beast. I set my feet on the bench in front of me and pulled, pulled away, my wake a pathway showing faint and pale. But there was no path ahead of me, by sea or by land. I had no life beyond the next dip of my oars. How tempting to ship them and simply drift, alone in the dark. But that would be death, and now I could see the dim flash of foam where the sea was breaking under the palace. There was no escape: I would wash up sooner or later. Well, I knew how to row, and so I kept to it, the corpse of Constantinople sliding by on the port side.

Chapter Twenty-Three

I moored the boat to a broken marble pole jutting from the slimy rocks. Everything was wreckage here, rubble and seaweed. I could hear the rattle of crab claws on the rocks as I clambered ashore, and the pop of bladderwrack under my feet. The round wall of the chapel was right in front of me, looming overhead, very high and forbidding. It sat upon a crumbling buttress of boulders and rubble which the sea had been chewing so intently that the whole building was nearly undercut. Another decade or so and the Pharos Chapel would be another heap of weed-slick rubble, home to the crabs and eels. I pulled the ladders from the boat and propped them against the buttress, then heaved the boat up on to the rocks, turned it over and draped it with rags of seaweed. Then I scrambled up until I stood on a sort of rough platform or shelf, the width of a couple of feet, under the wall itself. I rested for a little while, for my nose was throbbing horribly and one side of my chest felt as if it were lying upon hot coals. From here the roof seemed much closer, and I could see the moss that hung from the overhang of tiles. Chewing upon my lip to take my mind from the pain of my injuries, I pulled the ladders up next to me and lashed them together with the eelskin cords. Then, after a glance out to sea to make sure I was not observed, I shrugged on my pack and laid a foot upon the bottom rung.

The ladder shook and bowed, and I felt like a big grasshopper climbing a little grass stem. With every step the ladder's feet danced upon the loose earth, and the top scraped and jounced on the tiles. The higher I got, the more precarious I felt, and I fairly dived on to the tiles when at last I reached the roof. Somewhat shaky with pain and relief I pulled the ladder up after me and set about looking for a place to attach my rope. There was a sort of stone finial at the apex of the roof but when I tugged at it experimentally it grated and shook in its nest of loose mortar. Further behind me the palace rose in its decaying tiers, and in the wall from which the chapel jutted, a little stone window glimmered faintly, white against the surrounding brick. I went over and felt it: the window, really a block of marble with four holes bored through it, was solidly anchored, and so with a little fussing and scraping of knuckle-skin I managed to thread the rope in one hole and out through another. Twice more and a hefty knot, and I had something to which I could trust my weight.

Tying the rope around my waist, I sat on the roof's edge, legs dangling. The hammer and chisel were tucked into my belt, the empty pack limp against my spine. Before me the sea brooded, black upon black. Away in the distance some fishermen's lights winked very faintly, but below me the water was empty, and I could hear nothing save the slap of water against the rocks. I gave the rope one last tug, and swung myself over the edge, twisting as I dropped, and as my grip on the rope brought me up short I fended the wall off with my feet. There were old iron spikes sticking out of the wall here and there, doubtless meant to keep folk like me away, but they were placed wrong and I ignored them as I lowered myself, fist over fist, until my feet were planted on either side of the chapel window. Carefully I dropped another arm's length, then another, until I was looking at the square of slate. It had been mortared in once, but now it was just propped. I pulled it out and dropped it into my pack. A delicate breath of incense came from inside. With one hand I took hold of the rusty iron grille and tugged.

I had been right. Centuries of weather and of salt sea spray had gnawed at the iron where it was set into the lintels, and had rotted the stone and the mortar into nothing more than coarse gravel. Hanging free, I pulled out the hammer and chisel and gave one of the sockets a cautious tap. There was a low echo from within, and some loose gravel tinkled down the inner wall. I tried again, and again, keeping my blows light, for I did not wish to rouse the guards. After a couple of minutes I had exposed one arm of the grille and had set to work on the next. It took me no more than half an hour to work the iron free from its stone surrounding. When I judged that my work was done, I tied the loose end of the rope around it and heaved it out. With a grinding and a shower of rust flakes, it came. Wasting no time, I dragged myself back up to the roof, dumped the grille and the slate, and lowered myself down again. It was still dark: the guards had not heard, and I did not think they could, through thick stone walls and that heavy old door.

From the memories of one look at the inside of the Pharos Chapel when I had not been thinking about it, I had calculated – if my science, made up as it was of equal parts desperation, hope and the ever-tempting notion that if I believed it was so, it would be, could be called calculation of any sort, and not a nonsense akin to the casting of bones – that I would easily fit through the window. And so I could, with room to spare. But I was so wounded and bruised that I found that I could barely make my limbs obey me. Every move was a torment. Straining, feeling my clothing snag on the holes I had made in the sill, I found myself looking down at the ground, some way below, and at the belly of the rope that hung there.

Wiggling like a worm in cheese, I was horribly aware of the dark void in which half of me was flailing, a place that had terrified me when I had visited it with candles and company. My ribs, jammed against the stone, were howling in agony.

But with a heave, and remembering just as I began to slip backwards to grab the rope above the window and not below, I dropped into the blackness. Tugging the loop of rope through after me, I gingerly lowered myself, feet swinging, desperate to feel something solid beneath them. And then I realised. I was dangling, like a fly in a spider's larder, before the great painting of Our Lord in agony, that paean to torture and lingering death that covered the wall behind the altar. I could not see it, but I felt it: the pallid skin suffused with desolate luminescence, the blood-limp hair. With a choking cry I let go of the rope for a split second, but it was enough to send me sliding down, hands burning on the eel skin, until with a hollow thud I landed. Wringing my searing hands I stumbled forward and collided with the altar. The cold stone instantly soothed my palms and I laid my forehead down on the slab, which I could not see but which calmed me enough so that I could untie the rope and struggle out of my pack, into which I dived frantically, fishing for the tinderbox. I found it, and the candle-stub, and after a few clumsy attempts I had struck fire and a pinpoint of light grew into a glow, a halo that lit up the altar, but which seemed too feeble to force its way into the black air beyond. I lit the other candles on the altar, steeled myself, then turned round.

There was the gilded wall, and there the awful cross with its tormented giant. I felt sick and suffocated, as I had done before, but shook my head until it cleared. There was much work to be done. I looked around. It was clear where the great chest that held the Crown of Thorns had sat, for there was a rectangle of clear stone outlined in the plaster dust that

362

lay everywhere in a thin layer – plaster dust and dead flies, and the granulated emanations of the fatal treasures that were shut up in here. I felt the stifling weight of them all around me. But I was here to work. What had the Captain said? 'All these things: money and nothing more. Never forget that: money, and that alone.' It was hardly comforting, but I felt sharper when I muttered those words to myself. But where to start?

Most helpfully, the reliquaries – or most of them, at least – were sheathed in panels of hammered gold or silver which bore upon them some indication of what lay inside. The first one I examined showed, in beautiful relief, the washing of Christ's feet. There was the Virgin suckling her baby: Mary's Milk, no doubt. I had seen enough of that cheesy stuff being packed into vials aboard the *Cormaran* that I had no desire to look further. A long, slender case, I assumed, held the Staff of Moses. There was a small box, encrusted with gems, that showed the soldier Longinus at work with his lance. Curious, I opened it, and found an old, diamond-bladed spearhead into which a smith had cut four wedges to form a rough cross. A shiver of unease ran through me and I hastily shut the box. But I saw that it had been sitting upon an icon case whose cover also bore the image of Longinus. The icon inside was ancient and encrusted with a tarry patina, overlaid with a richly jewelled frame into which was set a small triangle of metal. Frowning to myself, I opened the box again, and saw that the spearhead was missing its tip, and it was this that was set into the icon. The *Inventarium* mentioned only one Spear, though. I considered. The icon was lighter, but the spearhead was more impressive and besides, the box would be worth something. I dropped it into my pack.

In short order I found the other relics: the Sponge, the Reed, the Swaddling Clothes. The Stone from the Sepulchre was, I guessed, the large stone sitting upon a gilded plinth, and the Chain was indeed a large and rusty chain. The three saints' heads were stacked one atop the other against the back of the rood-screen. Various vials of blood – there is no relic so fundamentally unconvincing, and yet so appealing to the customer, save wood from the Cross itself, and lo! here were two pieces of that very structure. I ignored them, for I had exhausted the smaller reliquaries and had not found what I sought. So now I turned my attention to the big chests that lined the walls.

I held a candle close up to the carbuncled metal of the reliquaries. The images glittered and swum before my eyes, so I opened one at random. A box within a box, and then a long thing wrapped in silk. I did not need to unwrap it, for I felt the hard claws at one end and the jagged, splintered bone at the other: the Baptist's arm. Had those stick-like fingers, so brittle and vulnerable, once held Our Lord under the waters of Jordan? I felt another twinge of dread, as if the lolling head on the wall behind me were about to speak. Time to banish all such thoughts. Money, remember: only money.

The next box gave me something I wanted: a suspiciously well-preserved pair of leather sandals, somewhat dried-out and crushed, the soles beginning to curl, but nonetheless, I thought, almost wearable. Christ's Sandals – it sounded like a prudish oath, but these were on the pope's list and not on Baldwin's. They were coming with me. I felt nothing when I handled them but a creeping respect for the men who passed things like this off to the credulous, century after century. To my delight, there were some authenticating documents in Greek and Aramaic. I made a parcel of shoes and papers with the silk they had rested upon, and opened another chest. Having heard not even a scrape or a cough from beyond the chapel I had more or less convinced myself that the guards were either asleep, drunk or were gone for the night, for who would be making the long and haunted journey through the ruined palace to their post at this hour? So I dragged the next box into the light with less care and let the lid fall back with a thud on one of its fellows. The thud, muffled and weak in the smothering atmosphere of the chapel, found an echo, an answering bump from beyond the rood-screen, out in the nave.

An explosion of panic hurled me across the floor to the altar, and I dropped down behind the stone and held my knees against my chest. I seemed to have grabbed my pack, at least. Oh God, the lights! I jumped up and pinched out the candles in a frenzy. But there were more alight over by the rood-screen. I hung there in a torment of indecision, not quite able to order myself across the sanctuary floor, nor yet daring to commit myself to the dangling rope behind me. As I stood there quivering, the smoke from the snuffed candles threading upwards around me, I remembered a word that Anna had told me long ago: not rood-screen. *Iconostasis*. And then the door opened.

I ducked down behind the altar again, my thoughts as ordered as a kicked ant-hill. I had no weapon, curse it! I had left the hammer and chisel up on the roof. I cast my eyes around in the gloom for anything else I could use, but all I saw were the painted nails pinning His feet, and the frozen dribble of blood from the gash in His side. Good Longinus, put me out of my misery now, for when they catch me they will flay me, I half-prayed. Longinus ... The door creaked open, and I heard two voices, very low and then, when they saw the light, very loud. They were speaking Venetian. Footsteps running up the aisle of the nave and stopping at the door into the sanctuary. I stood up and prepared to die fighting, the holy Lance in my fist.

'Oh, fuck me!' The nasal orison of London town cut the air like a blunt falchion. Letitia of Smooth Field stood there, open-mouthed. At her side, Dardi was already pulling out his dagger, a wide, single-edged thing like a butcher's knife.

'I thought they'd skinned you,' Letitia added, dropping her hands to her hips and regarding me with bemused impatience.

'Not yet,' I said, eyeing Dardi's knife. There was no time to think any more. I stepped smartly out from behind the altar and raised my weapon. Was Letitia armed? No doubt. But still ...

'Come and get it, you fat fucker,' I snarled at Dardi. His eyebrows shot ceilingwards.

'He doesn't speak English, love, or don't you remember?' said Letitia. 'Want me to translate?'

Dardi turned to her, chin raised in question. She pointed at me and muttered something. The big man laughed, then spat wetly on to the floor. I heard the gob splatter. How badly I hoped that it wasn't the last sound I would hear. I noted that he wiped his mouth and cast nervous eyes at the painted figure behind me, though.

'Get on with it!' I told him, in Italian. 'Come on, pig!' If I was hoping to goad him, it did not work.

'What have you got there, a plasterer's trowel?' he asked. 'You going to wall me up or something? I knew you had no balls the first time.' Again, he paused and crossed himself. 'Come on. Put that down. We'll do it outside. It will be quick, I promise.'

Letitia said something else in Venetian, and looked behind her at the door. Dardi shrugged, crossed himself again and squared his shoulders. He gave me the smile that butchers give to tied hogs. He wasn't scared of me, not even the tiniest bit. I felt the metal of the spearhead grow warm and slippery with sweat.

'Do you know what this is, you blasphemer?' I asked him, remembering dimly how I had almost, long ago, become a priest.

'Shut up,' Dardi told me.

'This is the treasure-house of Christendom. Do you see Our Lord in His Passion behind me? His grave-clothes are behind you. Do you see that wound in His side, and the blood pouring forth like a spring? This made that very wound,' I said, holding up the spearhead. 'The holy Lance. And it will pierce your liver, you dog.'

Dardi blinked, and his knife wavered. He crossed himself again, fervently, and when he raised his knife again it was less steady. His eyes darted up towards the dead face of Christ and his arms came up, as if he were being crucified in his turn by doubt. I stepped towards him, and he turned to Letitia, pleading. She stepped back, glanced at me, her face a pale blank, and with a mere flick of movement, like a fish darting through a strong current, she pulled out a blade and thrust it once, twice, into Dardi's ribs and held it there as his own knife dropped from his hand and he sank down to his knees and then backwards, arms still out, until he lay, legs twisted beneath him, a failed *pietà*. Letitia pulled out her knife with a grunt, squatted and wiped it on his jutting belly, took a deep breath, and turned to me. She had clamped her lower lip between her teeth.

'I was hoping *you* would do that,' she said at last, after we had regarded each other for a silent eternity.

I lowered the spearhead very slowly. 'What ... what the fuck is going on?' I rasped, mouth as dry as desert sand.

'Wait!' she said, holding up a finger. Turning in a flounce of skirts she ran lightly down the aisle and shut the door.

Locking it, she held up the key to me. Then she walked briskly back into the sanctuary.

'Right. What are you doing here?' she said. 'And, love, put that thing down. Is it really the ... holy Spear, or whatever?'

'I don't know. I mean, what ... Look, could you put your knife down as well?'

She looked down at her hand, all bloody up to the wrist, as if in surprise.

'Oh. This is yours,' she said, and held out the knife to me, hilt first. Through the darkening blood I saw that the hilt was carved from green stone. I took it, mute with shock. Letitia handed me the scabbard.

'Right. I came to kill him, and to nick something. What's the most valuable thing in here?'

I looked at her, slack-jawed.

'I said, Devonshire, what's the most valuable thing in this place? You know, don't you: that's why you came here.'

'Um.' I gave Thorn another wipe, sheathed her and tucked her into my belt. 'It's ... it's not what's valuable that counts.' Inside, I was screaming to myself: She has the key! She has the bloody key!

'Listen. I just saved your life – not for the first time either. Be nice to me, all right?'

'Letitia ...'

'Oh, and my name's not Letitia. Bloody Letitia. It's Letice. Letice Londeneyse, sometimes called Letice Pyefote. You'd better tell me yours now.'

'Petrus – Petroc. Petroc of Auneford.'

We were watching one another, panting as if we had just wrestled. I tore my eyes away and looked around the room. Dardi's sprawled body was taking up most of the sanctuary floor. There were scattered reliquaries everywhere. I decided that it might be possible to get out of here free and more or less alive.

'Why did you …' I began, jerking my head towards the corpse.

'Messer Nicholas … Listen, I am a whore, *Master* Petroc. Actually, a courtesan, as they say in Venice. Messer Nicholas is tired of me. He planned to give me to that fat fucker, that stinking, slobbering hog, and make me live out my days on some island he owns: a bare rock in the middle of nowhere. I wasn't going to do it. Dardi likes – liked – to give a woman pain, before, during and after. I wouldn't've lasted a year – Nicholas knew that, by the way.'

I looked at her closely. She seemed quite at ease with what she had done, but not happy: it did not seem to have filled her with that seething joy I had seen possess some after they had killed or maimed. She seemed weary, and businesslike. Upper lip curling a little, she gave me back my look.

'Listen to me,' I said. 'I came to get three things. Christ's Sandals, which I have. The *Maphorion* of the *Theotokos* – Mary's Robe. And something called the *Mandylion* of Edessa. They're on a list, an old inventory that I have, and they aren't on the emperor's own list – nor's that spear, and I am keeping it. As he's about to flog the whole lot off to your Master Nicholas, I thought I'd take them for my own …' I was going to say master, but it did not seem right. 'Help me look, would you? There are pictures on the boxes, to help nice thieves like us.'

In truth I was feeling almost light-headed, for here I was, more or less trapped in the second holiest place in the world with a dead man and a strange woman with warm blood on her hands. For a moment I felt like an alchemist's transmutation, something sealed in an alembic, changing into … what? Not a corpse, if I could help it.

'There's a lovely little virgin on this one,' Letice was saying. 'Shall I open it?'

'No! There's blood on your hands. I mean, let me. We don't want to leave traces.'

'Traces! What about him over there?' She jerked her head at the dead man.

I pointed to the window. 'Do not ask. We will do it.' I opened the chest, and two more within, until I found a small, flat casket of solid gold adorned with lapis lazuli. Inside was a square of linen or some such cloth; a plain, faded maroon, but with a faintly golden sheen. It was much folded, and I did not dare to probe further in case it was fragile.

'There's a lot of towels in this one,' called Letice.

'I told you, don't touch anything!' I hissed. I tucked the gold casket into my bag and went over to investigate.

'But it's all dry now, the blood,' she was protesting. 'Anyway, I only touched the chest.'

'Those, I will hazard, are the grave-clothes of Our Lord,' I said, peering in.

'Bloody hell!' she squeaked, jerking back and sitting down hard on the floor.

'Squeamish, are you?' I said bitterly. I did not want to touch these things myself, but, I reasoned, how many yards of Christ's shrouds already existed, out there in the world of the credulous? Enough to make sails for the English fleet, for sure. Still, I winced as I thrust my hands into the folds, but all was clean and dry. A faint smell of myrrh drifted up, nothing more.

'God, you're fishing around in there as if it were bed linen,' said Letice. 'Oh – there's a picture in this one.'

I looked over. She was holding up an icon, a big square of silver with a shape cut out of the middle, through which two dim, ancient eyes peered out. Letice's own blue eyes regarded me over the top.

'That might be the *Mandylion*,' I said, shutting the lid gratefully on the shrouds.

'What's a *Mandylion*, then?'

'Supposed to be a holy image, on a cloth, made into an icon. Can I have a look?'

The thing was very old. It looked older than the dead things I had seen in the hold of the *Cormaran*, but more alive, for the face, hollow-cheeked and thin of lip, seemed to appraise me with gloomy indifference.

'It might be,' I said. 'It *must* be.' I touched the face, very gently. Smooth paint, and the faintest ripple of woven threads beneath.

'Well, this is the last one. Doesn't look like much,' she added. I heard the creak of a lid and the click as it closed.

'What was it?' I asked over my shoulder.

'You said not to touch,' she said, coolly. 'Anyhow, it was just a big box, no gold or anything. Just wood.'

I was ready to leave with this thing I held, for at last I had found something that felt at least worthy of veneration in this storehouse of forgeries. As real, anyway, as the Crown, but not half as terrible. Still, another minute would not harm us, for dawn was still, I judged, an hour or two away. I knelt down and opened the chest, and tugged out the box inside. It was as plain as she had said, made of some scented wood that still felt a little oily to the touch. I opened it. Inside was another folded square of linen, and on it a painted face.

Except that it was not painted. It looked as if someone had just, in the last few seconds, drawn upon the cloth with water, for the image was a stain, I decided. Or a painting in blood – no, not blood. What ... what would Gilles use, for authenticity? But it looked like fresh water, just now soaking into the weave, with darker flecks of blood about the nose and forehead. The face was like that in the icon, but more alive, even though it was formed out of nothing but stains and suggestions. A young man with a beard, a long face, flowing hair and wide-set eyes that were nothing but smudges, but which held my gaze. I slammed the lid shut.

'It's this one,' I croaked. The face still hung in the air before me, like a ghost. It was a ghost, I realised: the artist, or whoever – I bit back hard on the thought of *whatever* – had somehow imprisoned a phantom in the weave of the cloth. I imagined it hanging there, folded in on itself, like smoke, like a shoal of fish hanging motionless in clear water. I set down what I had thought was the *Mandylion*. It suddenly seemed as crude a thing as I might have painted in an idle afternoon aboard the *Cormaran*. 'Let us leave now.'

We tidied up as best we could, put everything back in its place, and turned our attentions to the corpse. Dardi had hardly bled, and most of it had gone on Letice. We dragged him over behind the altar, Letice grabbing an arm without a word or a grimace. I told her to climb up through the window and on to the roof, and watched her haunches, bare under her dress, struggle up past Our Lord's face, her skin pale and alive against the balefully glowing, painted flesh. It occurred to me, too late, that she might just pull the rope out with her and leave me to be flayed, but after she had squeezed through the window, sending whispered curses flying like bats around the rafters, and disappeared, the rope stayed where it was and gave a companionable jerk when I pulled upon it.

I tied the end around Dardi's chest so that the knot lay against his throat. Then I pinched out the last candle and pulled myself, hand over hand, up the wall. It was easier getting out than in, after I had sent my pack through first and hung it from one of the iron spikes in the wall outside, useful after all. I climbed stiffly up to the roof and laid the pack down next to Letice, who was lying flat on the tiles, her chin on her hands, which were gripping the edge.

'Right, now for Dardi,' I told her.

I had not really had a plan, and it turned out that heaving a large dead man up a wall and through a window was not an easy task for two people, let alone a half-starved, battered man and a maid. But heave we did, and because I had hauled up many sails and anchors in my time it was not so very hard, except when the wretch jammed himself in the window. I had to take the slack out of the rope, climb down and wrestle him through, scrabbling at his clothing and manhandling his shoulders around so that he was propped at a diagonal, his head dangling, tongue clamped between blood-black teeth, above the drop. Then, feet on both sides of the window, I jerked and strained until, like a breech-birthed calf, he slipped out and fell for a moment before the rope brought him up and he swung, slowly. I got a good grip with one hand, drew out Thorn and cut him down. He landed with a ripe but brittle crash and rolled down on to the rocks.

After that it was simple enough to jam the grille back into the window and prop the slate up in front of it. I helped Letice over the edge and on to the ladder and followed her down in silence. She let me heave Dardi into the sea and launch the little boat. The ladders I smashed with a stone and scattered. When the pack was placed safely in the bows I turned to help her aboard.

She was kneeling at the water's edge, on a flat rock whose sea-lapped edge was encrusted, jewel-like, with sea-anemones. Her hands, palm to palm, hovered before her face, and her curving thumbs met the curved tip of her nose. I left her to her prayers and sat, fending off the boat, my spirit surging and lapping like the water. I felt relief, somewhat. I was tired, very tired. My injuries had stopped hurting very badly, so perhaps they were not so bad. Or perhaps I was just dying.

Letice dropped her hands at last, as the most grudging hint of light showed itself, moiled in cloud, in the far east. She stood up stiffly and tottered a little. Then she bent down again and washed her hands.

'Will that make amends?' she asked.

'No,' I said, without thinking.

'I didn't think so. I was very jolly in there, while I was damning myself. What about you? Aren't you bothered?'

I shrugged, with an unconcern I did not feel.

'I do it for a living,' I muttered.

'Listen, Petroc. I'm coming with you now. And I want us to be safe. There's things we need to be safe from, yes? I've ... you've seen something that I've done, something dreadful. So you have power over me.'

I shook my head. 'I don't care.'

'No. Do not make this a game. You are the kind of soul that can lie, and hurt, and come up smelling like a field of flowers. Tell me something. Give me some power over you, so we can be alike.'

I looked at her face. The light was flat and thin, but at least there was light, and it glimmered upon the flare of her nose and her upper lip that seemed, all of a sudden, like the bud of an apple-flower about to bloom.

'My name is Petroc of Auneford. I am called Patch. I am also the man they are calling the Gurt Dog of Balecester. They sing songs about me in London. Perhaps even in Smooth Field.' I looked at her. She cocked a fair eyebrow. Then she smiled, and then laughter was spilling up out of her, incredulous, amazed.

'You're not!' she said.

PART FOUR

At Sea

Chapter Twenty-Four

There was little strength left in my shoulders, and I stopped rowing when the little boat was safely away from the rocks. After I had hauled up the mast and secured it with pins and wedge, I raised the sail. It hung, a triangle of black against the brighter, star-sown blackness of the sky, as if I had torn the firmament itself. But the breeze, offshore as Michael had promised, licked at it tentatively and then filled it, so that the halyard creaked and the mainsheet grew taut in my hands.

It took little time to sail the quarter-mile or so back to where Michael Scot stood waiting with the stooped figure of the old Greek at his side. He took a step back when he saw that I had a companion with me, but I waved my arms to signal all was well, and, leaving the girl crouched in the prow, I jumped ashore.

'Do not worry, Doctor,' I assured him. 'We do not have time to explain. She will not trouble us, though, I do not think.'

Michael Scot was not convinced, but he had little choice in the matter, and between us we helped Mesarites aboard. He was much frailer than I had thought, and light as a child, and I lifted him clean off his feet and planted him amidships. Doctor Scot seemed as quietly proficient with boats as he was with all other things, and soon we were under way.

'What do you wish me to do?' I asked Scot, for the wind

was freshening and the sail had started to fret. He reached into his pack and produced a small dark cube.

'I have a compass,' he said. 'The French ship is sailing here straight from the Dardanelles, so that in order to intercept her we should be on a heading of ...'

'Good Doctor, the Sea of Marmara must be fifteen leagues across!' I protested. 'How do you expect to meet one ship in that great expanse of water?'

'*If* you hold this heading –' and he rattled off a string of numbers that meant nothing to me – 'by my calculations we will be in the middle of the sea roads from the Hellespont to Constantinople. They are narrow and not well travelled in this season. I'll wager the French ship will be the only one abroad upon the face of the waters. We will find her, if you can hold the heading.' And again he pronounced his tangle of numbers. I confessed that I had no idea what he was talking about.

'Well, hold the thing so that the needle points to *here*. That should be the right course,' he said impatiently.

'Do you think you can do that?' I asked Letice.

'Suppose so,' she muttered. I gave her the compass box and whispered Michael's instructions: keep your heading dead on south-south-east. She gave a little sigh of incomprehension, so I showed her how to keep the needle steady and line up the right arrow on the wind-rose with the bowsprit. Grateful, perhaps, for something useful to do, she hunkered down and threw the blanket I offered around her, blotting out the ghost-gleam of her yellow hair. I trimmed the sail while Michael and the old man settled themselves in the stern. I called softly to the shadow of the girl, and she held up a hand.

'Steer left,' she hissed. Smiling to myself, I let out the sail until the prow came around and the girl's hand went down. The water began to shush and crackle against the planks and we were away, sailing on a broad reach through the dark sea. I hoped Letice Londeneyse – or Pyefote, or whatever her name really was – had her eyes on the sea as well as the compass, for a floating log or spar would wreck a little boat like this in a trice. Yet as we rushed on, as the sail cupped the chill easterly breeze and the narrow hull jumped and skittered across the catspaws, I felt more free than I had since first setting eyes on Byzantium. Orion hung above us, his shimmering belt pointing the way to Sirius, low in the sky in the south-east. Letice Londeneyse could ruin her sight, staring at the all-but-invisible compass needle, but I would go by Sirius. The Dog Star, at least, I could trust.

No bells were ringing in the city behind us, but I judged that we were somewhere around the second hour of the morning. There was a fair wind now, and we were scudding along through white curls of foam. Nothing showed ahead save the night. And so we sailed, another hour, another, and then another. A faint purple line showed between land and sky to the north, and then the land showed itself, undulating low hills, still nothing more than shadows. As the light waxed, so the wind fell, and tendrils of mist began to creep across the sea, until we were passing silently through thick, cold fog. It was dark again now, and I heard – I could not see – Letice swear nastily and call to me to turn right. The fog seeped into me, and my hands, one on the tiller, one on the mainsheet, began to ache. Only the pitching of the boat, and the pull of the mainsheet, told me that we were still moving. I began to wonder how near the land had been.

And then the dawn returned. At first it was a cold glow, weak as waning moonbeams. But it warmed, and became golden, like honey poured into milk, until we were sailing through pure radiance. I let out a great sigh, and in the bow the girl held up her hands and laughed, deep and happy and full of relief. The tiller jerked in my hand, the sail snapped and filled, and all at once we leaped forward, the wind strong at our backs, and the fog began to rise from the sea. Like a veil lifted from a chalice, the white pall ascended, hovered for an instant high above the masthead, was caught by the breeze and blew away, breaking up and vanishing southwards. The sea spread out around us, flat, ruffled here and there by the breath of the wind. The coast was half a mile off our starboard side, flat land rising to dry, arid hills, near enough to see the pale line where the waves washed the rocks clean, and white buildings, first just dots, like scurf on the fur of an old brown dog, that grew with the coming light into cottages, houses, a church. And all of them deserted, I said to myself.

'Ship ho!' cried the girl, throwing out her arm. The blanket whipped from her shoulders and flew over the rail into the sea, but she seemed not to notice. For there before us, shaking the last rags of fog from its topmast, a ship, a big, high-prowed ship, was ploughing through the swell.

'Is it them?' I asked aloud.

'How the fuck should I know?' answered Letice, quick as lightning.

It was a merchantman, perhaps Genoese, a round-ship somewhat resembling the *Cormaran* but smaller and with the bulk of an overfed pony. The red and white flag of Pisa fluttered from the mast head. There were figures on the deck, sailors going about their morning chores. We were rushing towards each other now, on opposite reaches. On our present course they would pass a bow's shot away to starboard. Letice looked over her shoulder, her face white and anxious. She pointed again, in case I hadn't seen the ship. I nodded, and trimmed the sail. I could see faces now, too far away still to make out individual features. I wondered briefly if this was the right ship; if it might be a trap. But no: either it was the envoy's vessel or just another merchant, I reasoned, and feeling reassured, I pulled the boat as tight to the wind as she would go, the sail taut and humming, the little craft seething through the chop. Our prow was now aimed squarely at the rudder of the merchantman. A tall man appeared at the rail of the steering deck, and then two more beside him. I took a deep breath, pulled the boat's head to the wind and jumped to drop the sail before it began to luff and drag. We were drifting now, still moving fast. Letice shot me another look, worried this time, and began to clamber aft towards me. I began to steer us alongside, but we were still a slingshot from the ship when a loud snap rang out. Letice flinched and I looked up in time to see a great flag reach the limit of its unfurling from the stern rigging, a bedsheet of deepest blue constellated with golden lilies, the bed linen of the King of France himself.

I let out a great huzzah, and the girl cringed, thinking perhaps that I had been struck by an arrow. But I whooped again and waved my free hand in a delirium. Mesarites looked at me as if I had gone mad, but Michael Scot put a comforting arm around his shoulders.

'It's all right!' I yelled to them. 'It *is* all right! We are saved!' With a flourish that I would have been ashamed of at another time, I rammed over the tiller and let the boat slide broadside on towards the French ship. The moment of ecstasy I had felt as we sailed came back to me tenfold, a hundredfold, and I forgot all about the terrors of the last days. Another moment, and our boat came to rest gently against its salty planking. I looked up into the sun-haloed face of a deck-hand. A rope-end landed on the deck. The girl grabbed it, paused, and brought it over to me. I gave it a tug and pulled it tight.

'Up you go,' I said to her. She looked more worried than

ever, her upper lip clamped between her teeth and her eyes wide and black. I took her hand gently and laid it upon the rope.

'Do not worry,' I said. 'Go: climb up. You are safe, I swear on my life.' She stared hard into my eyes, set her mouth into a hard line and gave a curt nod. Grabbing the rope, she jumped and, fast as any deep-water sailor, swarmed up and over the rail. I threw the painter after her, hauled my pack on to my shoulders and climbed up in my turn. Strong hands grabbed me as I came level with the deck, and for a horrible instant my fears crowded back, but the next moment I was set upon my feet and steadied, as I rummaged for the pope's letter and tried to hide my tears from the wind-burned men around me: tears of joy, of relief and resurrection.

I had not noticed how beaten about I had become until I was seated under an awning, reclining Moorish-fashion upon rugs and cushions, Letice nearby, swathed in a fur cloak, for although the day was growing warm, in the shadows it was winter. Michael Scot and Mesarites were nowhere to be seen. Without the pressing need to survive, to crawl, to steal, to sail a bloody boat, my body was under no compunction to pretend it was anything other than very damaged. My face still throbbed and burned where Hughues the chamberlain had struck me, there was at least one broken rib in my chest, I was more than half-starved, and I could not remember the last time I had slept. The captain of the ship, a Genoese, as I had guessed, had summoned the barber, who had insisted on cleaning the suppurating gashes across my face at once, and had complimented me upon my brace of black eyes; and only then did I realise that, far from the handsome young fellow I had assumed myself still to be – we all allow ourselves such vanities, do we not, when mirrors are not to hand? – I was a scarred, pustular ghoul. No wonder Letice Londeneyse had been so quick to believe that I was indeed the Gurt Dog of Balecester, and great wonder that she had not knifed me out of hand when she had had the chance. Now she was eating quail and watching me from under her heavy-lidded eyes with what might have been amusement or indeed disgust. For I myself was addressing the victuals before me with all the refinement of a jackal, grease and wine dripping from me like blood. The Genoese captain was also watching me, a curious but polite smile upon his face. When I had finished, when my bruised belly could take no more and I felt more like the sun-bloated carcass of a seal than a man, he stood up and beckoned reverently to someone out on the deck. Two figures ducked under the awning and lowered themselves carefully on to the rug. Shielding my eyes with a greasy hand, I beheld two tonsured men dressed in the black and white garb of the Dominican order. One man was of medium height, well-fed and smooth-cheeked: an infant's visage, in fact, were it not for the broken veins in his nose that spoke of a fondness for wine. His fellow was taller and lean. He had the sunken cheeks and hollow eyes of an ascetic. No wine for this one, I guessed: nor pork chops neither.

'I am James of Paris,' said the smooth-faced one. 'And my colleague is Andrew of Longjumeau ...'

I raised myself stiffly and found myself stooping under the awning as I attempted a courtly bow.

'I greet the most worthy emissaries of His Majesty the royal and most pious King of France,' I croaked in my best French. The smooth-faced man beamed and motioned me to sit with the flat of his hand. I glanced at his cadaverous friend, and to my surprise I saw that he too was smiling, an honest grin that showed a row of yellow, horsy teeth.

'Please sit down, sir,' he said. He had a rich voice, a singer's voice, that belied his pinched visage. 'You have fallen on ill times, and come to us out of the night and the mists of the sea – and yet you bear a letter from His Holiness that pertains to our mission here in the Empire of the Latins. I find this exceedingly curious, to say the least.'

'My name is Petrus ... indeed, it is Petroc of Auneford,' I corrected myself. 'I serve Monsieur Jean de Sol, of whom I believe you will have heard.'

'De Sol? But of course,' cried James of Paris. 'Our travelling companion in Italy. He left us in Venice to come here, to Constantinople. He is here still ... ?' He left the words fluttering in the air between us, a question not quite asked.

'Alas, he is not,' I said, and bowed my head. The tall man, Andrew, leaned forward sharply, like a heron who spies a frog.

'Not here?' he said, carefully. 'And from your evident travails, I find myself drawing unpleasant conclusions. Tell us everything, please.'

'Monsieur de Sol, my dear master and benefactor, is dead – or so I fear,' I rasped, for my throat had gone very dry. 'I cannot be certain, but I have little hope.'

'But you must tell us,' said James. He had gone somewhat pale.

'I shall, but first I must warn you that nothing good awaits you in that city,' I said, pointing beyond the bowsprit to where Constantinople hovered, a rapidly resolving blur. 'Captain, I would suggest you take in some sail and let us slacken our pace, for I have a long tale to tell, and I would not have us at the quayside before I am done.'

The man looked somewhat taken aback, and turned to the friars. 'We have talked matters over with Doctor Scotus,' said the one called Andrew. 'He – I *did* think he was dead, but no matter – he has confirmed everything you have told me,

384

save the awful news of your master. Yes, Captain, do as he says.' James nodded urgently to him, and he left us to see to his men. Letice – I had almost forgotten about the girl, I realised – had sunk down into her swaddlings and I thought she might be falling asleep, but then her eyes flashed and I knew she was following the proceedings with every one of her needle-sharp wits.

'Good brothers, it began like this,' I started, and laid out my tale from the start – or not quite the start, for I passed over our first strained meeting with young Baldwin in the tavern, and gave matters a gloss of gentility that had, at the time, been sadly lacking. I was honest, to a degree; as honest as I believed I could be, but I left the girl out of the telling, and made my escape from Rome into a pleasant diversion. I said nothing of the *Inventaria*, those of the pope and of Mesarites, and made pretend there was but one list of the relics in the Pharos chapel, that of Baldwin. And, to be sure, I did not tell of my last visit to the Chapel, and of what had befallen there. I guessed Michael Scot had also left out this detail. Querini, I told them, had taken Jean de Sol with him, plotted with the Regent to have me killed, and then returned for the Crown of Thorns. Letice ... I had no idea what to do about Letice, or indeed who she really was, but to make matters simple I styled her as the sister of Querini's secretary, come to Greece to seek a husband, who had fallen under the threat of some terrible dishonour at the hands of Querini – I took care to be exceptionally vague at this point – and had helped me to escape in return for her own rescue. As I told this last piece of the tale I felt the girl's eyes upon me, and glancing at her, received a cat's languid, two-eyed blink.

When I had finished, the Dominicans, who had been listening to me in rapt attention, bent their heads together for a moment. Then James rose and, with a polite bow, ducked out into the sunlight while Andrew turned back to me.

'My son,' he said, 'you have had a most vexing time of it. And yet you appear to have done your master's memory some honour. You have escaped with your life and with His Holiness' letter. You have saved a most famous man, by which I mean the famed Scotus, and his venerable friend. And you bring to the midst of this disaster some hope that the task entrusted to my brother James and I might yet be fulfilled. For if, as you think, it is Querini's intention to hold the holy Crown as a security,' he curled his lip at the blasphemy of the thought, 'then it is simply a matter of transferring the, the *gratitude* of my royal sovereign from Baldwin to said Querini.'

'That is so,' I agreed, 'as far as I can fathom it.'

'It is tiresome,' said Andrew, cracking his knuckles briskly with annoyance. 'His Majesty did so want his cousin's empire to benefit. But the Regent's improvidence has rendered that impossible. But as Solomon the Wise said, "Go not forth hastily to strive, lest thou know not what to do in the end thereof, when thy neighbour hath put thee to shame."'

'Solomon also said, "He that maketh haste to be rich shall not be innocent,"' I said.

'If you mean Nicholas Querini, I would not put great store in his innocence,' agreed Andrew, amused. 'But remember the whole of the proverb, for the first part has some bearing on your own self: "A faithful man shall abound with blessings."'

'Blessed, but hardly faithful,' I said piously.

'Not at all. You have shown great loyalty to your master, and faith in the rightness of his – and our – mission,' said Andrew. 'And let it be said that I greatly enjoyed Monsieur de Sol's company. I grieve that I shall not enjoy it again, and I believe that King Louis will be saddened, for he spoke highly of de Sol, to me and to others.'

'My master had many friends,' I agreed. 'The Holy Father himself held him in some esteem. When we spoke with him, he …'

'Gracious me, you have met the Holy Father?' said Andrew, amazed. He seemed to be regarding me with new respect, which I confess had been my intention. And so I told him again of the journey to Viterbo, remembering that I had left myself out of the first telling, and realising that to profit now from telling something of the truth would do me no harm at all no matter what King Solomon might have to say.

While we were talking, the ship was drawing close to the city, and indeed we had rounded the end of the peninsula and were sailing through the boom and into the Golden Horn, until the captain ducked his head under the awning to ask Andrew what his pleasure might be. A pilot boat had met us some time before, and the news of our arrival (though not of my presence aboard) would already be at the palace. So I expected the order to be a meek retreat, but instead the friar stood up and beckoned me to join him. I left Letice, who had fallen into a trance of fatigue, and staggered out into the cold sunshine. There was the wall of Byzantium, jagged and rotten, and, towering above it, the vast and piled domes of Hagia Sophia, pallid in the sun. And there were the Italian wharves. We were close enough to see that upon one of them, a party waited: knights done up in their finery, fluttering pennants, and even the purple robes of a bishop could be glimpsed. I knew the Regent would be there, florid Anseau de Cayeux, and no doubt Chamberlain Hughues would be at his side.

The Genoese captain was a fine sailor. He had hung just enough sail to carry us sweetly and gently forward, and the fat ship was gliding like a swan, tacking up into the wind, trailing its own modest pennants in the lively air, for the royal standard had been furled at Andrew's request. We edged towards the quay, until I could see the red of the Regent's cheeks. A man in white robes stepped forward and raised his hand to us in a lordly greeting. There was a loud crack! and the great flag of France unfurled behind us. There was a cheer from the quay. At that moment Andrew gave the captain a nod. The Genoese gave a curt command. All of a sudden the deck was alive with scurrying men, all grabbing up ropes and hurling themselves into the rigging. There was a commotion of canvas and air, and the ship began to go about. With timing so perfect that I found myself sharply envious of the crew's skill, the hull drew a white circle upon the dirty waters of the Golden Horn, until it presented its stern to the Regent and his party. With another command, the crew heaved upon the lines, the sail filled, and the ship began to gather speed. The great blue and gold standard of Louis Capet waved a mocking farewell to Constantinople, and to the men on the quay, now milling about in consternation. But they were fading from view, for we were already out past the boom, out into the currents of the Bosphorus, with a fine, fast day's westward sailing ahead of us, out of the Sea of Marmara and the ruined city that squatted at its end, like a dead spider in an empty web.

Chapter Twenty-Five

'Nicholas Querini owns an island,' said Letice. They were the first words she had spoken to anyone – save a few mutterings to me, ill-tempered with fatigue – for she had slept her way across the Sea of Marmara and down through the Hellespont, and now that she had made her way on deck to join us for luncheon, we were out in the Aegean, with Lemnos far away to starboard and Tenedos behind us.

'I'm sorry?' said James, looking at her in some amazement, or possibly discomfort, for although his sensual complexion made this seem unlikely, he was the shyer of the two Dominicans.

'It is called Stampalia,' she went on, and I realised she was speaking Paris French, and well at that. 'Rich Venetians tend to have their own islands,' she explained, cutting herself a slice of salted ham. 'Querini has Stampalia, which lies to the south, near Naxos.'

'How interesting,' said Andrew, distractedly. He was attempting to eat a piece of dry and crumbling bread on which perched a tough sliver of ham while reading some official-looking document. Crumbs were showering over the parchment.

'And I was wondering if, perhaps, he is there,' she said primly, dabbing at her lips with her sleeve. 'With the holy relic.'

The Dominicans looked up as one.

'How far is this Stampalia?' asked Andrew.

'Three or four days' sail,' said Letice.

'Why would he not have carried his prize back to Venice?' I asked. James nodded in agreement.

'I do not know, but I wonder … these seas are dangerous at this time of year, and the news in Contantinople, again and again, was of the Greek Emperor's navy and their raids on the ships of the Latins. Perhaps he is holding court in his castle until spring comes. Or perhaps he has left the holy relic there under guard. In either case …'

'My dear daughter, you are not suggesting …' began James, a frown ploughing across his pink forehead.

'No, no, I am sure Mistress Letitia was not implying that we should *abscond* with the relic,' I said hurriedly. 'But …' and I stared hard at Letice as I spoke, 'if Messer Nicholas is at home, we will perhaps be able to treat with him there, and thus save us the long and uncertain passage to Venice.'

'I do not think that Querini has the authority to treat with us,' said Andrew kindly, a little as if he were addressing a child or perhaps a horse. I waited for Letice to bridle at his tone, but she merely smiled impassively. 'I have assumed, from what Master Petroc has told us, that Querini is merely acting as an agent for the Serene Republic of Venice, and that it is in Venice that we will conclude our business.'

'I do not know if that is actually true,' I put in. 'That is, I assumed the same thing at first, but now … if he were an agent of the Doge, he would not have made off with Monsieur de Sol, or tried to kill me. De Sol is a resident of the Republic. He is on friendly terms with the Doges' palace.'

'Well, then, I … how far is this Stampalia? Perhaps I will at least mention it to the good captain,' said Andrew, and returned to his battle with bread and ham.

'Good Brother Andrew, perhaps you can tell me how this

matter *is* to be settled?' I said. That question had been prey-ing upon my mind since first I had set foot aboard the *Seynt Victor*, and this seemed as good a time as any to broach it. For it seemed that, if Captain de Montalhac's company was to reap any reward from this ghastly mess, I would have to do the reaping. And indeed I seemed to hear the Captain's voice in my ear: 'Pay attention, Patch! Pay attention.'

The friar looked up again, crumbs flying, jaws working furiously upon a piece of pig gristle. 'It is a simple trans-action,' he said at last, after a mighty swallow. 'Possession of the Crown is transferred to His Majesty Louis, depending upon its exchange for a gift, a token of gratitude, from the king to the emperor or empire.'

'Exactly! And the size of this putative gift was, I hazard, known by my master?'

'No,' said Andrew, wiping his greasy mouth with the back of his hand.

'Oh?' I said, surprised. This was not going to be easy, then.

'It had not been decided,' said Andrew. '*Has* not, even yet. We were to adjust the magnitude of the gift to the needs, the requirements, of Baldwin de Courtenay. These needs, we hoped, we could estimate without putting His Majesty the Emperor to any embarrassing questions. As, now, the Crown is being held in surety for a loan, the gift, to my thinking, will be in the amount of said loan – for how better to reward Baldwin but to discharge him from onerous and shameful obligation?'

'Indeed. So …' I paused, my mind scurrying ahead to commissions and percentages. 'The mortgage imposed by Querini is in the sum of …' There was a sharp burst of pain in my lower shinbone. I looked around to see that Letice was glaring at me with her piercing eyes, the same docile smile upon her lips. She had kicked me smartly under the table.

'Querini's mortgage is the crux of the matter,' agreed Andrew, not noticing a thing. 'As soon as we find out what it is, we can send back to Paris and make arrangements. But it is to be assumed that we are concerned with a considerable sum – a very considerable sum indeed, to necessitate such a holy, an indeed priceless security. I would place the Crown's worth far above that of the whole empire, from what I have heard and seen of *that*.'

'Quite so, quite so,' I said smoothly, placing my chin upon steepled fingers, something I had seen Gilles do. I felt like a rank impostor, but nonetheless we seemed, incredibly, to have come to the nub of the matter. 'And what sum is in your remit to ... to disburse?' I enquired casually.

'Oh, good heavens!' cried Andrew. The piece of bread burst asunder in his fist, blasting crumbs everywhere. One caught in my eyebrow, and I spied another upon the ivory skin of Letice's neck. I bit my lip in frustration: I had gone too far. But no: Andrew was brushing his hands together and gazing at the clouds overhead, as if performing some kinetic prayer. I could see his great teeth. He was smiling.

'My dear son,' he said at last, tugging abstractedly at his earlobe, 'I cannot quite believe it myself, but I have the authority – and I tell you this only because you are now, to my mind, the successor of Monsieur de Sol ...' he broke off and glanced at Letice. She stood up and dashed the breadcrumbs from her tunic front. 'I believe we need a little more wine,' she said brightly, taking up the jug and wandering off towards the stern.

'An extremely well-bred young lady,' I murmured, sanctimoniously. The friar nodded his agreement.

'Indeed, yes,' he said. 'Most discreet, most discreet. Now ...' he leaned forward until his mouth was inches from my ear. 'It is King Louis' wish that James and I give whatever is necessary to secure the Crown.'

'Whatever necessary being ... ?' I could barely get the words out.

'When I said that the Crown was worth more than the empire, I was not indulging in rhetoric,' said Andrew, softly. 'Louis is willing to present Baldwin with ... with half the royal treasury of France!' he finished in a rush and regarded me, panting a little, as if he had relieved himself of a physical burden. And indeed he had, I thought. What could the kingdom of France be worth? I thought of the barber of King Midas, rushing out to bellow his secret to the bullrushes. Well, I would press on.

'My ... my merciful Lord!' I squeaked, blinking in unfeigned shock. 'That could be no less than ... than ...'

'One hundred and fifty thousand golden livres,' hissed Andrew, in a rapture of release. 'There. It is told. I would have told Monsieur de Sol ere now, and so I am telling you.'

'And I shall tell no one,' I assured him.

Andrew stood up and rubbed his cheeks briskly, as if to force the blood back into them. 'You see what a dilemma James and I have been in?' he asked. I nodded.

'Good brother Andrew,' I said, leaning forward over the food-strewn table, 'I see what a burden you have borne. But consider this. It may be that to find Querini away from Venice would put us to some advantage. If he should reach Venice, is it not possible, given the record of past Doges, that the Republic might be loath to surrender the relic, even to King Louis himself?'

'It ... it is possible,' Andrew conceded. He turned away and gazed eastwards, towards the golden backs of the islands that shimmered there. 'Four days' sail, eh? Not so very far. I shall consult my brother.' And without another word he drifted off, leaving me in possession of the table, and of the ham, on to which I fell in an ecstasy of greed, made sharper by relief, and by the appalling, wonderful secret with which I had just been entrusted.

I had not had time to think much about Letice of Smooth Field since we had escaped from the Pharos Chapel. I might have left her there on the shore, but my mind and body were in painful turmoil and it had been easier to take her with me. And strange to say, her kneeling to pray by the water had moved me in some way I could not have explained then or now. Since we had climbed aboard the *Seynt Victor* we had barely seen each other. But when she had insinuated herself into my conversation with Andrew, and that sly kick beneath the table ... All the desolate, impotent rage I had felt when Michael had revealed to me the circumstances of Anna's death had come flooding back. But I was trapped now, for I could not ill-treat any woman, no matter how evil; nor could I have her put ashore, for I was but a passenger on this ship. We had no power over each other here, and that very thought was a knife in my heart.

'Thank you,' I told her now. I had cornered her in the prow, where she was watching the land slip by in the distance. 'Thank you very much. Do not ...' I held up my hand, for she had turned to me in surprise. 'Do *not* mistake yourself, lady. I do not know what is in your mind, but I know what you are, and what you have done. That you and I are alive together on this ship is an accident, nothing more. You will keep out of my affairs, or by God I'll ...' I broke off, and smacked the rail in confused rage.

'Master Petroc, there is something I must say to you.' I rounded on her in fury, for how dare she address me? But her eyes were cast down and she was hugging herself tightly across the chest, and the unbidden memory of that day in Rome when I had witnessed Querini beating her stilled my tongue.

'I was in London when you were there,' she muttered. 'With some others. They were looking for ...'

'I know who you were looking for,' I said, quiet in my turn, for I feared that if I raised my voice I would lose control of my passions and strike her, or worse.

'Facio was riding the horse,' she said, eyes still down. 'He was the tall man with me in Rome, down by the river, the one who ...' She gave me a rueful look, and I narrowed my eyes. 'I told him not to kill you, though he had planned on it. He was a mercenary once, before he met Nicholas Querini, and can ride a destrier as well as any knight,' she went on. 'I did not know they planned to kill your woman. I thought they would take her back to Venice. I ... I would not have been party to it, I swear.'

'I do not believe you,' I told her. 'Why should I? You are a murderess and the tool of an evil-doer. You killed your own friend in front of me. And Fulk de Grez in Rome, and his companion, no doubt: why would you not murder ...' I could not utter Anna's name in the presence of this creature. 'It would surely be as easy, nay, easier by far, to strike down a defenceless woman.'

'You were there!' She pleaded. 'You saw!'

''Twas not you upon the horse,' I hissed, 'but you no doubt guided your friends to Cheapside. That is why you were in London, was it not?'

'Well, you are right,' she said, and her eyes met mine. They were rimmed with red, and the pale skin beneath them was bruised with exhaustion. 'We knew your plans – Nicholas keeps an army of spies to tell him of friends and enemies, and what the world's gold is doing; and at Pope Gregory's court there was a certain Peter of Verona, newly become Inquisitor General of northern Italy, courtesy of Querini gold ...' I closed my eyes. The trap that had caught us was monstrous. I saw Peter's jolly face and cold eyes, and how spittle had flown from his grinning mouth as he spoke of heretics and what he did with them. '... we were waiting for your ship,' Letice was saying. 'We had been there since November ...'

'But I do not care about this,' I snapped. 'What does it matter? I know. All of it: all the schemes, all the ... waste.' She opened her mouth in shock. 'Oh, do not play the virtuous one,' I told her. 'I have found out your master's plan at last – too late, but a simpleton like me is always late to the feast, eh?'

'We were to kidnap the lady, no more,' insisted Letice. 'I thought Nicholas was going to ransom her off to her uncle. And then I heard ... I saw her, out in the streets; followed her. She was a fine lady ...'

'She was a *princess*!' I cried. 'But that is not why – dear God, I cannot bear this!'

'That wasn't why you loved her,' said Letice, quietly. I stared at her, horrified. 'And Querini is not my master, no matter what you might think – I'd not blame you for thinking it, mind. No, listen,' she said hurriedly, for I had begun to turn away. 'I was his woman, it is true. He took care of me, and what I gave him in return should be obvious. And more: I was useful to him, for I have a quick mind, and men will betray themselves happily for a pretty face. Nicholas has grown rich on such betrayals. I am not dull enough to think I am the first woman he has used thus, and I shall not be the last. But he gave me a fine life and I was happy to do his bidding. Until that day. No: listen to me. I saw you in Rome that day, when Nicholas blacked my eye: remember? He had taken me out to buy me something, or so he said, but we were following you. When I realised, I told him I would have nothing more to do with it, that he had no right ...'

'Please, do not mock me with this morality play,' I scoffed, but she shook her head furiously.

'Whatever else I may not be, I am a woman,' she said, eyes blazing. 'I will not suffer to watch my sisters ill-treated. I am a whore, Master Petroc,' she said defiantly. 'Not a *princess*, but I know how men use women, how they hurt us, defile us, kill us as if we were beasts. Do you know why Nicholas had your woman killed? Because it was *easier* than carrying her off. If she had been a man, do not think but that he would have taken the trouble. That's what I told him, there in the market, and he knocked me down.'

'Much you have suffered,' I sneered.

'Oh, I have suffered all right,' she said, suddenly angry. 'We've all fucking *suffered*, haven't we? Do not come the high-handed one with me, Master Gurt Dog of Balecester, Master Priest-killer! You would not blanch at the killing of a lady, from what I've heard! The priest you once were is showing, you moralising popinjay!'

'I was never a fucking priest!' I hissed. 'I was a novice monk, no matter what the ... the stories, the songs about me – and they are not about *me*, no matter what the London street believes – are all of them lies, and ...'

'And you are innocent. You never done it, eh?' said the girl, with an angry smile. 'Well, you must have done something.'

'I am no priest, no priest-killer, and no—'

'No what? You have done your share, my lad. You've killed more men than I.'

'Is that so?' I asked, bitterly. 'You seem to know how to use a knife. Who taught *you* to kill, since we are speaking of such things?' She gave a grim little chuckle and and peered at me sidelong.

'Taught me?' she said. 'I worked it out for myself. Not very hard, is it? Who taught you, then?'

I was silent, remembering Sir Hugh de Kervezey, and the first words he had ever spoken to me: 'This is how you kill someone quickly and efficiently. Knife forward, your thumb on the blade. Strike upwards under the ribs, and keep pushing upwards.' And I remembered how the light had gone out of his eyes after I had killed him. He had proved a good teacher after all, and I a fine student. I found that I had clenched my fists so tightly that they had gone numb, and that the terrible agonising rage I had felt was quenched, although I could not have said why, or what was taking its place.

'Not hard?' I said at last. 'I suppose it isn't. But it makes everything else impossible.'

She gave me that sidelong look again. 'Depends on who it is, doesn't it?'

'Those who believe in the immortal soul would disagree.'

'Fuck. Of course, you used to be a priest. You aren't squeamish, though, Gurt Dog ...'

'Do you not listen? I was never a priest,' I growled. 'As for my soul, it is destroyed, beyond a doubt, but I have ceased to believe in salvation or a loving Saviour. I will not give myself that luxury, to be a murderer and a thief and still under His protection. I leave that to the soldier-priests and the crusaders.'

'I didn't kill your friend,' she said, suddenly. 'The German, in Foligno. That was Facio. You want to know if my arms are bloody to the shoulders? I will tell you. I killed a man in Venice, when I was a girl, and all alone. He beat me and fucked me in an alley, and when he had had his way he fell asleep from all the drink in him, and I stove his head in with a brick.' I heard her swallow hard, as if her mouth had gone dry.

'Will you hear my confession, Master I-was-never-a-priest? Here it is anyway: I have stood by while men were killed. I have brought a man to his death, once. In Smooth Field life was not accounted very high, and in Venice they will kill a man over the cut of his clothes. But Dardi was the second one I have slain, and he fucking deserved it,' she said through clenched teeth. 'Fuck! Fuck it! Ach ...' she sniffed, and I suddenly realised she was weeping. Reluctantly I raised my hand to comfort her, and she flinched. My anger flooded back.

'He deserved it, did he? Anna did not deserve it, but he did: you are as just as Solomon, aren't you? You kill your friend, and betray your master, as easy as ...' I shook my fist, as if to beat the words out of the air.

'The betrayal was not mine,' said Letice fiercely. 'Nicholas had thrown me aside.'

'He gave you to Dardi,' I said, all of a sudden remembering her hurried words in the chapel. I had not really listened then, for I had been awash with terror, confusion and relief, but now I began to recall that she had given me some explanation that had been enough for me then. 'But, really, what of it? You are a whore: you said so yourself.'

'Yes, I should not care, should I?' she was saying. 'Nor be surprised, for Nicholas bought me like a sword or a horse. Something to ride. But give me to Dardi? To Dardi! He knew it would mean my death. He had just made Dardi the warden of his island, and I was to sweeten the pot. Stampalia – it is a hideous, dry place, and the castle is—'

'This is nonsense! You would have had your own little kingdom,' I interrupted.

'Not with Dardi. He would have killed me sooner or later – no doubt sooner. Torture was what he really liked. Nicholas, Facio even – they are not cruel, not in that way. They do not hurt for pleasure, except when that might bring gain. They want what they want, and they will do the necessary. They have enough in their heads to keep them occupied: Dardi's head was empty: he must needs keep it filled with a store of horrors inflicted upon others.'

Despite the scorn I was trying to keep hold of, I shuddered, remembering all too well the smell of his breath that night by the Tiber. 'He looked too stupid for that,' I said.

'No, no. You men: so arrogant about your cruelty. You do not need to be clever to be cruel, you just do what your flesh tells you. Dardi – suffice to say he once fucked a girl to death, and she was a friend, and I had to clean her up. He *wanted* me to see.'

'But did Querini know what he was about, when he ...'

'Oh, he knew all right. He'd had enough of me. I think Facio was grown clever and bold enough that Nicholas could lean upon him – he didn't need me any more. And there's many a foreign whore in Venice, cleverer ones than me.'

'But ... but didn't he care about you? After all those years?'

'He put me clear out of his mind the moment he left me,' she said. 'I'm sure he doesn't remember me at all.'

We had fair weather and a fair wind out of the north, and so we quickly threaded our way down through the islands of Greece, past Scio and Scopello, between Icaria and Micono and down into the Duchy of the Archipelago, Venetian castles nailing Venetian rule on to barren hillsides and whitewashed villages cowering in their shadow. Late on the third day we raised Stampalia, and not wanting to arrive at night, the captain took the *Seynt Victor* into the lee of Amorgo. I passed a restless night, for, whatever the Dominicans intended to do should we find Querini at home, I – for all my eagerness to come here – had but one thought in my head. If Messer Nicholas were there, then to avenge my master, and Horst, I must try and take his life from him. This thought had been seeded on that last day in the Bucoleon Palace, and had grown slowly, in darkness, ever since. Out here in the pure light of the Greek seas, however, it had begun to uncurl and to darken, like a shoot pushing its way up from underground, and since the lady Letice and I had reached some strange, uneasy truce its full strength had been turned upon her erstwhile master. I had no idea how my need to avenge Captain de Montalhac could be squared with the extraordinary – nay, stupendous – opportunity offered by Andrew of Longjumeau's revelation. I had never before planned to hurt anyone and I did not wish to now, but there did not seem to be a choice if I were ever to return to the fellowship of the *Cormaran*. As the boat bobbed gently beneath a dazzling net of stars, I bitterly regretted that I had ever come eastward in the first place.

Letice, on the other hand, was seething with excitement. She had been acting her part with aplomb, so much so that she kept herself sharply to herself and had allowed the captain of the *Seynt Victor* to appoint himself her chaperon, which office he fulfilled in an absurdly grave manner, no doubt because he felt the eyes of the friars upon him. I had not passed more than the time of day with her since our disagreement, and I found myself urgently wishing that I could divine whatever it was she had going on in her head. I knew little more about her now than I had when I first beheld her in Rome. She fascinated and repelled me, and I did not trust her one hair's breadth. So I was startled to find her at my side as I leaned upon the rail, gazing out at the black silhouette of the island.

'Hello, Master Dog,' she murmured. I looked around, and

saw her sharp yet sensual profile outlined against the faint star-sheen on the water.

'Good evening,' I said. Dear God, could I do no better than that? I wished she would leave me be, to my dark and bloody thoughts.

'You're a well-mannered dog, aren't you?' she answered. 'I mean, for a blaspheming priest-killer and all.'

'Mistress Letice, you should not be here,' I said vehemently. 'The captain, the brothers ...'

'Bugger the brothers,' she said. 'Or, mayhap, they are buggering each other as we speak. That is what you get up to, isn't it, you priests?'

'I told you, I was never a priest!' I burst out, then saw she was chuckling.

'Like I said before, you must have done something,' she said.

There was nothing for it but to tell her. I thought perhaps then she might leave me alone. So I hurried through my sad tale, from the night I had met Sir Hugh de Kervezey in the Crozier tavern to that bloody morning on the Koskino beach.

'I have told you these things because I wish you to leave me be,' I told her sullenly, when I was done. 'We are not friends, make no mistake.'

'Well, we are thrown together, friends or not. And thank you for your tale, though it was less interesting than the songs. Now listen: you know nothing of me, although you assume much. So be silent, and I will tell you of my life, and then you may judge me – but only then. I was born in Smooth Field perhaps two-and-twenty years ago,' she went on in a rush, as if afraid that I would prevent her.

'Mam was a troubadour – nay, she *called* herself such,' she added with a grave smile, seeing me cock my head sceptically.

'She could sing like a blackbird, trip a neat step and play enough upon the lute. And she had a lovely body – "bumps in all the right places", as she would say – such that gentlemen like to stare at until their wives break jars over their heads. She, for there was no father around to do it, and I never knew who he might have been, earned us pennies by singing at parties, fine and not so fine. When I was starting to grow hair upon my quim she began to bring me too, for folk like to give coins to a pretty little girl, and when I passed the oblation cup around they would fall over themselves to fill it for me.'

'I saw Smooth Field – it is a grim place,' I said grudgingly.

'You would say that, wouldn't you?' she shot back. 'If all you knew was Balecester, I am sure that all of London seemed *a bit grim*.'

'Balecester? I am not from that poxy kennel,' I told her, laughing. 'I am a Devon boy – to me, Balecester might have been Babylon itself when I first came there. God rest you, girl, but since then I have seen some of the world, and Smooth Field is grim by any comparison.'

'Worldly-wise,' she said, shrugging. 'Well then, you are right: there are prettier and kindlier places to live. Yes, I grew up in a dung-heap, with people who would pay to watch two dogs fucking. And yes, I fingered purses, and watched my mam do things the quality don't. What of it? Do you want to hear my tale, or what?'

'Go to, go to,' I said, feigning unconcern, although in truth her company had become more welcome, for I had been alone save for my anger, and anger is a poor companion.

'When I was in my sixteenth year – I suppose I was sixteen, but … well, the year that the king locked up the Earl of Kent …'

'So five years ago,' I put in. 'That would make you one-and-twenty.'

'All right then, Ptolemy,' she said. 'Well, well: younger than I thought. Anyway, in that year my mam took up with a merchant from the Aldgate. A rich man, very rich indeed. She was dancing and singing for his company one night, he took a shine to her, and next thing I knew we were living in his house. My God, it was lovely! I mean, we were up in the attic and all, but still ... And that went on for all of three months, the nice clothes, having enough to eat, not being bothered by smelly old men with grey whiskers and dead-bird breath. I used to prance up and down Cheapside like royalty, I can tell you, and did I go over to Smooth Field and play the queen? Too right I did. So, all very lovely, until the bloody old fool of a merchant decides he has to crown his virtuous life with a pilgrimage to Jerusalem. He set about gathering a merry band of like-minded fellows, all as rich as himself, and servants, mules and muleteers – and of course such a party must needs have entertainment. My mam was bought for a fine purse of gold and the promise of saving her soul.

'She brought me along, of course, for I begged her, and I was useful, and the old codger had taken a shine to me as well. We set off in the spring, crossed the sea with everyone puking over the side even though it was flat as a millpond, and had a lovely time all the way through France: I even got my own donkey. Now it was easy living, for the old codger put us up in the best inns. Mam danced and drank at night and I kept to myself in the daytime, but there wasn't much pawing, for the whole crew of them had their minds on higher matters. So it was sweet, even crossing the mountains, which they'd all been dreading. Down into Italy we went, and very pretty it was. We were headed for Venice, there to take ship for Jaffa. It was before Frederick had returned, so there was peace all the way from Milan to the sea, and hot sun, ripe fruit ... and Mam getting closer and closer to the old codger, and hinting that I might be getting a new dad ...' She paused, and shook her head, a tiny, wry smile hovering on her lips.

'We came into Venice, and the very next day Mam wakes up with a fever. And the day after that, she didn't wake up at all. Just like that: a fever, a bloody flux, and she was dead in a shit-filled bed. Well, the purse of gold was gone, grabbed up by the old codger, who did not want to be my daddy any more. I tried dancing for the gentlemen, but they laughed at me. In their haste to save their souls they made sure to leave me behind when the ship sailed.

'There I was, in the clothes I stood up in and without a groat, wandering about in Venice, not being able to speak a word of their language. And if I thought I'd been pawed in London – Christ almighty! Venetian men are like lice: they get everywhere. I was ... you are looking at me with that expression men get, you know: how shocking! Tell me more!'

'Ballocks!' I spluttered, all wounded dignity. She was right, though.

'I was going to say that I was no maid of easy virtue, but I was no maid neither, if you catch my meaning. I was hungry, of course, but I knew how to steal, and it kept me going for nigh on a week, until I ran into a mob of bravoes who decided to rape me. I ran from them and kept running, into parts of the town I'd never been, until I stumbled into a square full of ... whores. Windows full of them, going up into the clouds it seemed to me, all shaking their tits and cawing at the men below like randy rooks. I was clever enough to work out that I would be safe from the bravoes in one of those houses, so I dashed in and begged the madam to hide me. She did. And before I knew it I was a Venetian whore. I could dance and sing, remember, so I paid my way; and the madam thought I was exotic – Smooth Field, exotic! – so she kept me by for the special customers ...'

'Ah. Like Nicholas Querini, perchance?' I ventured.

'Like Messer Nicholas. He took a fancy to me – a bit more than a fancy, in fact, for he bought me from the madam. Bought me, yes, for at some point I had become her *property*.' She hissed the word, and bit her lip. 'Bought and sold, that's me. Nicholas has a wife and a pretty family, so he kept me in an old palace round the corner from Saint Mark's. I was happy, I'll admit. There was a roof terrace, with flowers and a little tree, and do you know? I had my own monkey! Men do like to buy their courtesans monkeys, you know, and pappagallos. A hazard of our trade, you might say: they bite and peck and eat squishy fruits, which makes them shit everywhere, but you know, it is *exotic*. Tra-la. Nicholas would come around to bed me, and we would talk, and then the talking came before the bedding, and afterwards; and I liked that. He taught me to read, you know: bought me my very own tutor, an old monk – hated my guts.' She threw back her head and barked a harsh laugh. 'He didn't think women should read, and tried to teach me scripture by rote, but I would threaten him with the monkey – he hated the monkey – and in the end I did learn. Funny, it was the parrot killed him in the end, for they carry fever, dirty creatures. Why I didn't get it I don't know, but I didn't.'

'I like monkeys,' I said. 'They ...'

'Don't start!' she told me.

'All right,' I assured her. 'So you learned your words. Then what?'

'Nicholas brought me things to read, and he noticed that

406

I could pick them apart and find what they really meant, the gold in the dross, if you like. At first he did it for his own amusement – got him worked up, talking to a clever wench. Then he started bringing me other things, *his* things, papers to do with his affairs. I hadn't realised what a big man he was, but he is very, very … he has power, lots of it. He's as rich as the Doge, oh, more so, and he is always, *always* plotting. I used to think his skull was full of ants, never resting, always bringing in more ideas, building more schemes. He wore me out, really. Wears everyone out eventually.'

'But he looks like such a typical merchant,' I protested. 'Big and pleased with himself. Lots of food and drink and pats on the back.'

'Oh, he's all of that,' snorted Letice. 'That's how he keeps folk off their guard while he's pinching their stuff.' She saw my surprised look. 'Not pinching like you mean, Petroc. He doesn't steal things and shove them in a bag. He does it with paper and words and numbers. That's the way to nick the really big stuff. Like empires. He would love to be Doge, of course,' she said, thoughtfully. 'I've always known that. He started to let me out of the house, you see, to spy on his rivals. No one knew who I was, or *what* I was, and I caught on to the language pretty quick, so I could go anywhere. No past, not in Venice. That's when I met Facio and Dardi.'

'I was wondering about that,' I said.

'Dardi was a knife-man, pure and simple,' she told me. 'Anyone Nicholas wanted out of the way, Dardi took care of it. He was busy all the time, and Nicholas paid well, so he got rich. But he didn't get clever, or less like an ape. Facio, however … he's different. Very quick. He'd be a Nicholas if he'd had the right parents, but he's a fisherman's son, so he must needs claw and trample his way up. He's close to Nicholas now, close as can be. He thinks Nicholas will get him made a nobleman – perhaps he's right. He'd kill the pope for that. If it had been Facio in the chapel, we wouldn't be having this talk.'

We were silent for a while. The wind was picking up and it was getting colder. Letice leaned her shoulder against mine for a moment and then pulled away. I found myself wishing she would do it again.

'We are not so different, you and I,' I said. 'We have had our lot thrust upon us. It was my fate to fall into the hands of Captain de Montalhac, whom I would call a good man, although others would not. It was yours to be found by Nicholas Querini, who the world accounts a good and gentle man. But we have both been drawn into ... into ...'

'Into a stinking bloody jakes,' she said. 'By your leave I'll wish you goodnight, polite Master Dog, and I'll see you in the morning.'

PART FIVE

Stampalia

Chapter Twenty-Six

The castle of the Querinis, despite all Letice had done to proclaim it a grim and doom-laden place, was a great block of brand-new, blindingly white ashlar sitting almost cheerfully above its whitewashed village, and overlooking two coves of clear, deep water. Querini himself was gone, we saw at once: there was no ship in the harbour, and no flag flew from the battlements.

As soon as we had come within sight of Stampalia, the two Dominicans had begun pacing about the deck, whispering agitatedly to each other and getting in the way of the sailors.

It had been decided that only Letice and I should go ashore, so that suspicions should not be aroused. Master Lambertus found me a sword, an ugly thing that looked as if it had last been used to slaughter hogs; but it had a scabbard and a belt, and I was glad to gird myself with it, although there seemed to be no threat of danger. I put on my cloak, and Letice put on hers, and together we climbed down into the jolly-boat. As the sailors rowed us across the cove to where a line of fishing dinghies were pulled up on the narrow white beach, I saw the villagers milling about under the trees. They did not seem alarmed by our arrival, and I took that to be a good thing. When we had jumped ashore, a few fishermen wandered over to see what we were about, and I greeted them in their own tongue and told them we had business at the castle. The Lordos was away, they told us. We had just missed him – he had left but two days ago. When would he be back? They shrugged as one and, evidently relieved that we were not Venetians nor officials of any outside power, went back to mending their nets.

'They did not recognise you,' I said to Letice.

'Well, I was never allowed to wander about down here,' she answered. 'I was here for a month, three years ago. But I think I can find the path – here.'

We followed a narrow roadway, here cobbled, there rock-hewn steps, that wound up through the village, where old ladies sat in their doorways and children hid from us, and chickens looked down upon us from the olive trees. It was a short but steep climb up to the gate, and when we reached it there was no one in the guardhouse. I called through a grate in the thick door, and presently heard footsteps clipping towards us. A very young man-at-arms peered through, and then a thick, booze-blown nose appeared.

'Mistress Letice!' crowed a throaty Venetian voice, there was a scraping and clanking, and the postern door opened.

'Jacopo,' said Letice, 'I fear we have come too late, and must chase Signor Nicholas back to Venice!'

'Alas, yes,' said Jacopo. He was a well-fed and well-watered fellow in his middle years, with swollen hands and rheumy eyes. I guessed he took a keen interest in the running of his master's cellars. 'But you are expected,' he went on. 'And where is Signor Dardi?' he enquired, looking me up and down curiously as Letice and I stepped into the little courtyard, a high-walled space adorned with orange trees in clay pots and with carved plaques bearing what I assumed were the Querini arms. It smelled faintly of new mortar.

'Dardi sent me ahead. He remains in Constantinople,' said

Letice, as the gate shut behind us. 'I am to set things in order here in the meantime.'

'Good, good!' said Jacopo with evident relief. 'We are all *so* looking forward to Signor Dardi taking up his new position,' he added, his words oozing with desperately feigned sincerity.

'I am sure that you are,' said Letice, regarding him down the length of her nose. The man cringed slightly, or perhaps I was imagining things. 'Now. Master Nicholas left me instructions. Did he leave anything here, anything of importance he carried out of Constantinople?'

'No thing,' said Jacopo. 'No actual thing …'

'A chest, an extremely valuable chest,' Letice prompted him. 'I am to make sure that it is locked up in the strongest room you have.'

'A chest?' asked Jacopo, looking more and more puzzled. 'No, no, nothing like that.'

'Perhaps not a chest,' said Letice. 'A box. A, a package, about this big?' She glanced at me, and gestured with her hands, the width of a man's head.

'Absolutely not, I am afraid,' said Jacopo blankly. 'He brought spices for the kitchens and a bolt of silk for hanging in the great hall, but … no, apart from our guest, he left nothing more than that. '

'Your guest?' said Letice sharply.

'I speak lightly,' said Jacopo apologetically. 'The man whom my lord brought from Constantinople – we are to hold him until such time …'

'Holding him?' I asked, feeling as if I were about to fall down upon the flagstones, so strong was the blood running about my skull. 'The … the Frenchman?'

'Jacopo, I have not presented Signor Petrus, lately come into my lord's service,' said Letice smoothly, as Jacopo's wet eyes grew round with surprise.

'He is French, yes indeed,' said Jacopo. 'So you know of whom I speak. Good. I was beginning to worry that he would die before … ah, yes. Signor Dardi was going to ask him some questions.'

'Indeed he was,' I said grimly. 'Well, Signor Dardi has entrusted the asking to me.'

The man gave a great whooshing sigh of relief. 'How marvellous,' he wheezed. 'I … Signor Querini knows I am not the equal to such special tasks. I was sure I would fail him. Would … would you like to see him now? No, no, forgive me. I must settle you first. You are tired, you are hungry – you are waiting for your effects to come ashore. Signora, should I send men to fetch them?'

'No, no. The master of the ship has taken care of it. No, let us see this Frenchman of yours – Signor Petrus had better talk to him before he expires, eh?'

I nodded, trying to look cold and uninterested. Jacopo wasted no more time. He spun on his heel and led us into the castle. I was suddenly overcome by the urge to draw my sword and divide the fat little man down the centre, but I resisted it.

'How many men does your garrison number?' I asked, in what I hoped was a bored voice. I was not permitting myself the smallest morsel of hope, for false hope is a greater affliction than no hope at all.

'Five,' said Jacopo over his shoulder. 'And ten Greek lads – but they are all down in the village today, for they are celebrating one of their vile, schismatic holy days tomorrow.'

We passed through the hall, where a great fireplace adorned with the Querini shield had yet to be swept. Then we climbed, first one straight stair, then a winding one. I had expected us to descend, for were not prisoners kept in dungeons? But perhaps new castles did not have dungeons.

I glanced at Letice, but she was staring at Jacopo's quivering backside, a dangerous blankness upon her face. The memory of Dardi's shocked face came back to me, and I prayed silently that she was not planning some new revenge, for this was her world and I knew almost nothing about it, nor what she might be capable of.

'Here we are!' panted Jacopo at last. We must have reached the very top of the castle, for there were no more stairs, and we stood on a landing with two closed doors facing us. A rush lamp was burning down in a sconce. Jacopo turned a key and opened the nearest door. The room was small, but the walls were newly whitewashed, and the low winter sun was slanting in through the narrow window. It was far from a dungeon, but there was something cold and desperate about it: something dead. There were no furnishings of any sort save for a straw pallet on the tiled floor under the window. And upon it a naked man lay stretched out upon his belly, one hand lolling, palm up and fingers limp, upon the tiles. Letice stayed Jacopo and I with an imperious raised finger, walked briskly across the room and squatted down before the man. She reached down and grabbed a handful of his iron-grey hair and raised his head, but I could not see the face, for it was hidden by her thigh.

Letice dropped the lolling head and, straightening, she turned to Jacopo.

'It is he,' she said. 'You may leave us alone with him. We will ask some questions and, depending upon the answers – if answers there be – Signor Petrus will take the wretch onwards with him to Venice.'

Jacopo beamed and almost leaped from the room, closing the door after him. As soon as the latch clicked I hurled myself over to the pallet and dropped to the floor beside Letice. The man's face was sunk into the straw. I reached for him, then paused. His back was a contorted mass of scabs, some crusted over, some pink and suppurating, that roiled over the livid skin like a tangle of lobworms. There was a heavy stench of piss and spoiled meat. But the shoulders rose and fell faintly, so I swallowed and, wincing, gently rolled the head over.

Captain de Montalhac licked his blistered lips and his eyelids fluttered, but both eyes were bruised black and swollen shut. Dried blood had blocked both nostrils. But he breathed, he lived. I had held the things that witnessed the Resurrection of Our Lord in my hands, but they had been dumb. The dead are dead, and they do not return. The bones of Constantinople's Greeks; the withered clay of the relics I had stolen and sold; Anna ... they would not come back. It is not the dead who are abandoned, it is the living. But I had been alone, and now the Captain had returned to me. I bent down and kissed his brow.

'Patch?' he said, although it was no more than a sigh, and I had to lean so close that I felt his breath flutter upon my ear. 'Patch? They have you.' He seemed to go limp, and I took his shoulder and shook it gently, urgently.

'No, Master,' I whispered, smoothing the matted hair away from his burning forehead. 'I have come for you. You are safe.'

'They have the letter,' he said suddenly, clearly, his good eye opening very wide.

'No, no!' I exclaimed. 'I have it. And more. Let us be gone from here. Can you rise?'

He tried to roll himself over, but could not. Taking off my cloak, I draped it carefully over his wounded back, pushed my arm under his shoulder and tried to heave him up, but he was heavy.

'Letice,' I called softly, 'can you persuade friend Jacopo to

call out the guards? We must bring my master to the ship.'
She gazed at me for a second, eyes narrowed, then nodded
and went to the door. She left the room and I heard her
voice, raised and hectoring, and Jacopo's, wheedling and then
relieved; and then the sound of feet on stone stairs. Letice
peered around the door.

'He will fetch them, and a litter,' she said. 'He's fucking
delighted to be rid of your master, so if we play it very fine, I
believe we will be away from here without any trouble.' She
came and knelt beside me. 'Jacopo is a fool, but not much
of one. He hates this island, for he misses Venice and his
bum-boys. It is my guess he had nothing to do with this –'
and she laid her hand gently upon the Captain's matted head.
It looked very long and white against the blood-seized ropes
of black and grey – 'for he is not cruel, merely greedy. He
fears Dardi above all things, and believes that your master
will die, and that Dardi will want to make someone's flesh
suffer as a consequence – Jacopo's flesh, I mean. If we do not
push him I think he will believe what he wishes to believe.'
She gazed down at the Captain and crossed herself slowly.
'The guards did this, I expect. Nicholas would not soil his
hands. But he finds it a simple matter to squeeze cruelty out
of others,' she muttered, and her shoulders stiffened for a
moment. Footsteps sounded upon the stair.

The guards – the young lad from the gatehouse and three
others, stubbly and hungover Venetian stevedores, by the
looks of them – heaved the Captain on to a stretcher and,
cursing, manhandled him down the stairs. It seemed to take
hours, and I was terrified that they would drop him, but in
the end we reached the hall, and they dumped their burden
down upon the dining table.

'Did he come with any effects – clothes, documents, the
like?' I asked Jacopo. He considered for a moment, bustled

away and came back a while later, bearing a dark bundle. Although the cloth was filthy, I recognized the black damask of the robe he had worn the day he left Constantinople.

'And the rest?' I snapped. Jacopo, clearly expecting to be praised, cringed a little and shook his head.

'Nothing, Signor,' he said. 'He came ashore in these clothes ...'

I did not believe him, but the men-at-arms had stopped panting like blown carthorses, and we must needs be gone from here. I snapped my fingers as I hoped Facio might do, and the Captain was heaved up on to four shoulders and carried, wreathed in muttered curses, out of the hall and out of the Castle of Stampalia. Down through the narrow, winding alleys of the village, down through the olive trees, past the fishermen, who averted their eyes this time. The stretcher was edged on to the jolly-boat, and I began to help Letice aboard.

'Signora Letitia, where are you going?' Jacopo whined. He was dancing from foot to foot, as if in dire need of a piss.

'To give Signor Petrus his instructions, and to pay the ship's master,' she snapped. 'I have dealt with too many fools already today,' she added dangerously, 'to imagine that Messer Nicholas' instructions will be carried out merely because I wish them to be. I will send Petrus on his way and then come back to deal with things here. You will await me at the castle.' And with that she snapped her fingers at the oarsmen, and I pushed the little boat off the shingle and vaulted over the gunwale as the oars bit and we began to surge seawards. Jacopo watched us, still doing his dance of indecision, while the soldiers turned and began to trudge up the beach. Letice and I steadied the Captain, and as the swell took the boat and the oars began to kick up spray, he turned his head to me and opened his eye. We regarded each other for a while, silently, and then he took a great lungful of the cold, brine-sharpened air. The corners of his mouth turned up, perhaps, a fraction, and he laid his hand upon mine. I looked at Letice. She was watching the Captain, her white face tight with a bitter sympathy.

'Will you pray for him?' I asked. 'I cannot, and he would not wish me to. But if you will …'

'I will,' she said, and closed her eyes.

Chapter Twenty-Seven

There was a little space below decks, away from where the men slept and not too near the bilges, a nook surrounded by barrels and coils of rope, and there we made a bed for the Captain. There he lay for a long day and night, attended by Michael Scot and by the Dominicans who, after they had overcome their distress at his terrible state, became quite transported with joy. They knelt at his side, deep in prayer, while I watched from the shadows. I hoped the Captain would not wake and find them there, for the sight of two black-swathed agents of the Inquisition hunched over him like ravens might well finish what Nicholas Querini had begun. Michael had found tincture of poppy in the barber's physic chest, and he did not wake, even when we cleaned his wounds with sea-water – a measure Michael insisted upon, for the salve which the barber wished to use smelled like a mouse drowned and rotted in piss-thinned pine tar – and wrapped them in clean linen. He had been scourged, I guessed; beaten and kicked, and hung up by his wrists, for there were rope burns there and his elbows were swollen.

'I fear for him,' said Michael simply, after the Captain's wounds had been bandaged to his satisfaction. 'He is not young.'

I had never thought of that before. But Captain de Montalhac must be close to his fiftieth year, I supposed. He was not old, I told myself, but no, perhaps not young after all. I kept my vigil beyond the edge of the lantern light, wrapped tightly in my own thoughts, for a day and a night, and into the next day. At some point, Letice came to huddle with me, and tried to comfort me with soft words, but I could not be companionable, and so she left again. The Captain had started a fever, and Michael had rifled the barber's chest while the poor fellow looked on in horror, measuring out powders and essences, and dosing his patient first with one mixture, then another; and then, when nothing seemed to take effect, he joined the brothers in prayer. When I saw that Michael Scot himself had resigned himself to the Captain's death, and that my master was going to die in an airless hold amongst cargo and bilgewater, I called Michael aside and asked that the Captain be taken up on deck, for I knew that he would wish to die under the sky, in the salt air, and not in this hole. I thought he would protest, but instead he agreed, and the four of us, with the help of some crewmen, carried the limp body up into the sunlight. I laid a pallet for him near the prow, where he would not be tripped over by the sailors, and when he was settled I wiped the sweat from his forehead and waved the brothers away, for I wished him to be free of their pious mummery, at least until he was beyond its reach.

The wind was blowing away the stink of sickness and fouled wounds, and in the sunlight I noticed that the bruising on the Captain's face was fading a little. I bent down and whispered in his ear.

'Breathe, dear Master, breathe in the air. The gulls are wheeling, the sea is running, and we are sailing west. Breathe.'

I called for wine and, dipping my finger in it, wet his lips. The sun crept around and fell upon him, warming the black cloak with which I had draped his body. I hardly took my eyes from him, for I was expecting at any moment to see his chest cease its shallow heaving. But instead of failing, his breath began to steady and his chest to rise more strongly, until I could hear the air passing between his lips. Not daring to hope myself, I beckoned Michael over, and he bent down and searched the Captain's face.

'The fever has broken,' he said. 'That is very good. Keep watch, and give him wine if he will take it.'

I raised his head and trickled a thread of wine between his teeth, but too much, for he spluttered and gagged. And then he opened his eyes.

'Petroc,' he murmured. 'Do not say a word to ...'

'You are safe, Master,' I told him, tears welling up in my eyes. 'You are on a ship bound for Italy. We found you on Stampalia.'

'The Venetian ...'

'I know. I worked it out, too late of course. Do not worry: I have the letter, and ... and some other things.'

'Things?' said the Captain, and he tilted his head ever so slightly. I held the cup to his lips, and after he had drunk – a proper draught this time – he gave me a weak smile. 'Things, do you say?'

'I do say. Now sleep, sir, for you must be well soon. I cannot be expected to treat with kings and emperors by myself, can I?'

He smiled again and laid his head down, and watched the clouds for a while before drifting into a wholesome sleep. And I fell asleep too, like a dog, my head on his chest. When I awoke it was evening, and Letice was tucking a fur blanket around me.

'How is he?' I gasped, for I had been having dark dreams.

'He is well. He took some gruel, and now he sleeps,' she

told me, pushing me down firmly. 'Between you and Master Scotus you have cured him, I think.'

'He cured himself,' I said, closing my eyes in relief. I felt her lie down beside me. She stretched out, close enough that our bodies did not touch, but I could feel her there.

'Well, Master Dog, you are a physician as well,' she said softly.

'As well as what?'

'Oh: thief, murderer, priest – I mean *monk* – papal envoy ...'

'How do you know about that?' I demanded, sitting bolt upright. She did not move, but grinned up at me.

'I was laying you down, and your chest crinkled and crackled,' she said. 'Thought there was something amiss, but instead I found a letter with *a fucking great lead seal*.' She whispered the last words, and her smile widened, and grew even wider as I slapped my hand to my breast and felt the reassuring weight of the papal bull.

'Listen, Petroc,' she said, her smile fading. 'When your Captain wakes up – I mean properly – there will be a deal of explaining to do, and it seems quite likely that a certain girl from London might get slung over the rail; and I can't say as I'd blame anybody for doing it. But I'd rather make it to dry land alive. So suppose we explain things to each other first. I liked your Captain asleep, but awake?' She peered up at me, searchingly.

'What do you mean?' I said, looking down at her.

'I mean, you know half of what is happening, and half of why. I might know the rest. We can put it all together, and see if your master feels like being kind to his enemy's once, but now repentant, tart.'

'Go on,' I said.

'Well, Querini and the emperor. *You* go on.'

'Very well. My best guess is that Querini – he's a banker, is he not? – holds the empire's notes, and that was his way in: suck Constantinople dry, and give the husk to the Republic. They'd certainly make him Doge for that.'

'Oh, fuck. He's far more clever than that,' said Letice, shaking a finger. 'He helped the Regent mortgage himself away, but to other bankers – actually, to the Republic itself. He doesn't carry any of the risk.'

'But then, what of the Crown?' I asked. 'You mean, he's just doing the Republic a favour? He's simply a patriot?'

'Ha! It works! The scheme works!' she crowed. 'Querini the Selfless – the martyr, perhaps?'

'Very well, then,' I said, feeling mocked. 'Was that worth all those lives? My friend Horst? And Rollo, to say nothing of Fulk de Grez and the poor fellow in Spoleto – did they all die to advance Querini's selflessness?'

'Don't be a twat,' she told me, not unkindly. 'Constantinople – the whole of Greece. The trade routes, Petroc. The bloody trade routes. Querini will place the Republic's greedy fingers on the vein which pumps in all the silk, all the pepper, the ginger ...'

'Well, they'd make him Doge, all right,' I said, glumly. I lay down again, and sighed, gazing up at the mackerel sky, stained orange by the setting sun. 'The Regent's little debt is a pittance, isn't it? A pinch of salt to be thrown over the shoulder. Thirteen thousand livres – not much, is it, what is the commission on that, do you think? And how much is the damned Crown worth anyway?' I knew what I had done the instant the words left me, but I could not take them back. Screwing up my eyes, I cursed silently.

'To whom?' said Letice, turning to me. I felt her breath upon my ear.

'To ... to Querini it's plainly worth thirteen thousand livres,

424

and to the Regent, the same. Poor bloody Baldwin would probably be glad of five thousand – less. He is already robbing church roofs, so ... Louis will be disappointed, though.'

'Won't he just?' said Letice, thoughtfully.

I was suddenly attacked, and that is not too strong a word, by a memory. The Captain and I were sitting before Pope Gregory, and he was cackling like a punctured bellows as he handed us our wax-spattered bulls.

'I am certain that Our Lord will provide,' he had said. And then I thought of Baldwin in his mean lodgings in Rome, and the famished look that had tightened his young face when he spoke of his cousin, the King of France.

'Does Nicholas know about Louis?' I asked, wincing in anticipation.

'Of course. The Regent told him. We arrived after you, remember?'

'What, exactly, did he tell him?'

'That Louis was going to give Baldwin a present of gold in return for the Crown.'

'How much gold did the Regent mention, do you think?'

'I don't know. But thirteen thousand pounds of gold is an awful lot of money, don't you think?'

'Thirteen thousand?' I breathed.

'That is what Querini loaned the empire. I expect Nicholas will ask for that, and the same again for his pains. Twenty-six thousand pounds – *pounds!* – of French gold! Can you even imagine such a sum?' She sighed. 'That Brother Andrew seemed quite shocked when I told him.'

'You told Brother Andrew,' I said, as calmly as I could.

'Of course. I mean, he asked me. That was why he came all this way, wasn't it? 'Course he wanted to know. He didn't bat an eyelid, though. Made some pious little remark when I brought up the commission, but nothing else.'

'You were right, Letice,' I said after a long silence. 'That will help. I do not think anyone will pitch you overboard. You will like Captain de Montalhac. I think, as a matter of fact, he is going to like you.'

I felt the pressure of her shoulder against mine through the fur rug. I suddenly felt full of light and even, although I would not have dared name it, hope. Should I reach out and take her in my arms, I asked myself? I should, I certainly should. And, shutting my eyes to ponder upon how I should begin, I fell asleep.

Chapter Twenty-Eight

Winter sailing is harsh, even as a passenger, and although we had escaped until then, four days out of Stampalia the winds turned strong and icy. The Greek Emperor had his galleys out, preying on Frankish ships. Not until we had passed through the Cyclades did that danger pass, although we were running from the bitter north winds, and beating against them when we turned up into the Adriatic. It was passing miserable, for once again I could not join the crew, but needs must endure endless boredom. Letice might have been an entertaining companion, but she was ill most days, despite all her boasting, for, like James of Paris, she was afflicted by a dreadful seasickness. She kept to herself, wrapped in fur cloak and misery. I was not so callous that I did not understand how she felt, at least somewhat: she had come from nothing, and as far as she knew had returned there. She could not bring herself entirely to trust the Captain, no matter how much I tried to reassure her, and despite all his friendly advances. To her he must have been one more powerful man enmeshed in schemes that did not include her – or worse, that did.

She was often barely civil to me. When she was feeling less poorly we conducted ourselves as friendly acquaintances, and when she was suffering I gave her as wide a berth as I could. That was in a way not hard, because she had grown very cold and inward; but I could not forget how she had first stirred me, that morning in Rome, for as much as I distrusted her, the sight of her milk-white skin, and the soft pout of her upper lip made my mouth dry whenever I beheld her.

Letice Londeneyse did not need me, that was plain. No doubt she needed only herself. And there was the fact, as plain and dismal as a corpse laid out on a kitchen table, that she had had a hand in the death of a friend and of three other men, in the short time since I had first seen her. She had not held the knife that killed Horst, I could admit that much; but she had been in Foligno that night, as she had been in Spoleto. And I had seen with my own eyes how she had put an end to Dardi, I knew she was capable of it. And when I pondered this, I could only say that I had done such things as well: I had killed men who had had friends ... but such thoughts were profitless, and I had long since taught myself not to tread that path lest it lead to melancholy.

The Captain began to recover in earnest, although it was another week before Andrew of Longjumeau would let him rise. Andrew had taken over his care, for soon after we had passed Thira, Mesarites, who had hardly stirred from the cabin which he shared with the ship's master and with Doctor Scot, fell ill. At first Michael thought it was no more than the seasickness that had afflicted the others, but on the second day of his illness, when I went to offer my sympathies, I found the old man shockingly changed. He seemed to have lost pounds of weight, his eyes were sunken and his cheeks had fallen in. His gaze darted about, confused, and his lips were caught in a quivering moue. A silver trail of spittle crept across his silvery beard.

'What ails him?' I whispered to Michael, although I need not have, for the old Greek seemed not to hear anything.

'He has suffered an apoplexy,' he answered, bluntly. 'It happened in his sleep. I feared that all the disorder that has befallen him might do harm, and so it has.' He bowed his head, and for the first time Michael Scotus, so astute in divining the emotions of others, showed his own.

'Do not blame yourself, Doctor,' I told him. 'It was his great desire to make this journey. To achieve his great work – that is so, is it not?'

Michael nodded. 'It is so. But I came and plucked him from his family. He would have died, at least, in a Greek bed. As it is …'

'He will die, then.'

'Alas. All his higher functions have been destroyed by the apoplexy. He cannot eat or drink. The ancients called it a stroke of God's hand, but I think it is a crueller touch than that.'

'Amen,' I muttered, but I was remembering Anna's death throes. Why should God's touch not be cruel? I had seen nothing to the contrary.

I went and searched the old man's face, seeking in its all but abandoned furrows a trace of – what? The old Greece, the fallen empire that had been, whose spirit had run so hot in Anna's blood? I found nothing but the desolation of Constantinople as she had become, for the skull was plain to see under its veil of failing skin. I pressed Anna's ring to his lips, and kissed his forehead. That night, he died while Michael slept at his side.

The day after that, a foul storm swept off the Morea and tore our sail to shreds. We put in at Cerigo to bury Nicholas, and the man who had been Exarch of all Asia was laid in the crypt of the half-ruined Orthodox church, while an awe-struck country priest sung him to his rest. We lingered to make good the damage, and then another storm blew up and kept us in port for another week. We did not leave Cerigo until the middle of February, and then it was slow, miserable sailing against icy winds. We were forced to take shelter at Zante, and then the threat of a raiding party of John Vatatzes' ships sent the master running for Patra. And so it was not until the second week of March that we dared set out across the narrow waters of the Adriatic to Italy.

In the long weeks that intervened, Michael Scot had become withdrawn, and ever more wrapped up in his thoughts. He blamed himself for the death of his friend, I guessed, and mourned the old man who would never see his dream, of healing the great schism between Greek and Latin, fulfilled. And he had received some news at Cerigo from a ship's captain from Brindisi. What it was I did not ask, but it upset him greatly. James of Paris and Letice were rendered barely human by seasickness, as I have said, and Andrew of Longjumeau fell to nursing his friend. Only the Captain strengthened while the others declined, and soon, despite the misfortunes and setbacks that battered themselves against the *Seynt Victor*, he was up and about, weak but with the life slowly coming back into him, and he and I passed most of our time together.

He told me what had befallen him on leaving Constantinople.

'They set upon me,' he said, 'and beat me insensible. When I awoke I was bound, and soon I was passed over to Nicholas Querini's ship. Querini, whom I counted as a neighbour and an acquaintance in Venice, gloated over me, and tormented me with insinuations and threats until we came to his fortress.'

There he had been starved and tortured by a man who fitted the description of Facio. They had hung him by the wrist from the ceiling, and flogged him, and doused him with icy water.

'They wanted the letter,' he said. 'The pope's letter. I said I did not have it, for I did not. Bravery had nothing to do with it: I told them the truth. They left me there, for some other man was coming to put me to the question, someone they promised was far more terrible and merciless than they.'

'Dardi,' I told him. And I recounted what had taken place in the Pharos Chapel, how Letice had killed Dardi and how we had struggled to heave his fat carcass out of the window. The Captain took some grim amusement at that. I knew he was all but overcome with curiosity as to what I had brought out of the chapel, but we could not be open about that. My oilskin pack was locked in a chest in the master's private hold, and I had bought the only key from him. As we waited for night to fall and the others to go to sleep, I told him about the girl, and how I trusted her despite myself.

'She is hungry,' said the Captain. 'Someone or something will be consumed before she is whole again – take care it is not you.'

'She has had her chances,' I answered. 'I do not think it will be me.'

That night – it was the night before we came to Cerigo, and the seas were running high and fierce – we stole into the master's hold. The ship was pitching madly, but we were both used to such things, and when I had hung our lantern from the ceiling I took out the key, opened the chest I had bought, and pulled out my pack. The Captain watched, rapt and lupine, as I undid the ties and pulled out the contents one piece at a time. First, the broken spearhead.

'The Spear of Longinus,' I intoned, holding it out. 'There were two pieces, and Baldwin's list only mentioned a spear set in an icon – so I took this one.'

'You did well,' said the Captain softly, turning the lozenge of metal over in his hands.

'I thought I was going to have to fight with it,' I told him, reaching into the pack again. 'What would that have done, to shed blood with the holy Lance?'

The Captain shook his head and began to wrap the spearhead up again. 'We are in a realm that even I had never quite dared to imagine,' he said. 'As to their power – their metaphysical power, I mean – they have none. But as things, as gross matter, they can change the world. What is next?'

Next were the Sandals, which the Captain examined with an amused look upon his scabbed and bruised face. 'Dear oh dear,' he muttered. 'Could they not have done better than this?' But he nodded when I produced the authenticating papers. 'They are official, then: marvellous. We shall copy these, of course, and then go into the cobbler's trade. Do you think Gilles would care to turn sandal-maker?'

I laughed, for it was a merry thought, and we had need of such. 'Now this,' I said, 'requires a deal of care.' I opened the flat golden case that held the Robe of the Virgin. 'The *Maphorion* of the *Theotokos*,' I said. The Captain held out his hands, and I placed the case on them and opened it. He bent his head towards the faded cloth.

'This accords with all that I have read,' he whispered, carefully examining the folds. 'It is … I feel strange saying this, but did you know, Patch, that this is the talisman of Constantinople? The Virgin's veil protected the city. Emperors carried it as a standard into battle. What will happen to the city now that it is gone?'

I could not quite tell if he were serious, so I said, with care, 'The city's talismans have failed her, sir. But you do not mean that I should have left it be?'

'No, no,' he said. 'Nevertheless it is strange that you and I are here in this reeking ship's hold with the very thing that once girded the Empire of Rome itself with … with magic.'

'I hesitate to show you what is left,' I said, 'if we are going

432

to talk of magic. For there is something that I do not understand. Perhaps we should wait.'

'I am sorry, Patch,' said the Captain. 'I am not quite myself
yet. You know that I have no belief in magic, nor in miracles.
No, it is their power over the minds and hearts of men that
I find strange and terrible, and this thing . . .' he handed back
the robe, 'has kept an empire in its thrall. Now, what is it you
have to show me?'

I said nothing, but took out the plain wooden box and set
it on top of the chest. Opening it, I held my breath, reached
in, and took hold of the uppermost two corners of the cloth
that lay folded within. As I lifted, the watery, shimmering
face I had beheld in the Pharos Chapel slowly rose into view
from the shadows of the box. The Captain gasped.

'I think this is the *Mandylion* of Edessa,' I said, and my
words fell flat and lifeless about me. The Captain had bent
forward and was gazing at the cloth, mouth open. For an
instant I thought that he too had been stroked by the hand
of God, but then he tore his gaze away.

'How did you find this?' he hissed. I told him. And as
there did not seem any point in avoiding it, I also told him
of Mesarites, and his great and marvellous scheme to heal the
wounds of Christendom.

'Stand up,' said the Captain, suddenly. I was surprised, and
made to lower the cloth back into its box, but the Captain
stopped me. 'No, keep hold of it. Raise it up.' Obediently I
stood, and drew the cloth up with me until it hung before
me, the face – if face it was – level with my own. But no, it
was not the face. I was looking at the imprint or the stain
of hair, and only then did I understand that the cloth I held
was folded over, and I held the fold between my fingers. I
was looking at the terribly faint image of a man's back. It
was translucent, the cloth, and even in the dim lantern-glow

I could see the Captain behind it, examining every inch.

'What is it? What do you see?' I demanded, when I could bear it no longer. The dark suggestion of eyes in the face was beginning to oppress me.

'You are right,' said the Captain at last. 'This is the *Mandylion*. I wish I could have talked with Mesarites, for we might have understood each other despite ...' He did not finish, and did not need to. The heretic and the schismatic contemplating a thing I could find no name for: what strange discourse would have been born from such a meeting?

'What is it?' I asked again. 'It is not a painting,' I offered, 'but is it woven into the cloth? It frightened me when I found it, and I did not want to take it.'

'But you did,' said the Captain, 'and perhaps you will never do so great a thing again. Here,' he added, and took hold of the cloth himself. 'Let me hold it for you.'

I went round into the light and stood where the Captain had been, facing the cloth. I licked my dry lips and forced myself to stare. It was a piece of yellowed flax that I beheld, about a yard's width, and upon it was painted – I had to say painted, for I could find no other explanation that I could give words to – the image of a naked man with hair that curled to his shoulders and a full beard, his hands crossed modestly over his shame. There were dark stains on the cloth, darker than the image itself, around the head, in the side and upon the left wrist. I instinctively looked down, but the feet were still folded.

'De Clari was right,' muttered the Captain. 'And Mesarites – of course, Mesarites. If only he ... no matter. "The Shroud in which Our Lord had been wrapped, which every Friday raised itself upright so one could see the figure of Our Lord on it" – that is what de Clari wrote of what he found in 1204.'

434

'This must be it,' I stammered. 'Does that mean ...'

'That it is real? How can it be? But I cannot tell how it was done. It is not paint.'

'Is it branded in some way?' I said, squinting reluctantly at the blank-eyed face. 'It is horrible,' I confessed with a shiver of revulsion. As if I had given him some signal, the Captain lowered the cloth carefully into its box and hastily shut the lid.

'The image of a tortured man,' he said, when we were both sitting on some handy bales of silk. I was shocked to find that he was wide-eyed and smiling. It was an expression I knew, but had never thought to find upon that face: the ecstasy of faith. 'What a symbol of love that is, eh? I hate it too,' he burst out. 'My people revile the cross and the Crucifixion, for—'

'But to you, Christ was a spirit,' I put in. 'He had no form, so how could He be crucified?'

'Indeed! He could not be, but it has long been our belief that the Crucifixion was a dreadful mummery concocted by the Dark One to shame Christ, to humiliate him, by spreading the lie that He had suffered death. No matter that He was resurrected, for what has never had life, not as we imperfect ones know it, cannot be reborn, can it?'

'I suppose not,' I muttered. Then I understood. 'And because this seems to be real ...' I could not believe I was saying this, but I pressed on. 'Because this is, somehow, the burial cloth of an actual man, you think that your belief is proven? But – forgive me, but I was once a Church scholar, if a dreadfully indolent one – it also seems to prove the presence of the miraculous.'

'There are no miracles,' said the Captain. 'No – there may be, but they are illusion, tricks of the Devil made to snare us and lure us from the pure way. If this is proof of a miracle, then ...' To my horror, he buried his face in his hands and gave an awful, sobbing laugh. I hugged him around the shoulders.

'You are tired,' I soothed. 'I should not have shown you these things yet.'

He took a deep breath, and when he turned to me he was himself again.

'Forgive me, Patch,' he said. 'I have lived for so long with my people's agony. The reason I was overcome is not hard to explain. The Good Christians have brother sects in the East, even in Constantinople, where they are called other things – Manichees, Bogomils – and when I was a child, the *perfecti* in my country heard, from merchants coming from Greece and the land of the Serbs, of an image of Christ crucified with three nails, thus proving that the cross venerated by the Church was false. The Good Christians used this image to taunt their enemies, and even made images of their own, with which they mocked the priests of Rome. I wondered if the stories had their origin in something they had seen in Constantinople, and when I read Robert de Clari ... Now you see. Here it is, in the flesh, as it were. And that is the point. This thing, miracle or not, is the imprint of flesh. We cannot deny it, can we?' He took a deep breath and swallowed as if his own Adam's apple were choking him. 'And if this is the image of the crucified Christ ...' He sat back and reached his unsteady hand towards the wavering light of the lantern.

'So this is your proof,' I said after a long silence. 'What will you do?'

'What can I do? Doctor Scot will carry out his friend's wishes, and give it to Frederick Hohenstaufen, who in turn will give it to the pope – is that not the plan? I cannot let that happen, but what is my choice? We cannot – *I* cannot do away with the doctor, for that would be a foul sin indeed, to pay such a friend out for his good deeds. I do not know. I will think.' He rose, and clapped me upon the back. 'And now I will go to bed. Master Petroc, you have done well. You are the equal of any man I know, and the better of most. Thank you for saving my life, and ...' he looked towards my pack where it lay upon the chest, fat with secrets, gleaming black and smug.

.'I fear I have brought a deal more trouble into the world,' I muttered, but locked away our dreadful treasures and helped the Captain to his bed. But I did not sleep well that night, nor for many nights to come.

PART SIX

Venice

Chapter Twenty-Nine

We sighted the long coast of Italy on a clear morning in early spring, after a short, squall-fretted night crossing from Corfu. The *Seynt Victor* made landfall near Otranto and turned her prow north. The weather improved, and the sea settled down, and one by one the recluses emerged from their places of torment, and turned their white faces towards the sun. Only Doctor Scot stayed in the cabin, writing endlessly in a great black ledger. He had become a quite different man since Mesarites had died, and I, who had always been in awe, and indeed a little terrified of him, left him well alone. He was looking and acting more like a necromancer every day, and I did not wish to tempt the Fates.

It was time to make plans. The Captain wished to travel straight to Venice and face Querini, but much as I hated to admit this even to myself, he was still far from recovered. He was dreadfully thin, for the victuals aboard a ship are barely enough to keep starvation at bay at the best of times. If he had been active for too long he would begin to tremble in his hands, and his eyelids would droop and twitch. He looked older, too: his beard had gone almost white, and the streaks of grey in his hair had widened. So I argued against that, saying we should wait, perhaps in Rome, and take the good Dominicans with us to see the pope. Andrew and James, though, to my surprise, were all for haste. They had been sent on a mission by their beloved king, and felt it was within their means to fulfil it without more time being wasted. To this end they argued good-naturedly and then not so happily with the Captain for a day or so, until I could bear it no longer. I called them to the prow, and, as we sailed past the cloud-capped peak of Monte Gargano, told them that I would go to Venice alone.

'Listen to me,' I told their sceptical faces. 'Querini thinks me dead, and no one else in Venice knows me. I will find Baldwin, for he must be a guest of the ... the ...'

'Doge,' said Letice. Uninvited, she had appeared at the Captain's shoulder. We all turned to stare at her.

'The Doge. I will come with you, Petroc. I know Venice – you, plainly, do not. And I am afraid to say that Baldwin is more likely a guest of Nicholas Querini, who is not the Doge, at least not yet.'

'But you are Querini's companion,' said the Captain. I admired his tact. 'I am not certain that we should take your advice, if you will forgive me.'

'I will forgive you: you are right to look at me askance. I will not spare your blushes. I am a woman cast aside, plotted against and almost deprived of her life. You should know that I want my revenge of him. I will hazard that your plans involve redeeming the Crown from Nicholas. I think that might be difficult, unless he has done the honourable thing and turned it over to the Republic. If he is a good son of Venice, he will have. But as he is a scheming, plotting creature whose only loyalty is to Nicholas Querini, I believe he will not. Now, he is how many days ahead of us?'

'Not many,' said Andrew. 'A week, perhaps?'

'Then we must act fast. Petroc will seek an audience with Doge Tiepolo, and show him his papal credentials. Good brothers, can you provide him with letters of your own, to make him a representative of King Louis?'

The brothers grudgingly said they would consider it. Andrew shook his head angrily. 'If only we could steal the Crown back from the thief!' he cried. The Captain and I exchanged weighty glances.

'And then what?' asked the Captain. 'I mean, should such a thing be possible.' Now it was the turn of Letice to raise her eyebrows, but Andrew spoke first.

'Querini is a proven thief. I am sure that the legal position is clear: the Constantinopolitan Regent's debt is transferred to the Republic, and our king shall redeem the Crown by making his gift to Venice. Indeed, payment of the debt shall be a perfect solution, for it sidesteps the issue of simony.'

'But someone still has to steal the Crown,' James pointed out.

'Hmm. I wonder if I could have a word, in private, with these two young people,' said the Captain.

Much later that night, huddled in the master's hold once again, Letice, the Captain and I went over the plans we had made. The girl and I were to make our way to Venice in secret, and go straight to the Ca' Kanzir, which was the palazzo where the Captain and the company of the *Cormaran* lived when he was in the city, and was the closest thing to a home that he possessed in the whole world.

'I do not have the keys,' said the Captain, crossly. 'I managed to throw them overboard, with my purse, before I was overpowered. With any luck, Querini will not have ransacked the place. You will have to make a set of picks, my lad. Do you know how?' I shook my head. 'I will show you,' he said, and drew an admiring look from Letice.

Andrew of Longjumeau, hoping against the odds that matters could be handled in an official manner, and giving me the strictest instructions not to implicate Louis Capet in any skulduggery, had written me an official letter, and sealed it with the royal seal. That should be enough to get me an audience with the Venetian Council. The Captain advised me against using the pope's letter except in the direst need.

'I really do not want you even to take it, Patch,' he said. 'It is worth more to us than you can even imagine – no, I am sure you can imagine, in fact. I beg you, guard it with your life. But – ' and he held up a hand and placed it gently upon my head – 'your life is worth more. Probably. Now, Mistress Londeneyse.' He turned to Letice. 'What are your intentions towards Nicholas Querini?'

'I wish him dead, of course,' she said bluntly. 'But I'm not a fool. I would rather that he were humiliated, in truth, that his spirit were staved in. He would die inside, that way. It would eat him like a canker.'

'And how would that be achieved?' asked the Captain.

'If he were made to look foolish, if he lost face. If he were ruined – but that will not happen. He is almost the richest man in Venice.'

'I like Venice,' said the Captain. 'It is a useful place for us. I would not have it made dangerous for my company.'

'I understand,' said Letice.

'Do you?' She nodded, gravely. 'What do you want, young woman?' asked the Captain, softly.

'I want respect. I want to be the equal of men,' she said, vehemently. 'I do not want to end my days in the purgatory of whoredom, and I do not wish to pull the strings for idiot puppet-men, just because the world regards a quim as … as disqualifying its owner from receiving all that her brains and courage can earn her!'

'Well said,' the Captain said, and although Letice was shaking with fury, she gave him a curt nod. 'Brains and cour- age are all that I and my company require. Patch has vouched

444

for you: that is almost enough for me. Almost. You know much about my affairs. You have, in fact, some power over me. Do not abuse it. Do not: for I would welcome you when this affair is settled. Do you understand?'

Letice stiffened, and nodded. 'Thank you,' she said.

We put into Ravenna on the fifteenth of March, 1239, for it was decided that it was a safe port and far enough from Venice, but not too far. An inn was found, and the two Dominicans, Michael Scot and the Captain bid farewell to the master of the *Seynt Victor*. I went with them. The friars were in raptures to be on dry land again, although I had noticed that Andrew of Longjumeau was far from the pious milksop that at times he pretended to be. Even Michael Scot was almost happy, and glided greyly along, looking something like his own self.

The four men found beds, and while baggage was being carried up and prices agreed upon, we adjourned to the dining room and called for wine. We all, friars included, took a cup, and while we were drinking and reminiscing, although the voyage had only just ended, there was a thunder of hooves outside and much shouting, then a growing clamour of voices, as if a crowd were gathering. The innkeeper went outside to see what had happened, and came back a few minutes later, looking worried. We all asked him what could be the matter.

'His Holiness has excommunicated the Emperor Frederick,' he told us, and poured out more wine. 'It happened three days ago, so it seems. That fellow outside just arrived from Rome. The war will not stop, then.'

'War?' said the Captain, curiously. 'There has been fighting in the north for a year now. Is it still going on?'

'Frederick declared that he would take the papal states for the empire,' said Michael Scot, hollowly. 'I found out at Cerigo. Now this. I expected it, I suppose, for what else could Gregory do? Surrender the Patrimony of Saint Peter? But … so it begins.' He rubbed his temples, and stood up.

'Leave my things,' he told the innkeeper. 'I must depart right away.' And he bade farewell to us, although we could do no more than nod and murmur in return, so surprised were we. But when he went to the door he beckoned to me, and as the innkeeper found him a horse, he looked up at the sky, which was lowering.

'I will be riding into snow,' he said.

'Where are you going?' I asked him.

'My good Petroc,' he replied, 'my plans are at an end. The two great giants of the world are lumbering towards one another, and nothing will stop them. They will tear Christendom apart with their greed and their pride. I am glad, now, that Nicholas did not live to see this.'

'Shall I bring you the *Mandylion*?' I whispered, dreading his reply, but he only shook his head.

'What good would it do?' he said. 'The world is slipping into chaos. The Beast's jaws are widening. Keep it for me. Your friends are, after all, the experts in such things. If I think I can use it to do some good, I will find it in good hands.'

The horse was being led out, and Michael picked up his bag.

'Doctor Scotus,' I said, as he slung it over the saddle and set his foot in the stirrup, 'thank you.'

'For what?' he asked, looking down at me. I felt again that strange sensation, as if the air were shimmering before his face.

'For Anna – for healing Anna.'

'Gladly done,' he whispered.

'Where will you go?' I asked again. He settled himself in the saddle and threw his hood over his head.

'I shall ride towards the mountains,' he said. 'Sooner or later I shall come to a crossroads. Frederick is in the north, Gregory the south. I will choose, somehow, as I have always chosen. Or maybe I shall not. Goodbye, Patch. Perhaps we will see each other again.'

'I hope so, good Doctor,' I said.

The next day the *Seynt Victor* sailed north again. We put into Chioggia late in the afternoon, and I was glad of it, for the wind was blowing cold off the Po marshes and there was a wearisome smell of rotting weeds in the air, lowering to the spirits. Chioggia itself was a small city, squatting cheerfully upon the great sandbank that lay between the sea and the lagoon on which Venice lay, further to the north-east. There was a bristle of belltowers and a stubble of masts, and into this we nosed. The Captain had given us a name, of a silk merchant, whose cousin had a brother, a trustworthy fellow, a discreet man, who owned a fishing boat. And so it was arranged.

We passed through the Lagoon lying on the cold, brackish deck, hidden beneath a mound of old sacking that stank of fermenting fish. The cousin and his mate had made us hide as soon as the lights of Chioggia had faded. I squeezed myself tight against the side of the boat and stretched out, trying to see stars between the tight mesh of the sack-cloth. There was no sound except the rush and knock of the water beneath us, and the creaking of the sail. Letice wriggled herself tight against me, and her fingers wrapped themselves around mine. I did not say anything, for I was too cold and too nervous – about Venice, and now, truth be told, about her warm hand. Sometimes one of the fishermen muttered something or hissed a curse, and now and then, from very far away came the hollow plea of a night-bird. It was not an unpleasant way to pass the time, despite the nose-searing fish stench, and indeed I fell asleep, only realising I had done so when Letice prodded me awake. I opened my eyes to see the blaze of the Milky Way above me. The snow-clouds had blown away. I took a chestful of sharp, rush-scented air and sat up.

I was blinking the sleep from my eyes when I felt her hand, cold and strong, slide up my spine until it lay, fingers trembling slightly, against the back of my neck. My hair rose to meet it, and as I leaned, eyes closed, to meet her lips with mine, I knew that I was stepping from the known world into the blank lands at the edge of a map: here be monsters. Her lips had been cool against mine, and I had almost drawn back, sensing that she was about to do the same, when her mouth opened slightly and I brushed against her teeth. We both shuddered, and for a long moment it was all heat and bruising, crushing, growling. I tasted blood and sweet spit, smelled her powdery-sharp sweat. Then, as if we were puppets and our mountebank had snapped his fingers, we jerked apart. But her eyes held mine for another desperate moment, and then she raised her pale hand and pointed. At first I could see nothing save the velvet shimmer of stars upon smooth water, and deepest shadow all around. Then, following her outstretched arm, I saw that the first inkling of dawn was lightening the east, turning the night from black to the blue of a magpie's wing. And there, faint, no more than the play of blue upon blue, the domes and spires of a city rose out of the starry brocade of the water.

Chapter Thirty

I saw nothing more of Venice until the boatman prodded me with his foot and I peered out from beneath the nets and the burlap to behold a wall of cut stone, crusted with wet moss and alive with little grey crabs, and a thick pole striped with ancient yellow and black paint. Letice poked her head out beside me and took a shuddering breath. Her hair was plastered against her skull and her nose was running.

'Go!' hissed the boatman. I dumped my bag on the top of the quay and clambered up, pulling Letice after me as soon as my feet were set. The boatman, without a backwards glance, began to heave at his oar, and in less than a minute we were alone. But where were we? I looked about us. The canal upon which we had arrived was no more than a tiny channel trapped between towering walls of brick, into which, here and there, had been let a marble-framed window. To our left the canal ended unceremoniously in another wall, and to our right was a narrow oblong of daylight through which we could glimpse blue sky, white buildings and boats passing on choppy water. That, then, must be the Grand Canal. In front of us were more striped poles, a little thicket of them, leaning this way and that. Sparrows hopped around their bulbous finials, and tiny silver fish flicked through them as they sank out of sight in the hazy canal. I kicked at some loose mortar between two mossy steps and looked up, to find that above us an ancient palace squatted, its stones streaked with grime and blotched with lichen like the hands of an old man. The steps led up to a row of plain columns that supported light, simple arches. Behind these I glimpsed two heavily barred windows and a large doorway. Above the arches another row of arched windows were set into the face of the building, interspersed and surmounted by stone plaques that seemed to show long-legged birds and stars. Above that, a plainer storey rose up, pierced here and there with more windows, these ones pointed.

I climbed the steps and walked cautiously between the columns and into the damp, mossy shadow of the arches. Stepping up to the doorway, I laid my finger upon the bronze knocker, a toothy fish pop-eyed in amazement at the taste of its own tail. I heard Letice climb the stairs behind me.

'You remembered the key, didn't you?' she asked, casting a somewhat querulous look up at the looming palace. Glancing about, I made sure that we were not observed, but the windows that faced us were bricked or boarded up, and it seemed likely that the little canal had been left to itself for quite some time. I pulled out the set of burglar's tools I had made aboard the *Seynt Victor* and addressed the lock. After an uncomfortable few minutes of scraping and cursing the hasps surrendered, the hinges rasped and groaned, and we stepped inside the Ca' Kanzir.

The Ca' Kanzir was not the true name of the palace on the Rio Morto. To the Venetians – those who even remembered its existence – it was the Palazzo Centranico. It was one of the oldest buildings in the city, and had survived floods and fire, for it had been built from stone at a time when most of its fellows were of wood, two hundred or more years ago. It had once housed a Doge, and the Captain had bought the place from the last member of that noble family. Over the years he had transformed it, inside if not out, into his one earthbound refuge. All this I had learned as we made our way up the eastern shores of Italy, and as the Captain found his voice and began slowly to mend. So, as I sat with pliers and files and a collection of ships' nails, making lockpicks for myself, he had created the Ca' Kanzir in the air between us, each word brought forth carefully and with love. He had guided me through its halls and up its stairways, explaining, in loving detail, how the Venetians built their houses, until I marvelled that a man who had always seemed as rootless as one of the Athingani could be so wedded to a pile of ancient stone and brick.

Beyond the door stretched a wide, damp hallway, sequestered in mouldy gloom. I knew it would be there, for the Captain had drawn it for me in words. The walls were of wooden panelling, simply painted, with many doors leading off on either side. It was very dark, but I could make out huge, ungainly chairs and benches standing between the doors. The floor over which our shoes clicked was a simple chequerboard of white and red marble flagstones. At the far end was another door, which was not locked. We stepped through it and back into sunlight, into a small courtyard with high walls on all sides. In the centre stood a marble wellhead carved with spiky leaves and birds. Big pots of red clay lined the walls, and from them grew trees, some of which I recognised – there were lemons and oranges rotting upon the branches, and lying in green and mouldy heaps upon the ground, a fig and a small olive tree – and some I did not, strange plants with thick, hairy trunks and glossy leaves like huge ferns. Everything was dry and neglected and near death. Vines festooned the outer walls, and a tall rose-briar was scrambling up towards the sky. Odd carvings in many kinds of stone were set into the brickwork, seemingly at random, so that faces of birds and beasts, shields with noble devices, and swirling knots of carved greenery peered from among the leaves. A stone staircase with an ornate, though worn, rail of marble led up the side of the palace. It should have been beautiful here, for the Captain had described it as his refuge, his Eden. But old cobwebs cloaked the leaves and branches in grey and refuse-mottled tents and all was silent save for the rustle of a wren somewhere. It suddenly began to screech and scold us with its tiny voice. I shivered, and beckoned to Letice, who was peering down the well.

'No one there,' she said with a grin, but I knew she had not been jesting. Silently we climbed the stair and stepped into another long hallway paved with smooth, worn brick and lined with long benches strewn with plump silk cushions, silvery with dust. At the end was a long gallery that formed another loggia with the windows I had seen from the canal. There were tapestries on the walls, and old shields and lances. Strangely, the windows at both ends of the hallway held no glass, and an icy draught was flowing down towards us. As below, the hallway was lined with doors, and I opened one at random. Beyond it lay a large, white-walled room hung with far richer tapestries and strange, barbarous-looking weavings. Candles stood ready in tall, gilt candle-holders. There were wide, high-backed chairs brightly painted and stacked with pillows. A round table stood empty. Dust lay everywhere, criss-crossed with the roadways of mice and spiders.

'No one has been here,' I said. No one had come to this house since Gilles had left, two or more months ago. That meant that Querini had not yet thought to search the place – or perhaps, hope against hope, he had not even arrived in the city, and we had overtaken him somewhere upon the ocean. But that thought, tempting though it was, could not be clung to.

'We might stay here, but it is not safe,' I whispered, so that the dust could not collect upon the words. 'Querini will come here sooner or later. It is less safe than if he had already ransacked it. Where shall we go, then?'

She said nothing. I turned to find her gazing into an enormous mirror. I had seen such things before, but they had been little discs of burnished silver that gave one a reflection little better than could be had from a puddle of water. This one was almost as big as my head, and I could see that it was curved like the face of a soap-bubble. Curious, I went to her side. In the mirror the room was duplicated as if through a window. Another Letice stood there, fey and dishevelled, looking out at me with mocking eyes. And next to her another man stood uncertainly. He was sunburnt and his thick brown hair was in need of trimming, and had not seen a comb for many a windblown day. There was a rutted track of newly healed scars across his face, pink and livid, and his clothes were rough and salt-stained. His nose was somewhat askew, and his eyes were at once suspicious and resigned. The only thing bright and lively about him was the sheathed knife at his belt with its hilt of green stone set with rubies. I swore under my breath and stepped back hurriedly. Letice's eyes watched me from the mirror. Then she shook her head, and for a moment the glass was a blur of whirling golden threads. Then it was empty save for the empty room.

'We can go somewhere very near,' she said at last, after a long silence.

I took the trouble of locking the doors behind us, scraping away with my crude tools while Letice kept watch. We had left through the street door, and had found ourselves in a little square. There were unfinished brick walls on three sides, their windows boarded up with weathered planks. The Ca' Kanzir formed the fourth side. A low marble well-head stood in the middle, its carvings softened by years of rain. Ahead of us a low tunnel led under the sagging, abandoned building. The Calle Morto, the Captain had called it: the Alley of the Dead. Inside the tunnel, the stench of cat was almost solid in the air. White stalactites dripped like livid toadstools from the roof. It was narrow enough that I could easily touch both sides as I walked, and shadows lurked here as thick as soot, or ashes. Letice seemed as oppressed by the tunnel as I was, and hurried along, pausing only when she reached the end and looked out into a wider alley.

'I thought so!' she hissed triumphantly. 'The Calle dei Morti. We are only just around the corner.'

'From what?' I whispered back.

'You will see,' she crowed, stepping out into the street. There were a few people about, but no one gave us a second look, and I followed Letice, who turned left and began to bustle along. We passed over a little bridge and into the square beyond.

It was a small square and one side of it was a church. But the other three sides were all high walls of brick with many pointed windows. And in those windows, in each one, stood a woman, sometimes two or more; women with painted faces, with curled hair of every unnatural hue and – I stopped dead in my tracks as I took this in – all of them with clothing pulled up or down, or no clothing at all, shaking their breasts, offering them, caressing their bellies, even flicking aside their tunics to give a glimpse of bush. And down below, men, scores of them, some furtive, some strutting with stirred-up lust. Every one of them had his head thrown back and his mouth hanging slack, gawping up at the tarts ...

'Oi, fishface,' Letice said loudly in my ear. 'You can do that later.' She grabbed my hand and led me through the throng, my nose wrinkling at the acrid, hog-house scent of rutting men, trying not to look up at the festoons of juddering pink flesh above me. And then I saw: Letice was leading me into one of the houses. I tried to protest, but too late, for she had rapped out some signal upon the door, and in another instant we were inside, and a grave man with a monkish face and a humped back was closing the door behind us.

This was not my first time in a brothel, I must confess, but if I had intended to make some pretence of virtue I need not have bothered, for no one was paying the slightest attention to me. Instead, a gang of women had leaped up, leaving assorted men behind them in various stages of arousal and indignation, and had surrounded Letice like bees about their queen. They poked and stroked her, laughing, scolding and gabbing, and her voice rose above them in happy protest, until an older woman, her grey hair gathered under a sort of starched wimple and dressed in a sombre robe of shimmering, lead-hued silk, emerged from the shadows and began to belabour the tarts none too gently with a silver-tipped staff. They squealed and did not seem to mind, but when the blows continued to fall they trotted back, chattering and swearing cheerfully at each other, to their impatient customers.

'Magpie!' said the madam, for so she must be. She did not smile, but held her arms out stiffly from her sides. Letice embraced her around the neck and hung there, as if embracing a crucifix. The woman patted her upon the head and pushed her away gently with the head of her staff.

'My little London Magpie,' said the woman. 'Or rather, Signorina Querini, eh? What are you doing here, Letice?' There was affection in her voice, but a palpable edge as well. Letice bowed her head.

'Messer Nicholas has let me go,' she said. 'He gave me away to Dardi Boldù.' Something appeared for a moment in the madam's face, but vanished as quickly as it had come.

It was a lean visage, planed and chiselled and sanded, lips thinned by time but still full, eyelids thin and sagging but beneath them, eyes of startling green. She had probably never been beautiful, but no doubt she had always terrified and bewitched.

'Oh, dear,' she said, emotionlessly. 'But you have found yourself a new benefactor, I see. My, he looks important. Welcome to Il Bisato Beccato, Signor.' She gave me a flat, scouring look. I thought of bowing, and thought again.

'No, Mother, this is Petroc. He is a friend. We are ...'

'Not fucking,' finished the woman bluntly. 'That is plain. Why are you here, little one?'

'We need a ... a bed,' said Letice. It was the first time I had seen her ruffled. 'Not for that! I mean, we need a place to stay, not for long, just a few days.'

'And why should I let you stay here, in trouble as you plainly are?' said the woman. Nothing showed in her face. Letice nodded to me, and I pulled out my purse.

'We will pay what we would at the finest hostelry in Venice,' I said, fumbling out a gold piece. At the sight of the coin one of the woman's eyebrows lifted fractionally. She tapped Letice upon a breast with her cane and treated us both to a frosty smile.

'Well, my dears, sentiment is my weakness,' she said, her voice showing not a glimmer of any weakness whatsoever. 'You may stay five days. Any longer and I shall put you to work – both of you.' I felt the tip of the cane brush my crotch and cleared my throat noisily. 'You may have your old quarters, Magpie. The girl who was using them died last week.'

'Thank you, Mother Zaneta,' said Letice fervently, dropping a deep curtsey. Now I did bow, but Mother Zaneta's cane caught me under the chin.

'Do not put that purse away, young man,' she said. 'The

terms of my house are very explicit. Payment in advance, for any and …' the cane found the coin and there was a chink of silver upon gold, '… *all* services.'

Our room was up at the top of the house. It was a square, cramped box, and faced, not the seething square, but a decorous canal.

'Not a prime spot,' said Letice indifferently. 'Good enough for a dying girl, though, I expect.'

There was a bed, a linen chest, and nothing else: no adornment of any kind. I thought of the last occupant and shuddered. Had they kept her working, the poor wretch? I pictured the girl and her rough, oblivious customers, and felt a breath of desolation pass through the close, stuffy air.

'Tell me about Mother Zaneta,' I said, to drive the ghost away.

'I broke her heart,' she replied, inspecting the sheets suspiciously. 'Well, they did change the linen. Now then, Mother … I told you about her. She took a shine to me – let me learn things. *Made* me learn. Perhaps I was going to be Mother one day – I'll never know, will I?'

'She didn't like Dardi, did she?'

'Oh, you are sharp. Dislike might be the wrong word, though. Remember I told you about the girl he killed? Well, that happened here. Not in this room,' she added, seeing my horror. 'Her name was Amelia. I don't think Mother thought she was special, but no whore-mistress likes it when the customers fuck the girls to death, do they?' Her voice was light, belied by the hardness of her words. She flicked a feather from the bolster.

'What does "Il Bisato Beccato" mean?' I asked.

'"The Trapped Eel,"' she said, flatly, and went over to the window, where she propped her elbows on the sill and slumped wearily.

'Now what?' she said.

'Now we find Querini,' I told her.

'Easy enough. Come over here.' She pointed out across the rooftops, south-west. I saw a forest of tall chimneys, each topped with an odd inverted cone, and here and there a taller belltower. Pigeons strutted and wheeled everywhere. Further east was nothing but a blurred confusion of land, sea and sky.

'The Querini Palace is just over there,' she said. 'See those chimneys there, the bright ones, next to the dragon weather-cock?' I saw: the place seemed within pissing distance. 'We can walk there in the time it takes to eat an apple.'

'Let's not,' I said quickly. 'We can't very well march in and demand to see Baldwin, and by the bye, would they mind giving back the Crown? You know the building. Is there a postern door, a ...'

'A thief's way in?' she finished. 'No: there's a front door and a back door, like all Venetian houses. One on the square, one on the canal. And really they're both front doors, if you take my meaning. You could swim up the canal, climb the wall and get in through the pantry window, but you'd freeze to death in the water, and the wall's sheer.' She leaned upon the sill and gazed out over the city, eyes, I guessed, seeing nothing; or perhaps seeing what her younger self had once beheld. I turned back to the room. I knew now what was troubling me: it was Anna. The first night we had spent together as lovers had been in a brothel. It was as clear to me in all its strange, mortifyingly wonderful detail as if I were seeing it painted upon the walls: a summer night in Bordeaux, the candlelight, the rutting in the room next door, the terrible mural with its fat little people who bulged their eyes at us as we played.

'I am going to have a look anyway,' I said, to break the spell. 'You can take me there.'

'I think I had better not,' said Letice. 'These streets are likely to be full of Querini's people. I might bump into Facio, or it might be Agneta the cook on her way to the fish market, which would be worse.'

Instead, she drew me a map in the dust behind the bed, the way to the Palazzo Querini and a crude outline of the city and its various islands. I changed into my sadly abused but patched and clean Venetian clothes and left Letice alone at the window, her yellow hair bright against the blue sky and the darting grey of pigeon wings.

I let myself out of the brothel, ignoring the curious stares of the whores. The square – the Campo San Cassiano, as I now understood it to be – was as busy as before, and I slipped unremarked through the slobbering, randy fools and, trying to remember the twists and turns that Letice had described, set off into the maze that is the city of Venice. My legs felt light and weak, for I had been a month at sea, but I followed my directions – left, second right, over the bridge, round the corner, sharp left, left again – and in no time I had reached the busy little square where the Palazzo Querini stood, its back to a wide canal. I held back in the shadowed mouth of the alley and took stock.

It was far bigger than the Ca' Kanzir, and far newer, a towering edifice of chestnut brick into which were set an exotic congeries of pointed, tracework windows, carved plaques and bosses, and even fragments of mosaic and ancient statuary. I suddenly understood where the glory of Constantinople had ended up: here, in the strongrooms and on the walls of Venice, for the people of that city have decorated their houses and churches with whatever they looted from their great and ancient rival, haphazardly, as a hedgehog in an orchard will roll over in the windfalls to see what will stick to its spines. A nation of thieves indeed, and they were by no

459

means coy about it. But Letice was right. There was no way in save through the delicately pointed door, and although I took the trouble to skirt around and steal a look at the backside of the palace from across the canal, there was no way in that way, either.

Crestfallen, I started back towards the brothel, but I could not face that desolate room again so soon, and so I wandered, and came to a teeming marketplace that ran along the bank of the canal. It was loud and bustling, and I wove my way between the stalls, gaping at what was on offer there: fish, and every kind of grotesque beast from the depths of the Lagoon. I would have marvelled at the things like pink spiders, the seething baskets of eels and the creatures that seemed to be nothing but eyes or spines, but before long I found myself at the Riva Alta and its bridge of boats: the Quartarolo Bridge, Letice had called it. I made my way across, enjoying the heave and sway of the boards beneath my feet, and fell in with the crowds on the other side, who all seemed to be heading either for the bridge or for, I guessed, the heart of the city: Saint Mark's Cathedral, and the palace of the Doges. I had intended to go there tomorrow, but I had the pope's letter and Andrew's, and the crowds and the strange luminous air of Venice had given me an unaccustomed feeling of confidence. I would try my hand now, I decided, and let the crowd carry me forward.

I was in a river of Venetians, chattering and squawking at each other like a flock of gaudy starlings. No part of Venice is ever empty save very late at night. Vacant space fills with people like a footprint in a mire fills with water. The pale morning sun was picking out marvels on every side, and I felt a surge of joy rising in my chest that seemed to lift each hair on my head and make it quiver. In a sort of daze I meandered along more streets, through squares thronged with people bedecked in the finest clothing I had ever seen, until I stepped through an archway into a wide square, at the far end of which stood the most extraordinary building I had ever seen.

'San Marco,' I said out loud, as if that might be explanation enough, though it was not.

The church – for so I realised it was – rose before me out of some fevered dream. Enough travellers have described it, and I will not enter the lists with pens more worthy than mine, save to say that it took several paces across the wide space of the square before I was sure that what I beheld was in truth a building and not a panoply of giants' armour or a wondrous spinney of trees whose leaves were gold and whose fruits were jewels. So intoxicated had I been rendered by the wonders I had already seen that I do not believe I even noticed the soaring tower of the campanile as I tottered towards the church across the herringbone bricks of the square, my sea-legs barely up to the task, and saw winged figures – humans and, it seemed, lions – swarming over the swoop and jut of the façade. There were real people up there, too, and now I could see a filigree of scaffolding over the front and the four great domes.

This, I knew, was how Constantinople must have been before the Franks had destroyed her – destroyed her, and then built their own city in her image, for Saint Mark's, I saw, was a Greek church, and everywhere about me – on the church, on the walls of the buildings around the great square, on the columns that guarded the waterfront – were treasures that could only have come from the East. It was horrible to see, with the ruin of that other city so fresh in my mind; but Venice is a strange and terrible place, but also a lovely one, and when the sun shines, its warm stone and brick, the outlandish skill of its builders and artisans, and the gentle

461

music of light and water, work a powerful conjuration upon the spirits. So I did not curse the Serenissima, but instead let myself fall under her enchantments.

Enchanted or not, I knew better than to expect an audience today, but nevertheless I screwed up my nerves and walked through the open doors of the palace of the Doges. There were people everywhere in the hall beyond, milling about, gossiping and doing business, all dressed in peacock-bright silks of outlandish cut, their tunics in the main even shorter than my own. I looked in vain for someone who might be official, and at last I asked a guard if he could direct me to where I might arrange an audience with the council. He gave me a crooked look, as if marking me for a moon-struck fool, but pointed out an old man in the black robes of a cleric, who was standing near some grand stairs and nodding, polite and extremely bored, at the men who assailed him on all sides.

I had to wait my turn, for it seemed everyone in Venice wanted an audience, and each one of them had to go through the bored old man. I finally planted myself in front of him, and gave a brisk bow.

'Good sir, I seek an audience with the Council of the Republic. I have several very pressing matters of business, even of state, to discuss ...'

The man looked me up and down. He had a beaky nose, from which a great number of white hairs bristled, and watery blue eyes, yet even so he managed to look quite implacably important.

'Your name?' he interrupted.

'Petrus Zennorius, sir, from ...'

'And your business is?'

'Pertaining to Baldwin, Emperor of the Latins and of Constantinople,' I said, garbling the title. The man's glistening eyes blinked, and one shaggy eyebrow twitched. 'I believe he is in Venice, and I would speak to him and to the council on urgent matters of ...'

'No doubt.' I thought I had hooked him, but now he was lost, already turning to another face in the surging crowd. What had I done wrong?

'I have papers,' I said desperately, groping in my tunic for them. The man rolled his eyes in horror, and turned to the man beside me, who launched into his own desperate patter.

'But, sir!' I cried, but already I was being shouldered and elbowed backwards, and I saw it was useless. The guards were already looking my way, and so I stood up straight and marched out of the palace, looking, so I hoped, like a man who had got just what he had come for.

I was out in the cold sunshine again, on the waterfront that the Venetians call the Molo, and it was such a fine sight that I lingered, admiring the ships that were docked there, as thickly as in the port of London, for this was the city's main wharf. There was a veritable wall of masts, and I walked slowly, reading the names painted upon the prows, wondering where they had been and where they would go next. But I felt exposed and nervous out here in the light, and turned back towards the domes of Saint Mark's. Crossing the canal next to the palace I stumbled a little and, with that reflex of embarrassment, glanced around me to make sure no one had noticed. Of course no one had: a man could disembowel himself in the middle of Saint Mark's Square and the Venetian throng would chatter around him, making certain, of course, not to bloody their clothes. But as I straightened up I glimpsed a man dressed in a brighter-than-usual yellow silk tunic stepping into the mouth of a nearby alley. A lovely yellow it was, like the necks of goldfinches or cowslips in spring. Still I thought no more about it, save to wonder

463

whether – unbidden thought! – it might look fetching upon Letice.

I walked on, forcing myself not to hurry. Little round white clouds drifted above me, seeming to wander through the thicket of masts. I doubted I would ever get used to the way the city hung between sky, sea and land, seemingly made from all three elements but belonging wholly to none. The way the marble on the palace façades seemed more spun than carved; the tall windows and columns that echoed both the masts of ships and the wavering shafts of light that danced wherever the sun met the water; the great cathedral, barbaric and glittering, a vast chest full of pillage upturned on the square.

I strolled along past eel-sellers and touting boatmen, past whores and whoremongers, money-changers and cut-purses. A man was selling little grilled birds on wooden skewers – sandpipers or something of the like, to judge by the long, charred beaks – and because they smelled so good, and I had eaten nothing since last night's supper, I bought two sticks. As I handed over my money I caught a flash of yellow away to my right: that tunic again. I began to crunch my way up the first beak and as I bit into the head, the hot, unctuous brains bursting in my mouth made me sigh with pleasure and forget, once again, about tunics of yellow. I went on my way, munching and leaving a trail of small bones in my wake, and soon reached the twin columns that stood at the entrance to the square of grass known as the Piazzetta, which is the one place in all Venice where one may gamble, and where the executions are held. Gamblers had their tables set up between the bronze lion and the saint perched upon his crocodile, and the dice rattled out the tunes of *marlota* and *triga* and *riffa* as men cursed and coins glinted. There had been executions the day before, and the grass was rucked up and thick with dried blood and vomit, but the gamers did not notice or care as their shoes became stained darker and darker while they shuffled in joy or frustration.

I walked on towards the campanile. There was a shout behind me and a clatter, and I looked back to see a table overturned and an angry man set upon by the table-owner's footpads, hidden in the crowd until needed, as always. And there, to one side of the strugglers: a man in a yellow tunic, who stepped quickly behind the pillar that held up the lion as if hiding from me. And he was hiding, I realised. He had seen me notice him, and clumsily dodged out of sight. Someone was following me.

I was so surprised that I just stood there and took another bite of sandpiper. This is ridiculous, I thought. He'll peep out from behind that pillar in a moment. And so he did, like a child playing hide-and-seek with a younger boy who has not quite grasped the fundamentals of the game. But perhaps secrecy was not at stake here, and all he needed to do was get close enough to stick something sharp through my liver. I dropped the last sandpiper and dodged into the throng that filled Saint Mark's Square.

I tried to seem nonchalant as I wove and barged my way through the back-ways of San Marco towards the bridge at the Riva Alta, following the river of Venetians through the Calle del Fabbri and then through the square in front of Saint Salvadore's Church. A gaggle of tarts were arguing on the bridge there and cursed me in their rasping slang as I shoved past. Then I found myself in the midst of a busy cloth market that had all but blocked the alleyway beyond. Finally I turned a corner and saw, at the far end of a small square, the two halves of the Quartarolo Bridge writhing like trapped snakes. A big, deep-water galley had just rowed through and churned up the water, and its wake slapped against the stone walls of the Grand Canal, each slap making more wavelets that rushed to the canal's middle, where they fought one another and the poor, soaked wretches who were stoically drawing the bridge together. The pontoons bucked and twitched, the ropes snapped, went slack and snapped again, and inch by turgid inch the flimsy wooden causeways approached each other, jumping and nervous, like two horses brought to stud.

They were making a meal of it, the bridge-men. It would be minutes yet before anyone could cross safely. And the street behind me was filling up with Venetians, chattering and squawking at each other like a flock of gaudy starlings. I glanced back and saw that the square was bursting with a crowd anxious to cross over to San Polo and too idle or poor to pay for the ferry, which in any case was lurking on the far side, its boatman too lazy or spiteful to row through the waves. Then I saw the follower: a flash of cowslip silk at the corner of an old church.

Frantically I pushed my way to the front of the crowd, past more quarrelsome tarts and some young rakes in garish striped hose. Another glance behind me: the follower was at the last corner before the street opened on to the waterfront and as I watched began to shove forward, not caring any longer if I noticed. In front of me the bridge-men had got their bucking pontoons under some degree of mastery and were heaving the two sides towards each other. Two yards of fretting green water separated them. I saw very clearly what I would do next, and it surprised me so much that my head had no time to argue with my legs. That was fortunate, as they had begun to sprint at full tilt over the flagstones and on to the heaving, slippery planks of the bridge. Suddenly I felt weightless as the wooden causeway yielded beneath me, banging with every footfall. I might as well be running on the waves themselves. The bridge-men's mouths were hanging open like empty feed-bags.

'Keep pulling those fucking ropes,' I yelled in English. The bouncing of the planks was forcing my knees up into my chest as I ran and I knew I would fall if I slowed even a little. But I would have to plant my feet for the leap. The ropes were slack in the hands of the bridge-man, who was fighting to keep his balance, and as I crashed towards him he dropped them and grabbed at me. I saw his huge hands in front of my face and open water ahead and then suddenly, incredibly, I was in the air. The other bridge-man stepped aside and I was across, skipping like a stone along the twisting, rearing causeway. I had solid ground beneath my feet when I staggered to a halt and turned to see one bridge-man in the canal, his mate heaving him towards the planks, and a cheering, jeering crowd on the other side. The two halves of the bridge were drifting apart once more. And there, fists on hips at the edge of the water, a slight young man in a wondrously shimmering tunic of yellow Venetian silk.

Chapter Thirty-One

For a moment I felt as light-hearted as a child who has scored some little victory over a rival. I wanted nothing more than to taunt my follower, but crushed that urge and instead slipped into the nearest side street. I was beginning to get the hang of the city, and allowed myself to become half-lost, all the while heading roughly northwards, checking at every corner for any sign of pursuit. But there was none, and soon I began searching for the Campo San Cassiano, which was not too hard, for I followed the most furtive-looking men, and soon I was back in the square of brothels, where the tarts were still touting their wares, and the men were still gazing aloft, rapt, as if God and his angels were descending from the heavens.

The hunchback let me in to The Trapped Eel, and I hurried upstairs to find Letice.

'I've been followed,' I told her breathlessly.

'Here?' Her voice was sharp.

'No, no.' I told her what had happened, and how foolish my pursuer had looked, stranded on the wrong side of the canal.

'Describe him,' she demanded. I did, as much as I could: blond, fresh-faced, a dandy.

'Sounds like Righi,' she said, scowling. 'One of the Querini bravoes. You were marked, all right. And they did not follow you here? You are sure?'

I was, for I had been taught well in such villains' crafts these last few years. 'He was making it bloody obvious,' I added.

'Well, he is not the cleverest of God's creations,' said Letice. 'But even so ...'

She was interrupted by a clamour from downstairs, men's voices raised in anger, and women's shrieks. Letice rubbed her cheeks in vexation.

'This bloody place,' she muttered.

'What is it?'

'Drunken men in too much of a hurry to get their eels trapped,' said the girl wryly. 'It is always so. Do not worry. Luchas the Hunchback will see to them – beat their brains out, most likely. Christ, I hope we do not have to stay here long.'

But the noise did not abate. It grew in ferocity, until I opened the door and stuck my head out on to the landing. We were four flights up, but I could hear doors being hammered upon, and outraged cries from disturbed revellers.

'Something's wrong,' I said. 'Quick – is there another way out?' Letice shook her head. I could see a blue vein darken in her temple, so pale had she become.

'One staircase. The roof – too far to leap to the next building.'

I looked out of the window. It was a long drop into a narrow canal, and who knew how deep it might be? No escape there.

'We'll have to go down,' I told her. 'Perhaps they won't recognise us. Because it must be Querini's men, mustn't it? Quick – tie up your hair, and ... and put these on.' I picked up my travelling clothes from the floor and flung them on to the bed. She looked at me for an instant, about to speak, and then in one motion she turned her back on me and pulled her robe up over her shoulders. I caught no more than a glimpse of her long back, as white and supple as cream poured out from a ewer, before I wrenched my head away. When I turned back, she was draped in the ugly, salt-stained things of black fustian, busily stuffing her tresses into my dark coif. But such thoughts I had had meanwhile, thoughts I could not keep away, that had swarmed and bitten like midges, a thousand tiny ghosts that were the shards of one shattered spirit. How I loathed this room.

'Take this,' I said, unhooking Thorn from my belt and holding out the hilt to her. She reached for it, and stopped.

'You take it,' she said.

'No. You. I am ... I'm stronger than you. The knife will make us equal.' She bit her lower lip, and grasped the green stone of the hilt. Our eyes met, and, like the first pangs of sickness or the hidden stab of joy when the hidden meaning of a thing reveals itself, I felt as I had those many months ago, when she had looked up at me from the floor of Baldwin's chambers in Rome. The curve of her long lip, the perfect sculpture of her nose ... all at once, the tormenting ghosts were gone, and I was alone with Letice in an empty room, just a room where people had lived, fucked and died, a room like every other in the world.

'I am ready,' I told her. 'Are you?'

She nodded once, briskly, and, holding the knife by the scabbard, tucked it up under her left sleeve and curled her fingers over the hilt so that it was hidden. I looked around the room, spied the big, crude chamber-pot and snatched it up.

'Right then,' I said, and opened the door.

There was pandemonium going on below us, and I led the way down towards it, fast, taking the stairs two at a time. The first landing was empty, and I did not pause, but grabbed the banister and leaped down the next flight. There was a man coming up towards us, red-faced, holding a club of bog-oak. He had time to look shocked before my foot caught him under the chin and he fell backwards, arms out, into space, and then into the wall at the bend in the stairwell. He lay still, head crooked. I picked up the club in my free hand, for the man was insensible or dead, and kept moving. I could hear Letice behind me, the stiff cloth of her clothes rustling but no words, no sound from her lips. Around the next corner another man was puffing up the stairs, but he was stark naked and red as a robin's breast, and so we pushed him aside and kept going down.

I could hear a loud female voice. It was high, but as tightly controlled as the others were panicked. 'By what right?' it said. 'By whose authority?' Mother Zaneta, apparently, was having none of it. There was a piercing yelp beside me. Through an open door, I saw a big man with a scratched face pinning a young whore against the wall by her throat. He was fumbling somewhere between them: going either for his knife or his cock. I took two strides across the room and slammed the club across the back of his head. He buckled, his face smearing blood down the girl's breasts as he fell.

'Don't waste time!' hissed Letice. I grimaced: she was right. We abandoned the girl, who was picking her tormentor's purse, and charged down the next flight of stairs. No one there, and the doors were either shut tight or open to reveal empty rooms. There was a peal of cursing and then barked orders from below – the ground floor. We had come to it. I paused and looked at Letice. She shrugged and bared her teeth in a desperate grin. Her face was flushed, the darker red that lies at the centre of a pink rose, and she shook back her sleeve and jerked Thorn free of her scabbard. A laugh that was not fuelled by joy rose like a bubble in my chest. I switched the chamber-pot to my right hand and shrugged helplessly, grinning myself, feeling the fingers of madness upon my face. With Letice at my back I hurled myself down the stairs. We turned the corner together, and ran straight into the young man in yellow. His hands were empty, and he took one look at Thorn and fled with a clatter, with me treading upon his heels. We reached the downstairs hall together. I had time to see Facio, sword drawn and laid casually across his shoulder, and another man; and Mother Zaneta, who was staring them down like some ancient martyr facing the pliers and the saw.

Then the boy, in his panic, pitched headlong into the man next to Facio, who fended him off with an indignant shout and sent him flying into the old woman. The two of them fell in a tangle, and a cacophony of shrieks and laments rang out, for now I saw that beyond Facio a huddle of girls clung to each other, shaking and whimpering in fear. Facio had whipped around and I found myself surging towards the gently wavering point of his blade. I had no time to stop, but reflexively put up my right hand to cover my breast, and the gaping mouth of the chamber-pot swallowed the sword point. The sword was stout but the pot was stouter, and did not break; but its heavy bottom banged into my chest and stopped me short. Facio drew back his blade to strike again and without thinking I hurled the pot at him. He got his hand up and the pot glanced off his knuckles and smashed into the side of his face. He staggered and, awkwardly, wildly, I swung the club with my left hand and bludgeoned him on the ear. He went down awkwardly and I sprang forward and stamped with all my weight upon his crotch. The other man had meanwhile tugged out a hideous short sword, more a cleaver than a sword, and was raising it to chop me down when there was a flash of quicksilver beside me and the man's arm opened to the bone – I glimpsed its blood-netted yellow – and he dropped the cleaver with a scream.

Instantly Letice struck again, stabbing him in the upper shoulder. He flailed with his good arm and caught her wrist, twisting it. My foot was caught between Facio's legs and as I tore myself free and brought up my club, the man's knees buckled and he fell in a heap. Behind him stood a whore, a long-handled copper kettle in her hands. She raised it up and hit him again, and then, as if some terrible mechanism had been triggered, the kicking body was being belaboured from all sides by women wielding fire-irons, pots, clogs, even a wooden stool. The boy in yellow had got to his knees, but Mother had him by the collar. I raised my club, but saw in time that he had no weapon and was a boy, younger than me, and weeping in terror.

'Tie him up!' I yelled at Letice. Everyone was yelling now save the men on the floor, for Facio was doubled up in agony and his companion would never make another sound. She nodded as if in a fevered trance, eyes showing white all around. I straddled Facio to keep the whores from him while Letice bound the boy's wrists together with his own belt and forced his head down to the floor as he sobbed and shook in a palsy of terror. I held out my hand to Mother Zaneta and helped her to her feet. Then I bent down and hauled Facio up by the neck of his tunic until he was sitting, his face ashen, panting with the pain of his crushed stones, eyes screwed shut. I took hold of his hair and shook him until he opened them. He did not seem to recognise me. I shook him again.

'Remember me? From Tiber-side? Querini sent you to find me, did he not? Tell me!' I was mad with rage; my spittle was flecking his cheeks. He shook his head, then nodded.

'It was you who killed Anna ...' He tried to shake his head. 'No, no, you charnel rat,' I told him urgently, 'you did:

473

you rode her down in Cheapside and broke her skull. You trampled her face into the mud ...' I had twisted his hair so tightly around my fingers that they had gone numb. He was wincing in pain, but still he held my gaze. 'And Horst – do not shake your head at me, filth! – the man you butchered in Foligno. And the boy in Spoleto, when it should have been my head on the flagstones, what about him?'

'Petroc,' said Letice, quietly.

'No! He will tell me why!' I shook the club under his nose, then threw it away in disgust.

'Letitia?' gasped Facio, seeing her for the first time.

'Good morrow, Facio. Why did you come here?'

'To take you and this one to Messer Nicholas. You were seen coming into Chioggia. I thought he was chasing ghosts ...'

'Ghosts? No,' said Letice. 'Nicholas wouldn't waste time on ghosts.'

'Why?' I pressed. He panted and shook his head.

'The letter?' he winced. 'Baldwin's letter. Christ, you know better than I.'

'No, you do not understand,' I said, all the fury suddenly draining from me. 'Why? I want to know why.'

'Gold, what else?' he said, eyes narrowing. He was almost master of himself again. 'Oceans of gold. See? You *already* know, you fool.'

There was a stillness in the room, a breathlessness. The whores, with their gory, hair-crusted pots and shoes; the hunchback, who had appeared from somewhere, a bloody rag clutched to his head; a customer, who cringed by the fireplace; the boy, whose shoulders heaved, though he made no sound; Facio, who was rocking gently in my grasp, eyes still fixed on me; Letice, who had gone quite pale again, save for a constellation of sprayed blood across her face; and Mother

Zaneta. Someone had found her cane, and she was gripping it, standing straight and sombre as a poplar tree. She was staring at me too. Everyone was. I had become the centre of the room. Mother smoothed back her hair, for her wimple had been knocked off, and her heavy tresses, the colour of burnished pewter, had come free. Then she held out her hand to Letice.

'Give it me,' she said softly, and took Thorn from her, almost sweetly, as if prying a rattle away from a tired baby. Then she held the knife out to me.

I still had a hold of Facio's hair. Without thinking I reached for my knife, and a ripple went through the room, a shiver, a scurrying of thought, skittering like mouse-feet. Letice reached for my hand, but Mother Zaneta warded it off with her cane. The green stone hilt did not waver. Mother's eyes were the same green. I took the knife.

Facio set his jaw. He raised his chin and glared at me. I looked past him, at the faces arrayed there: young, smooth, ravaged, keen and simple. Luchas' lips were pulled back like a fox at bay. Righi sniffed, his eyes gone soft, distant, as if he were trying to will himself away from here with all the useless conjurations of a trapped mind. Mother Zaneta drew herself up even straighter, trembling with the effort. A lock of hair had fallen down across her face, making her seem at once a girl and terribly old, a rain-smoothed idol dressed up for some heathen rite. She pushed it away and, closing her eyes, bowed her head.

I looked at Facio. There was nothing much in my own head, I found, save for the memory of Anna as the apoplexy took her, and her fingers as they had scrabbled at my palm and then gone still. There was Horst, teaching me to ride amongst the thistles on the Janiculum hill, and the hollow knock of the poor servant Giovanni's skull against the stones of Spoleto. And now the Captain turned his head to me, eyes swollen shut, the stink of rot about his body. I shook my head and they left, but I still had hold of a man's hair, and of a knife. I did not wish to do this.

Here was Anna's killer, the half-seen, barely remembered figure on a rearing horse whose face I had strained again and again to make out in dreams and in bitter memories. He was a pale man, tall and thin, whose face bore the deep lines of worry; not very old, but not so young either. He was afraid – the smell of his fear was coming from him like an old fox skin – but not surprised. He knew what we were doing here far better than I did. And he was ready to die.

I did not wish to do this; but now, I found, I had no choice. I turned to Letice, but she was staring at Facio, her face tight, revealing nothing. Every eye in the room was fixed upon the man before me save those of Mother Zaneta. It was I whom she watched curiously, expectantly. Then I knew. I no longer had the stomach for revenge, and if we had been alone I would have let him go. But now Facio was a dead man whether I killed him or not. His life had brought him here to this room, with this audience, and no way out. And I had arrived at the same place. I would not leave here alive if I did not kill this man. Vengeance and justice were but a dream. There was nothing left for me but survival.

I closed my eyes, trying to gore myself with the pain of memory. But all I saw was Anna running away from me, skipping up on to the stepping-stone over the kennel of Cheapside, hair flying. She turned back to me and smiled.

'Goodbye, Anna,' I said. I wrenched Facio's head back, and cut open his throat before he had time to make a sound.

Chapter Thirty-Two

When he was dead, when his legs had ceased to scrape and thrash upon the floor, I stepped back. The faces of our audience – or my audience, for Facio had departed and left but one mummer upon this stage – had come back to life, and suddenly everyone was busy, straightening their clothes, staring in bemusement at the blood-caked implements in their hands. I turned to Letice, and she lowered her eyes. On the floor, Righi had stopped shaking, though he had pissed himself. In his eyes, the artifice of bravery battled with overwhelming fear.

'Not you, boy,' I said, and my voice sounded strange to me. I found Thorn's scabbard on the floor and, wiping her upon my tunic, put her away. My hands were shaking so hard that I had to trap them beneath my arms, yet even as I hugged myself I shook. Facio's blood had soaked me from my navel to my feet. I had better have someone wash them, I thought, and then I was sitting on the bottom step and staring at the soles of the dead man's shoes, swallowing back the bile that had risen, scalding, in my throat. Mother Zaneta leaned over and spat loudly and neatly on Facio's chest. Then she clapped her hands.

'Gather this filth up and take it to the storeroom. Take this child and lock him in there as well. Now, are any of my dear customers hurt?'

*

I was led to the bath-house, for of course there was one, a somewhat dank and cavernous room at the back of the house that smelled of mildew, sweat and rose-oil; stripped naked and helped into the hot water by three girls, who scrubbed Facio's blood from me and left me there. I sat amongst the curls of steam, and my teeth chattered. My blood is cold, I thought. How strange: the doctors are right about that. Nothing else seemed real. I had stepped into a different life, and I was not who I had been. Perhaps this was survival.

I did not notice when Letice came into the bath-house, only when she swung her leg over the edge of the tub and stepped in. She slid beneath the water and came up with her hair plastered to her head. Pale hair; pale, naked skin; glistening water: she glimmered like a fish, like quicksilver. I did not look at her, for she seemed hardly there at all: perhaps just a vision conjured by my frozen blood. But she straddled me and wrapped her arms about me, and at her touch my body began to remember what it was to be warm, and then all of a sudden I was Petroc again. I took her head in my hands and felt the hard vault of her skull and all the thoughts, all the life inside it. We said nothing, but rocked together until life returned, and heat, and sweat; and until I did not care whether or not she saw my tears.

My clothes were declared ruined – but by some lucky fate the letters hidden within them were only a little stained – and more were found for me from among the great store left by careless or insensible customers. I couldn't have cared less, so the choice was made by the girls: a short tunic with long flared sleeves in a maroon and chestnut striped silk damask, dark-blue hose, and a cycladibus of black, arm-holes, hem and collar scalloped and trimmed with dark red ribbon. I let them dress me like a mannequin while I stared at the blackened heap of my old clothes, my gift from Anna. The whores were chattering, debating the relative merits of this costume – how I would blend in just enough, but not too much, how rich it made me look, how manly. At last, Mother Zaneta appeared in the doorway.

'I must have words with you,' she said.

It was a command, and I obeyed. She led me through the girls and serving boys who were scrubbing the floor with lye. The bodies had already vanished. We went upstairs to a finely appointed chamber and she called for wine, which I sipped at, then gulped. When the cup was empty she took it from me and set it down out of reach.

'You have killed an important man,' she said. I opened my mouth to speak, though what I would have said in my defence, or perhaps in self-condemnation I did not know then, nor do I know now.

'It was well done,' she went on, before I could say anything at all. 'It was necessary, and you did well. He came into my house with his bravoes, and that could not be tolerated. Do you know who he was?' I nodded, glumly.

'The capo of Nicholas Querini's company,' she went on. 'The coming man in this quarter. Many friends, and many more enemies, as such a man must have. What do you know of Venice, young man?'

'What I have heard is that the water in its streets is no match for the fire of its people,' I said, half-remembering some words of my friend Zianni. She wrinkled her eyes at me, questing.

'I know what you are thinking,' she said at last. 'You fear for yourself, for what will befall you as a consequence of what you have done. And you fear for *this*.' She leaned forward quickly and placed her hand flat against my breast, over my heart.

'You are young, and you have seen and done much,' she went on. 'It is cut into your face. And you hold yourself well, for which I have reason to be grateful. So I will tell you this. The first of your concerns is nothing. Do you think that you have spilled the first blood that has ever stained my floors? Do you understand what manner of place this is, what manner of city? We kill each other for taking the wrong side when crossing a bridge. Men die here, and my girls die, and if an explanation is sought I give one, but I tell you that I do not often need to do it. Signor Facio was a man of standing, but as such a man stands taller than those around him, so will he be cut down, sooner or later.'

'But Querini ...'

'Will find another Facio. It is business for him, for me, and what I must tell you, Englishman, is that what you have just done was a fine piece of business for yourself and many others. Querini will not thank you if he ever finds out, but others will, and Messer Nicholas, I am certain, will not take it personally. He is a great man, but when the whores of San Cassiano are angry, even great men's balls shrivel in fear.

'And as for this ...' and she patted her own heart, 'if you had not slain that man I would have, and then I would have slain you too, for bringing trouble to my door. If you thought you had a choice, you chose well, and if you knew you did not, you are wise. I thank you for what you did, and for bringing Letitia back to me. Now you must go. The girl will stay here, for I can hide her but not you. Go to the mainland. Letitia told me that your master is in Ravenna – go and find him. You can do no more alone.'

'And the boy?' I asked, fearing what the answer would be.

'Righi?' she said with something like a chuckle. 'I know his mother. He is a good lad, but a fool. We will terrify him, then give him wine and a girl, and send him back to his master, where he will tell such tales of the fearful Englishman that Messer Nicholas, and all the quarter of San Polo, will wish to be your friend.'

'Is that so?' I said, bitterly.

'Perhaps,' she shrugged. 'Now. There is a stunned man upstairs. We will send him home today, with Facio and his two dead friends – the man on the stairs, his neck was snapped.' And she rose. I followed her out of the room, but she paused in the doorway, and raised the silver tip of her cane so that it hung in the air between us.

'Letitia is safe here,' she said. 'You do not know, O dealer in treasures, what a marvel you have brought back. Such a thing that not even the storerooms of the Palazzo Centranico have ever seen.'

'But how ...' I began.

'And you may give my compliments to Messer de Montalhac,' she said. 'The quarter of San Polo is small, and full of secrets, but every secret, like a strand of spider-silk, ends here.' The cane tapped the floor between her feet. 'I tell you that as my gift of thanks. Now go.'

I had four things to my name in this world: the pope's letter and that of Brother Andrew, a purse of gold and silver, and my knife. A strange and powerful burden, to be sure, but now, I knew, quite useless save for the gold and, alas, the knife. I hid the letters inside my tunic and buckled on Thorn and purse. I wondered where Letice could be – or had Mother Zaneta meant me to go at once, with no leavetaking? Perhaps so, for one of the younger girls hurried over to me and held out a travelling cape with a large hood. She actually curtsied, and then tripped back to her companions, most of whom were lolling about as if nothing untoward had happened.

And indeed, there was little evidence to the contrary. As I pulled on the cloak I looked around the room. Everything was back in its place. The floor was wet but clean. Two new customers had come in, and were taking their ease, oblivious. Then I felt a touch upon my shoulder. Letice stood behind me. Her hair was plaited and coiled on top of her head, and she wore a simple shift of white cambric. I blinked, for she was suddenly very pure and fair.

'Go up to the north shore of Castello,' she said, 'and take a boat to the island called Cavana del Muran. The fishing fleet gather there in the morning and evening. Find someone to take you across to the mainland. It is too dangerous any other way.'

She took my face between her two hands and looked straight into my eyes. Her long fingers were digging into my temples and quivering minutely. The tip of her tongue brushed my upper lip. Then she was gone, a blur of white vanishing up the stairs. I stood there for a long moment, then I unlatched the door and went outside.

The square was busy again, and I shouldered my way, head down and hood up, through the teeming, flesh-tranced Venetians, feeling every eye upon me. Not looking back, I ducked into the Calle dei Morti, walked briskly past the entrance to the Calle Morto and found myself at the end of the street. I could turn left or right: on the right, the alley ended in a doorway. I turned left, following the alley until it turned again and deposited me in a narrow square. There was an ancient, Greek-looking church on one side and houses on the other. I heard the clack of shoes on stone ahead, turned a corner and stepped on to a busier thoroughfare. Slipping in amongst the people I slowed my pace.

I needed to get across the Grand Canal, but there was only one bridge, and as Letice had pointed out, it was the easiest place in the city to keep watch over. If I could find the canal, though, I could hire a boatman to take me across, or perhaps there were ferries. The Grand Canal was somewhere to my right, I knew, and I looked down each side street in the hope that I would find some clue as to how I might cross. But each passage or alley ended in a wall, and only the canals gave out on to the broader waterway, until at last my stream of people joined a larger stream crossing us from left to right, and looking that way I saw the water and a small crowd gathered on the embankment. It must be the ferry.

It was. A long, sharp craft was bobbing towards us over the canal, laden with figures all standing bolt upright despite the choppy water. It slid up against the dock and I marvelled at how the people all managed to get ashore without tipping the boat over. I edged forward with the crowd, hoping that I would be able to board as it seemed as if there were far too many of us for the slender ferry. But the two ferrymen, barking in dialect, guided every passenger to a precise spot, and at last I had handed over my coin and was stepping down on to what little deck remained free. The boat felt alive underfoot, twitching yet firm. My fellow passengers stood around me, stolid and uninterested, gossiping or silent. I felt as if I were naked and wet with smoking blood. The ferrymen heaved upon their long oars and turned us around. We slipped out into the open water of the canal.

The Grand Canal is wide – wider than the Tiber in Rome, yet narrower than the Thames in London – and crowded. Its shores are lined with palaces built of red brick and white marble, and churches great and small. To me it seemed as if a whole sea had been squeezed in between the buildings. The little black boats of Venice, the gondolas, were everywhere, darting about like water beetles. Bigger craft loaded with crates of fruit, live geese, piles of mortar, bricks and lumber ploughed up and down, and fishing boats, sails furled, were being rowed by weary fishermen. But I felt horribly exposed, and bit my lip nervously as our own boat sidled closer to the gaggle of striped mooring poles that marked the landing stage on the right bank.

Suddenly the ferryman in the prow cursed and began churning his oar furiously, hurling oaths to left and right. The ferry began to pitch alarmingly, and the passengers to stagger and mutter, and I looked about us to see, as I guessed, if we were about to be run down by a larger vessel. There was no big boat, but it seemed as if we had steered into the middle of a small fleet of gondolas. I counted seven of them, all fitted with odd little hutch-like structures that seemed to be made of half-barrels covered with black cloth. The gondoliers were wearing livery of red and white. The ferryman yelled to the nearest one in Venetian.

The gondoliers said nothing in return, but leaned carefully against their oars until, three on each side and one behind, they had closed in and were matching our pace exactly. I was beginning to doubt that this was an everyday occurrence on the canal when a flap opened in the side of the nearest cabin and I found myself looking at the polished head of an arrow.

'What the …' I gasped, and felt the other passengers go rigid beside me. The ferryman had shut up at last. Very slowly I looked around. Arrows pointed at us on three sides, and now I could see that within each cabin crouched a man, each armed with a small, curved Saracen bow. Their bowstrings were not taut, but I had seen such bows in the hands of Saracen mercenaries when we had put in to port at Messina. They had been shooting at butts, and at the time I had marvelled at the way they had seemed merely to pluck at the string to send their arrows deep into the target. Now it was very clear that, if the archers wished it, we would be dead in the blink of an eye. So I barely noticed that the seventh gondola, bigger than its fellows and rowed by two men, and with its own, larger cabin, had come across our bows.

'What is this?' I hissed. I knew, though: but how had they found me so quickly? A man next to me understood my poor Roman speech and whispered back, 'The Doge's men. Someone hasn't paid their taxes.' He jerked his chin towards the ferryman in the prow, but then a black curtain hung across the end of the cabin on the big gondola, which a ringed hand pulled open. The owner of the hand bowed through the opening and stood up. He had the balance of a gondolier, for the boat kept quite still in the water. He was of medium height, very thin, and his austere black robe hung close about him. He might have been a priest, but he stood like a warrior. The lines of his face were deep and precise, and his eyes did not blink. They were eyes that would have been terrifying had they stared out from the slits of a helmet, but even so I found myself wishing I could simply roll out of our boat and sink into the muddy canal just to escape them and what they seemed to promise. He raised his hand and pointed straight at me.

'Signor, in the name of the Serene Republic of Venice, you will accompany us.' He clapped his hands and the arrows were drawn back inside. Then he pointed at the ferrymen and crooked his finger once. Without another word he ducked back inside the cabin and the gondoliers began to row his craft off down the canal in the direction of the Quartarolo Bridge. The ferrymen, white as geese, had brought us to a stop and a gondola had come alongside. Its bow-man had grabbed the side of the ferry, and held out his hand to me. For one moment I considered jumping overboard, but pictured arrows slicing into me as I flailed in the water. So I took the bow-man's hand and stepped across. My host took up his bow once more and indicated that I was to sit in the prow, outside the cabin. As soon as I had settled myself we began to make our way, the boat in front setting a regal pace, and I feeling like a crippled sparrow surrounded by a flock of hungry crows.

The Rialto boat-bridge was opening for us, the bridge-men heaving on their ropes while the curses of indignant citizens rained down upon them. I saw fear upon their faces as we passed by with our escort.

Then followed an eternity drifting in the flat Venetian light, until we rounded the last gentle sweep of the canal and the columns of the Piazzetta hove into sight, the exuberant domes of San Marco behind them; and beyond the church the palace-fortress of the Doges. Now the walls of the palace were slipping past, heavy and glowering. At last we turned and nosed into the narrow canal that ran along its western side. The gondolas fell behind us, all but the leader, which slowed, turned to the left, and seemed to disappear into the wall. The bow-man muttered something under his breath, and the gondolier heaved us around and we glided under a high, massive archway.

We were in a sort of roofless, water-floored room, arcaded on three sides, with steps of white marble that led down to the water's edge. The big gondola pulled up to a mooring pole and the black-clad man slipped from his cabin and jumped lightly on to the nearest step. He gestured brusquely towards us, and the gondolier brought our craft in behind the other and held her steady as the bow-man stood up and nodded to me to go ashore. I stepped out, knowing that I made the gondola rock clumsily beneath me, and feeling the eyes of the Doge's men upon me. As soon as my feet touched dry ground, it seemed, a small company of armed men, all wearing the same red and white livery sported by my escort, appeared from among the columns and stood to attention. I followed the man in black, for I had no choice, as he stalked through a huge, balefully iron-bound door and into a long, torch-lit hallway, something like the hall of the Ca' Kanzir, but far bigger, grander and gloomier. The walls were bedecked with the trophies of war: shields, some very old and archaic in shape, some familiar, others strange and barbarous. There were swords, lances and mail coats, and here and there old banners hung, some torn and stained. It was a display calculated to humble anyone who beheld it, and I felt the last remnants of my courage give way like a walnut in a vice. Behind us marched the men-at-arms. I could hear the leather of their equipment creak softly in the thick, warm air.

The silent man in the black robe led us to the end of this corridor, up a short flight of stairs, down another corridor, this one lit by many windows, up more stairs until we came at last to an ornate stone doorway over which presided a carved image of the winged lion of Venice. The door swung inwards and the man stalked inside. I followed, not before snatching a look over my shoulder at the expressionless faces of the men-at-arms. We had entered a quite small room lit by a long row of windows that faced west. There was a long view of the Molo and the wharfs, the tip of the island and the hazy lagoon beyond, islets dotted here and there on the water. From this height the masts of the ships tied up along the Molo were a dense forest, thick as the bristles on a boar's back. That was my world, down there. I doubted I would ever feel the deck of a ship beneath my feet again.

Chapter Thirty-Three

I found myself looking down a long table of dark wood. Three men in red robes sat on either side, and at the end, on a throne of red and gold, sat the Doge of Venice, Giacomo Tiepolo himself. He too wore a long red robe, and on his head perched a strange hat of gold and silver, part crown, part bishop's mitre. He was not a young man, and his face showed the signs of hardship as well as privilege. Indeed all the men at that table had the hard faces of sailors and soldiers and the cunning eyes of merchants. The black-robed man indicated that I should stand at the foot of the table.

'Signor Petroc of Auneford, Your Excellencies,' he said, and stepped off to the side. In truth, I was so dismayed by everything around me that I was not particularly surprised when he spoke my name. Spies, spies everywhere.

'Signor, do you know why you stand before the Signoria of the Republic?' asked one of the seated men. His mouth snapped shut and he leaned back. Seven pairs of eyes bored into me. There was no hostility, merely an awful intent, a razor-edged scrutiny, as if I were a stanza of Catullus being analysed by Sorbonne grammarians.

'Well, I …' I floundered.

'Why did you come here? What business do you have with the Serenissima?' enquired another man. It was plain that he knew very well what my business was.

I took a deep, queasy breath. 'I … I sought an audience

yesterday,' I stammered, trying to sound calm. 'But I do not believe I gave anyone my name ... If I have transgressed or ... or broken some protocol, I humbly beg the council's pardon.'

'We have your name from a trusted source,' the man interrupted, and made a swift, neat gesture to the guards. I tensed, expecting them to come for me, but instead they opened a door that was cleverly hidden in the panelling of the room. A thickset man in clothes of a smouldering, ruby-red silk stepped into the chamber.

'Messer Nicholas Querini,' drawled one of the councillors. 'Is this the man you know as "Petroc of Auneford"?'

Querini gave me a casual glance. 'No, your honour, I know him as Petrus Zennorius,' he said, his voice making it plain that he cared not one whit about me or my names.

'An alias? Ach, how tedious. Sit down, Messer Nicholas. I am sure you have far more important things to do, but if you might offer a few minutes to the Republic ...'

'I have already offered her my life,' said Querini smoothly, 'and so another few minutes are gladly given.' He took the proffered seat, at the corner of the table next to the Doge's right shoulder, and leaned back, the picture of ease.

'Messer Nicholas has just returned from Constantinople,' said the councillor who had first spoken. 'He brought news that certain interests were at work there, interests with the intent to harm the Serene Republic's efforts to aid the most Christian Empire of the Latins in their struggle against the Greeks.'

'Your name was brought up in connection with this,' said another councillor. 'Your name, but more particularly that of one Michel de Montalhac, known to many as Jean de Sol. You are an associate of this man.'

'I am,' I said, drawing myself up as straight as I could.

'It is our understanding that de Montalhac is no longer a threat to us. Is that not so, Querini?'

Querini nodded, and steepled his fingers upon his chest. He stared at me like a well-fed tomcat. 'Just so,' he said. 'De Montalhac, or de Sol, will not trouble the Republic further.'

I opened my mouth to speak, but paused, for I heard the Captain's voice very distinctly within my skull: 'Pay attention!' I shut my mouth again, and took a deep breath.

'He was seeking to defraud the empire of its most valuable possessions,' Querini was saying. 'Claiming the authority of the Holy Father and of King Louis of France. It was audacious, I will grant you, but if the empire was not in such a lamentable state he would have had no chance at all. As it was ...'

'The situation is in hand,' finished the Doge. 'You are returned safe to us, for which God be praised. But now, when this Petrus, or Petroc, came to our doors yesterday, enquiring about the Emperor Baldwin, naturally the honoured council thought it more than coincidental. You recommended this man's arrest, did you not, Querini?'

'I did, Your Honour. I observed him in Constantinople, and he is dangerous – not so much as his master, but nonetheless ...'

'Young man, you face the gravest of charges. This man, Nicholas Querini, who is a person of the highest standing in the Republic, has brought accusations against you of thievery, sedition and fraud. Far more seriously, he has raised questions of simony, a traitorous attack upon the integrity of the Holy See, and heresy. What do you say to that?'

I looked at each man in turn, but they were implacable, unreadable. I thought briefly of charging at the windows and throwing myself out, but then I recalled Querini's words about the Captain, and the smug certainty in them, and a grain of hope began to whirl, tiny as a dust mote, through my clanging mind.

'I am no fraud,' I said. 'I have spoken with His Holiness in person, and I can attest that Captain de Montalhac's mission was authorised by Gregory himself, and blessed by him too. As for thievery, I have committed no such deed. Sedition? To accuse one man of weakening the empire of the Latins is akin to blaming the fall of a rotten house on one solitary woodworm – and besides, our mission and our intent was to strengthen the empire, not destroy it. We were acting under a commission from Baldwin himself, and he will confirm it. As for heresy . . .'

'De Montalhac is a Cathar.' The Doge was patting a sheaf of papers on the table before him. 'He and his lieutenant, one Gilles de Peyrolles, and many others of his company. Do you deny it?'

My bones turned to water and my heart seemed to be made of unfired clay. Christ, what could I do? They would have me condemn my master and my friends, and then doubtless myself. It was hopeless; and yet I had met the pope – that had happened. Surely someone could be sent to Viterbo? Then I remembered jolly Peter of Verona, the Pope's Inquisitor, and how he had railed against Venice.

'Is this the Inquisition, Your Honour?' I asked. 'We are discussing temporal affairs. I will not be drawn into slanderous accusations of heresy, slanders aimed at souls who are not even present, unless it be before the representative of the pope himself.' I was feeling almost angry now, and I fixed my glare upon Nicholas Querini.

'Of what, specifically, am *I* accused?' I asked. I almost wanted to hear the word now. If I was to hang for Facio, at least I had had my revenge upon him. 'With every respect to the honour of this chamber, I have heard only slanders and libels. If you would talk to Baldwin de Courtenay, all your questions would be answered. Happily, he is in Venice.'

'His Majesty is in Rome,' said the Doge, dismissively.

'Ah – I believe he is in France,' a councillor put in.

'England, I thought,' said another.

'At any event he is not *here*,' said the Doge, impatiently. 'Messer Querini's word is enough.'

'Specifically,' said another man, 'you are charged with attempting to steal from Constantinople a relic beyond price, to whit, the Crown of Thorns of Our Lord's Passion.'

'How can that be, Your Honour?' I asked, summoning wounded innocence. For some reason they had not yet cried murder, but that would come next. 'The holy Crown left Constantinople before I did. This man took it.' I pointed at Querini, who smiled coolly.

'Indeed? I am sure that Messer Querini, one of this Republic's most honoured lords, would have mentioned such a thing to this council,' said the Doge, watching me carefully. 'Your slander is wearisome, but happily we will not have to suffer it any longer.' I tried to keep my face impassive, but in truth it was another terrible blow. I saw now that I must be doomed, for my word counted for nothing against that of Querini, and I would be dead long before anything I said could be proved. And yet still that seed of hope remained, growing, strengthening me with its tendrils. 'Messer Querini acted entirely within the bounds of propriety. He lent a very considerable sum to the Latin Regent, who, honourable man that he is, gave his creditor an exceptionally sound piece of security. And so honourable is Messer Querini that he has allowed the treasure to remain in Constantinople.'

'But we were acting for Louis of France ...' I began, but the Doge raised a cautioning finger.

'Louis will have to pay Messer Querini,' he said. 'You

expected, of course, that he would pay *you*.'

Suddenly hope flowered into revelation. I placed my hand to my breast, and felt the crackle of parchment there. They had not searched me – had not even taken Thorn, which had terrified me, for it meant that they feared no resistance, resistance being unthinkable. But now I had something far more dangerous, and it was not the knife.

'Your Honour, Honourable Council,' I said, 'your concerns for the safety of your interests in the Latin Empire are unfounded. I sought audience with you on a most urgent and weighty matter of state, although it seems you heard only my enquiry as to the whereabouts of Baldwin, which seem to be something of a mystery.' I shot a look at Querini, but he was gazing, bored, at the ceiling. 'Although I have been taken by force of arms in broad daylight, like a common scoundrel, I am an accredited agent of His Holiness the Pope, and of His Majesty Louis Capet, most pious monarch of France.' I was spooning on the diplomatic unction a little thickly, but judging by the room's silence, not entirely in vain, so I reached into my tunic and pulled out, first the letter from Andrew of Longjumeau, and then the papal bull itself.

'This,' I declaimed, holding up Andrew's letter, 'appoints me an agent of the King of France.' I handed it to the nearest councillor, who began to study it curiously and a little gingerly, as if he expected something scurrilous. 'And this,' I went on, holding up the bull, with its massive seal, 'is a decree issued by Pope Gregory in person, dated September of last year, and signed by His Holiness at Viterbo in my presence.' That had their attention, for every eye, especially those of Messer Nicholas Querini, were now fixed upon the great, ominous seal of lead. Seizing the moment, I gave a stiff, grudging bow.

'I would guess that this is not the usual welcome accorded

493

to weary ambassadors in your Republic,' I said, coldly. 'But I am young in years and my person does not, I will admit, reflect the gravitas of my commission. Nevertheless ...' and I tensed every sinew in my body as I said this, 'nevertheless, I wish to address the Doge in private, for I have matters of high state that I would rather not speak of in public.'

Querini pushed himself up out of his chair. 'How dare you insult the Serenissima, you verminous—' he barked, but the Doge, who was scanning Andrew's letter, took hold of his arm.

'Nicholas,' he said, pleasantly, but there was a taste of iron in his voice. Querini shut his mouth and sat down, his face tight with fury. Around the table, the councillors had their heads together, whispering, but the Doge stared directly at me. I felt myself grow pale, but allowed myself one single blink in return. At last one of the councillors, the man who had first addressed me and who now held Andrew's letter, turned to the Doge and gave him a simple, measured nod.

'Good, good,' exclaimed the Doge. He looked around the table. 'Sirs, with your permission I will withdraw to my chambers with this gentleman.'

One by one the red-robed men nodded their assent. The man who had arrested me left his post by the window and walked past me to an inner door. He opened it and stood by while the Doge entered. We followed him into a small, surprisingly sparse room lit by two narrow windows. Tiepolo seated himself in a smaller version of his throne in the council chamber, and, prompted by the official, we took two smaller seats. I looked around me furtively. The walls were painted, but it had been done many years ago – centuries, perhaps – as the paint had faded into the plaster, which was itself cracked in places. There were stars, waves, winged lions, done mostly in gold upon a red field. It must have been splendid once, but now the room was almost homely and in spite of my fears I began to grow more easy.

'Thank you, Giustiniano,' Tiepolo told the man in the black robe, who nodded and left the room.

'Giustiniano Zeno is one of our most trusted captains,' said the Doge, when the door had closed. 'A man whose discretion matches his capability. I trust you were not inconvenienced in any way.'

'Not at all,' I said hurriedly. It was clear that, to Doge Tiepolo and to Giustiniano Zeno, being abducted by archers on the Grand Canal did not count as an inconvenience.

The Doge leaned forward. 'I regret that you were not shown more *politesse*, Signor Auneford,' he said. His voice was low but distinct, commanding, the French word a hiss: the hairs stood up on the back of my neck.

At that moment a pair of servants entered with trays of food and drink. Tiepolo insisted I eat, which given the state of my nerves was a particular refinement of cruelty. But, eager to give no offence, I picked at some unpleasant little fish smothered in raisins and vinegar. The wine, however, was an excellent Monemvasia, and I allowed myself a good draught or two. Finally the Doge spoke again, wiping the remains of a minced-meat cake from his chin.

'Young man, it grieves me to hear that Messer de Montalhac will not be returning to our city. Your master, despite what you heard out there, was known to us, as was the nature of his business. Rest assured, that does not concern us.' He leaned back in his chair and slowly folded his arms across his chest. 'I doubt you will be surprised to learn that we have had you under observation, Signor, since your arrival this morning, for we have been watching the Palazzo Centranico, your master's residence on the Rio Morto. You may find it helpful to learn that your master fascinates – fascinated – us, and that he ought to have been flattered by our attentions, for we in turn were flattered that he chose our Republic as his home. Rest assured,' the Doge continued, 'that if his company chooses to return, our attention will not prove to be, in this case …' he raised a jewelled finger to his cheek and rubbed it gently, distractedly, '… malign.'

'The company of the *Cormaran* will return to Venice,' I said, 'and with its captain. For Michel de Montalhac is not dead, he is merely in Ravenna, although that is not necessarily preferable.'

'But Querini assured us …' said the Doge, looking genuinely surprised. I pressed home.

'Querini, perhaps in his great love for the Serene Republic, has withheld certain truths, I believe,' I said. 'My master was abducted from Constantinople and taken to Querini's island of Stampalia, where he was woefully ill-used. I was able to rescue him, and at this moment he is recovering from his many hurts. But he is not a young man, and it will be a matter of some time before he is well again. Querini told you that he had done away with him?' The Doge nodded, slit-eyed. 'As he tried to do away with me.'

'This is nonsense,' snapped Tiepolo, beginning to rise from his chair. 'You have postponed the moment of your judgement, I see, with slanders and …'

'I will tell you why Querini has misled the Republic,' I cried, 'and why he has murdered and plotted. Nay, I will show you!' And I held out Gregory's decree. The Doge snatched it from me, but sank back into his cushion. He cast a hawkish eye over the letters, and suddenly his shoulders dropped and his brow crumpled into a deep frown.

'This is an absolution from simony,' he muttered, and glanced up at me. I nodded.

'Given to Captain de Montalhac so that he might

accomplish Gregory's fervent wish: that Louis of France bestow upon Baldwin of Constantinople some part of his great wealth, as gratitude for a certain gift that was to be made to him – that gift being the holy Crown of Thorns.'

'But you say Querini has the Crown,' said Tiepolo, head cocked in puzzlement. 'And … if that is so, he has every right to it. And moreover, he does great honour to our city by bringing it here, and by arranging the loan to …'

'Querini did not loan his own money, though, did he?' I asked quickly.

'No: it was a consortium, although Querini put up perhaps the greater part.'

'Thirteen thousand livres of gold,' I said. 'A colossal sum. That such a strange, plain thing as a plaited ring of thorns could be worth so much. But who can put worth on such a thing? That is simony.'

'Young man …' snapped Tiepolo.

'What would the Crown of Thorns be worth to the highest bidder?' I asked him.

'Such a question is blasphemy!' he protested.

'And yet that is what Querini wishes to find out,' I said. The Doge stiffened again, but I went on: 'He has it. Querini has the Crown. It is here in Venice. I saw him take it from the Pharos Chapel with my own eyes. He abducted Captain de Montalhac and tortured him, for he believed he had this letter. Querini has need of the decree of absolution, for he intends to negotiate with Louis himself.'

'What of it?' said the Doge. 'He will recoup the thirteen thousand for the consortium. The Querinis are the richest family in Venice: they are very sharp in matters of business.'

'Ah. The thing of it is, that Querini does not know what the highest bidder is willing to pay, and I do,' I said. I picked up the pope's letter from the table. 'Louis of France has already decided what he wishes to pay for the Crown, and it is not thirteen thousand livres of gold.' I leaned forward over the low table. Reluctantly, Tiepolo did the same. I found myself very close to his dark, diamond-hard eyes.

'Well?' he muttered.

'Louis will pay one hundred and thirty-five thousand gold livres,' I said.

There was utter silence in the room, save for the pounding of my own blood. A bloated winter fly alighted on the sweet fish, and I heard the skitter of its claws.

'Impossible ...' breathed the Doge at last.

'No. Two Dominican friars – one of them is the Andrew of Longjumeau who wrote this letter – wait with my master at Ravenna. They have the authority to treat with the holder of the relic, and will authorise any payment up to that sum. I swear it. And I, young as I am, and a poor substitute for Captain de Montalhac, have the power, invested in me by the pope, to agree to and legalise the transaction.'

'What ... what exactly are you saying?' asked Tiepolo, groping for his wine cup.

'That the Crown of Thorns is here in Venice, in the illegal possession of a possibly, but not certainly, treasonous citizen. I am sure it would be much more to King Louis' taste to deal with the Most Serene Republic of Venice than with Messer Nicholas – do you not agree?'

'Undoubtedly. But he has a right to hold the Crown. And treason ... we have no proof, no proof at all.'

'Your Honour, I can supply the proof, today.'

'I doubt that,' barked Tiepolo, haughtily.

'Where is Baldwin de Courtenay?' I asked him.

'Rome,' he said.

'Or France?'

'The Republic is not a party to Baldwin of Constantinople's

plans and whims,' rasped Tiepolo. 'We have another emperor to concern ourselves with, a far more dangerous one.'

'And if he were here?'

'Here, he would be a revered guest,' said the Doge.

'Well, he *is* here. Querini is holding him captive. He was taken from Rome last summer, by force. One of his companions, a Fulk de Grez, was killed – this I know for certain. Doubtless the other companion also died.'

'He would not dare …'

'For half the treasury of France? What man alive would not dare? The pope's decree does not specify one transaction. It has no limit. Do you know, Your Honour, what lies in the Pharos Chapel? Treasures beyond the world's dreams. Querini will sell it all. He will buy the poor Latin Empire – dear God, he can probably afford it already. And then he will buy Venice.'

I regretted those last words the moment they left my tongue, for I had overstepped, I was sure. But to my utter amazement, Doge Tiepolo had risen to his feet and was pulling open the door.

'Querini, would you come in here, please?' he called. I heard a councillor give an unconcerned reply, and then Tiepolo threw up his hands and beat upon the frame of the door.

'WHEN?' he bellowed.

Nicholas Querini had excused himself from the council chamber as soon as the Doge and I had withdrawn, and no one had thought anything of it. After Doge Tiepolo's outburst and the shocked silence that had followed it, an icy efficiency descended upon the council. Taking his place at the head of the table, the Doge, as calmly and carefully as a surgeon carving out a canker, laid out what I realised was my case against Querini. There was no dissent. But for

Tiepolo's cry, there was scarce anything to show that these men were made of warm flesh and blood, so icily did they go about drawing up their orders. Giustiniano Zeno was to go at once to the Querini Palace with a company of soldiers, place Messer Nicholas under arrest, free the emperor should they find him – and there was marked scepticism on that point – and take possession of the Crown of Thorns.

I insisted on going with him. For, I told them, I was in effect not only the pope's agent but also Louis' and, at a stretch, Baldwin's as well. If the Crown were there it was my duty to ensure that it was safe and genuine. So far had the wheel of my fortune turned in the short space of time since I had stood before them as a hopeless wretch that they agreed without argument, and I was about to follow Zeno from the chamber when the Doge laid his hand upon my shoulder and crooked a finger at the soldier.

'Zeno, I do not wish any scandal to fall *too* hard upon the house of Querini,' he said softly. 'You will manage that?' Zeno nodded. 'Excellent. You look puzzled, young man,' he said to me. 'Hear this. The Querinis are, with the Tiepolos, the most powerful family in Venice. If they are weakened, the Republic weakens. I do not think Nicholas will be at the palazzo in San Polo. Please make a fuss, Zeno, a diversion. And then leave with Signor Petroc, and find Querini and this damnable Baldwin. Do it quietly, and settle it, if you can, to everyone's satisfaction.'

'Everyone's?' I asked him, daring to hold his gaze for the first time.

'The Republic comes first. The emperor will require some sop. Querini must not lose too much face. Otherwise, I care not. Ah. And my young friend. If you are playing us false, you shall not escape,' he told me, fixing me with his pitiless eyes.

'I have too much at stake,' I assured him.

'Such as?' he enquired.

'The confidence of popes and emperors,' I said, tapping the pope's letter and tucking it away in my tunic. 'But far more important than that, my commission.' And I took my leave of him, but not before I had caught a flicker of something in his face – not respect, to be sure, but perhaps a hint of recognition. *All thieves, these Venetians*, the Captain had said. Well, perhaps I would be welcome here after all.

Chapter Thirty-Four

A company, a full thirty men, had formed a column in the street behind the palace. They were mail-clad and armed with sword and buckler, and the first ten held pikes. Zeno took his place at the head, and I, having no idea what to do, fell in behind him. We set off in a jingle and stamp of iron-shod boots, and marched through the piazza of San Marco, dividing the crowds before us, and sending whirring clouds of pigeons into the sky. I found I knew the way we were going: back to the Quartarolo Bridge. People pressed themselves against the walls to let us by, some scowling, others catcalling, and the ever-present whores calling out their invitations. The bridge was whole again, and we made it writhe and skip as we banged across. One of the boatmen recognised me and called out some imprecation, and I, feeling somewhat tipsy with the turn my fortunes had taken, reached for my purse and threw him a gold piece, his pay for a month, no doubt, and he snatched it from the air and cursed me again, laughing this time.

The way is almost straight from the Riva Alta to the square where the Querinis' palace stands, and before we had gone far we could see some commotion in the distance, and soon the sound of women crying out in anger and mockery. Clattering into the square, we saw before us something that stopped every man in his tracks. For the place was full of women. The whores of San Cassiano had laid siege to the

Palazzo Querini. They yelled up at the windows, and some were throwing old fruit and eggs, daubing the brick with juicy spatters. In front of the mob, standing before the palace door, stood Mother Zaneta, silent and grim, and beside her was Letice. When she saw me she gaped and thrust a fist into her mouth. I shook my head furiously and stifled my happy cry with both hands, for Zeno had scanned the crowd and found its leaders. I followed him towards the two women.

'Ladies, what means this?' he asked gruffly. The whores behind us were pulling up their clothes and flaunting themselves before the soldiers, who were beginning to shuffle their feet like bull-calves on a summer's day. Letice had stepped behind the older woman and was attempting to question me with her eyes.

'We have come to make a protest to Signor Nicholas Querini,' said Mother, with tight dignity. 'Some members of his household came to my place of business with weapons drawn, and disturbed my customers. Ah. And one of my employees has a broken arm,' she added. 'I require restitution, and these other delegates from the Campo San Cassiano are here in sympathy.'

'And the attackers? What of them?' said Zeno. He was running his gaze across the face of the building, no doubt looking for armed defenders. There seemed to be none.

'I am fortunate to have a doughty household myself,' said Mother Zaneta, icily. 'There.' She jerked her chin towards the canal, where three bodies lay, feet towards us.

'Good Christ, Signora!' exclaimed Zeno. 'But the Republic cannot allow ...'

'The Republic, Giustiniano Zeno, cannot allow its highest functionaries to be disturbed as they take their hard-won ease,' she said. 'And well you know it. Now. I would have you open that door.'

As if commanded by the Doge himself, Zeno gathered himself and stalked over to the palace door. Drawing his sword with a flourish, he banged three times upon the wood. He had raised it again when the door swung open, to reveal a terrified woman, by her dress the housekeeper or governess. She was in a veritable ague of dread, and Zeno hurriedly sheathed his sword and, beckoning to me, stepped inside. Unbidden, Mother Zaneta and Letice followed.

'Messer Nicholas is not here!' squawked the poor woman. 'No one is here! Not Master Dardi, for he is in Greece; not Signor Facio ...'

'Who lies dead outside,' said Mother Zaneta, almost kindly. 'You should see to him. It does a man no honour for his corpse to be lying in the public way.' The housekeeper blinked and I thought she might faint, but Zeno helped her to a bench. The andron was filling up with servants, all peering from doorways and hiding behind pillars.

'Where *is* Messer Nicholas?' asked Zeno kindly. The woman shook her head, hands pressed, white-knuckled, to her mouth. 'Do you know?' he pressed, with less patience. I knelt down and grasped the arms of the chair.

'You must know,' I insisted, letting a little anger into my voice, for it was boiling up within me. But I got no answer, for now indeed the lady had fainted dead away.

'Let the soldiers in!' called Zeno to his sergeant, who was hovering in the doorway. 'Search the building. And post someone on the canal side.' There was a surge of noise outside, hootings and lusty laughter, as the soldiers filed in. They stamped into the hall, and the servants disappeared like rats in a haybarn when the doors are opened. There began a great clamour of banging doors and feet upon stairs, and Giustiniano Zeno had bent down to revive the housekeeper when Letice, with a glance at Mother, a glance that was met

504

with the subtlest tilt of the old lady's head, stepped to my side.

'Gentlemen,' she said, 'I believe I know where Nicholas Querini is to be found.' Zeno straightened so fast that he almost sent her flying, and I took her arm to steady her.

'Where – and who are you?' he barked.

'This is the Widow Letitia of Smooth Field,' I told him quickly, 'and I can vouch for her as a lady of impeccable … of integrity. We should heed her.'

'Querini's brother has lately become the Abbot of San Giorgio Maggiore in the Lagoon,' she said. 'Messer Nicholas spends much time there in prayer and meditation, indeed he keeps rooms in the abbey so that he may retreat there, as he is often given to do.'

Zeno left the houskeeper to her vapours and pulled me aside. 'To the monastery, then. We will go alone. Do you know what you will do when we get there?'

'I will do business,' I said.

Within a few minutes one of the Doge's gondolas had arrived, complete with sinister little cabin, in the canal by the square. The bodies of the three men had been carried inside, and I was glad not to see Facio again, although I cast a look at the smeared cobblestones where he had lain. While we stood waiting for the boat, Letice appeared at my side and took my arm.

'Take me with you,' she whispered, urgently.

'No – I have led you into enough harm already, and the sun is not yet sinking,' I said firmly. She sighed with exasperation and presented herself before Zeno.

'Sir,' she told him, 'the Abbey of San Giorgio is very large, but I know where Messer Nicholas is to be found. I can take you straight to him.'

'Certainly not,' said Zeno, scowling, as if sizing her up for arrest. I prayed she would not push matters further, but she did.

'If you arrive on the island and go asking for Nicholas Querini, the word will spread amongst the brothers, and your quarry will escape, with ...' she cocked her head inscrutably, '... with something and some*one*. Let me hazard that such would not be in our best interest.'

'And your interest, wench?' Zeno was getting angry.

'Is that of this man here, Messer Petroc.' She glanced at me, and her eyes danced like the blue butterflies of an English summer. I found myself smiling.

'That is so. She knows Querini's habits. And you can trust her – I give you my personal guarantee.'

The look on Zeno's granite face told me that he valued my guarantee as highly as that of a spoiled oyster, but to my amazement he gave a curt nod and a grunt of assent. And thus I came to be huddled against Letice in the cabin of the gondola while the two oarsmen rowed like fury across the basin of Saint Mark towards the Abbey of San Giorgio, standing beneath its campanile on its own island at the tip of that quarter of Venice called Dorsoduro. Zeno was hunched opposite us. He was not the most voluble travelling companion, indeed he was silently terrifying. But having seen him ordered about by Mother Zaneta, I found I could bear his inquisitorial stares, and even managed an airy smile in reply.

When we were drawing near to the island, Letice leaned across to him.

'Only the three of us will go ashore,' she said. 'The boatmen are in livery and will frighten the monks. I will take you to Nicholas' quarters. Keep your weapons out of sight. If we are stopped, do not say a word. I am known here, and I will talk. Agreed?'

Zeno looked at me. '*I* agree,' I told him. 'Letice, if Nicholas

thought he was to be arrested for treason, would he fight?'
She gave an affirming snort in reply.

'Very well,' said Zeno. 'But if it comes to blows, and I find
you have betrayed me, you will pay for it.'

'I am sure that I shall,' I said.

We tied up at the landing place between the usual bristle
of mooring poles and made our way towards the church. The
island itself was small, and the abbey and its church took up
most of it, sprawling in every direction over the flat, reedy
earth with barns and well-ordered fields and orchards. I felt
a stab inside at the sight of the monks, who were going about
their chores and paid us no mind, but then I saw that they
were oblivious, and cared not one whit for three laymen come
to say their prayers.

Letice led us past the church and into the cloister. I found
myself treading quietly, as had been my duty years ago. It
was a calm, lovely place, with a garden of clipped box-wood
surrounding a pond; and there were orange trees, in which
finches sang and squabbled. We came to the end of the
colonnade, and passed through a gate of worked iron, that
was unlocked, into a long stone hallway. I guessed it led to
the refectory and the monks' cells. We made our way along
it for a few paces, and then Letice paused and pointed to her
right, where a doorway led to a flight of stairs leading steeply
up out of sight. Zeno gave her a look, and she pointed again.
I realised that none of us had spoken since we had landed.

'Shall I go first?' I whispered.

'Let the woman go first,' said Zeno. 'Then you. I would
not have either of you at my back,' he added darkly. Letice
gave a tiny curtsey and began to climb. I followed, and Zeno
took up the rear. The way was steep and narrow, and I could
feel the soldier behind me, blocking the way down. We were
halfway up when Letice stopped suddenly and I bumped into

the small of her back with my face. Peering around her waist I saw a pair of bare legs and feet in monks' sandals, and the hem of a black robe.

'My dear Abbot!' sang Letice.

'What means this?' said a loud but courtly voice. The owner was indignant, but more surprised.

'Is Nicholas here?' she asked sweetly. 'I am just back from the East, and he summoned me. I thought ...'

The feet began to climb backwards. I did not know what to do, but I knew that this man, if he was indeed the abbot, was also Querini's brother, and must be prevented from sounding the alarm. So quickly and roughly I pushed past Letice, scraping along the plastered stone of the stairwell, and – before the man had time to turn himself around – past the abbot as well. I planted myself two steps above him and looked down at the top of his tonsured pate. He twisted round and stared up, red-faced and indignant.

'Young man, I ...'

'Lord Abbot,' said Zeno, peering in his turn past Letice's hips, pushing past her as he spoke. 'We have come to find your brother, Nicholas, on the Republic's urgent business. You will bring us to him.'

'I will do no such thing,' said the abbot, haughtily. 'You have *no* business here, Giustiniano Zeno, and no jurisdiction. Does Doge Tiepolo think himself above the Church?' He made to push past me, but I put out my arm and barred his way.

'It seems that at this moment I am above *you*,' I said. I could see that in one more heartbeat he would scream for the monks and they would swarm to us, armed with staves and sickles. Zeno had had the same thought, for I saw that he had freed his sword from the folds of his cloak and was grasping the hilt. So before the abbot could make a sound I pulled out the pope's letter and thrust the seal into his face.

His mouth had already opened, but all he could muster was a half-strangled croak.

'This man is sent by the Doge, but I have the authority of Pope Gregory,' I said. 'Will you leave us be?'

'What do you want with Nicholas?' he asked, face quite pallid now. He knows, I thought; of course he knows.

'I cannot tell you,' I said.

'Then I cannot help you,' he replied, and I saw his indignation begin to spark again. I opened the letter and held it for him to read, my finger pointing out the relevant passage.

'Et cetera, et cetera,' I said. 'Read this. The word "simony" and the words after it. Do you understand? Let us pass, go to your church and say your prayers. If you do this, I give you my word that the abbey shall have, from my hand, a precious relic that will bring even more glory to this glorious and holy place – my word on it, and the pope's authority. We will not harm your brother, and we will not disturb the good monks. What say you?'

Pietro Querini stared at the paper, mouth working, pride and avarice striving in the muscles of his face. Avarice won, as I suspected it might. He crossed himself.

'Nicholas is in his chambers,' he said. 'The door is locked.'

'And you have one of the keys,' I prompted him, for I knew he must. He drew out a great ring and selected a slender key from the many that hung there, detached it and held it out to me.

'I had no part in any of this,' he muttered. 'Do you hear me, Zeno?' he demanded, louder now, and I shushed him. 'I would not have any stain upon this abbey,' he cried and, with an oath not often found upon the lips of abbots, he thrust himself down the stairs past Letice and the soldier, and was gone in a clattering of leather soles.

We climbed the rest of the stairs in silence, but when we reached the top, Zeno stopped me.

'What did you do to him?' he demanded under his breath.

'My dear sir, I am afraid I bribed him,' I replied. 'But do not worry. I have the pope's blessing.'

'This way,' Letice interrupted, perhaps fearing that I was about to be throttled. She set off down a plain whitewashed corridor with doors lining one side, windows the other. At the end was a narrower passageway, and at the end of that, a door. My two companions paused and looked at me. I held up the key, and Zeno nodded. He loosened his sword in its scabbard, and let his cloak fall lightly over it. I slid the key into the lock, thanking the Lord of Thieves that it had been newly greased, and turned it. As soon as the hasp clicked I lifted the latch and put my weight against the door.

Nicholas Querini was standing by the window. He turned towards us, an indignant question starting from his mouth, which turned into a snarl when he saw who had burst in upon him. It was a meaty, bestial sound, and I saw then what I had not remembered: that Querini was a meaty and power-ful man, a brawler. I fumbled for my knife, but as I did so, Giustiniano Zeno strode past me, sword straight out at the end of his arm, and in two strides the tip of the blade was resting upon Querini's breastbone.

'Nicholas Querini, by authority of the Republic of Venice, I am …'

'Jean de Sol?' came a voice from the other side of the room. 'Monsieur de Sol?'

I looked around. Querini's chambers were hardly monastic. There were two glass-paned windows, a Moorish rug, chairs, and a large and comfortable bed. A table was covered in dirty silver platters and the remains of a fine luncheon, and dice and chess-pieces were scattered about. In the corner of the room, next to a large black chest, a young man sat upon a stool. He was just getting to his feet, and I saw, with enormous relief and a pang of disdain, the smooth, slack visage of Baldwin de Courtenay, Emperor of Romania. He looked angry.

'No,' I said gently. 'I am not Jean de Sol. Your Majesty, I am Petroc of Auneford, and I bring you news of Constantinople, and the loving words of your subjects.'

'How ... how *dare* you? I remember you now: de Sol's associate! Did you kill Fulk? Or Gautier? Nicholas, they have come for me! You said they would, and they have ...'

'It was Querini who killed your men, Your Majesty,' I told him. 'And he abducted your royal person.'

'Abducted, you say?' cried the emperor with as much disdain as he could. 'I am here as a guest of Venice. Or rather ...' He looked confused.

'As surety for a loan?' I enquired.

'Yes, that is right! I ... I offered to stay here while Nicholas settled my Regent's debts to the Republic. And the Serenissima has been most kind.'

'Sire, you are a prisoner. Nicholas Querini intends you and your empire nothing but harm. And your Regent is a scoundrel, but ... but Querini can tell you of that.'

Zeno had lowered his sword, but he had taken the liberty of disarming Querini, whose long, thin knife glinted in the soldier's belt. Querini, however, was not paying the slightest regard to Zeno. Rather, he had stepped back so that he leaned against the window frame, and his eyes were fixed upon Letice.

'Surprised to see me, Nicholas?' she asked. 'Thought I would be dashed to pieces by Dardi's love, I suppose?'

'Dardi?' said Querini, carefully.

'Dead, alas,' I said. 'He fell out of a window.' Querini

turned to me. 'But you will be delighted to hear that Jean de Sol lives! Oh yes, he waits in Ravenna, waits to pick the last shreds of pride from your bones.'

'Petroc,' said Letice, warning me.

'My bones?' said Querini, scornfully. 'I doubt that! I have done nothing.'

'You have ...' My hand was on my knife and I was shuddering with rage. I had him, here, at my mercy: Anna's destroyer. But then I remembered Facio, and how he had gasped and kicked, as Anna had done, and my gorge rose. 'No,' I shouted, shaking the images from me. 'Done nothing? You have killed a princess, and kidnapped an emperor!' I pointed to Baldwin, who was standing, open-mouthed.

'He is my guest,' said Querini. 'Is it not so, Your Majesty?'

'I have been living here while Nicholas has been paying off my debts,' said Baldwin, happy to have lines to speak.

'Do you say that to Querini's friends, who come here masquerading as officials of the Republic?' I asked. 'Do not trouble yourself: we are not his friends; we are yours. You are free to leave, Your Majesty. You do not have to remain here, while this man, your friend, twines himself like a basilisk about your empire, sequestering its little treasures for himself.'

'Treasures?' asked Baldwin. 'What new trick is this?'

'Trick? Why should it be a trick?'

'Because people come here and ask me things! Ask me to sign things. I have not. I will not! I have been locked in this room for months! I have been here since the summer, I think – although I am not certain. Nicholas ... this swine Querini, for I would have you, sir, place your blade upon his breast again, and the monks, the poxy, bloody monks of this place have made me a prisoner.'

'You have been a captive since Rome,' I said. 'Now what is in that chest, Your Majesty?'

'I ... I do not know. It is locked. I ... good sir, do not be angry.'

'I would not presume to be angry with you, Your Majesty.' I paused. 'I am sorry about Fulk de Grez, and Gautier. They were good men.'

'My brave friends,' whispered Baldwin, and covered his eyes. 'I know, sir, by the way you look at me, that you think me a fool, and a boy, and a knave. I am no knave! And no fool neither, though I am young. If I am a fool, it is because I have gone mad stripping my empire, my birthright, of everything of worth, that I may save it from the Infidel and the Greek! Stripped it, as I have stripped, with my own hands, the wood from the buildings of my own city so that my people will have warmth! I ...'

The Emperor was trembling, and tears were running freely down his face. I noticed what I had not seen at first, that he was very thin, and there were heavy shadows beneath his eyes.

'Have you been ill-treated, Your Majesty?' asked Zeno, gravely.

'Ill? What is ill? I have been a hostage, a hostage to my own fortune,' he answered, half-choked with tears. 'I have had the saving of Constantinople dangled before me, and my good behaviour as security for it.'

'How?' asked Letice, coming to my side.

'Fair lady, I have been promised that business was being conducted on my behalf, under the aegis of the Holy Father himself, to bring some great affair to a head,' said Baldwin. 'Sometimes it is a crusade, sometimes a fortune in loans, in gifts. There have been letters, from the pope, from my royal cousins ...' he waved at a much crumpled, much reread heap of parchments and vellums under the table. They would all be bad forgeries, I knew at once. 'But nothing has been forthcoming. I mean, I have not been ill-treated, if you do not consider exile to a shitten little island all full of monks to be ill treatment.'

'Your Majesty! Have I not kept you supplied with companions?' said Querini, with feigned hurt.

'Whores! Nicholas, they are whores! A whore is all very well, but they are not capable of ...'

'Of courtly behaviour?' asked Letice kindly.

'My lady, you have it exactly,' said Baldwin gratefully.

'I grow tired of this talk,' said Zeno, gruffly. 'We have the emperor, and the ...'

'Ah!' I cut in quickly. 'Messer Nicholas, will you tell your guest what is in yonder chest?'

'Yes, what is it?' said Baldwin. 'Querini arrived not two days ago, and has left that thing to scowl at me and torment me, for I am under pain of death not to open it, and what else do I have to occupy me than thoughts of what it contains? You are a fiend, sirrah, a fiend!' he cried to Querini, dragging his fingers through his hair with a sudden mad fury, so that I began to wonder if he had, in truth, been deranged by his captivity.

'Tell him!' said Letice.

'Yes, do tell us all, and be done with it,' said Zeno, 'for I would fain have your head on a spike right now than listen to this drivel.' He scraped the tip of his sword impatiently across the floorboards.

'The chest contains the Crown of Thorns,' said Nicholas Querini, with a fine simulacrum of boredom. 'I have it as surety of a loan I made to Anseau de Cayeux. You see, you doubted me, but I have been working on your behalf.'

Baldwin fell to his knees and clutched his face with his

hands. When he looked up, I saw a new purpose in his face.

'You think me so starved and confused that I have gone mad,' he said, 'for a madman would suit your purpose. Sir,' he said, turning to me, 'you spoke to me of my subjects.' There was a light in his eyes, unsteady, to be sure, but more than I had seen there before. 'What do my subjects say of me?'

'They would have you with them,' I said. 'Sire, some are disloyal, like the Regent and his faction. But many more are loyal. They love you, and want only that you come back to them. They need your hand to lead them. Do you know a man called Aimery de Lille Charpigny?'

'De Lille Charpigny … no,' said Baldwin, shaking his head distractedly.

'He saved me from this man's plots, sire,' I told him, pointing to Querini. 'He is but one of your loyal men, who would risk their lives to have you back. There are others.'

'And what of your debts?' sneered Querini. 'They are real enough. Thirteen thousand pounds of gold, mark you well. Men die every day in the prisons of the Doge for owing one-hundredth of that sum. The Republic deserves your gratitude, Majesty. Not only do we strive to save your honour and your reputation, but your rotting Constantinople as well.'

'Silence!' screamed Baldwin. He tottered, and I grabbed him around the waist so he would not fall. 'Sirs,' he said, when he had mastered himself, 'and my lady, I know not if you be another masquerade designed to undo my mind yet further, but if you are, what I say shall make no difference. Please, arrest this man, and you shall have the gratitude of the Latin Empire, for what little that may be worth.'

'Zeno?' I said. He shook his head in disgust.

'Nicholas Querini, it is the council's pleasure that you sur-render the Crown of Thorns, which you removed from its

515

rightful home without licence. And it is their *suggestion* that you leave Venice and limit yourself to your realms in Greece from this moment on.'

'And if I say no?' said Querini, folding his arms across his chest.

'The pope shall hear that you kidnapped the only hope of the Church of Rome in the East,' said Zeno.

'And perhaps were planning an alliance with Frederick Hohenstaufen, who is a friend of John Vatatzes,' I said. 'Although, since you murdered the *Vassileia* Anna Doukaina Komnena, who was Vatatzes' niece, I wonder how that plan would have fared. Further, King Louis of France shall be told that you seized his cousin, and planned to extort money from the French patrimony,' I said. 'I do not think that the Doge or the council would be best pleased by that.'

'So! I will go to Stampalia,' snapped Querini. 'With pleasure. But what of my thirteen thousand pounds, eh? Eh, Baldwin? Who will give me satisfaction? You worm. My grandsire climbed the walls of Constantinople and took it from the Greeks! You dishonour his memory!'

'All well and good, Messer Nicholas, but the loan you made to Anseau de Cayeux was funded by a consortium,' I said, 'of which you happen to be a minor stakeholder. Giacomo Tiepolo has bought up the debt. You are owed nothing.'

'Lies!' snarled Querini. He seemed to be growing more bold. At that moment he could have walked past us and through the door, and perhaps we would not have stopped him. And then Letice moved. She left her place in the door-way and came slowly over to me.

'Andrew's letter, Petroc,' she said. Wordlessly I gave it to her. She walked across the room, daintily, carefully, choosing every footfall, and went up to Querini, so close that their knees were brushing together. She handed him the letter, and, laying a long white hand against his ruddy cheek, she reached up on tiptoe and breathed something in his ear.

It was as if she had run him through. Worse, for if you have ever seen an ox brought to slaughter you will remember that the great beast stood, indifferent, secure in his bulk and power, until the very instant when the butcher's axe cleaved through his backbone. Then everything is done: the solid legs turn to water, the massive body plummets to the ground with a dismal crash, the hooves churn the beast's own excrement into gory mud. Thus was Nicholas Querini felled, for as he listened to the girl's whispered words his eyes scanned the letter, and the blood left his face quicker than if she had cut his throat. He leaned heavily against the wall, groped for a chair and dropped into it. His jaw went loose, and I thought that he had suffered an apoplexy.

I did not want Baldwin to hear any more, so I helped him to his feet and out into the hall. I could hear Querini beginning to speak, disjointedly, as if in a trance. Steadying Baldwin by the shoulders, I walked him to the stairs and helped him down. When we had reached the cloister I let him sit on the low wall of the colonnade.

'Will you go back home now?' I asked.

'In penury?' he said. 'How can I? You think me a fool – oh, it is nothing, sir, I have been counted a fool since the day I was born. I know what has happened. Querini stole the Crown of Thorns from me, and Venice has stolen it from him. So Cousin Louis will pay Venice for my property. You might let me die here: it would be a kindness.'

'You are right,' I said. 'That is about the size of it. But all is not lost. You still have the Pharos Chapel.'

'What do you mean?' he asked, barely interested.

'I mean that you are wealthy in relics beyond man's reckoning.'

'But I cannot sell them!'

'No. But I can,' I said.

From far away, glancing along stone walls and trickling down stairs, there came the sound of a man's angry tears. Nearer, a woman's light footfalls were coming down the passage. I looked up and saw Letice walking towards us, her hair a pale glow, wrapping her in a light of her own, sunlight and starlight, like primroses shining in a lane at nightfall. I felt the weight of the pope's seal just below my heart.

'You can trust me,' I said. 'I bring you absolution.'

Epilogue

Venice, August 1239

There is a narrow little tavern in the weave of narrow streets east of the fish market of Venice. It is indistinguishable from two score or more others, the low-ceilinged, stuffy places where the fishermen and labourers of the Republic go to quench their endless thirsts for wine and for sharp-edged gossip. Doubtless I could not find it again now, and if I did I might not recognise it. Perhaps that was why Michael Scotus had summoned me there. A note had come to the Ca' Kanzir just after the house had risen, and I had slipped out and searched the alleys until I had found the tavern's sign, proclaiming – what? A bunch of grapes, a fox, two ravens? I do not remember. But there in the shadows was a slender form I recognised at once. Doctor Scotus pushed back his cowl and regarded me with his grey, timeless stare.

'Well met, Petroc of Auneford,' he said. 'I hoped we might see each other again.'

'But not so soon!' I cried. 'This is an unexpected—' He silenced me with a raised finger.

'Let us be quiet, and quick,' he said calmly. 'I am supposed to be somewhere else altogether.' He let the words hang in the close, ham-scented air, and for a moment I wondered where exactly he meant, for he did not seem to be entirely here. But I blinked and he still sat before me, no phantom, but an old man in a travel-stained cloak.

'The war that my dear old friend Mesarites hoped to ward off has come,' he said, and I nodded. The news had been bad, if one loved the pope: the whole of Italy's middle portion had been taken by the Emperor Frederick, and his lieutenants were barking at the edge of the Lagoon: every morning new pillars of doleful battle-smoke rose across the water, black and shimmering against the hazy mountains. 'Perhaps it is not Armageddon – not yet,' he went on. 'But there will be no getting between these two dogs now, not until they have destroyed each other. In any case, I did not come to give you the news. No: I heard of your … of your survival, and rather more. The Crown of Thorns will be in Paris by now, I suppose. And you look well.'

I nodded. It was true: my body had healed, and I had discovered that, underneath the scabs of grief and hurt I was still a young man after all. Joy and delight had begun to uncurl their shy petals again, but slowly. 'I am well,' I agreed.

'I thought so. Now then: to work. Nicholas Querini.'

'He is fled to Stampalia,' I said, surprised. 'In disgrace.'

'A mild sort of disgrace though,' said Doctor Scotus. 'It would not do for the Doge to cut Venice off from all the Querini riches, especially with battle so near.'

'He is ruined,' I protested. 'Exiled. He will never sit on the council, and his enemies are crowing.' But then I shook my head. Once I had wished the man dead with such vehemence that I feared it had poisoned my blood. And although I had seen him brought low, seen his spirit felled like a rotten tree, thoughts of revenge still came back to taunt me.

'Men as powerful as Querini are hard to ruin for good,' said Scotus. 'Which brings me to my point. When I left you I made my choice and went south, to Gregory. I cannot say that it was the right choice, but at least I was able to whisper some words into his old ears.'

'Meaning what?' I said, puzzled.

'Meaning, my lad, that the pope knows that it was Querini who foiled his plans to wed Baldwin to …' He paused, but I nodded him on. He caught my eye and smiled. 'Well, then. And he knows that Querini has been guilty of simony. The one, the other …' He made a balance with his hands. 'But together?' His hands dropped to the table with a thump, palms up. 'His Holiness does not enjoy being thwarted or toyed with, and if he was ever a patient man he is one no longer. Did you know that simony is a heresy? Of course you did. Peter of Verona, as the pope's Inquisitor here in the north, has decreed that Querini be tried as a heretic.'

'Peter of Verona?' I remembered the shrewd-eyed, half-jolly friar from Viterbo. 'But he will not hurt Querini! He was the man's spy!'

'Ah.' Doctor Scotus snatched a bluebottle out of the air and smeared it into the table. 'There is no justice in this life, as you have found to your cost,' he said softly. 'But there is always cruelty. As a physician I was taught to balance the humours of the body. Let us think of this as redressing the cruel humours of the world, if only in the smallest way: hardly more important, really, than the death of a fly.'

'So the Inquisitor will turn on his paymaster?'

'Oh, the saintly Peter did not spy for money. Querini gave him influence in the lands of Venice, the better to carry out his hunt. Who used who? It is a moral question I should not dare to answer.' He gave a faint smile. 'All this Gregory knew: he chose his Inquisitor well. You knew that Peter was once a Cathar? Well, like many converts he is a fanatic. Gregory allowed him to play up to Querini, for he has no need to doubt his loyalty. Indeed, he used Peter to take a closer look at the Captain and, I dare say, you yourself. Apparently you satisfied His Holiness that you would be worthy instruments of his will. '

'*Instruments?* Dearest Doctor, if you can discern some form in all these past horrors, indeed you deserve your reputation.'

'Oh, there was form, certainly there was. Three wills, those of Gregory, Querini and Captain de Montalhac – and latterly your own, lad, if we talk of reputations – twining and striving like serpents for mastery. You should not be so very disappointed that Gregory has won, for he is the greatest prince on earth – he is fighting this war to prove it.'

'So we are the losers,' I muttered. I did not wish the night of despair, so recently faded, to return again, but the darkness seemed to be gathering.

'Did you not hear what I told you? Querini has been summoned to answer charges of heresy. He is at this moment sailing towards Rome.'

'A rich man need not fear such a charge,' I scoffed. 'No one is ever declared a heretic because of simony.'

'Peter has been diligent. Querini will land in Ostia to find himself an outcast. But there is an invitation, a friendly one, inviting him to the Castel Sant'Angelo to explain himself to a sympathetic Holy Father. My dear lad, he will find that Gregory is not there. The Castel Sant'Angelo is the pope's fortress, and his prison. It used to be a tomb, did you know that? Hadrian's tomb. It has depths that you, delicate soul that you are, ought not even to imagine, wormy tunnels gnawed through ancient mausoleums and sewers, into which the Tiber seeps like dead men's sweat. Querini will be set there to wait, in hope of a trial, of forgiveness, and he will wait for ever.'

I found myself looking into Michael's grey eyes, and in

their depths, where time seemed to quaver like faded grass in the wind, I glimpsed a sudden darkness. A chill shot through me, but then the old man smiled, and I found myself letting out a great sigh of release.

'The worthy Peter's eyes are many and sharp, lad, so I had better be on my way. Ah: one other matter. Would it give you any satisfaction to triumph after all, even if neither Querini nor old Gregory ever knew about it?'

'Of course!' I laughed. 'But I ask for nothing. I am glad to even draw breath, if you would know the truth.'

'Then my physician's work is done. Now: that thing you took from Constantinople, so beloved by Mesarites?' I nodded.

'It is safe,' I said.

'Good. I think de Montalhac has a plan for it. I renounce my claim. Do what he wishes, and there is your victory. Best do it quick, though, while the Inquisitor's gaze is elsewhere.'

He rose, and we embraced, and then he was gone, and I was left alone in the bright sunshine, blinking like a barn owl, catching the faint smell of burning on the north wind.

Two days later, very early in the morning, only the fish market was awake. Boats were coming in, and dripping baskets of eels, crabs, cuttlefish, clams and mantis shrimp were being slapped down on the slimy stone pavement. Michel de Montalhac and I walked through the throng, and paid the drowsy traghetto men to row us across to Santa Sophia. We walked quickly through the empty streets as the mist trickled over the edges of the canals and the sparrows started complaining to one another from every tree and rooftop.

Past churches and monasteries, past sleepy priests and famished monks who did not give us a second glance, across the Rio del Paradiso and through the square of Santa Maria

Formosa. We were silent, but it was a companionable silence, and we were not in any great hurry. Anyone watching us would have seen two friends, one older, with the suggestion of a limp, the other a younger man carrying a small seaman's pack of oiled cloth.

We walked for a long while, and the streets began to grow narrower and more down at heel. There was more life here. Workshops were already clanking and sawing away, children were running errands and even a few optimistic whores were seeing if anyone could possibly be in the mood, for it was going to be a lovely day, and what better way to begin it? But we pressed on until the acrid stench of boiling pitch began to sting our nostrils, and we knew we had reached our destination.

The Captain knocked four times on a door up a narrow alleyway no wider than a man. The door opened, and a black-swathed figure beckoned us inside. We found ourselves in a large room, very clean and bare, empty save for two old women sitting on a bench, and three men in plain black robes. Someone was leaving soon on a long journey, for saddlebags and a bedroll were lying by the door. The Captain exchanged greetings, while I hung back. The man who opened the door asked the Captain a question. He nodded, and the other man stepped back and spread his arms wide. His fellows did the same, and the Captain sank to the floor and prostrated himself. I heard murmured prayers in the soft, lilting tongue of Provence, and to my surprise it was the Lord's Prayer. I wondered if I should kneel as well, but felt awkward, and so remained standing.

The Cathars' prayers were at an end. The Captain was helped to his feet, and concerned questions were asked about his leg, his hip. He waved them off, and signalled to me. I undid my pack, and laid it on the ground. I drew out a plain box of ancient wood, shiny from centuries of touch. The Captain gave a nod, and I opened the lid and drew out a square of cloth, wide as a bedsheet, stained and yellow with age. He rose to his feet, and the cloth unfolded and rose with him. The men in the black robes gasped. They recoiled, and then one by one they came closer and examined the cloth. Now the women rose and looked also. They shook their heads in dismay, and one hugged the other, hiding her face in her friend's head-cloth.

The Captain laid his hand on my shoulder, and, very relieved, I hastily returned the cloth to its resting place and closed the lid.

Everyone stepped back, and the box was left there in the middle of the floor. There was a long silence. The old women went back to their bench. Finally, the man who prayed took the Captain in his arms and they swayed together as they took their leave. I felt awkward once more, and offered my hand, which was shaken warmly. The other two men picked up the box gingerly, and I gave them my empty pack. The *perfecti* bowed once more, and the Captain gave a strange smile in which joy struggled with longing, and turned towards the door.

Outside, the streets were full of noise. The great Arsenal of Venice was about to give birth to another galley. We hurried down alleys and across bridges until at last we came out on to the wide seafront. We paused and looked at the ships, and began to stroll, easily, unburdened. We were almost at the palace of the Doges when the bells in the campanile of San Marco started to chime, a low, liver-shaking knell, and then every bell in Venice began to ring, until the very waters of the Lagoon were trembling, rilled by the throbbing waves of sound. It was Sunday, and away to the south, past the zone of war, past the disputed areas, across the mountains in

Rome, the pope was rising, stiff and crippled, from his throne in the Lateran. In Venice, a Good Christian was setting off for his home outside Toulouse.

Leaning against the wall of the palace, Captain de Montalhac and I began to laugh. No one could hear us, and we stood there for a while in the sun, mouths open, eyes watering.

'Is this really hell?' I asked the Captain, suddenly. He frowned, and then started to laugh again. A couple of Franciscans, late for Mass, scowled at us as they hurried by.

'Oh yes,' he said at last. 'Yes, my friend. This truly is hell.'

Historical note

This is a work of fiction, and as such is constructed from a jumble of 'what if?'s. But here are some facts:

The Crown of Thorns was taken to Venice in 1237 by one Nicholas Querini as security for a debt of 13,134 pounds of gold.

King Louis IX of France, through the agency of Andrew of Longjumeau and James of Paris, redeemed the Crown from Venice for 135,000 gold livres, half the annual worth of the kingdom of France. He built the Saint Chapelle in Paris to house it, and went on to 'buy' most of the other items in the Pharos Chapel.

Baldwin de Courtenay did not return to Constantinople until 1240. He was always desperate for money, and at one point was reduced to mortgaging his own son to Venice.

John Vatatzes' successor finally took back Constantinople in 1261. The Franks had crippled Byzantium beyond repair, though, and it finally fell to the Ottoman Turks on 29 May, 1453.

Baldwin spent the rest of his life as an emperor without an empire, wandering about the courts of Europe in the vain hope that someone would get Constantinople back for him. No one did. He died in Sicily in 1273.

In 1238, the Abbot of San Giorgio Maggiore, Pietro Querini, obtained the body of Saint Eustichius from Constantinople.

In 1310, the Querinis, together with the Tiepolos, attempted to overthrow the Venetian Republic and set up a despotate. Their rising failed, and the Querini Palace in San Polo was confiscated and turned into a slaughterhouse.

The *Mandylion* of Edessa vanished some time after the Franks sacked Constantinople in 1204. Nicholas Mesarites saw it in 1201, and Robert de Clari says it was in the Bucoleon Palace in 1205. Then it disappears from history.